JOSEPH O'CONNOR

Joseph O'Connor was born in Dublin. His books include seven previous novels: *Cowboys and Indians* (Whitbread Prize shortlist), *Desperadoes*, *The Salesman*, *Inishowen*, *Star of the Sea* (American Library Association Award, Irish Post Award for Fiction, France's Prix Millepages, Italy's Premio Acerbi, Prix Madeleine Zepter for European novel of the year), *Redemption Falls*, *Ghost Light* (Dublin One City One Book Novel 2011) and *Shadowplay*. His fiction has been translated into forty languages. He received the 2012 Irish PEN Award for outstanding achievement in literature and in 2014 he was appointed Frank McCourt Professor of Creative Writing at the University of Limerick.

ALSO BY JOSEPH O'CONNOR

Novels

Cowboys and Indians
Desperadoes
The Salesman
Inishowen
Redemption Falls
Ghost Light
Shadowplay

Short stories/novellas

True Believers
The Comedian
Where Have You Been?

Plays

Red Roses and Petrol
The Weeping of Angels
True Believers (adaptation)
Handel's Crossing

Film Scripts

A Stone of the Heart
The Long Way Home
Alisa

JOSEPH O'CONNOR

Star of the Sea

Farewell to Old Ireland

THE IRISH-IBERIAN   THE ANGLO-TEUTONIC   THE NEGRO

From *Harper's Weekly: A Journal of Civilization*

VINTAGE

5 7 9 10 8 6 4

Vintage
20 Vauxhall Bridge Road
London SW1V 2SA

Vintage is part of the Penguin Random House group
of companies whose addresses can be found
at global.penguinrandomhouse.com

Penguin
Random House
UK

First published in Great Britain by Secker & Warburg in 2002
First published by Vintage in 2003
This edition reissued by Vintage in 2019

penguin.co.uk/vintage

A CIP catalogue record for this book is available from the British Library

ISBN 9781529112634

Printed and bound in Great Britain by Clays Ltd, Elcograf S.p.A.

Penguin Random House is committed to a sustainable future
for our business, our readers and our planet. This book is
made from Forest Stewardship Council® certified paper.

FOR ANNE-MARIE
AGAIN AND ALWAYS

INTRODUCTION

Visitors to Connemara, that wilderness of stony beauty in the west of Ireland, sometimes stop at the village of Letterfrack. It's a charming little hamlet, with thatched cottages and cosy pubs; picture-postcard pretty, on the face of it untroubled. Not far from the town is the manor where Yeats honeymooned. (Like many Great Houses, it is now a hotel.) Nearby you can stroll on a shingled beach. Sea-wrack, gull-call, Atlantic breezes – the strange loveliness of coastal places. There's a sense of continuities, of things unchanged for generations. But that is illusory, the wishful thinking of the outsider. Modernity has indeed touched Letterfrack. *Father Ted* might be playing on the TV in the bar. The guesthouses offer *en suite* bathrooms, as well as turf fires.

We tourists take pleasure in the emptiness of Connemara. There are reasons why such a silence exists. You would not think, as you amble the sleepy lanes, as you are stilled by the twilight descending on the mountain, that you are walking through a space that was once a disaster zone: the Ground Zero, perhaps, of Victorian Europe. These meadows, those pebbled fields, saw astonishing suffering. There was heroism, too; there was extraordinary courage and love. But these wine-dark boglands and rutted boreens witnessed tragedy so immense that those who observed it, like Grantley Dixon in my novel, would never forget the sight.

All this happened in the 1840s, that decade in which a million of the Irish underclass died as a consequence of famine. Residents of the richest kingdom on earth, they lived only a few hundred miles from the empire's capital, London. But that did not save them; nothing saved them. Abandoned by the dominant of Ireland and

Britain, perhaps two million of the desperate became refugees. We might call them 'asylum seekers' or 'economic migrants'. They fled their homeland by any means possible, often on ships like the *Star of the Sea*. Their language, Gaelic, among the oldest vernaculars in Europe, already in decline, virtually disappeared overnight. '*Mharbh an gorta achan rud,*' one Gaelic speaker remembered. 'The famine killed everything.'

Like the age we live in now, this was an era of technological advances, of artistic brilliance and scientific progress. Great novels were written; there would be revolutions all over Europe; democracy began to flower; new engines were invented. But little of that mattered to the starving of Letterfrack, as little enough of it matters now to the starving of Africa. The world was organised as a pyramid of power, with the affluent at the summit and the poor bearing their weight. Those who worked the hardest possessed the least wealth. Those who did nothing at all owned the most. Down at the very bottom were the nobodies of Connemara: white Ethiopians of the Dickensian world.

Tens of thousands of them died. Whole communities, sometimes. Many thousands more would also have perished, were it not for the efforts of two gentle English people. James and Mary Ellis were a prosperous couple from the industrial city of Bradford. (Like Captain Lockwood in my novel, they were Quakers or Friends.) Despite having no familial or business connection with Connemara, they moved from Yorkshire to what is now Letterfrack in 1849, where they paid for the building of cottages and roads, a school, a food store, a doctor's dispensary. They employed the locals fairly and treated them with respect. The couple, who were elderly by the standards of the time (most people died in their sixties in the 1840s) forsook the comforts of home and privilege to live in solidarity with the poorest of the poor. They were not politicians, nor were they missionaries. Indeed, they were motivated by nothing more than compassion, a faith in the certainty that we are all connected, no matter what we are told by our rulers. They believed that the world need not be a slum; that we live in a society, not just an economy; that every human life is unutterably precious. The imagery of holocaust is sometimes used about the Irish famine. If that's what it was, James and Mary Ellis are our Schindlers. There should be a statue of them on Dublin's

O'Connell Street – but there isn't, of course. The possibility of the famine story including heroes who were English was not part of Ireland's thinking for a very long time.

It was not part of my own thinking when I came to write *Star of the Sea*. The novel's beginnings were more intimate and tentative. About seven years ago, the image began to come to me of a criminal walking the decks of a nineteenth-century tall ship at night. In my mind's eye I saw him as a haunted, lonely man, who had once been good, and who yearned to be again, were it not for a past that boiled with secret shames. I had never written historical fiction – nor had I read much of it – so I was surprised by the persistent drifting into my consciousness of this limping ghost. Wherever the apparition came from, I was intrigued by who he was. I wanted to know his story.

The nightwalker turned out to be Pius Mulvey, a central character in *Star of the Sea*. If Mary Duane is the book's hero – and to me, she is – it is Mulvey who lives at the centre of its web. The novel's opening pages describe him exactly as he was when he shuffled out of the ether and into my life. I didn't know it then, but he would become my close companion. Mulvey and I would spend many an hour together, as the book slowly sprouted out from that first sighting of him. Who were the women in this mischief-maker's past? Was he Jack the Lad or Jack the Ripper? What transgressions had he done? Who were his enemies? As I began to think of what was happening in my part of the world in Pius Mulvey's era, it became clear that this would be a novel set during the famine.

I had the notion that he might once have been a singer or a song maker. I don't know why, it just seemed right. And other characters were suggested by the Irish ballad tradition, too: that complex and deeply beautiful body of art created by geniuses whose names we will never know. Irish (and English) songs of the age feature landlords and labourers, police and thieves, star-crossed lovers, betrayed serving girls. David Merridith and Mary Duane had their birth in song, as did Merridith's father, and the mudlarks of London, and the Liverpudlian recruiting sergeant who tempts the Mulvey brothers with the King's shilling. I tried to take these archetypes and write about them as though they were real – just as Mulvey, one of several aspiring artists in the novel, borrows the melodies of the past and fills them up with new words.

There have been relatively few novels about the Great Famine. Joyce, Wilde, Yeats, Beckett – the gods of Irish literature hardly mention it at all. As the critic Terry Eagleton has observed: 'If the Famine stirred some to angry rhetoric, it would seem to have traumatized others into muteness.' Certainly, to read contemporaneous accounts is harrowing. Even to glance at the bare statistics is unforgettable. In 1841, four years before the start of the catastrophe, the recorded population of Ireland was 8,175,124. In 1851, the year after it ended, it had fallen to 6,552,385. The historian R.F. Foster has noted that by the 1870s there were three million Irish immigrants living in America - 39% of all those alive who had been born in Ireland. Inevitably, there is scholarly disagreement as to the reliability of the nineteenth-century records. But most agree that Ireland's population today is three million less than it was on the eve of the Great Famine.

A character in Roddy Doyle's novel *The Commitments* jokes: 'The Irish are the blacks of Europe.' How true that was in the time of Mary Duane. And the comparison was made with notable frequency in the nineteenth-century. (In 1892, even Sidney and Beatrice Webb, those sanctified champions of the British Left, remarked of a visit to their neighbouring island: 'We detest them, [the Irish] as we should the Hottentots.')

As I sketched out the novel, its intentions slowly cohered: without hatred or propaganda, to tell the story of this astounding cataclysm, of the culture that allowed it to happen. To celebrate the courage of those who were betrayed; to honour those who attempted to live with love and dignity in a world that regarded them as surplus to requirements. But beneath all that, what I was trying to do was something much more personal: simply to learn the story of Mulvey, my ghost. Where did he come from? Where was he going? Why was he traipsing those starlit decks?

I studied nineteenth-century fiction to try to get the background correct. And I found that I loved those well-upholstered stories from the era when the novel was still a relatively young form. The early novelists had a license to make mistakes, I suppose, and I was excited by the punkish verve of their work. There was also the belief, during the novel's adolescence, that words could portray absolutely anything. Authors were so tenaciously ambitious for language. Dickens, the Brontës were such daring writers, unafraid of large casts of characters or real historical events. To borrow a line from *Spinal Tap*, they weren't afraid to turn the amp up to eleven. No setting was too epic, no technique of narration too audacious. Some novels in our own time seem watery by comparison.

I read first-person accounts by nineteenth-century sea travellers, and eye-witness testimonies of conditions in Ireland and England at the time. Much of this novel is set in 1840s London; the pioneering journalism of Henry Mayhew brought that gloriously gaudy metropolis to life for me. Other sources included ballad-sheets, collections of immigrant letters, engravings from old journals, ships' logs and manifests. But my hope was to write an engaging novel, not a work of history or a textbook. I used nothing that wasn't a direct help in building characters or telling a story.

I must admit that I don't care for many historical novels, with their diligently researched stenches and obsession with inadequate dentistry, their rumbustious heroes and capering paupers. Indeed, while I hope that my book is faithful to the verities of the past, I don't think that being a chronicler alone is enough of an aim for a novelist. So the book touches on many preoccupations of our twenty-first century: sex, the body, gender roles, parenting, music, terrorism, war, religious intolerance. More than that, I hope it also celebrates the solidarities which fill life with joy: friendship, loyalty, home, commitment, the bravery of the emigrant, the indomitable boldness of human desire. *Star of the Sea* has been read in different ways, but to its author, at any rate, it is simply a story about love.

The book took a deal of planning, before ever a word was written. I sensed that it would need many disparate elements, but to discover the order that might make the structure float – that took work and time. Every novel has a secret architecture, and it's important to get that right. Writing is an art, but it is also a craft. It felt important to use a wide variety of storytelling strategies, differing perspectives, voices and time zones – even some laughter, as a kind of hope. The background would be dark: I tried to flood it with light. Otherwise, the book might turn out to be yet another slab of windswept Irish misery, which would sink before its voyage even began.

The thriller, the mystery, the romance, the Gothic suspense tale: all these have traces in *Star of the Sea*. Merridith is a Jekyll (and a Douglas Hyde), Mulvey an Irish cousin of Frankenstein's freak. He is the Artful Dodger with a Galway accent, the trickster who scuttles through folklore gleefully ruining the crops. And behind all that, he is a frightened outcast, desperate to cast off these roles even as he stumbles further into them. The reader needs to be drawn into a novel through its language and atmosphere, through the struggles of recognisable characters, their choices and rejections, and should only absorb whatever it has to say about history through a kind of unnoticed osmosis. First and last, a novel must be an involving read. As David Merridith is fond of claiming: 'Everything is in the way the material is composed.'

But that isn't the whole truth. Composition is not everything. At the nucleus of the story of the *Star of the Sea* are real events, real men and women. To regard such a tragedy as raw material for a novel may be morally ambiguous, to put it mildly. But as Grantley Dixon insists, to remain silent is to say something powerful: that it never happened; that it did not matter; that there was never a Letterfrack, never a Mary Duane, no brutal Commander Blake, no merciful James and Mary Ellis. People like my characters all existed at the time. More to the point, they exist now, too.

On Cashel Hill, Connemara, there is a famine-era cemetery that is still in use today. Ard Cashel in Gaelic ('High Cashel' in English) is one of those lofty and lonesome places that the folk music shared by Ireland and Appalachia somehow translates into sound. Atlantic windstorms buffet Cashel Hill; the trek up is sheer and arduous. On the afternoon I last made the climb, Christmas Eve 1999, a small stars-and-stripes pennant had been placed on a tombstone. It marked out the grave of a young man of Cashel whose family had American connections, as have numberless Connemara people. He was too young when he lost his life, so very far from home. He should be alive today, dandling grandchildren, but that was not to be his emigrant's fate. Born in Galway, he would die on the far side of the planet, on 31 March 1969 – a few months short of his twenty-second birthday. Locals recall that on the icy morning when the American military came to bury him, the jeep that bore his casket could not manage the steepness of Cashel Hill. So he was carried up the mountain to his final resting place, up the rocks to Ard Cashel, as his ancestors had been before. He lies among those others whose names are long forgotten, who were abandoned in the latitudes of hunger.

His grave is a reminder of many things: among them, the awful cost demanded by patriotism, the wrongs we have done to one another for love of country, the dreadful waste that is racism, all those unaccepted friendships, but the hope that the world can yet be a fairer place. I respectfully add his name to the text of this novel, in memory of his short life and of all the nameless who lie around him – or wherever in the land of Connemara they lie.

Lieutenant Corporal Peter Mary Nee: Galway/Connemara
United States Marine Corps
Born August 15, 1947
Died March 31, 1969
Vietnam

– Joseph O'Connor

[The Famine] is a punishment from God for an idle, ungrateful and rebellious country; an indolent and un-self-reliant people. The Irish are suffering from an affliction of God's providence.

Charles Trevelyan, Assistant Secretary to Her Majesty's Treasury, 1847
(Knighted, 1848, for overseeing famine relief)

England is truly a great public criminal. England! All England! . . . She must be punished; that punishment will, as I believe, come upon her by and through Ireland; and so Ireland will be avenged . . . The Atlantic ocean be never so deep as the hell which shall belch down on the oppressors of my race.

John Mitchel, Irish nationalist, 1856

THE MISSING LINK: A creature manifestly between the gorilla and the Negro is to be met with in some of the lowest districts of London and Liverpool by adventurous explorers. It comes from Ireland, whence it has contrived to migrate; it belongs in fact to a tribe of Irish savages: the lowest species of Irish Yahoo. When conversing with its kind it talks a sort of gibberish. It is, moreover, a climbing animal, and may sometimes be seen ascending a ladder laden with a hod of bricks.

Punch magazine, London, 1862

Providence sent the potato blight but England made the Famine . . . We are sick of the canting talk of those who tell us that we must not blame the British people for the crimes of their rulers against Ireland. We do blame them.

James Connolly, co-leader of the Easter Rising
against British Rule, 1916

PROLOGUE

FROM

AN AMERICAN ABROAD:

Notes of London and Ireland in 1847

by G. GRANTLEY DIXON

of the *New York Times*

A LIMITED,
Commemorative One-Hundredth Edition.
REVISED, UNEXPURGATED
and with Many New Inclusions.

THE MONSTER

A PREFACE; IN WHICH ARE SKETCHED CERTAIN
RECOLLECTIONS OF THE STAR OF THE SEA; THE
CONDITION OF HER PASSENGERS AND THE EVIL WHICH
STALKED AMONG THEM.

All night long he would walk the ship, from bow to stern, from dusk until quarterlight, that sticklike limping man from Connemara with the drooping shoulders and ash-coloured clothes.

The sailors, the watchmen, the lurkers near the wheelhouse would glance from their conversations or their solitary work and see him shifting through the vaporous darkness; cautiously, furtively, always alone, his left foot dragging as though hefting an anchor. A billycock hat was crumpled on his head, a ragged scarf wound around his chin and throat; his tattered military greatcoat so utterly dirty it was impossible to imagine it ever having been clean.

He moved with a deliberation that was almost ceremonial, a curious strain of threadbare stateliness: as a king in a story in disguise among his lessers. His arms were very long, his eyes needle-bright. Frequently he had a look of bewilderment or foreboding, as though his life had come to a point that was beyond explication or was drawing ever closer to such a point now.

His mournful face was disfigured with scars, cross-hatched with the blemishes of some affliction much exacerbated by his bouts of furious scratching. Though slender in build, made like a feather-weight, he seemed to carry an indescribable burden. Neither was it a matter of his deformity alone – a distorted foot in a brick of a wooden clog which was stamped or branded with a capital M – but the air of anguished expectancy he bore; the perpetually frightened watchfulness of the abused child.

He was one of those men who attract great attention by making a great effort to attract none. Often, although they could not explain it, the sailors had a sense of his presence before seeing him. It became their amusement to wager on his whereabouts at a given hour. 'Ten bells' meant down by the starboard pigpens. Quarter after eleven found him up at the scuttlebutt where by day the destitute women of steerage prepared what little food they had – but even by the third night out of Liverpool the contest had lost its power to kill the time. He walked the ship as though following a rite. Up. Down. Across. Back. Stem. Port. Stern. Starboard. Materialising with the stars, stealing below with the sunrise, he came to be known among the ship's nocturnal denizens as 'the Ghost'.

Never did he engage the sailors in conversation. The night-stragglers, also, he completely eschewed. Not even after midnight would he speak to another, when anyone still above boards would talk to anyone else; when the dark, wet deck of the *Star of the Sea* saw a fellowship seldom apparent by daylight. Gates were left open at night on the ship; rules relaxed or quite ignored. It was illusory, of course, this witching hour democracy; darkness seeming to obliterate station or creed, or at least level them down to a point where they were not worth acknowledging. An acknowledgement in itself, perhaps, of the axiomatic powerlessness of being at sea.

At night one sensed the ship as absurdly out of its element, a creaking, leaking, incompetent concoction of oak and pitch and nails and faith, bobbing on a wilderness of viciously black water which could explode at the slightest provocation. People spoke quietly on the decks after dark, as though fearful of awakening the ocean to savagery. Or one pictured the *Star* as a colossal beast of burden, its rib-timbers straining as though they might burst; flailed by an overlord into one last persecution, the hulk half dead already and we passengers its parasites. But the metaphor is not a good one for not all of us were parasites. Those of us who were would not have admitted it.

Below us the depths which could only be imagined, the gorges and canyons of that unfathomed continent: above us the death-black bowl of the sky. Wind pounded down in an outrage of screams from what even the most sceptical mariner was careful to term 'the heavens'. And the breakers thrashed and battered our shelter; like wind made flesh, incarnate and animate, a derision of the hubris of those who had dared to invade them. Yet there was an all but religious tranquillity among those who walked the decks at night:

the angrier the sea, the icier the rain, the more palpable the solidarity among those withstanding them together. An admiral might chat to a frightened cabin boy, a hungry man of steerage to a sleepless Earl. One night a prisoner, a maddened violent Galwayman, was brought from the lock-up to take his doleful exercise. Even he was included in this communion of the somnambulant, quietly conversing and sharing a cup of rum with a Methodist minister from Lyme Regis in England who had never tasted rum before but had often preached its evils. (Together they were observed kneeling on the quarterdeck and quietly singing 'Abide With Me'.)

New things were possible in this Republic of night-time. But the Ghost showed no interest in possibility, or novelty. He was immune; a crag in the vastness surrounding him. Prometheus in rags, awaiting the avid birds. He stood by the mainmast watching the Atlantic as though expecting it to freeze over or bubble with blood.

Between first bell and two bells most would slip away; many alone but some together, for tolerances flowered under night's kind cover; nature and loneliness bedfellows in the dark. From three until first light, little happened on deck. It rose and it fell. It climbed. It plunged. Even the animals slept in their cages: pigs and chickens, sheep and geese. The clang of the watch-bell would sometimes puncture the ceaseless and numbing susurration of the sea. A sailor might sing shanties to keep himself awake: he and a comrade might tell stories to each other. From down in the lock-up the madman was intermittently heard, yelping like a wounded dog or threatening to brain the other prisoner with a handspike. (There was, at that time, no other prisoner.) A couple might be glimpsed in the shadowed alleyway formed by the aft wall of the wheelhouse and the base of the funnel. Still he would stand, that man from Connemara, gazing out at the awesome darkness; facing like a figurehead into the sleet, until the webs of the rigging emerged from the murk, so black against the reddening sky of dawn.

Just before sunrise on the third morning, a seaman approached to offer him a pan of coffee. Beadlets of ice had formed on his face, on the back of his coat and the brim of his hat. He did not accept the benevolence nor even acknowledge it. 'As poor as a pox-doctor's clerk,' the Mate remarked, watching him shuffle silently away.

The sailors sometimes wondered if the Ghost's nightly ritual was a religious observance or exotic self-punishment, such as the Catholics of Ireland were whispered to favour. A mortification, perhaps, for some unspeakable transgression, or ransom for the souls ablaze in Purgatory. They believed strange things, these Aboriginal Irish, and a mariner whose profession took him among them might expect to witness strange behaviour. They talked in a nonchalant, matter-of-fact manner about miracles; saintly apparitions; statues that bled. Hell was as real as the city of Liverpool, Paradise as mappable as Manhattan Island. Their prayers were like spells or voodoo incantations. Maybe the Ghost was a holy man: one of their gurus.

Among his own tribe, too, he evoked confusion. The refugees would hear him opening the hatch, hobbling down the ladder and into the gloom of candles; his hair wild, his clothes sodden, his glazen eyes like those of a half-dead mackerel. They knew it was dawn when they saw him coming, but he seemed to bring below the stinging cold of the night. Darkness clung around him, a cloak of many folds. If there was noise, as there often was even at dawn – a huddle of men colloguing, a woman deliriously chanting the Mysteries – his arrival would cause much of it to die. They watched as he shivered the length of the cabin, as he dragged himself down through the bundles and baskets, flaccid with exhaustion, dripping and coughing, a battered puppet whose strings had been cut. He would peel the drenched coat from his shuddering torso, fold it and roll it to the shape of a bolster and slump in his blanket to sleep.

No matter the happening, he would sleep all the day. Invulnerable to the noises of babies or seasickness, to the quarrels and tears and fighting and gaming that made up the clatter of life below decks, to the roars and oaths and wooings and ragings, he would lie on the boards like a corpse. Mice scuttled over him; he never gave a twitch; roaches ran under the collar of his semmit. About him the children would canter or puke, men would scrape fiddles or bellow or argue, women would haggle for a little spare food (for food was this waterborne dominion's only currency, its disbursement a matter of fevered speculation). From the heart of the din came the groans of the sick, rising like prayers from their paltry bunks; the sick and the healthy sleeping side by side, the tormented moans and fearful invocations mingling with the buzzing of the innumerable flies.

The line for the only two water closets in steerage formed directly past the coffin lid of squalid floor that the Ghost had silently claimed as his berth. One lavatory was cracked, the other clogged and over-flowing; the cubicles infested with legions of hissing rats. By seven in the morning the ammoniac stench, constant as the cold and the cries of steerage, would have invaded that floating dungeon with savage force, would be filling it up like an erupting spirit. The stink had an almost corporeal presence; it felt like something you could grasp in gluey fistfuls. Rotten food, rotten flesh, rotten fruit of rotting bowels, you smelt it on your clothes, your hair, your hands; on the glass you drank from and the bread you ate. Tobacco smoke, vomit, stale per-spiration, mildewed clothes, filthy blankets and rotgut whiskey.

The portholes intended to ventilate steerage would be thrown open in an attempt to quell the astounding putrescent reek. But if anything, the breeze seemed only to make it worse, blowing it into the hollows and alcoves. Saltwater would be sluiced over the boards twice a week, but even the freshwater stank of diarrhoea and had to be laced with vinegar before it could be faced. The malicious fetor oozed its way around steerage, a steaming, noxious, nauseating vapour that stung the eyes and inflamed the nostrils. But that choking effluvium of death and abandonment was not baneful enough to wake the Ghost.

Since the start of the voyage he had remained imperturbable. Just before noon on the morning we left Liverpool a great shout had gone up from a group on the maindeck. A barquentine had been sighted approaching from the south, heading up the coast towards Dublin. *The Duchess of Kent* was her honoured name. She had carried the remains of Daniel O'Connell, M.P. – 'the Liberator' to Ireland's Catholic poor – from his death-place at Genoa in August of that year, to be laid to rest in his motherland.* Seeing the ship was like seeing the man; so it appeared from the passengers' tearful praying. But far from joining the Novenas for the fallen champion, the Ghost had not even come up on deck to watch. Heroes did not interest him as much as sleep; nor did their hallowed vessels.

At eight o'clock the galley crew distributed the daily ration: half a pound of hardtack and a quart of water for each adult, half that

*In my memory the sails on that ship were black, but when I consult my notes I see I am mistaken. – G.G. Dixon

banquet for every child. Roll call was taken at a quarter after nine. Those who had died the night before were removed from steerage to await disposal. Sometimes the slumbering Ghost was mistaken for one of them and required the protection of his dilapidated fellows. The plywood bunks would be hastily hosed down. Swabs were mopped across the boards. Blankets would be collected and boiled in urine to kill the lice that spread scabies.

After they had eaten, the people of steerage would dress and wander up to the deck. There they would walk in the clean, cold air; would sit on the boards and beg from the sailors; would watch through the cast-iron double-locked gates as we First-Class passengers took pastries and coffee under the shelter of the silken awnings. Exactly how the cream was kept fresh for the rich was often vigorously discussed by the poor. A bead of blood dropped into the mix was said by some to be effective.

The first days passed with agonising slowness. To the passengers' stupefaction, they had learned at Liverpool that the ship would be taking them back to Ireland before setting out to confront the Atlantic. The news led to frustrated drinking among the men, which in turn had led to frustrated fights. Most in steerage had sold all they owned to gather the fare across to Liverpool. Many had been robbed in that unhappy and violent city, swindled into parting with their few possessions; sold heaps of crudely stamped pewter washers which they were informed were American dollars. Now they were being carried back to Dublin, from where they had fled in the weeks before, resigned – or endeavouring to become resigned, at least – to never setting eyes on their homeland again.

But even that small blessing was to be denied them. We had chopped across a filthy-tempered Irish Sea and docked at Kingstown to take on provisions; then crept down the jagged south-east coast, making for Queenstown in the county of Cork. (Or 'Cobh', as it is known in the Gaelic language.) Seeing Wicklow glide past, or Wexford or Waterford, seemed to many a bitter taunt, a poultice being ripped from a putrefying wound. A consumptive blacksmith from the town of Bunclody jumped the upperdeck rail near Forlorn Point and was last seen swimming weakly towards the shore; every last shred of his will employed to bring him back to the place where his death was certain.

At Queenstown a hundred more passengers came on, their condition so dreadful that it made the others seem as royalty. I saw one elderly woman, little more than an agglomeration of rags, barely gain the gangplank only to die on the foredeck. Her children beseeched the Captain to take her to America anyway. No means were available to pay for her burial but they could not support the shame of dumping her body on the wharf. Her aged and crippled husband was lying on the quayside, too afflicted by famine fever to be able for the journey, a few short hours from death himself. He could not be asked to witness that sight as one of his last sights on earth.

The Captain had refused to acquiesce. A sympathetic man, he was a Quaker by faith, but bound by a set of regulations he dared not to transgress. After almost an hour of weeping and begging, a middle course was discovered and carefully plotted. The woman's body was wrapped in a blanket from the Captain's own bunk, then placed in the lock-up until we had left the port, at which point it was discreetly thrown overboard. Her people had to do it themselves. No seaman could be asked to touch the remains in case of infection. It was later recounted by the Fourth Engineer, who against all advice had been moved to assist them, that they had disfigured her face terribly with some kind of blade, fearful that the current would drift her back to Crosshaven where she might be recognised by her former neighbours. Amongst those so poor that they deserve no shame, shame lasts even longer than life. Humiliation their only inheritance, and denial the coinage in which it is paid.

The batterings of recent crossings had taken their toll of the *Star*, a vessel approaching the end of her service. In her eighty-year span she had borne many cargoes: wheat from Carolina for the hungry of Europe, Afghanistan opium, 'blackpowder' explosive, Norwegian timber, sugar from Mississippi, African slaves for the sugar plantations. The highest and the most hideous instincts of man had been equally served by the *Star*'s existence; to walk her decks and touch her boards was to feel in powerful communion with both. Her Captain did not know – perhaps nobody knew – but she was bound for Dover Docks when this voyage was completed, there to finish out her days as a hulk for convicts. A few of the steerage people were offered work by the Captain's Mate: coopering, caulking, doing odd bits of joinery, stitching up shrouds out of lengths of sailcloth. These were envied by their comrades who had no trade or whose trade back in Ireland had been tending sheep: as useless an occupation aboard the ship as it would surely prove in the slums and rookeries of Brooklyn. On-board work meant extra food. For some, it meant survival.

No Catholic priest was among us on the *Star of the Sea*, but sometimes in the afternoon the Methodist minister would recite a few uncontroversial words on the quarterdeck or read aloud from the scriptures. He favoured Leviticus, Maccabees and Isaiah. *Howl, ye ships of Tarshish: for your strength is laid waste.* Some of the children found his fiery style frightening and pleaded with their parents to be taken away. But many remained behind to listen, as much to kill the boredom as anything else. A small-headed, dapper, compassionate man, he would stand on his tiptoes and conduct them with his toothbrush as they sang the adamant hymns of his denomination, the lyrics starkly majestic as granite-stone graves.

> *O God, our help in ages past,*
> *Our hope for years to come;*
> *Our shelter from the stormy blast,*
> *And our eternal home.*

Down in steerage, the Ghost slept on through the singing.

And then the darkness would descend again. He would rise from his flea-ridden heap of stinking bedding and devour his ration like a man possessed. His food was left for him in a pail beside his berth and though theft of food was far from unknown on the *Star*, nobody ever stole the Ghost's.

He would take a drink of water. Every other day he would shave. Then he would don his ancient greatcoat, as a warrior putting on his armour of battle, and bluster his way up into the night.

The steerage cabin was situated directly below the maindeck, its half-rotted roof planks here and there as brittle as the biscuit that kept its inhabitants one swallow from death. So sometimes in steerage, as the dusk came down, they would hear the *clug* of his wooden shoe above them. A thud, and a shower of powdery splinters, causing children to chuckle into their gruel or take a kind of delicious fright. Some of the mothers would seize on their trepidation: 'If you're not good this minute and do as you're bidden, I'll put you above for Lord Ugly to eat you.'

The Ghost was not ugly but his face was unusual. Pale as milk and slightly elongated, its features might have been stolen from several different men. His nose was bent and a little too long. His ears protruded slightly like those of a harlequin. His hair, as a hideously overgrown black dandelion, might once have belonged to a pantomime ghoul. His wan blue eyes had an unearthly clarity which made the rest of his face seem dark despite its pallor. A smell of wet ashes hung around him, commingling with the odour of the long-time traveller. Yet he was more careful than many in his habits and was frequently observed to use half his water ration to wash his comically tangled hair, as meticulous as any débutante preparing for a ball.

Tedium was the god who reigned over steerage, commanding the acolytes of restlessness and dismay. The Ghost's eccentric demeanour soon began to attract speculation. Any assemblage comprising human beings, any family, any party, any tribe, any nation, will bind itself together not by what it shares but ultimately by what it fears, which is often so much greater. Perhaps it abhors the outsider as camouflage for its own alarms; dreading what it would do to itself were the binding to fall asunder. The Ghost became useful as the stranger of steerage, the freak come among the terrified normal. His presence helped to cultivate the illusion of unity. That he was indeed so very strange only increased his value.

Rumours adhered to him like barnacles to a hull. It was said by some that he had been a moneylender back in Ireland; a 'gombeen' in their slang; a hated figure. Others pronounced him the former master of a workhouse, or a landlord's agent or a deserted soldier. A candle-maker from Dublin insisted the Ghost was an actor and swore he had seen him playing his namesake in a production of *Hamlet* at the Queen's in Brunswick Street. Two Fermanagh girls who never laughed were certain he must have served time in a bridewell, so cold was his expression and so calloused his small hands. His apparent fear of daylight and love of the darkness led some of the imaginative to call him 'a cithoge'; a weird supernatural of Irish legend, the child of a faerie and a mortal man, possessed of the power to curse and conjure. Yet nobody was sure of exactly what he was, for he gave away little in conversation. Even a question of platitudinous unimportance would draw only a mumble by way of response, always evasive or too quiet to be understood. But he had the vocabulary of a scholar and was certainly literate, which many of those in steerage were not. Approached by one of the braver children, he would sometimes read in an oddly tender whisper from a tiny book of stories which he kept in the depths of his greatcoat and never allowed anyone to touch or examine.

When drunk, which was rare, he had his countrymen's habit of talking in ironies that do not seem ironic: of turning a question back on the interrogator. But most of the time he did not speak at all. He took pains to avoid one-to-one conversation completely, and in company – which was often unavoidable, given the merciless realities of steerage – he would bow his head and gaze at the boards, as one lost in prayer or hopeless recollection.

It was said by some of the children he tolerated that he knew the names of an astonishing number of species of fish. Music, too, seemed to interest him somewhat. One of the sailors, from memory a Mancunian, claimed to have seen him studying a broadsheet of Irish ballads – and laughing at its contents for some unrevealed reason: 'cackling like a crone on Hallowe'en night'. When asked with absolute directness he would give an opinion of a fiddler. But the opinion was always briefly expressed, and almost always approving in tone, and as happens with those who only give approving opinions, the others soon wearied of asking him.

He had something of the younger priest; an unease around women. But clearly enough he was no sort of priest. He read no breviary, dispensed no blessing, never joined in the Glory Be. And when the first of the passengers was taken by typhus, two days out of Queenstown port, he did not attend the obsequies such as they were: a dereliction that caused a certain amount of muttering in steerage. But then it occurred to someone that the Ghost might be 'a Jewman', or possibly even some kind of Protestant. That, too, could have explained his unease.

It was not that he did anything unpredictable – in truth he was the most predictable man on the ship. It was more that his very predictability made him strange.

It was as though he was certain that someone was watching him.

Even at that greener and youthful interval, I had happened upon men who had taken life. Soldiers. *Presidentes*. Gangsters. Executioners. Since that terrible voyage I have met many more. Some killed for money, others for country: many, I think now, because they found pleasure in killing and used money or country as varieties of disguise. But this inconsequential little man was different to all of them: this monster who haunted the decks at night. To observe him shuffling that vessel of miseries, as he shuffles, still, across my memory, even at this interim of almost seven decades, was to witness one who was curious in his behaviour, certainly; but no more than many in the strangle of poverty. No more than most, if the truth be told.

There was something so intensely ordinary about him. It could never have been guessed that he meant to do murder.

Farewell to old Ireland, the land of my childhood,
Which now and forever I'm obliged for to leave.
Farewell to the shores where the shamrock is growing.
It's the bright spot of beauty, the home of the brave.
I will think of her valleys with fond admiration,
Though never again her green hills will I see.
I am bound for to cross o'er the wild swelling ocean
In search of fame, fortune and sweet Liberty.

CHAPTER I

THE LEAVE-TAKING

The FIRST of our TWENTY-SIX days at Sea: in
which Our Protector records some essential
Particulars, and the Circumstances attending our
setting-out.

VIII NOV. MDCCCXLVII
Monday the eighth day of November, Eighteen Hundred
and Forty-Seven
Twenty-five days at sea remaining.

The following is the only register of Josias Tuke Lockwood, Master of Vessel, signed and written in his own hand; and I attest it on my solemn honour a compleat and true account of the voyage, and neither has any matter pertinent been omitted.

Long: 10°16.7′W. Lat: 51°35.5′N. Actual Greenwich Standard Time: 8.17 p.m. Wind Dir. & Speed: S.S.W. Force 4. Buffeting Seas: rough. Heading: W.N.W. 282.7°. Precipitation. & Remarks: Mild mist all the day but very cold and clear night. Upper riggings encrusted with ice. Dursey Island to starboard. Tearagh Isld visible at 52°4.5′N, 10°39.7′W, most westerly point of Ireland and therefore of the United Kingdom. (Property of the Earl of Cork.)
Name of Vessel: The *Star of the Sea* (formerly the *Golden Lady*).
Builder: John Wood, Port Glasgow (prop. engines by M. Brunel).
Owner: Silver Star Shipping Line & Co.
Previous Voyage: Dublin Port (South Docks) – Liverpool – Dublin Kingstown.
Port of Embarkation: Queenstown (or The Cove). 51°51′N; 008°18′W.

PORT OF DESTINATION: New York. 40°.42′N; 74°.02′W.

DISTANCE: 2,768 nautical miles direct: to be factorised for tacking into westerlies.

FIRST MATE: Thos. Leeson.

ROYAL MAIL AGENT: George Wellesley Esq. (accompnd. by a servant, Briggs).

WEIGHT OF VESSEL: 1,154 gross tons.

LENGTH OF VESSEL: 207 ft × beam 34ft.

GENERAL: clipper bows, one funnel, three square-rig masts (rigged for sail), oaken hull (copperfastened), three decks, a poop and topgallant forecastle, side-paddle wheel propulsion, full speed 9 knots. All seaworthy though substantial repairs required; also damage to interior fittings & cetera. Bad leaking through overhead and bulkheads of steerage. Hull to be audited in dry dock at New York and caulked if required.

CARGO: 5,000 lbs of mercury for Alabama Mining Co. The Royal Mail (forty bags). Sunderland coal for fuel. (Poor quality the supply, dirty and slaggy.) Luggage of passengers. Spare slop in stores. One grand piano for John J. Astor Esq. at New York.

PROVISIONS: sufficient of freshwater, ale, brandy, claret, rum, pork, cocks, mutton, biscuit, preserved milk & cetera. Also oatmeal, cutlings, molasses, potatoes, salt or hung beef, pork, bacon and hams, salted veal, fowl in pickle, coffee, tea, cyder, spices, pepper, ginger, flour, eggs, good port wine and porter-beer, pickled colewort, split peas for soup; and lastly, vinegar, butter, and potted herrings. Live beasts (caged) to be butchered on board: pigs, chickens, lambs and geese.

One passenger, a certain Meadowes, is lodged in the lock-up for drunkenness and fighting. (A hopeless out-and-outer: he shall have to be watched.) Suspected case of Typhus Fever moved to the hold for isolation.

Be it recorded that this day three passengers of the steerage class died, the cause in each case being the infirmity consequent on prolonged starvation. Margaret Farrell, fifty-two yrs, a married woman of Rathfylane, Enniscorthy, County Wexford; Joseph English, seventeen yrs (formerly, it is said, apprenticed to a wheelwright) of no fixed place but born near Cootehill, County

Cavan; and James Michael Nolan of Skibbereen, County Cork, aged one month and two days (bastard child).

Their mortal remains were committed to the sea. May Almighty God have mercy upon their souls: 'For here have we no continuing city, but we seek the one to come.'

We have thirty-seven crew, 402½ ordinary steerage passengers (a child being reckoned in the usual way as one half of one adult passenger) and fifteen in the First-Class quarters or superior staterooms. Among the latter: Earl David Merridith of Kingscourt and his wife the Countess, their children and an Irish maidservant. Mr G.G. Dixon of the *New York Tribune*: a noted columnist and man of letters. Surgeon Wm. Mangan, M.D. of the Theatre of Anatomy, Peter Street, Dublin, accompanied by his sister, Mrs Derrington, relict; His Imperial Highness, the potentate Maharajah Ranjitsinji, a princely personage of India; Reverend Henry Deedes, D.D., a Methodist Minister from Lyme Regis in England (upgraded); and various others.

As we sailed this day came heavy news of the wreck of the *Exmouth* out of Liverpool on the 4th ult. with the loss of all 239½ emigrants on board and all but three of the crew. May Almighty God have mercy upon their souls: and may He bestow greater clemency upon our own voyage; or at least observe it with benign indifference.

. . . poeple that Cuts a great dash at home when they come here [to America] the[y] tink it strange for the humble Class of poeple to get as much respect as themselves [but] when they come here it wont do to say i had such and was such and such at home [for] strangers here the[y] must gain respect by there conduct and not by there tongue . . . i know poeple here from [Ireland] that would not speak to me [there] if they met me on the public road [but] here i can laugh in there face when i see them . . .

Letter from Patrick Dunny, Irish immigrant to Philadelphia

CHAPTER II

THE VICTIM

The SECOND evening of the Voyage:
in which a certain important Passenger is
introduced to the Reader.

12°49′W; 51°11′N.
— 8.15 P.M. —

The Right Honourable Thomas David Nelson Merridith, the noble Lord Kingscourt, the Viscount of Roundstone, the ninth Earl of Cashel, Kilkerrin and Carna, entered the Dining Saloon to an explosion of smashing glass.

A steward, a Negro, had stumbled near the doorway, bucked by a sudden roll of the vessel, letting slip an overloaded salver of charged champagne flutes. Someone was performing an ironic slow-handclap at the fallen man's expense. An inebriated mocking cheer came from the farthest corner: 'Huazzah! Bravo! Well done, that fellow!' Another voice called: 'They'll have to put up the fares!'

The steward was on his knees now, trying to clear the debris. Blood was riveting down his slender left wrist, staining the cuff of his brocaded jacket. In his anxiety to collect the shards of shattered crystal he had sliced open his thumb from ball to tip.

'Mind your hand,' Lord Kingscourt said. 'Here.' He offered the steward a clean linen handkerchief. The man looked up with an expression of dread. His mouth began to work but no sound came. The Chief Steward had bustled over and was barking at his subordinate in a language Merridith did not understand. Was it German, perhaps? Portuguese? Saliva flew from his mouth as he hissed and cursed the man, who was now cowering on the carpet like a beaten child, his uniform besmirched with blood and champagne, a grotesque parody of commodore's whites.

'David?' called Merridith's wife. He turned to look. She had half risen from her banquette at the Captain's table and was gaily beckoning him over with a bread-knife, her knotted eyebrows and pinched lips set in a burlesque of impatience. The people around her were laughing madly, all except the Maharajah, who never laughed. When Merridith glanced back towards the steward again, he was being chivvied from the saloon by his furious superior, the latter still bawling in the guttural language, the transgressor cradling his hand to his breast like a wounded bird.

Lord Kingscourt's palate tasted acridly of salt. His head hurt and his vision was cloudy. For several weeks he had been suffering some kind of urinary infection and since boarding the ship at Kingstown, it had worsened significantly. This morning it had pained him to pass water; a scalding burn that had made him cry out. He wished he'd seen a doctor before embarking on the voyage. Nothing for it now but to wait for New York. Couldn't be frank with that drunken idiot Mangan. Maybe four weeks. Hope and pray.

Surgeon Mangan, a morose old bore by day, was already pink in the face from drinking, his greasy hair gleaming like a polished strap. His sister, who looked like a caricature of a cardinal, was systematically breaking the petals off a pale yellow rose. For a moment Lord Kingscourt wondered if she was going to eat them; but instead she dropped them one by one into her tumbler of water. Watching them with a sullen undergraduate expression sat the Louisiana columnist, Grantley Dixon, in a dinner jacket he had clearly borrowed from someone larger and which gave his shoulders a boxy look. Merridith disliked him and always had, since being forced to endure his socialistic prattle at one of Laura's infernal literary evenings in London. The novelists and poets were tolerable in their way, but the aspiring novelists and poets were simply insufferable. A clown, Grantley Dixon, a perfervid parrot, with his militant slogans and second-hand attitudes: like all coffee-house radicals a screaming snob at heart. As for his imperious guff about the novel he was writing, Merridith knew a dilettante when he saw one, and he was looking at one now. When he'd heard Grantley Dixon was going to be on the same ship, he had almost wanted to postpone the journey. But Laura had told him he was being ridiculous. He could always count on Laura to tell him that.

What a collection to have to abide over dinner. A favourite expression of his father's came into Merridith's mind. *Too much for the white man to be asked to bear.*

'Are you quite all right, dear?' Laura asked. She enjoyed the role of the concerned wife, particularly when she had an audience to appreciate her concern. He didn't mind. It made her happy. Sometimes it even made him happy too.

'You look as if you're in pain. Or discomfort of some kind.'

'I'm fine,' he said, easing into his seat. 'Just famished.'

'Amen to that,' said Surgeon Mangan.

'Excuse my lateness,' Lord Kingscourt said. 'There are two little chaps I know who insist on being told bedtime stories.'

The Mail Agent, a father, gave a strange, baleful smile. Merridith's wife rolled her eyes like a doll.

'Our girl Mary is ill again,' she said.

Mary Duane was their nanny, a native from Carna in County Galway. David Merridith had known her all his life.

'I don't know what's come over that girl,' Lady Kingscourt continued. 'She's barely left her cabin since the moment we boarded. When usually she's hale as a Connemara pony. And quite as bloody-minded as one too.' She held up her fork and gazed at it closely, for some reason gently pricking her fingertips with the ends of the tines.

'Perhaps she is homesick,' Lord Kingscourt said.

His wife laughed briefly. 'I hardly think so.'

'I notice some of the sailorboys giving her the glad eye,' said the Surgeon affably. 'Pretty little thing if she didn't wear so much black.'

'She was bereaved of her husband not too long ago,' said Merridith. 'So she probably shan't notice the sailorboys I should think.'

'Oh dear, oh dear. Hard thing at her age.'

'Quite.'

Wine was poured. Bread was offered. A steward brought a tureen and began to serve the vichyssoise.

Lord Kingscourt was finding it difficult to concentrate. A worm of pain corkscrewed slowly through his groin: a stone-blind maggot of piercing venom. He could feel his shirt sticking to his shoulders and abdomen. The Dining Saloon had an ashy, stagnant atmosphere, as though pumped dry of air and filled up with pulverised lead. Against the cloying odour of meat and over-bloomed lilies another more evil stench was trying to gain. What in the name of Christ was that filthy smell?

The Surgeon had clearly been in the middle of one of his interminable stories when Merridith had arrived. He resumed telling it now, chuckling expansively, enfeebled by duckish clucks of self-amusement as he gaped around at the dutifully simpering company. Something about a pig who could talk. Or dance? Or stand on its hind legs and sing Tom Moore. It was an Irish peasant story anyway: all of the Surgeon's were. *Gintilmin. Sorr. Jayzus be savin' Yer Worship.* He tugged his invisible forelock and puffed out his cheeks, so juicily proud of his facility for imitation. It was something Merridith found hard to stomach, the way the prosperous Irish were never done lampooning their rural countrymen: a sign, they often claimed, of their own maturity on matters national, but in truth just another form of cringing obsequiousness.

'Will you tell me now,' the Surgeon chortled, his bright eyes streaming with excess of mirth, 'where else could that happen but darlin' auld Oirland?'

He spoke the last three words as though in inverted commas.

'Wonderful people,' agreed the heavily perspiring Mail Agent. 'A marvellous logic all their own.'

The Maharajah said nothing for a few long moments, grim-faced and bored in his stiff robes. Then he muttered a few gloomy syllables and snapped his fingers to his personal butler who was standing like a Guardian Angel a few feet behind him. The butler brought over a small silver box, which the Maharajah reverently opened. Out of it he took a pair of spectacles. He looked at them for a moment, as though surprised to have found them there. Cleaned them with a napkin and put them on.

'You'll remain at New York for some time, Lord Kingscourt?'

It took a moment for Merridith to realise whom the Captain was addressing.

'Indeed,' he said. 'I mean to go into business, Lockwood.'

Inevitably Dixon gave him a look. 'Since when did the gentry stoop to working for a living?'

'There's a famine in progress in Ireland, Dixon. I assume you stumbled across it on your visit there, did you?'

The Captain gave an apprehensive laugh. 'I'm sure our American friend meant no offence, Lord Kingscourt. He only thought – '

'I'm quite aware of what he thought. How can an Earl be fallen low as a tradesman? In a way my dear wife often thinks the same thing.' He looked across the table at her. 'Don't you, Laura?'

Lady Kingscourt said nothing. Her husband went back to his soup. He wanted to eat it before it coagulated.

'Yes. So you see my predicament, Dixon. Not a man on my estate has paid rent for four years. My father's death leaves me with half of all the bogland in southern Connemara, a great deal of stones and bad turf, a greater deal of overdue accounts and unpaid wages. Not to mention the considerable duties owing to the government.' He broke a piece of bread and took a sip of wine. 'Dying is rather expensive,' he smiled darkly at the Captain. 'Unlike this claret. Which is muck.'

Lockwood glanced uneasily around the table. He wasn't accustomed to dealing with the aristocracy.

A young woman had begun to pluck the ornate harp that was sitting near the dessert table in the middle of the saloon, beside the dripping ice sculpture of Neptune Triumphant. The melody sounded tinny and just slightly out of tune, as harp music habitually sounded to Merridith, but she played with a seriousness he found affecting. He wished the Dining Saloon were empty except for himself and the young woman. He would have liked to sit there and drink for a while: drinking and listening to the out-of-tune music. Drinking until he felt nothing.

Connors? Mulligan? Lenihan? Moran?

Earlier in the day, through the cast-iron bars that fenced off the people of steerage from their betters, he had noticed a man he had often seen in the streets of Clifden. The fellow was in chains, and either drunk or half mad, but Merridith still recognised him, he wasn't mistaken. He was a tenant of Tommy Martin's at Ballynahinch. Apparently – so the Methodist minister from Lyme

Regis had said – he had been flung in the lock-up for being drunk and violent. Merridith had been quite astounded to hear it. That wasn't at all how he remembered him.

Corrigan? Joyce? Mahony? Black?

He would come in to Clifden on a Monday morning to sell turnips and kale with father, a smallholder: a pugnacious little jockey of a typical Galwayman, full of spit and strength and snap. What the hell was his name? Fields? Shields? A widower, anyway. Wife died in '36. He'd scraped a living for himself and seven children out of a perch of quartzite shale on the slopes of Bencollaghduff. Ridiculous to say, Merridith had often envied them.

He knew himself how ridiculous that was. And yet the father was clearly so proud of his son. There was a tenderness between them, an embarrassed affection, even though they were never done goading each other. The farmer would accuse his son of idleness; the son would retort that his father was a drunken gawm. The man would clip his son across the head; the son would fling a half-rotten turnip at him. The women of Clifden would congregate around their rickety stall as much to watch them trade imprecations as to buy what meagre goods they offered. Abusing each other had become a kind of pantomime. But Merridith knew that was all it was.

Meadowes?

Very early one December morning, driving the phaeton to meet his sister off the mail-coach at Maam Cross, he had seen them kicking a ragged football in the middle of the empty marketplace. The morning was still: a little misty. Their stall had been set up near the gates of the church, the turnips polished like gleaming orbs. The whole town was asleep except for the father and son. Leaves were drifting in the deserted streets; the fields in the distance were silvered with dew. He remembered it all now, as he sat in the Dining Saloon, plunging through the rolling darkness of the sea. The strange beauty of everything in the Connemara morning. Their shadowed forms gliding through the mist like celestial beings. The *thuk* as one of them would hoof into the ball. The muffled shouts. The impish obscenities. The extraordinary music of their unrestrained laughter echoing against the high black walls of the church.

In all his childhood Lord David Merridith had never kicked a football with his own father. He wasn't sure his father would have *recognised* a football. He remembered saying as much to his sister when he met her off the Bianconi that morning, weighed down with Christmas parcels and boxes of candied fruits; brimming with news and gossip from London. The way she had laughed and agreed with his remark. Probably, Emily said, if Papa had ever seen a football, he would have rammed it into a cannon and tried to shoot it at a Frenchman.

He wondered where his father was now. His body was buried in the churchyard at Clifden; but where was *he*? Was there any shred of truth to it, after all, the pietistical absurdity of life after death? Could the story be metaphor for some other, more scientific reality? Would the sages of the coming times be able to decode the allegory? And if such a truth existed, how did it work? Where was Heaven? And where was Hell?

Am I all my fathers? Are they all me?

Three weeks before embarking on the *Star of the Sea*, Merridith had locked up the house in which he and his father and grandfather had been born, shuttered up its shattered windows, closed it and locked it for the last time. He had handed the keys to the valuer from Galway and walked around the empty stables for a while. Not a single former tenant had turned up to see him off. He had waited until dusk but nobody had come.

Accompanied by his bodyguard – the man had insisted – he had ridden out from Kingscourt to visit his father's grave at Clifden, only to find that it had been desecrated again. The granite sea-angel had been smashed in two, the words ROTTIN BASTARD whitewashed across the tombstone, along with the emblem of those who had put them there. His grandfather's grave and those of the ancestors had all been marked with the splattered badge of their loathing. Merridith's own name appeared on several of the stones, and those ones, too, had been defaced. His mother's tomb alone had not been touched, a pardoning which had merely made the despoliation around it seem starker. But looking at the scene, he had been able to feel nothing. Only the misspelled words had truly taken his attention. Did they mean that his father was rotten or rotting?

He wondered about that now: the awful inadequacy of his response. And what precisely had they meant to say, these men who had ruined his father's grave? Their symbol was an H enclosed in a heart, but what heart was it that could violate the dead? 'Hibernian Defenders', his bodyguard had explained; the name the local troublemakers gave to themselves. Another name they went by was 'the Liable Men', primarily because they dealt out liability; also they were gruesomely reliable in doing so. And Merridith had quietly pretended not to know these etymologies already, had feigned his usual interest in the customs of the indigenous, as though the constable had been enlightening him about jig steps or fairytales. Had they truly hated his father quite so much? What had he done to deserve their repugnance? Yes, he had been an inflexible landlord, in the latter years especially; that was undeniable. But so had most other landlords in Ireland, and in England too, and everywhere else: some far worse and many more cruel. Didn't they know, these night-stalking mutilators, how much his father had tried to do for them? Couldn't they understand he was a man of his time, a conservative by instinct as well as politics? That politics and instinct were often the same thing, in the pebbled fields of Galway, in the statued halls of Westminster. Probably in every other place, too. 'Politics' the polite word for antediluvian prejudices, the rags put on by enmity and tribal resentment.

For some reason Merridith found himself thinking about his children: a memory of his younger son as a baby, sobbing in the night with the pain of teething. The puppet-stuffed nursery in the London house. Stroking the child's head. Holding his hand. A blackbird hopping on the rain-spattered windowsill. The tiny fingers tendrilling around his own, as though mutely to plead, 'stay with me'. Like Christ in the garden. Watch with me one hour. The heart-rending smallnesses we finally want. Strange thought that Merridith's father had been a baby once. And in the minutes before he died he had seemed so again; that vast, indignant, iron-hearted seaman whose portrait hung in galleries all over the empire. He had reached out his frail, white hand to David Merridith and squeezed his thumb as though trying to break it. There was fear in his eyes; gleaming terror. And David Merridith had wanted to say, It's all right. I'll stay with you. Don't be afraid. But he had not been able to say anything.

As though waking from a sleep that has lasted too long, he realised the people around him were talking about the Famine.

The Mail Agent was loudly contending with Dixon. 'The landlords aren't all bad, you know, dear boy. Many of them subsidise their tenants to emigrate.'

The American scoffed. 'To rid their estates of the weakest and keep the best.'

'I suppose they must run their lands as a proper business,' attempted the Captain. 'It's a hard thing for everyone, but there it is.'

The thrown-back glower was wholly predictable. 'And is it proper business to accommodate the steerage passengers as you have on this vessel?'

'The passengers are treated as well as my men can hope to treat them. I must work within the constraints laid down by my owners.'

'Your "owners", Captain? And who might those be?'

'I mean the owners of the ship. The Silver Star company.'

Dixon nodded grimly, as though having expected the answer. He was the kind of radical, so Merridith assumed, who is secretly relieved that injustices exist; morality being so easily attainable by saying you found them outrageous.

'He has a point, Lockwood,' the Surgeon said. 'Those people down in steerage aren't Africans, after all.'

'Nig-nogs are cleaner,' the Mail Agent chuckled.

The Surgeon's sister emitted a hiccup of tipsy laughter. Her brother gave her an admonishing glance. Quickly she arranged her features into an expression of sorrow.

'Treat a man like a savage and he'll behave like one,' Merridith said. His voice had a tremble that frightened him a little. 'Anyone acquainted with Ireland should know that fact. Or Calcutta or Africa or anywhere else.'

At the mention of Calcutta some of the company surreptitiously glanced at the Maharajah. But he was busy blowing on a spoonful of soup. A surprising thing to do, perhaps, given that the soup was already chilled.

Grantley Dixon was staring at Lord Kingscourt now. 'That's rich, Merridith, coming from you. I don't know how a member of your class can sleep at night.'

'I sleep very well, I assure you, old thing. But then I always peruse your latest article immediately before retiring.'

'I am aware that your Lordship has learned how to read. Since you wrote to my editor to complain about my work.'

Merridith gave a low-lidded, disdainful grin. 'Sometimes I even snore a little and keep my wife awake in bed.'

'David, for heaven's sake.' Lady Kingscourt was blushing. 'Such talk at the dining table.'

'Quite a sight, the periodic eruption of Mount Dixon the Lesser. As for when your long-awaited novel finally delights us all by appearing, no doubt I shall find it as conducive to tranquillity as the rest of your effusions. I dare say I shall sleep like Endymion, then.'

Dixon didn't join in the round of uneasy laughter. 'You keep your people in abject penury, or near it. Break their backs with work to pay for your position, then put them off the land with no compensation when it suits you.'

'No tenant of mine has been put off the land without compensation.'

'Because there's hardly anyone left to put off it, since your father evicted half of his tenants. Consigned them to the workhouse or death on the roads.'

'Dixon, please,' said the Captain quietly.

'How many of them are in Clifden Workhouse tonight, Lord Kingscourt? Spouses kept apart as a condition of entry. Children younger than your own torn from their parents to slave.' He reached into the pocket of his tuxedo and pulled out a notebook. 'Did you know they have names? Would you like me to list them? Ever once visited to read a bedtime story to *them*?'

Merridith's face felt as though it were sun-scorched. 'Do not dare to impugn my father in my presence, sir. Never again. Do you understand me?'

'David, calm down,' his wife said quietly.

'My father loved Ireland and fought for her freedom against the vicious scourge of Bonapartism. And I have used what you term "my position", Mr Dixon, to make strenuous argument for reform of the workhouses. Which would not be there at all to offer what help they do were it not for the likes of my father.'

Dixon gave a barely audible scoff. Merridith's tone was becoming more strident.

'I have spoken about the matter frequently, in the House of

Lords and other places. But I shouldn't suppose your readers would be interested in that. Rather tittle-tattle and muck-raking and simplistic caricatures.'

'I represent the free press of America, Lord Kingscourt. I write as I find and I always will.'

'Don't delude yourself, sir. You represent nothing.'

'Gentlemen, gentlemen,' the Captain sighed. 'I implore you. We have a long voyage ahead, so let us leave aside our differences and remain good friends and companions together.'

Silence settled over the discomfited company. It was as though an uninvited guest had sat down at the table but everyone was too embarrassed to mention the fact. A dribble of unenthusiastic applause sounded through the saloon as the harpist finished a sentimental Celtic melody. Dixon pushed his plate away desultorily and downed a glass of water in three quick gulps.

'Perhaps we shall postpone the political discussion until later in the evening when the ladies have retired,' the Captain said, forcing a laugh. 'Now. More wine, anyone?'

'I have done all I can to improve the situation of those in the workhouses,' Merridith said, trying to keep his tone steady. 'I have lobbied, for example, to relax the conditions for admission. But this is a very difficult question.' He allowed himself to meet Dixon's now unmeasurable gaze. 'Perhaps you and I can have a talk about it on another occasion.' He added once more: 'it's a difficult question.'

'It certainly is,' Merridith's wife said suddenly. 'Unless strict conditions are imposed they take advantage of the help offered them, David. The conditions should be a great deal stricter, if anything.'

'That is not the case, dear, as I have told you previously.'

'I believe it is,' she calmly continued.

'No, it isn't,' said Merridith. 'And I have corrected you on this question before.'

'Otherwise we merely encourage that same idleness and dependency which have only led to their present misfortune.'

Merridith found his anger rising again. 'I'll be damned if I'll be given lectures on idleness by your good self, Laura. Damned, I say. *Do you hear me now?*'

The Captain put down his cutlery and gazed bleakly at his plate.

At the next table the Methodist minister turned to give an owlish stare. Dixon and the Mail Agent sat very still. The Surgeon and his sister bowed their heads. The Maharajah continued quietly eating his soup, a soft whistle through his teeth as he blew on it.

'Permit me to apologise,' Lady Kingscourt said hoarsely. 'I am feeling a little unwell this evening. I believe I shall go to take some air.'

Laura Merridith rose stiffly from the table, dabbing her lips and hands with a napkin. The men half-stood and bowed as she went, all except her husband and Maharajah Ranjitsinji. The Maharajah never bowed.

He removed his spectacles, breathed carefully on to the lenses and began wiping them scrupulously on the hem of his golden scarf.

The Captain waved over one of the stewards. 'Go after the Countess,' he quickly muttered. 'Make sure she stays behind the First-Class gates.'

The man nodded his understanding and left the saloon.

'Natives restless, are they?' the Mail Agent smirked.

Josias Lockwood made no reply.

'Tell me something, Captain,' said the Maharajah with a perplexed frown. Everyone at the table gaped at him now. It was as though they had forgotten he was capable of speech.

'That pretty young lady who is at present playing the harp?'

The Captain gave an embarrassed look.

'You shall enlighten me, I know, if I am speaking in error.'

'Your Highness?'

'But isn't she actually . . . the Second Engineer?'

Everyone turned or stretched to stare. The harpist's hands were sweeping across the loom of strings, weaving a climax of ardent arpeggios.

'By the holy powers,' said the Mail Agent uneasily.

The Surgeon's sister made an attempt at laughter. But when nobody joined in, she suddenly stopped.

'It didn't seem right to have a man,' the Captain murmured. 'We do like to keep up appearances on the *Star*.'

CHAPTER III

THE CAUSE

In which the Author gives his frank account of
certain Controversial and CALAMITOUS EVENTS in
IRELAND; and defends himself against Denigration
by a certain Lord.

THE NEW YORK TRIBUNE,
WEDNESDAY NOVEMBER 10, 1847

TODAY'S TALKING-POINT

WHY IS THERE A FAMINE IN IRELAND?

by Our London Bureau Assistant,
Mr. G.G. Dixon.

The present reporter demands to respond to the letter lately printed in this newspaper from a correspondent who signs himself "David Merridith of Galway" but who is also known as Lord Kingscourt of Cashel and Carna, on the subject of the Irish Famine.

The Apocalypse now raging through the Irish countryside has been detonated by the fearful conspiracy of four Death Riders. Natural disaster, crushing poverty, the utter dependency of the poor on one susceptible crop, and the utter indolence of their Lords and Masters; by the same terrible forces which wreak famine everywhere among the destitute. It is not "an accident" but an inevitable consequence. What but evil could sprout from such pestilent soil?

Anyone with the Oxford education Lord Kingscourt has received – paid for in full by his family's tenants – must be presumed to know this fact. As with every deadly Famine, it has been preceded by many another. (Fourteen in the last thirty years in the case of Ireland, and a cataclysmic blight in the middle-18th century.) The spark for this tinderbox was the appearance two years ago of a fungal canker that annihilates the potato, the staple food of the Irish poor. The name of the disease is not known.

The name of the economic system within which the catastrophe is occurring is very well known indeed. It is called "The Free Market" and is widely reverenced. Like David Merridith of Galway it also has an alias. Many criminals do, and most aristocrats. Its *nom de guerre* is *"Laissez-Faire"*; which preaches that the lust for profit may regulate everything: including who should live and who should die.

This is the Freedom which permits Irish food merchants to quadruple their prices in hunger-struck areas; which allows cargoes of unblighted produce to be carted by Irish ranchers under armed protection to Dublin and London while their countrymen starve in the putrid fields. (There is notably little Famine in the dining rooms of Dublin's wealthy, neither at the palace of My Lord Archbishop.)

No other manifestation of humanity may be allowed to

intervene in these magnificent workings of Freedom. Not man's Imagination, which gave us the glories of the Renaissance. Neither his desire for Liberty which gave us America. Not his natural Sympathy to his suffering brother, but the grind of the Profit-Engine, first and last.

This is not an exaggeration. The contention that the one task required of the unemployed aristocracy might be to prevent those on whom it leeches from starving to death, is considered bizarre by My Lords of England and Ireland. Indeed it is *de rigueur* to chastise the poor for their poverty while regarding one's own riches as a matter of Divine entitlement. Those who toil the hardest possess the least wealth; those who do nothing but eat have the most.

It is a matter of record that a great number of the powerful who are permitting the decimation of the Irish poor are British; and also that many are Irish themselves. Of those who are British much has been written already, but of those who are Irish, not nearly enough. Some have found it convenient to blame "Britain" for such a decimation; though it is not "Britain" which is inflicting it, nor "Ireland" which is suffering it. What is happening is more sophisticated but no less brutal.

Most of the British establishment abjures responsibility, while millions of those they rule in Ireland are left to the cruellest destruction in a long, cruel history; all the while many of the better-off Irish with whom the victims share nationality (if not much else) quietly look the other way. As Lord Kingscourt contends, in his memorable phrase: "Hunger kills the poor. It does not ask their flag." Doubtless if the Famine were laying waste to Yorkshire the government's response would be less dismally ineffective. But if anyone truly believes that the Right Honorable Lord John Russell (the British Prime Minister, the 1st Earl Russell, the Viscount Amberley of Amberley, the Viscount of Ardsalla, the third son of His Grace the 6th Duke of Bedford) would raise the tax on his Lordly "chums" in order to succor the famished of Leeds, he needs to have his butler run him a long cold bath.

Food has indeed been sent by the Russell government, as Lord Kingscourt's recent epistle so proudly maintains. But too often it has been woefully insufficient in some way; poorly planned, poorly organized, poorly distributed, inadequate in quality to the point of uselessness; in the wrong places at the wrong times; far too little and far too late. And his many Irish admirers – the very many indeed – must share the culpability with Lord Russell and his government.

Numerous Irish farmers of the richer class have done absolutely nothing to assist the hungry; indeed they have greatly augmented their wealth by fencing in holdings deserted by the poor. An army of landlords who claim to love Ireland's people have in fact evicted thousands from their inherited fiefdoms. Lord Kingscourt's own family is one such gang. He says he is "an Irishman, born and bred in Galway." One wonders if he says it in his usual home at Chelsea.

It is maintained that "the people of Britain" are to blame for the Famine because they have supported governments that exert themselves so feebly to assist. This is measurably incorrect. Literally not one of the wealthless class of that kingdom has ever voted for the corrupt regime that is worsening the sufferings of Ireland's hungry. The evidence is simple. The people have no vote.

The right to vote in the benighted motherland of democracy (in whose unelected "House of Lords" David Merridith contentedly burbles) is apportioned exclusively on wealth, not on citizenship. Indeed no Briton is actually a citizen, but a subject of Her Imperial Majesty. Nineteen of every twenty Britons have no vote whatsoever. The opinions of "the people" are of precisely no importance in that scepter'd isle of oligarchs which used to over-rule ourselves. How happy that we continue their quaint olde custom of the disenfranchisement of that half of our population which does not possess the capacity of growing a beard.

Recently Lord Kingscourt has cautioned in this newspaper: "everything about this Irish Famine is more complicated than it appears." So it is. Unlike the legion of victims His Lordship enjoys the luxury of being alive to debate its complications.

Granted, the division of rustic Ireland into wealthy and completely destitute is not entirely accurate. There are small farmers and others whose meager resources put a blade's width between themselves and the glorified Gaol called the workhouse. Many have even enough to purchase a coffin; though most do not, as Lord Kingscourt will see if he rises from his writing-desk and looks out his window. There is a great deal of unofficial sub-division of land among poor tenant families (for no rent, or very little), leading to massive over-cultivation of already exhausted soil and thereby more hardship and hunger. There are also the abject poor, who own nothing at all. Lacking the eight dollars it would cost to emigrate (the price of a supper at Lord Kingscourt's London club), or any possession they might sell in order to get it, they are dying in their tens and hundreds of thousands while we ask ourselves interestingly complicated questions. Quarter of a million have died this year alone. More than the combined entire populations of Florida, Iowa and Delaware.

Everything about the Famine is indeed complicated. Everything except the agonies of those who are its victims: the old, the young, the defenseless and the poor. Their labors have supplied a gracious leisure to the gentry of Ireland, who like their siblings in England languish in bed half the day. Their Lordships and Ladyships are so understandably weary. A look though the *Illustrated London News* for the last several years will reveal how hunts, balls, and other fatiguing diversions of elegant country living have merrily continued in disaster-struck Ireland, while the hungry have the temerity to die on the roadside.

To where might they turn for assistance now, these people cruelly abandoned by those who had squeezed them dry? To our esteemed colleagues in the British Fourth Estate, perhaps. Here is a recent editorial from the London *Times* (a publication in which Lord Kingscourt holds considerable shares): "We regard the potato blight as a blessing. When the Celts once cease to be potatophagi, they must become carnivorous. With the taste of meats will grow the appetite for them. With this will come steadiness, regularity and perseverance."

An enforced scheme of mass emigration had been advocated in a recent number of the journal *Punch* (an anti-American rag whose editor has been a frequent guest in Lord Kingscourt's own home). "We are confident, if this scheme was properly carried out, it would be the greatest boon to Ireland since SAINT PATRICK drove out the vermin."

The exodus is indeed being undertaken now. Within the next thirty years, more Irish will live among us in America than live in the cruelly inequitable place where they were born to be regarded as an infestation.

It is not a calculated act of national murder, the distorted teachings of some notwithstanding. This is another matter on which Lord Kingscourt is quite correct. (Profound the consolation to a mother watching her children starve that their starvations have not been calculated.) Neither has the Famine been brought upon the victims by idleness and stupidity (not their own, at any rate), despite the flagrantly hateful claims to that effect often made in the London newspapers now. Mr Punch is far from the only leering puppet to have likened the Irish to beasts and thugs. And such imbecilities are being repeated on all sides. Many an Irish clergyman is already tutoring his flock that an Englishman by definition is a godless degenerate, devoid of civilization, a bloodthirsty Pagan. Others are also girding for battle, a little more secretly if no less dangerously. A member of a revolutionary society in rural Galway (an evicted tenant of Lord Kingscourt himself) recently remarked to the present reporter:

"I despise the English as I despise Satan. They are filth. They were savages and idolaters when our people were saints. There will be a holy war in this country to put them out. All of them. I do not care tuppence how many centuries they are here, this is not their country; they have it by torture alone. They will be sent scurrying back to the cesspit they came from, the mongrel dogs and their bitches with them. Every one of the pack I slaughter, I will count as a blessing on my name."

Many of us have true friends in Great Britain and Ireland, and all of us owe those countries a deal of our heritage. It is thus imperative that America exert whatever influence she may wield upon the London government at this terrible time. Otherwise the Famine will poison relations between the decent and moderate peoples of those islands for a century to come.

A million will surely die as a result of this Famine. If something is not urgently done to help the poor, thousands more will die in its hideous aftermath: by the blade, the bomb, the bayonet, and the bullet. A number of Noble Lords might even be among them, which would of course be a very unfortunate development. The letters pages of many American newspapers would be profoundly impoverished by their utter extermination.

I am sorry that the priest put such a hard penance on you. You will have to come to the country where there's love and liberty. It agrees very well with me. You would not think I have any beaux, but I have a good many. I got half a dozen now. I have become quite a Yankee, and if I was at home the boys would be all around me. I believe I have got no more to say.

Letter from Mary Brown to her cousin in Wexford

CHAPTER IV

THE HUNGER

THE FOURTH EVENING OF THE VOYAGE: IN WHICH AN
ACCOUNT OF THE PLOTTING OF THE MURDERER IS GIVEN;
HIS CRUEL INTENTIONS AND MERCILESS CUNNING.

17°22′W; 51°05′N
— 5.15 P.M. —

The killer Pius Mulvey walked the drenched foredeck, his dead foot dragging like a sack of screws. The sea was knife-grey, flecked with eddies of blackness. Dusk was creeping down on the fourth day out of Cobh. A thin crescent moon like a broken piece of fingernail was visible through the rolling, charcoal clouds, some in the middle distance pouring bright streams of sleet.

Mulvey was in pain. Already his legs were aching. His knuckles and fingertips were smoulders of cold. Like a hag's poison, the spirit-murdering chill of wet clothes against wet skin.

For several days after they had left Cobh, herring gulls and guillemots had screeched in the wake of the *Star*, whirling and swooping, diving at the billows, alighting in screechy unison on the deck rails. Some of the men of steerage would try to snare them on baited hooks, more sustenance in the rivalry underlying the effort than in the fishy, cordlike meat yielded by the astounded prey. Cormorants and puffins had been seen skimming the whitecaps, even when Ireland had receded from view; inhabitants of the rocky and long-abandoned islands that stretched away from the south-west coast like ink-blots splashed by a careless cartographer. There were no birds now. Now there was nothing.

Except the ceaseless groans and heart-stopping creaks of the ship. The alarming ruffle of the unstiffening sails. The bawling of the sailors when the wind rushed down from the north. The crying of children. The roars of the men. The cacophonous music they made at night, the maudlin songs of love and vengeance, the strangled blaring of uillean pipes. The screeches of the animals caged on the deck. The endless chirrup of the chattering women, the younger ones especially.

What would New York be like? What kind of clothes did they wear in New York? What kind of animals were in the zoo in New York? What kind of food? What kind of music? Were Chinamen truly yellow? Were Indians red? Was it true that black men had larger what-you-knows than Christian ones? Did American women reveal their bosoms in public? Often, in the days of his youth especially, Mulvey had thought going to sea would be a silent existence; a life in which a man might well escape his past. In fact it was like being in the Hell he deserved. As for his past, it was attached to him like a mooring rope. The further the ship travelled, the more he felt its pull.

He could not be around the women, especially the younger ones. Partly because it pained him to see their emaciated faces: their lightless eyes and skeletal arms. The awfulness of their hope, the way it was burned into them: a brand of absolute dispossession. He would walk the ship all night to avoid them, and sleep all day to avoid the men.

The men were mainly evicted farmers from Connaught and West Cork, beggared spalpeens from Carlow and Waterford; a cooper, some farriers, a horse-knacker from Kerry; a couple of Galway fishermen who had managed to sell their nets. The poorest of the poor had been left on the dockside to die, having neither the money to purchase a ticket nor the strength to beg a mercy of those who might.

And the men suffered from seasickness more than the women did. Mulvey couldn't understand it but it seemed to be true. Two fishermen from near Leenaun got seasick more than anyone. They had lived on the high cliffs of Delphi Hill, trapping for crabs and lobsters in the deepwaters of Killary. Neither had been further out to sea in his life. They joked of being landlocked, these two ludicrously handsome brothers. They talked about themselves in the ironic third person, as though they found their own impotence and fear amusing. *The fishermen that never went to sea.*

It saddened the murderer to see them play-acting with the girls, wrestling each other, running races on the deck in their stocking feet. Even their kindness was somehow saddening. They were never done offering their rations to the children of steerage; singing patriotic ballads when their comrades were low. The younger one would die soon; that much was clear. There was desperation in his gaiety. He couldn't last.

Mulvey knew about hunger, its deceptions and strategies: its trick of letting you think you weren't hungry and then suddenly hammering into you like a wild-eyed, shrieking robber. He had known it in Connemara, on the roads of England. All his life it had shadowed him, a sneaking spy. But now it was limping the decks alongside him. He could almost hear its siren laugh and smell its stinking breath.

The night before last he had glanced towards the mainsail summit and seen his dead father staring down from the crows' nest. Later on the forecastle, a small fierce bird, an eagle-beaked assassin with bright blue wings, when there couldn't be a landing bird so far out to sea. And yesterday evening, close to dusk, through the cast-iron gates that fenced off the First-Class passengers, Mulvey had seen another ghost. The dark-eyed figure of a girl he had once wronged, walking hand in hand with a weeping child.

Looking at the vision, Mulvey had realised something strange. Had a banquet been set out on golden dishes before him at that moment, he would not have been able to eat a single morsel. Rather he would have heaved with disgust.

He would have to be careful now. This was how hunger worked its spell. It wasn't when you felt hungry that you were in the greatest danger. It was when you stopped. That was when you died.

Mary's Violet Eyes Make John Sit Up.

It had started on the second morning out of Cobh. Just before dawn Mulvey had been standing near the upperdeck ladders, gazing up at the dying stars. He was thinking about a Scotsman he had known in his childhood, an engineer called Nimmo who worked for the government. Nimmo had been sent to Connemara back in '22 when crop failure struck the western seaboard. Mulvey and his brother were among the local boys who were still healthy enough to be given relief work, hefting rubble for the new road from Clifden to Galway. The Scotsman had been an unselfish overseer, spending time with the boys, sharing in the hauling and breaking, sometimes explaining aspects of science or engineering. He had amused them by explaining in terms of Newton's Second Law why a river might never be made to flow uphill. They didn't actually need that fact explained but to watch him explaining it was better than working. 'And thou shalt not attempt to divide by zero. That, my men, is the eleventh commandment.' He had taught Pius Mulvey a nonsense phrase by which to remember the positions of the planets in relation to the sun: Mary's Violet Eyes Make John Sit Up.

Mulvey had been running the sentence over in his mind as he stared up at the brightening eastern sky. The words gave him comfort. He liked their rhythm. When suddenly he thought he had seen a whale. Off the starboard bow, perhaps a mile and a half in the distance – a hulking, blue-grey finback bull, such as he had once seen in a bestiary in a London bookshop window. The tail had appeared first, slapping the waves. A moment had passed. Mulvey was astonished. Then its obscene bulk had slid up from head to fin: impossibly long, impossibly black, a gush of frothing water spilling from its jaws – so sleek and vast as to be unnatural; something horrible and awesome from the depths of a nightmare.

The plunge was like a mountain collapsing into the sea.

Unable to move, he had stood still and watched, appalled at the immensity of what he had seen. Uncertain, in fact, that he *had* seen it. For nobody else had seen anything at all. None of the passengers. None of the crew. If they had, they said not a syllable about it. And surely they would have. They couldn't have remained silent. The creature was half the length of the ship.

He had kept watch for an hour – maybe more – wondering if finally he was losing his mind. He had seen it happen to the starving before. Had seen it happen to his poor, mad brother. While he watched the towering waves came a memory of the last night he would ever spend in Connemara. He could not ignore it. It broke against his mind, like the guilt of an old man for the crimes of his youth.

How he had beseeched, but they wouldn't be persuaded. 'We'll have men on the quay in New York. We'll have men on the ship.

If that English scum ever walks down that gangplank, you're a deadman and buried. Don't think we're lying. And you'll get the traitor's death you deserve, you devil's bastard. You'll watch your own heart getting cut out and burnt.'

Stone-hard brothers with bog-oak fists. He had pleaded to be spared this patriotic task. Whoever had denounced him must have made a mistake. He wasn't a murderer. He had never killed anyone. That, said their captain, was a matter of opinion.

'I'm leaving my land. Is that not enough?'

It's well for you that has land to leave.

'The man has children,' Mulvey said.

What about us? Do we not have children?

'Anything else. But I'll not do this.'

That was when the beating had started again.

He remembered their eyes; so frightened and convinced. The black-stained sackcloth of the hooded masks they wore. The slashed-out holes where their lips appeared. They were wielding the tools of their livelihood, but as weapons – scythes, hoes, loys, billhooks. Now they had no livelihood left. Centuries stolen in one stunning moment. Their fathers' labours; their sons' inheritances. At the stroke of a pen, they were gone.

Black soil. Green fields. The green of the banner draped across the table, splattered with ribbons of Mulvey's blood. The glint of the weapon they had made him take, the fisherman's knife pressed to his quaking chest while they raged at him about freedom and land and thievery. The words SHEFFIELD STEEL etched into the blade. He could feel it now, in the pocket of his greatcoat, nestling next to his lacerated thigh. He remembered the things they said they would do with that knife if he didn't stop whingeing about murder being too heavy a burden to put on him. When they held him down and started to cut him, Mulvey had screamed to be allowed to kill.

A man he had never met, let alone spoken to. A landlord and an Englishman; therefore an enemy of the people. A landlord without land; an Englishman born in Ireland – but there was little enough point in seeking definitions. For his class, his genealogy, the crimes of his fathers, for the pedigree bloodline into which he had been born. For the church he attended and the prayers he uttered. As much for his name as anything else – a single word he'd had no part in choosing.

Merridith.

That trinity of syllables had sentenced their bearer to be slaughtered, had marked him down as one of the culpable. The family tree had grown into his gallows. It counted for nothing that he might have done nothing; that was to bring in gratuitous complications. The men beating Mulvey had done nothing either, but that had not spared them when the reckoning came. Their land was gone. They were men without a purpose. Hungry and beaten; finally conquered.

Once they had been harrowers; now they were the harrowed. They still smelt of their land as they smashed him half stupid. Their canvas gloves, their farmer's boots, still caked with clumps of dead, black soil. Fingers which had tended and planted and coaxed now choking, wrenching, tearing at his face. They had let him escape and then caught him again – as though to say *there will be no escape*. One had a mongrel, another a hunter. The yaps, the howls were the worst things to remember: the hot, wet breaths of the starving hounds, the scrape of their claws and the urgings of the men. A clod of gravelled earth was snatched from a ditch and forced into his choking mouth until he gagged. Stones rained on his body and still the beating did not stop. He felt something of what they themselves must have felt, in every kick, in every gouge and spit and punch. Even through the blood trickling into his eyes, they looked so diminished, so completely afraid. They had been made to look small, and they were, and they knew it. What had happened to his attackers was a kind of rape. 'You'll do this, Mulvey, or you'll never see daylight again. And you'll be watched on that ship to make sure you do.' Through broken teeth, he had agreed. He would do it.

The reasons why things are the way they are could be ferociously complicated, Mulvey knew; but in this corner of the empire they worked themselves out into cadences of mathematical inevitability. A man named X would have to die. And a man named Y would have to kill him. You could call it the dictum of the Free Market of murder: the cravings and exigencies of supply and demand. Easily the equation could have set itself the other way around, and for all Mulvey knew, one day it might.

But this time it hadn't.

This time it wouldn't.

Christ had spilled his blood to redeem the debts of the guilty, all the inheritors of original sin. No crippled Christ was Pius Mulvey. No innocent martyr awaiting the nails.

Let X equal Merridith and Y equal Mulvey. Impossible to fight the power of mathematical law. A river could never be made to flow uphill.

He felt for the knife. Ice-hard in his pocket.

All night long he would wait for his chance. Perception was clearer in the absence of daylight, in the starlit cold of the decks after dark. People's habits and movements. Their places for strolling. Shadowy corners. How locks worked. Which doors were chained. Which windows might be left open. Whispered exchanges you were not supposed to hear: like the one between Lady Merridith and the handsome American the other night.

How long more must we keep up this childish deception?

For God's sake – he's my husband.

A man who speaks to you as though you were a servant?

Please stop, Grantley.

I don't remember you saying that when you were in my bed.

What happened was a mistake and mustn't happen again.

You know it will.

I know it can't.

Mulvey shuffled on, drawing up his damp collar, clasping his sodden greatcoat around his quaking frame. The moon had turned scarlet; the clouds fiery gold. Small lights were being lit in the windows of the First-Class cabins.

Some way behind the *Star* he saw the sails of a ship that had been following steadily for several days. The sight seemed an intimation of approaching violence, as though Vengeance was riding the second vessel. The knowledge he was being observed hung heavily around him, like a hex bestowed by a 'spoiled' priest. That was a curse from which no flight was possible: the anathema of a man who had once known holiness. He wondered which of the passengers was watching him even as he walked. The girls from Fermanagh, who never laughed. Maybe one of the Leenaun brothers. Even the American – a sympathiser perhaps? Plenty of Americans were sympathisers now. Certainly he was never done skulking around steerage and scribbling like a constable in his little snitch's notebook. And then there was the possibility that it was only a bluff; that nobody was watching; that Pius Mulvey was alone. But he wasn't sure. You could never be sure.

A grunted snivel of languor made him turn and stare. Near him, by the half-open door of the galley, a shabby black bitch was nuzzling its vomit. Inside the cookhouse a neat little Chinaman was renting through the carcass of a pig with a hacksaw. Mulvey watched for a time, his tongue soaked with longing. Hunger roared up in him like a hopeless lust.

He walked the ship as though following a chart. Up. Down. Across. Back. Stem. Port. Stern. Starboard.

The churning of the waves. The ropes clanking on the masts. The blind of salt water. The wind ripping at the sails.

And the women talking. Always talking.

The younger ones especially.

I cant let you know how we are suffring unless you were in Starvation and want without freind or fellow to give you a Shilling But on my too bended Neese fresh and fasting I pray to god that you Nor one of yers may [neither] know Nor ever Suffer what we are Suffering At the present

Letter from Irish woman to her son in Rhode Island

CHAPTER V

THE ORDINARY PASSENGERS

Friday, 12 November, 1847
Twenty-one days at sea remaining

LONG: 20°19.09′W. LAT: 50°21.12′N. ACTUAL GREENWICH STANDARD TIME: 11.14 p.m. ADJUSTED SHIP TIME: 9.53 p.m. WIND DIR. & SPEED: N.W. Force 4. SEAS: Choppy all last night but middling fair now. HEADING: S.W. 226°. PRECIPITATION & REMARKS: Extremely cold. Heavy rain and thunder all the day. The *Kylemore* out of Belfast two miles to the aft. Ahead of us the *Blue Fiddle* out of Wexford Town.

Last night four of the steerage passengers died: Peter Foley of Lahinch (forty-seven yrs, land labourer); Michael Festus Gleeson of Ennis (age unknown, but very aged, a purblind); Hannah Doherty of Belturbet (sixty-one yrs, a onetime domestic) and Daniel Adams of Clare (nineteen yrs; evicted tenant farmer). Their mortal remains were committed to the sea. God Almighty have mercy upon their souls and receive them unto that anchorage where reigns His peace.

The total of those who have died since this voyage commenced is eighteen. Five are in the hold this night, suspected of Typhus. Two, it is certain, will not see the morning.

I have given orders for burials to be conducted from the stern from now on and held at dawn or after dark. It is a habit of many of the women of steerage to indulge in 'keening' at such sad moments;

a peculiar variety of wailing ululation where they rend their garments and pull at their hair. Some of the First-Class passengers were complaining about the disturbance. Lady Kingscourt, in particular, was a little concerned that her children might be distressed by the queer proceedings.

Large number of steerage with dysentery, scurvy or famine dropsy. Smaller number (about fifteen) with all three. One seaman, John Grimesley, is quite smitten with a fever. A steward, Fernão Pereira, has a septic wound to the hand, caused by a cut from a broken wineglass. Both men were seen by Surgeon Mangan, who put leeches on the first, and a pasted opiate poultice on the second. He is of the view that they will recover presently if excused from duty and so they have been. (Both are good honest men; no idlers or scrimshankers. I do not propose to dock any pay.) The Maharajah is also unwell, though only with seasickness, and has retired to his stateroom, not to be disturbed. I myself had a poor chest earlier in the day, and took a quarter-grain of opium. Found it vivifying.

Instructions have been issued for the men to desist from referring to the steerage passengers as 'steeries', 'steeragers', 'raggers', 'shawlies' & cetera. (These terms are employed not only to disparage certain passengers that were better assisted with kindliness, but are used among the men themselves as varieties of insult.) Leeson has informed them this will not be tolerated. Every man, woman and child on this vessel will be addressed with respect, the common run of person as well as the better. They are Steerage or Ordinary Passengers, and will be known as such.

A troubling matter must be reported:

This forenoon it was brought to my attention by First Mate Leeson that very late last night some person – presumably male – had sawn through the bars in the lower foredeck gate, which leads to the First-Class compartments. At first I was perplexed, for in accordance with the regulations all the steerage passengers' belongings were carefully searched on boarding the vessel; such items as knives, saws, swords, blades, skewers & cetera being confiscated until we debark at New York. But Leeson being a diligent and thorough Mate – who has long since deserved promotion, though receiving none – had enquired of Henry Li the cook. The latter attested that a small hacksaw used for butchery had been pilfered from the galley some time last night, along with some pig innards and a flagon of freshwater.

A number of items have been stolen from First-Class; viz: a silver-plate watch belonging to Minister Deedes, a pair of cuff-links from the Mail Agent George Wellesley and a quantity of American dollar paper currency from the Maharajah. All are agreed that to search the entirety of steerage would probably prove fruitless, if such an endeavour were possible, which it is not now. I have promised that the thefts will be repaired by the Company's insurance policy and requested the victims to keep the matter to themselves, as I do not wish to cause wider alarm than is necessary. Meanwhile I have arranged for extra watchmen at night and other measures.

Leeson has said he will put it about steerage that the Minister is very saddened by the loss of his watch, a gift from a number of grateful parishioners on his retirement. We shall see if such a stratagem brings results.

Such petty thievings have happened previously on similar voyages and in my experience will happen again. Human Nature being the drama it is, a certain degree of resentment may be thought inevitable; indeed, I might venture, understandable.

The London office will by now have received my official notification of the 8th inst. written from Queenstown, on the perennial matter of overcrowding. Again and again in this past fourteen years, I have insisted that you, as the directors of this company, bear a legal, and indeed a moral duty to maintain the fundamental protection of those who entrust their lives to this vessel and to my own captaincy of same. And yet again, despite my unending protestations, too many steerage tickets have been sold for this voyage, by a factor of thirty percentage at the minimum.

I fail to comprehend why my passengers and my men must habitually be thrust into peril of this most immediate and outrageous nature, simply for the sake of the profits accruing from so doing. Nor can any satisfactory cause be advanced for the disgraceful failure to provide a physician or at least a nurse on board; nor a safe place for the purpose of accouchements for the women. Perhaps the shareholders think babies come from under the cabbage leaves. I can assure them they do not, though it were easier if they did. It is only a blessing of providence that we have Surgeon Mangan among us now; and if his efforts are tireless and his charity unstinting, he is not a young man and is already being overwhelmed.

Directly we dock at New York, I once more insist, arrangements must urgently be effected to ameliorate the lot of the steerage passengers, if any, on the return leg. If this is not done, another Captain will be required. I will have no more innocent blood on my hands, nor either on my conscience.

In the meantime I have had Leeson arrange for expeditious repairs; also for supplementary bolts, chains, hasps and morticed locks to be put on all gates, windows, hatches, frames, casements & cetera, this programme to be undertaken over the next several days. The cost of compleatly emptying our store of these items will no doubt be considerable to the Company. Greater, indeed, than the sum which might have been required to give every soul in steerage a daily dish of broth, or the children of steerage a pannikin of hot milk. Those more learned in matters of accounting than your humble employee may wish to reflect upon the above, for future reference.

Otherwise the ship seems peaceful enough, if restlessly so; and we continue to progress in adequate time.

The sea appears unusually tranquil for this time of year.

Greater number of sharks than is usual.

. . . We are all without a place to lea our head And this day we are without a Bit to eat and I wood Be Dead long go only for two Nebours that ofen gives me A Bit for god Sake But little ever I thought that it wood come to my turn to Beg Nomore

Letter to an immigrant in America

CHAPTER VI

THE VISIONS AT DELPHI

Christmas Eve, 1845, Rosroe⋆

Dearest Mary Duane, my only beloved wife,

Pen could scarcely put down what I feel now. All is lost, my sweetest Mary, and can never return.

I have just come back from Delphi Lodge at Bundorragha near Leenaun, where I went up to try and see the Commander. Having walked all the way from our present shelter up to Louisburgh in the County of Mayo, I was told by a man in the town that the Commander was not there at the present time but was after going up to Delphi with Colonel Hograve and Mr Lecky.

Hundreds of people were all about the town and they trying to get a docket to get into the Workhouse, but all were turned away by the Relieving Officer, it being too full, and the constables beating the people back from the gates.

The bright windows of the stores had Christmas fare in great

⋆Document written (in Irish) twenty-two months before commencement of voyage of the *Star of the Sea*. Found by New York Police Officer, in the cabin of the Merridiths' maidservant, several days after the voyage's end. The translation is by Mr John O'Daly, scholar of the Gaelic language and editor of *Reliques of Irish Jacobite Poetry* (1847) and *The Poets and Poetry of Munster* (1849). – GGD

abundance, geese and fowl and all such; but just as in Clifden the
traders have greatly multiplied the prices. How they can do it to
their own people at this awful time I cannot understand.
Everything now is the fault of the English and the landlords, the
people do say; and Jesus help us, so much of it is. But it is not the
common man of England who is preying like a vulture on the
poor people when they have nothing, but the Judas Irish merchant
with his greedy eye to whatever mite he can screw out of his
wretched countrymen and they so down.

The town was a dreadful sight, I could never forget it; with a
multitude half dead and weeping as they walked through the
streets. Worse again to see those for whom even weeping was too
much effort, and they sitting down on the icy ground to bow their
heads and die, the best portion of life already gone out from them.
I saw John Furey from Rosaveel and thought him asleep; but he
was dead; and to see that great strong man who could at one time
pull a hedge out of the earth with his mighty left hand now lying
so still was a terrible thing. But to witness the sufferings of the tiny
children; to hear the sounds they made in their agonies. I cannot
write it.

It can never be written, Mary.

People would not believe such things could have been
permitted to happen.

I faced out alone for the mountain track from Louisburgh. The
sun was going down by now. All along the road were unspeakable
sights. Cabins and shielings had been torn down and burned. In
one house at Glankeen the entire of a family had died: the parents,
all of their children and four old people. Two neighbourmen told
me the last to die, a boy of six or seven years, had locked the door
and hidden under his bed, being ashamed for his people to be
found in that way. The men were tumbling the cottage around
them as a grave, having no other place to put them.

Higher up the track there was hardly a living soul to be seen.
Where some of the poor people had died, dogs and rats were
about. The carrion crows and foxes were gorging also. And then a
wretched old woman whose bothy I passed beseeched me for a
scrap of food; and when I said I had none she begged me to put an
end to her life, for all of her sons were gone and she was quite

without support. All I could think of to do was to lift her up and carry her with me along the way. This I did. Christ be my judge, Mary, she weighed as a pillow; but even so, I could barely carry her. As I bore her in my arms she began to utter the Rosary that she and I might live this night. But before long she died and I laid her down and covered her as best I could with stones. I should like to say that I knelt and said a prayer but Jesus forgive me I did not, for I felt that if I did not get up at that moment I would never get up again in my life.

As I made along, I rehearsed in my mind some words I might say to the Commander: that I was an honest-hearted and industrious tenant who bore him no ill despite our former differences. That I begged his forgiveness for having spoken disrespectfully to him that time when I was angry, that on the life of my child my debt to him would be paid for certain if only he would overturn the eviction and that way allow me the means to pay it. That for all our differing stations he like myself was a Galwayman, no foreign planter come across the sea, and might help another Galwayman who was down on his luck. That he himself was a father, after all, and surely to Jesus could pity my situation, for if he were to put himself into my shoes he must imagine what it is to see your only child scream with the hunger and be able to bring no ease nor comfort.

The road was hard and fearsome cold. Near Cregganbaun the lake was after bursting its banks and so I had to wade across the road up to my chest in my clothes. The water was cold as a stinging fire. But I felt a kind of courage inside whenever I thought about you, Mary. I truly felt you were with me then.

At length the lights of Delphi Lodge appeared in the distance. How happy I was! Up to the house I went with haste. Courtly music was coming from the inside of it. A serving girl answered the door. I took off my cap and said I was a tenant of Commander Blake, much in distress, and was after walking three days and nights for to see him, and gave my name. She went away but shortly returned. The Commander was playing cards, she said, and would not come out and see me.

At this I was astonished.

Again I asked – Mary, I begged – but he would not come out.

Once more I gave my name but she said she was after telling it already and he had answered it with oaths so obscene I would not defile your eyes by writing them down for you to read.

I looked in the window of the withdrawing room at the front. A strange kind of ball was in progress, with elegant ladies and gentlemen in frock coats and they wearing the masks of goblins or angels and supping hot punch. I could not see the Commander anywhere within, but his horse and trap were in the yard.

I sat down on the snowy ground beneath a pine tree, intending to wait. It was dark now. It was very quiet all around. I was thinking strange thoughts, all sorts of thoughts. I do not know what I was thinking about. After a while I must have fallen into a sleep.

I dreamed that you and I and our child were in Paradise together, with warmth and plenty all about us. Music was playing. Your father and mother were there with my own, as hale and young as could ever be hoped; and many old friends, and all of us were happy. Our Lord came among us, as I thought, and gave us bread to eat, and wine to drink. A strange thing was that He had a newborn pig in his bloodied hands and when I asked him why, Our Lord said in our own Gaelic language: *he is holy*. And then Our Lady came in to the place where we were – not a chamber but a kind of shining meadow – and She touched our faces one by one and we became full of light, as water. And Our Lady said in the English language: *blessed be the fruit of my womb*.

When I woke up it was black-dark and the music was after stopping. I could taste the bread I was after eating in the dream, as sweet and luscious as any I ever knew. But then the cramp came back, harder than before – Christ stand between us and all harm – like a blacksmith's iron aflame in my guts. I thought my time had come to die but it stopped, then, and I could feel myself weeping for the pain of it.

All the lights were put out in the house. The lower portion of my body was covered in snow, and I could scarcely feel my legs no more. Such a dreadful stillness over the icy land I never heard before. Not the cry of a beast nor the croak of a bird. Just blackness and stillness all over the fields. It was as though the whole world was quietly dying.

Someone was after coming out and putting the horse inside in the stable and blanketing him. I went and waited beside the trap for a time.

But he never came out.

At length I went and knocked on the door again. One of the other servants, an old footman this time, said I would have to go on for myself. Otherwise he was after being told to set the dogs on me and it was more than his life was worth to give me admittance to the house for His Lordship the Commander was in a drunken fury. He gave me a cup of water and pleaded with me to go on for myself.

At that a terrible raging anger swept through me like a torrent. I tried to strike the man – God pardon me the raising of my hand to an aged person – but he slammed the door shut on me.

I prowled around the house like an animal for a time. But all inside must have gone to their beds for the windows were darkened now and shuttered. The madness came up again in me then. I let a roar out of me.

I cursed the living name of Henry Blake, and prayed to Christ that neither he nor his will ever know rest so long as they live, all seed and breed of them that ever sees Galway. That they may never sleep a night in their lives again. That they may die in agonies and have a dishonoured grave.

Mary, I would have murdered him if he came out of the house. Christ forgive me, but I would have got pleasure out of watching him suffer so I would.

Wind was coming up hard and biting off the lake. Now I heard a wolf crying in the hills behind. Down the mountain to Leenaun I went, thinking I might beg a place for the night in some haggard or even a morsel of bread itself or a sup of milk for the child. But the people would not stand for it, being afraid of the fever and they whipped me out of it with shame and scorn. Some troopers went past in the rain but gave me nothing either. They said they had nothing to give.

I came back here to find your sister looking over the child who was bestraught with the hunger. She said you were after going walking all the way over to Kingscourt to ask about help. That was shutting the stable door when the horse is after bolting,

Mary, because I know there is not a soul in that place at the present. I have sent her away now, for the pitiful screams of the child were distressing her.

They will stop soon.

Do you remember, my gentle Mary, how we used to go out walking together when we were young? The simple happiness of the days together and the sweetness and friendship of our nights. What a life we thought we should have, a life of buttermilk and bees, you once said. Even though I knew I was not your first choice for a companion of life, there was no happier man in all of Ireland than myself at that time. Nor would I have translated my place with any king or landlord, neither with the Sultan of India himself. All the gold in Victoria's throne would not have given me lure or temptation: nor every gem in her crown. O my own wife. My own Mary Duane. I felt that love would flower if watered with consideration and gentleness and I believe it did, at least for a time.

There are so many kinds of love in the world. If we were more like sister and brother sometimes, that would have been more than sufficient for myself; for no man ever had a better friend and helper than you and it was all my happiness to care for you.

But then a rat came into the wheatfield.

The meaning seems to have gone out of it all lately. Even the face of our innocent child now only seems a mockery.

I beg you pray mercy on my soul for all I have done and for the terrible thing I am about to do.

Forgive me for failing you, when you deserved so much more.

Perhaps after all you should have married that other creature of Satan who has brought me so low. Well now you are free.

I am so cold and afraid.

She will not suffer, Mary, I will do it quickly and be not long after her.

Say a prayer for me sometimes, if you can bear to remember your loving husband.

N

patt, for the honour of our lord Jasus christ and his Blessed
Mother hurry and take us out of this . . . [Your infant brother]
longs and Sighs Both Night and morning untill he Sees his
two little Neises and Nephews And . . . the poor child Says 'I
would not Be hungary if I was Near them.'

Letter of Kilkenny woman to her son in America,
pleading for help to emigrate

CHAPTER VII

THE SUBJECT

THE FIRST OF A TRIPTYCH IN WHICH ARE DEPICTED
CERTAIN IMPORTANT RECOLLECTIONS OF THE
GIRLHOOD AND LATTER LIFE OF MARY DUANE,
MAIDSERVANT; AND IN PARTICULAR HER REMEMBRANCES
OF A PERSON TO WHOM SHE ONCE RETAINED A TENDER
ATTACHMENT. HERE WE ENCOUNTER MISS DUANE ON THE
SEVENTH MORNING OF THE VOYAGE.

24°52′W; 50°06′N
— 7.55 A.M. —

Spears, maybe. Muskets? Maybe. Grey as Dog's Bay in the early morning. And the bullets must have been big to pierce his hide. And what did they use to hack him to pieces? A hatchet, maybe. A crosscut-saw. Trumpeting blaring bellying down. Trees all around as they went to work on his tusks. A scurf of blood flowing over the slick leaves. Black men, brown men with blood on their feet. Red men watching the black men cut.

Mary Duane glanced out the porthole at the monotonous dawnscape of the heaving Atlantic. In six long days it hadn't changed. She knew it wouldn't for another three weeks. Never would she have dreamed, this fisherman's daughter, that the sight of water could be so detestable: if you could even put the name of water on that colourless billowing desert.

Grey the fish that skulked down there. Grey the dolphins; grey the sharks. How could anything live in its depths? Grey as a shroud. Grey as a deadman. Grey and crinkled like a fibrous, shrivelled skin; as the elephant's foot she had often seen in the hallway at Kingscourt Manor. It was every bit as deathly and repulsive as that.

'Would you wash your hands again, Mary. Before touching the children.'

'Yes, Lady Merridith.'

'Their skin is so sensitive, Jonathan's especially.'

'Lady.'

'Make sure to change the sheets after breakfast, won't you? The counterpanes and pillowcases also, of course. If Robert doesn't get a comfortable sleep, we all know what happens.'

'I don't get your meaning, ma'am.'

'His nightmares, of course. What else would I mean?'

'Lady.'

'And I hate to say it, Mary, but would you wash your armpits too. I notice you have a habit of putting your hands in there when you're hot. It's really most unhygienic.'

Mary Duane wondered if she should tell her mistress that almost every night for the last seven months the lady's husband had come to her quarters at midnight to sit on her bed and watch her undress. That might soften her cough for her.

Usually all he wanted was to watch her undress. It was odd, she supposed, but men often were. Most men were queer as a five-legged dog. When they took off their masks that was all they were. The howling of a drunkard in the filth-strewn street was not so crude as what some of them wanted.

The dishonesty of how it had begun was below him, she thought, an insult to her intelligence, as much as to his own. Late one April night he had knocked on her door and slunk in with his sketchpad, saying he would like to draw her. A sour odour of whiskey was colouring his breath. He wondered if she might possibly 'permit him that privilege'. His choice of language had been unexpected, for they were unusual words to be spoken by a master to his servant. She had sat by the window and permitted him that privilege. A loosening of the hair was all he required that night. And the next night he had come up the stairs again. It was not his house but the house of his friends. 'A temporary shelter', was how he had put it. His friends were in Switzerland, walking in the snow. He moved like a man in another man's house. After ten minutes of drawing, another privilege was requested.

I wonder, Mary, if it might be possible. If you're uncomfortable at all I would absolutely. Friends since the days of childhood and so on. Brotherly sisterly. No suggestion of any sort of sordid. Just the bare arm perhaps. The light on your shoulder. If you could possibly unbutton unhook untie. Contrast of tones. Nothing more. Overall composition so important to get right. Not a matter of the material itself, do you see, but of the way the material is composed.

Without replying, she had removed her robe and nightgown. She could not bear to listen to any more lies.

It was the first time he had seen her naked body but he had said nothing and the silence had not surprised her. He wanted it to be regarded as a normal situation; a stripped woman, a clothed man watching her; his clothes and his art a kind of disguise, as much, perhaps, as her nudity. He had held a stub of charcoal up into his eyeline, squinting solemnly as he gauged her measure, closing one eye and then the other. As though she were an arrangement of bottles on a windowsill. The fact of her exposure was not to be mentioned: nor the careful manner in which it had been commanded. There was no sound at all, just the faintness of his breathing and the scuff of the charcoal moving across the paper. Grey the charcoal; grey his face. And after a while he had quietly moved his sketchbook from the ends of his knees and into his lap. She had looked away, then; down through the window. Down into the filth-strewn Dublin street. And he had kept drawing. And kept on looking. And the subject kept looking away.

The next night he returned, and most nights afterwards. At midnight she would hear his faltering footsteps on the bare stairs which led to the servants' attic. The timorous knock. The rancid reek of liquor. Ah. Mary. I hope I'm not. I thought we might. If you're not too tired. Perhaps the divan. Or with the pillow under. You're sure now, are you? And once again if it isn't asking. Natural beauty of the unclothed womanly. Nothing of which any of us should ever feel the slightest. Greatest of artists down through the ages. Maybe with your back turned. The sheet around. A little degree lower if you feel quite comfortable. Perhaps if I moved just a tiny bit closer. You don't object? Better light.

There was a time when she had thought to go to her mistress about it. ('Mistress' was such an interesting word.) But she knew what would happen if she dared to do that. It would not be Lord

Merridith who would be flung from the house to walk the streets or beg for a bed. In these everyday situations of privilege granted it was never the master who was ordered to go. She was one of His Lordship's charity cases: the local girl he rescued from beggary in Dublin. She knew her role and he knew his. As though they were characters in a hymn.

Very occasionally if he was badly drunk, he would ask for permission to touch her. She had the idea that it somehow pleased him to ask; it enabled him to pretend what was happening was consensual. That appeared to be important to him: that she didn't mind, or at least that she kept it quiet if she did. Some men found in their power a reason for arousal; others were aroused by the fiction of parity.

He never asked to be touched himself. He wanted to look and to touch: nothing else. Mostly he seemed not to find her body actually stimulating but a kind of problem he did not understand; as though its declivities and enfoldings and hardnesses and softnesses were geometrical conundrums he had to decipher. His whisperings and murmurs barely stopped for a moment. *It's all right, is it, Mary? Please say if it isn't. We're friends, aren't we, Mary? You don't object?* He caressed her with his fingertips, as something fragile and valuable, a precious possession that was worth protecting. An object from his father's collection of rare and extinct animals. An auk's egg, perhaps; a dinosaur's skull.

Sometimes he made small mewls of appreciation, like a whimpering tom clawing at its prey. She would close her eyes while he touched her and imagine being somewhere else. It helped quell her desire to weep or vomit. She would think about the faces of people she had known, the sound of a bell on a Sunday morning; the way a tolling bell causes ripples on a lake. She would say to herself: *it will be over soon. It means I will not starve. That is all it means.* Loathing him was something she attempted to avoid. Since he deserved no part of her, she tried to feel nothing.

One night he had begun to kiss her breasts. *Mary, I love you. I have always loved you. Have mercy on me, Mary; forgive me what I did.* She had looked down as his lips moved to one of her nipples, and quietly she had said without moving away: 'I would rather you did not do that, My Lord.' A moment had passed. She wondered if he would rape her. But he had nodded without saying anything and clambered to his feet. Gone back to his sketchpad as though nothing had happened; as though he had only knelt down to tie a bootlace.

Each time she undressed seemed a revelation to him. He would gape at her like a man who has just been stabbed in the heart, and who knows, in that instant, that his death is certain. Often she wondered about himself and his wife. He was like a man who had never seen a naked woman. When surely he must have. Was it possible he hadn't? Surely he must have seen Lady Merridith's body? They did not sleep in the same bed any more, she knew; but they had made two children together, after all.

Three weeks ago was the last time he had come to her quarters; the night he had returned to Dublin from closing his house in Galway. He had been like a different man that night. She was tired that night. His sons had been troublesome. When she had opened her dressing gown the way he usually wanted, he had asked her to stop, just to sit and talk for a while.

There was a darkness in him she had not seen before; not the gloom of lust but that of culpability. He had sworn to her that what had happened would not happen again; that he was ashamed of his conduct and meant to make amends. The phrase 'what has happened' he kept repeating, as though it had happened like weather happens. What had happened was completely unforgivable, he said; so he had not come to dare to ask for forgiveness. Merely to say how sorry he was, and to vow on the lives of his children not to bother her again. He had been very weak. His private life was unhappy. He had given in to his unhappiness and weakness: to his shame. Loneliness had led him to actions he now deeply regretted. It was no excuse at all for such unmanly behaviour but the past could not be altered by remorse, however necessary. If there was anything she needed – anything at all – she only had to say what it was and he would help her.

'I need no help from anyone,' she had answered quietly.

'We all need it sometimes, Mary.'

'Not me, My Lord.'

He hated it whenever she called him 'My Lord'. It reminded him of realities he would rather forget.

'The boys – would be most upset if you did not want to come

to America. We should all be upset, Mary. You have made such a difference. They have not had the easiest time of late.'

'Nothing remains for me here. As Your Lordship knows well.'

'So you'll still come, then. That is happy news. Will you take a position with us there?'

'I will leave your family's employment the moment we arrive at New York. I ask only what I am owed in wages, and a reference.'

'Mary.' He bowed his head slowly and gazed at the knotted floorboards. 'Do you think me an animal? I imagine you must.'

'It is not for a servant to have thoughts of her master.'

He could not bear to meet her eyes. 'So very much has happened between you and I, Mary. Perhaps there is some way we could make a fresh beginning. Maybe think on times when we were younger and happier. I find the thought unendurable that my disgraceful actions would end our friendship.'

'Are you finished with me, My Lord? I would like to sleep.'

He looked up at her, then, as though he didn't know her. The clock on her dresser struck for half-past one. He rose heavily from the chair and stared around the room; as a man who has taken a wrong turning in a museum. Placed his sketchbook on the washstand and quietly crossed to the door. Pausing in the doorway, without turning he had said: 'Will you shake my hand, Mary? For old times' sake.'

She made no reply. He nodded a few times. Closed the door behind him with the softest of clicks. She heard him descending the rackety staircase; the squeak of the door to the portrait landing.

Inside the cover of the sketchbook was a five-pound note folded into ragged quarters. She had burnt the book without further examination and given the banknote to a charity for the starving.

Since that night he had barely uttered a word to Mary Duane. She supposed he was afraid she might tell his wife. He was the saddest breed of man in the living world; the kind to whom women seem a kind of crucifixion. But the women around him would always be sadder. He was thirty-four now. He would never change.

Perhaps it was something to do with his mother. She had left him in Ireland for the first six years of his life and returned to London to live with her people, taking her two daughters but not her son. Nobody knew why. It didn't matter any more. Mary Duane's own mother had been employed to take care of him then.

'*Buime*' in Irish: a wet nurse, or a nursemaid. A woman protecting children; a seasonal mother. 'Nanny' was the English word for a woman who did such work. The same as the noun for a female goat. For all its beauty, its churchy magnificence, English could be a strange language sometimes. Mary Duane of Carna; daughter of the nanny. She was now a nanny herself.

She thought she could remember the first time she had set eyes on Laura Merridith's future husband. On her fifth birthday her mother had taken her up to the big house at Kingscourt. The rooms smelt of leaf-mould and beeswax polish. They were crammed with gleaming silverware and strange stuffed animals; faded paintings of earls and viscounts, barons and countesses, generals and dowagers, all long dead now and buried at Clifden, but who had once lived here, in Kingscourt Manor. A portrait of Lord Merridith in his magistrate's robes was hanging on the landing that led to the music room. Another, much bigger, the full length of a wall, showing him in his scarlet sea-clothes and feathered black hat, hung in the library like a poster for the circus. A grand piano sat in the drawing room. (A drawing room was not a place for people to draw.) 'Sébastien Erard' was the man who made the piano – her mother showed her the graven gold letters. The carpet on the staircase was a bleached-down red, patterned with a crest of crossed swords and a gryphon. *Fides et Robur* was the Merridith family motto. 'Faith and Strength' in the Latin language. The family of Duane possessed no motto and she wondered what it might be if they ever acquired one. There was a stand for umbrellas in the storm porch beside the front door. It was made from the foot of an elephant.

Lord Merridith was waiting by the hearthstone in the dining room with his hands behind his back and his feet a yard apart. He looked like one of Christ's apostles, with a neat, white beard and a severe mouth and eyes that seemed to smoke their way into you. He was bald as an egg and had no eyebrows. A bomb had exploded beside him at Trafalgar and burnt the hair off his head but not his beard. He had seen Admiral Nelson shot through the spine. He had helped to carry Admiral Nelson's coffin. His eyebrows and his hair had never grown back. There was a model of a ruined tower on a plinth by the sideboard. He was planning to build it in the Lower Lock meadow, near to the hillock where the Faerie Tree stood.

Why anyone would want to build a ruin was something Mary Duane could not understand, but her mother had told her to ask no questions. Lord Merridith had an interest in ruins and ruination. He was entitled to an interest in whatever he liked.

At first she had found him too frightening to talk to. But soon he had smiled and ruffled her hair. Somewhere inside him was an intense kindliness; she could see it. Like thinking you could make out coins at the bottom of a muddy river.

There were crusted, leaf-sized blisters on the backs of his hands, speckled with smears of pale pink lotion. He had given her a black penny and told her a joke she didn't understand, because he told it in English, and she didn't know much English at that time. He had poured her a tumbler of lemonade from a pitcher, wished her the compliments of a happy birthday. (Many Happy Returns. What did it mean? Did it mean she could come to the house when she liked?) Then he had pointed to a sad-looking boy who was squatting beneath the vast mahogany table, humming quietly and playing with a hoop: a priesteen of a fellow in velvet britches. 'That's my Admiral of the Fleet. Hup, hup! Stand to attention and say good day, won't you, David. Where's your manners, for heaven's sake?' (Her mother had told her what an Admiral of the Fleet was – the name of a beautiful English butterfly.)

He was five; like she was. Maybe he was four. He had tottered across the room and given a solemn little bow to Mary Duane and then to his nanny. Lord Merridith and Mary Duane's mother had laughed. And the boy had looked up at his father with a puzzled expression, as though he couldn't comprehend just why they were laughing; as though he himself, like Mary Duane, was listening to a language he did not know.

Mary Duane knew that look well. She had seen it on his face five thousand times as they grew up together in the fields around Kingscourt. Sometimes she saw it even now, as the flash of an after-image of something dark in sunlight. The look of a boy who needs something obvious explained.

Often his father was away at the war. There was always a war in some place or another. An aunt had come from London to help take care of him. She was a soft-hearted, widowed, funny old lady who had a thin moustache like a furry grey caterpillar and was often so drunk that she couldn't walk straight. She drank Three Crowns brandy 'like a randy sailor'. That's what Mary Duane's father had said.

Admiral Nelson was coffined in brandy. The brandy stopped his body rotting. The rooks in the battlements kept her awake at night. Sometimes she was seen shooting pebbles at them with a catapult. Johnny deBurca groomed the ponies at Kingscourt. He had to stop her firing the catapult; she was shattering the upper windows. She was cracking the guttering. She was cracked in the head. 'Aunt Eddie,' she was called by David Merridith. (He said she was 'a native of Barking, Madbury'.) Mary Duane's mother said Aunt Eddie's real name was the Dowager Lady Edwina.

David's name was Thomas David but everyone called him David or Davey. His other names were 'His Lordship' or 'The Viscount' or 'Viscount Roundstone'. All of David's family had three names, at least. It must have made dinnertime confusing.

Spifflicated. Ossified. Under the influence. One over the eight. Three sheets in the wind.

Sometimes if his aunt was in bed, or drunk, her mother would bring him down to her own house for a few hours. He liked to play in the ash-pit or to wrestle with the dog. He liked the way her mother would empty the great black cauldron of potatoes straight on to the table. He loved to eat potatoes with his small, bare hands, licking the butter from his knuckles like a puppy. Some days he went out in the currach with her father and her brothers, out past Blue Island and Inishlackan, where the mackerel and sea salmon were fat as piglets. He'd come back to the house with the men at dusk, quivering with glee, riding on her father's shoulders; brandishing a switch of blackthorn as a cutlass. 'Tan-tarah! Tan-tarah!' One night he wept bitterly when Mary Duane's mother was bringing him back up to Kingscourt to put him to bed. He wanted to stay where he was, he said. He wanted to stay for ever and ever.

But it wouldn't be right for him to sleep down here, her mother had told him. When he asked her why, she had quietly answered: 'Just because it wouldn't.'

Mary Duane thought her mother was cruel. Other children were sometimes allowed to stay, even though they had mothers of their own at home. Poor David Merridith had no mother to mind him. Really he had no father either, because his father was always away at the war. He was all on his own in that big dark house, except for his drunken mustachioed aunt and the rooks. And there might be ghosts up there, when you thought about it.

'There certainly might,' her father remarked.

He had looked across at Mary Duane's mother then, but she had given him that little head-shaking signal she used when she didn't want something discussed in front of the children.

In the middle of the night they had woken to a frantic hammering on the back door. It was David Merridith, wailing tears of dread. He had run all the way down in his nightshirt and nightcap, even though the thunder was shaking the ground and the lightning was splitting the sky in two, and the rain was so torrential that November night that the lowlands of Galway were flooded for weeks afterwards. His feet and his calves were flittered with thorn-cuts, his abject face splattered with mud. *'Please let me in. Don't send me away.'* But her father had put a coat on him and taken him back up to the manor.

Her father was gone a long time and when he came back to the cabin he looked older. He gazed around the small, dim kitchen, like a man who was lost, or in the wrong house, or waking from a dream in which he had seen something frightful. The latch gave a rattle in the draughting wind. Mice were scuttling in the walls of the cottage. Her mother had gone to him but he had drawn away, as he always did when upset about something. He took a jug of 'beestings' milk from the press, the milk of a cow that has recently calved, and drank it down in six big gulps. Mary Duane had run at him and tried to bate him. He had held her closely and kissed her hair, and when she looked up she saw he was crying himself, and so was her mother, though Mary didn't know why.

On Easter Sunday morning, 1819, Mary Duane was on her way to the well at Cloonisle Hill when she saw a beautiful lady in a sky-blue hooded cloak descending from a coach outside Kingscourt Manor. Her father explained. That was David Merridith's mother. She must have come home from London to mind him.

He didn't come down to her cottage quite so often now, but whenever he did he looked happy and well. He wore a white sailor suit she had fetched him from Greenwich. Sometimes he brought soft little sweets called marshmallows. Greenwich was the place where time was invented. The King of England invented time. ('I don't know why the Jaysus he did that,' said her father. 'We'd all be a track happier if he hadn't.')

His mother was the most graceful human Mary Duane had ever seen. Immaculately dressed, willowy and poised, elegant as the blossom of an English Bramley, she seemed to Mary and her sisters to glide across ground. 'Verity' was her Christian name: an English word for truth. She was related to another Admiral: Francis Beaufort. He was the man who discovered the winds. Her shoes were always exquisitely made. Her eyes were the green of the Connemara marble on the steps of the pulpit in Carna church.

Lady Verity was beloved by the tenants of Kingscourt. When a woman on the estate gave birth for the first time, the Countess would call to the cabin with fruit and wheatcake. She would insist that the man of the house go out so she could sit and talk privately with the new mother for a while. She would leave a gold guinea to hansel the baby. She visited the sick, the older people especially. She set up a laundry for the use of the tenant women in an obsolete stable on the bank of the watercourse, so that even in bad weather they might have somewhere to wash clothes. Every year on her birthday, the seventh of April, she gave a party in the Lower Lock meadow for the children of the estate. It was known among the people as Verity Day. The servants and farmers sat down with the gentry.

When potato murrain struck Connemara in 1822, Lady Verity herself ran the Model Farm soup kitchen, ten-year-old Mary Duane and David Merridith helping to chop the turnips and pump the water. Tuppence a bushel of whin-tops she would pay Kingscourt's children, who roamed the estate collecting them in baskets, mashing them up for His Lordship's sows. David Merridith used to steal them out of the pigsty and smuggle them back to Mary Duane's brothers, who would sell them again and give him a ha'penny. Lord Merridith's tenants, the people of Kingscourt, were envied by those on the neighbouring demesne, that of Commander Blake of Tully. He didn't give a devil's damn for them, blight or not; that was what Mary Duane's father had said. He was only a bloody devil himself: no better than any absentee rack-renter. He had scuttled up to Dublin as soon as the crop failed, the dirty cold-hearted whoremaster.

He'd steal the spittle from an orphan's mouth. The Blakes were turncoats who'd changed from Catholic to Protestant. If he saw an Englishman walking the highway without britches, he'd walk it without underdrawers to go one better.

Ninety of his tenants had died already and his agents were evicting families who had fallen into arrears. Masked men would come, usually early in the mornings. They had to wear masks, these filthy traitors, for if they were recognised they would get what they deserved. They'd be captained by a 'driver-out-man', a bailiff or sheriff, who would order them which cabins to smash and which ones to spare. They would clamber onto the roofs of the doomed cottages and saw through the mainbeams until the walls collapsed. Sometimes they'd simply burn out the people. The families would have to live in the woods or in 'scalpeens' of turf-sods on the side of the road.

Lady Verity sent the men of Kingscourt into the woods to find them. They could come and be fed at the manor, she said. Nobody hungry would be refused. It was a time for all Galway to stand together.

Sometimes David Merridith wept with fear when he saw them approaching across the wheatfields, the battalion of white-faced, lurching phantoms, and he wanted to run away. But his mother wouldn't let him. She always made him stay. She was never unkind but she was firm all the same.

One day Mary Duane heard her say to the little Viscount: 'In the eyes of God that poor man is exactly the same as you or I. He has a wife and family. He has a little son. And he loves his little son just in the way that I love you.'

Another day, just as the blight was ending, Lady Verity and Mary and Mary Duane's mother were cleaning the gigantic copper boiler from the soup kitchen when suddenly Lady Verity fell down on her bottom, as though she had been shoved by a bullying boy. Mary Duane laughed to see her on the ground. Her mother told her crossly not to be laughing but Lady Verity laughed too as she got back up, dusting off the skirt of her beautiful dress. Brushing the wisps of eelgrass off her bottom. She said she had a little headache and might go up to the house for a nap.

Later that day Dr Suffield from Clifden had called, remaining in the house until well after dark. For six months nobody on the estate had seen Lady Verity. Her son was sent away to friends of his parents at a place named Powerscourt in County Wicklow. She didn't go visiting the sick any more. Babies were born, and old people died, and still Lady Verity didn't come out of the manor. The laundry on the riverbank fell back into disrepair. Snipegrass began to sprout in the thatch. It was said by some of the very old tenants who remembered the starvation of 1741 that Lady Verity must be struck by the death kiss now; that she must have inhaled the breath of someone suffering from blight fever, or looked too directly into his eyes. Mary's mother told her those were only silly superstitions. You couldn't get the fever from somebody looking at you.

One morning at dawn Mary Duane and her father and her youngest sister, Grace, were gathering mushrooms in the Lower Lock meadow when they heard a scream coming from Kingscourt Manor. A long moment passed. Wind buffeted the scutch-grass. A rabbit looked up from a clump of whins. Another scream came, then: louder than the first. So loud that it drove the blackbirds rocketing out of the Faerie Tree.

'Is that the banshee?' Grace Duane asked, frightened to stone by the terrible sound. Never before had she heard the banshee, but she knew what her wail was said to mean.

'It's nothing at all,' her father said.

'Is it the banshee calling out for Lady Verity?'

'It's only auld cats,' Mary Duane said. 'Isn't that right, Dada?'

Her father turned around like a rusting weathervane. He stared, unblinking, into her eyes, the dew-soaked puffballs in his mud-stained fingers. It was the first time she had seen him appear afraid. 'That's right, my kitten. That's it exactly. Now hurry along and we'll all go in home.'

She dated her adulthood as having commenced at that moment. The first time she had donned a mask for reason other than play.

Physicians from Dublin arrived at the house. A famous surgeon travelled from London with a flock of nurses in crisp, cream uniforms. One midnight Lady Verity was seen by the gardener, passing an upper window with a candle in her hand. On St Patrick's Day, 1823, at six o'clock in the morning, she died.

Her funeral was the largest ever known in Galway. Seven

thousand mourners crowded into the cemetery at Clifden and filled the streets half a mile around; Protestant and Catholic, planter and native, the rich and the ragged side by side in the rain.

Lord Merridith's two daughters had been brought from London. Mary Duane could not remember seeing them before. One was tall as a beanpole, the other short and pudgy. Natasha Merridith. Emily Merridith. They looked like two sisters who had escaped from a nursery rhyme.

A rector from Sligo had recited the prayers. Reverend Pollexfen, a name Mary Duane had never heard. He was an angry looking, blond-haired, barrel-chested prophet with enormous hands and unpolished brogues, and when he spoke the sombre words of the Psalms, he trembled like an oak in a storm.

Lady Verity's coffin had been lowered into the grave. The bell had rung. A cow uttered a bawl from a nearby field. A loose buckle was clinking on Lord Merridith's belt. Drops of rain were spattering on the epaulettes of his uniform. The wind rustled quietly in the chestnut leaves.

And then another sound had begun.

A single voice, from the crowd behind her. An old woman's voice. And then another.

Soft at first, but quickly loudening: spreading out around the crowd in twos and threes. Men, now: and small children. Rising as people took it up, as a new part of the crowd began to add itself to it. Growing in volume, swelling like a wave, echoing against the granite-stone walls of the church until it seemed to Mary Duane that the sound was coming up from the wet, black earth and might never be stopped.

The Hail Mary, spoken in Irish.

Till the moment of her own death, she would never forget it. David Merridith – her David – in his father's raincoat, staring into the open grave, praying in Irish with his future tenants, mumbling the words as though speaking in his sleep, lifting his beautiful face upwards to the rain, and the terrifying sight of Lord Merridith weeping.

Anois, agus ar uair ár mbáis: Amen.

Now, and at the hour of our death.

CHAPTER VIII

THE THING NOT SAID

Lord Merridith began to neglect his appearance. His trim, white beard grew ragged and coarse, his fingernails dirty, his teeth discoloured: yellowed and blackened as antique piano keys. The blisters Mary Duane had seen on the backs of his hands now appeared on his face and his neck. They looked so painful. Sometimes they bled. She saw him walking the Lower Lock meadow one dawn, flailing his cane at the broken stones. He looked up and roared at her to get out of his sight. It was said by some that he smelt like a busted drain. Others reported that he had taken to drinking whiskey. His clothes were often dirty now.

Sometimes at night, in her family's cabin, quarter of a mile across Cashel Bay from the manor, they could hear Lord Merridith bawling in the yard. Strange rumours about him began to go around the estate: that he beat his son until the boy screamed for him to stop; that he had made a pile of his late wife's gowns and burned them. It was whispered by his stockmen that he was cruel to his animals; had whipped to its death a horse which had belonged to Lady Verity. Lord Merridith doing that was unimaginable to Mary Duane. He loved his horses.

'More than his people,' her father said.

As a magistrate he became feared all over Connemara. Once widely admired for being scrupulously fair in his judgments, for taking the side of right against influence, now he was dreaded from Spiddal to Leenaun. He would rage at the prisoners who came before him. If a man addressed him as 'Lord David', or even 'Lord Merridith', as has always been the local custom, he would stand up and bellow: 'My name is Kingscourt! Address me properly! Disrespect me again, I'll have you flogged for contempt!'

On the fourth of May, 1826, he sentenced a local man to death. The prisoner, an evicted tenant of Commander Blake of Tully, had stolen a lamb from the Commander's meadow and fatally stabbed the gamekeeper who had tried to arrest him. The case was closely watched in Connemara. The accused had five children; his wife was dead. Even the gamekeeper's wife had pleaded for clemency. What the man had done was a terrible thing but one day his God would have to be faced. One day we would all have to face our God. There had been too much killing in Ireland already. She did not want to see more children made fatherless. But the man was hanged in Galway Barracks a week to the day after sentence was passed; his body dumped in a quicklime grave in the yard. His children were sent into the almshouse at Galway, as, within the month, were the gamekeeper's children. And the seven children fathered by killer and victim were buried in the same pit-grave before the year was through.

A ballad was made about Lord Kingscourt's cruelty. Mary Duane heard it one morning in Clifden market.

> *Come all true native Connaughtmen, and listen for a while,*
> *Of the tyrant lord of Carna and his breed that blights our isle.*
> *The maker of misfortunes and the breaker of our bones;*
> *To keep him up, he keeps us down, and grinds us on the stones.*

She went up to the ballad-singer and told him to stop it. He was an ugly little man with one seeping eye. Lord Merridith was a man who'd had troubles of his own. There was nothing in the song about those, she said. And this shite and '*raiméis*' about 'true native Connaughtmen'? Wasn't His Lordship born thirteen miles out the road, like his father and six generations of his people before?

'Where in Hell were *you* born?' she asked the ballad-singer.

But he scoffed and pushed her away with his elbow. 'He can make his own bloody songs if he wants to, the murderer.'

That night she dreamed of the laundry on the riverbank. Women washing clothes and singing a hymn. Lady Verity rubbing her bottom: laughing. While around her the white sheets fluttered like sails. Wet with water and stained with blood.

✱

David Merridith was sent away to a boarding school in England. When he came back to Connemara for his half-term holidays he described the school in detail to Mary Duane. Its motto was 'Manners Makyth Man'. It was near to a place called the Water Meadows. It was founded nearly five hundred years ago, in 1382, three centuries before Cromwell's lieutenants ever came to Connemara. She liked saying the beautiful words of its name.

Winchester College, Hampshire.

Winchester.

Hampshire.

David Merridith goes to Winchester College, Hampshire.

It had eleven 'houses' and its own special rules for football. The village of Carna had eleven houses too, but the word 'house' meant something different in Hampshire. A house was a building where many boys lived, but no girls or ladies. The boys slept in dormitories, like soldiers or lunatics. They had 'masters' but not like a servant would have a master. If you lived in a house you hated all the other houses. You stuck up for the honour of your house to the end. But if it came to a fight you'd fight fair and manly. You never gave a chap a biffing when he was down or injured, and you never *ever* peached on him to his master. If you did you were a bladger, a croucher, a toady, Even under attack, there were rules.

Hampshire was a county on the south coast of England. She questioned her parents about it a couple of times – as a young man her father had gone to England in the summers to find farm work – but they didn't have anything to tell. One day she sneaked up to Kingscourt Manor and asked Tommy Joyce, Lord Merridith's valet, to show it to her on the atlas in the library, which had a gazetteer.

Hampshire was across the sea from France. It wasn't just historic; it was 'steeped in history'. It was widely valued for its chalky cliffs, the pleasant character of its charming people and its fascinating formations of fossiliferous rocks. ('Mother of Christ,' said Tommy Joyce. 'You'd sprain your lips.')

Winchester was the county town. King Alfred had died there and Henry III was born there. It was whispered by many in the world of letters that the authoress of the widely noted and delightful entertainments *Sense and Sensibility* and *Pride and Prejudice* ('published under the mysterious note 'by a lady'') resided within the county of Hampshire. The celebrated Mr Brunel, inventor of engines, resided nearby, at Portsmouth. Lord Palmerston, the Secretary at War, had his family seat at Romsey. King Arthur's round table could be witnessed in Winchester. It hung on the eastern bastion of the city's Great Hall, that noblest exemplar of magnificent construction whose mighty stones and oaken beams sang the stirring hymn of England's glory; the genius of her people from commoner to king. ('There's a spake for you now,' Tommy Joyce sighed dreamily. '*The genius of her people from commoner to king.*')

Nobody celebrated came from Connemara. There were no singing stones, no magnificent constructions. No literary whisperings. No tables hung on walls. No kings had been born there, or lived there, or died there; if they had, it was so long ago that nobody remembered their names. No inventors, no authors, no Secretaries at War. What a wonderful place Hampshire must be.

The rules of Winchester College Football were complicated. The teams had mysterious or indecipherable names. Scholastics versus Inferiors. Old Tutors versus The Worlds. Nobody had ever written down the rules, but you had to learn them anyway or the shags would biff you. They'd dig you; they'd prune you; they'd give you a pandying. ('Shag' was the English word for a cormorant; also a friendly name for an English boy.) A shag had to stand in the middle of a field and hold up the ball while shouting: 'Worms!' That, said David Merridith, was one of the rules. To know the rules was to know a language, though no book existed from which they might be gleaned.

The food at Winchester College was horrible. 'Bloody ghastly', according to David Merridith; a wonderful word Mary Duane had never heard before, yet one she thought sounded like its own meaning. ('*Ghaarst,*' you might groan, if you were being sick, for example.) But some of the fellows were decent chaps. There were a lot of other shags from Arland there, and they knocked about together no matter what happened. They weren't ghastly. They were blooming bricks.

Stones sang in Hampshire. Bricks bloomed.

But David Merridith didn't. Often he came back from Hampshire sickly and pale. He would take off his neatly pressed worsted trousers, his Winchester College blazer and schoolboy's cap, and don the rough clothes he wore at home in Connemara: the peasant's canvas britches, the bawneen '*bratt*' or smock. He seemed to think they concealed his status but for some reason they tended only to underline it. A boy in a disguise nobody believed in, an actor playing a part he didn't understand, he would trudge every rocky field and quaking bog, every pot-holed road and tortuous boreen, each of the thirteen villages on his father's estate, speaking the Irish he had learned from his father's servants.

The tenants found it difficult to attune to his changing accent; the exotic music of Connemara Gaelic spoken in the tones of the English public school.

'Ellorn,' he'd say, meaning *oileán*: an island. 'Rark' was his way of pronouncing *radharc*, a view. 'Rark. Rark.' He sounded like a shag. He *was* a shag. The shaggiest in Galway. Many of the people simply couldn't understand him. Mary Duane was one of the few on the whole estate who could make out what on earth he was talking about. Even when speaking in his native English, his brogue was harder to decipher now. 'Wistpawt' had become his word for 'Westport'. 'Arland' he'd say, when actually he meant Ireland. (Some of the people thought he was saying '*Ourland*' and thereby making some political point. They tended merely to nod and back away, smiling.)

He loved to speak in the Irish language. He would address her mother as 'Woman of Duane', her father as 'Friend' or 'Esteemed Person'. As he entered their cabin he would grin and announce: 'Christ between us and all harm!' He'd say 'the Lord bless all here' in the Gaelic idiom, and 'God and Mary be with you' for hello or good morning. Her father found it strange and faintly annoying. 'He'd give you an ache the way he carries on. And as for God-bless, he's a God-blasted Protestant. He doesn't even *believe* in God.' Her mother had told him not to be blethering like a geck, but her father thought David Merridith's behaviour suspicious. 'He wants to be something he's not,' he'd say. 'He's fish, that gossoon, and he wants to be fowl.'

'Just because they teach manners at Winchester College,' said Mary.

'Manners Makyth the Man,' her mother said.

'It was founded in 1382,' said Mary.

'So was my arse,' her father said bleakly.

Seasons passed. He took up drawing. She would happen upon him sometimes on her way to the market or returning from the well at Cloonisle Hill, seated with a sketchpad and a box of charcoals. He had a talent for capturing the rocky landscape especially, its sense of implied drama and sudden changes of light. A few scrawls of his chalk and you'd see it materialise: marl, shale, sea-wrack, basalt, the marbling of pebbles like bullets in the fields. Buildings, too, he was able to draw, with an exactitude Mary Duane thought almost miraculous. His people were always a little too idealised; stronger and courtlier than they were in the flesh. But people were already his favourite subject, the tenants and servants and workers on the estate. It was as though he was drawing them as he wanted them to be: not quite as they were, or ever had been. Perhaps not even as they would have wanted to be themselves, for he never asked them that. He simply drew them.

For all his pallor and delicacy he was growing up handsome, not at all like his stony-faced father. People often said of David Merridith: 'His mother will never be dead while that lad lives.' The broth of your father. The spit of your mother. The cut of your sister. The ghost of your aunt. His manner was gentle, amiable to everyone; though only when drawing a portrait could he look anyone directly in the eyes. A small occasional stammer, and the blushes it caused him, made him appear more timorous and incapable than he was. Though oddly he never stammered while talking in Irish; perhaps, Mary thought, because he had to think more clearly before speaking a language not his own.

For some reason bees and wasps stung him often. Perhaps he was simply more careless than others; or maybe there was some sweetness in his blood that attracted them. Whatever the cause, it seemed to happen daily. She would see him sometimes in a distant field, thrashing at the air around his head, jumping and flapping in a crazy jig. To some on the estate he was vaguely amusing – 'a long drink of water' or 'a great stuttering dodo' – but to Mary Duane, his companion of childhood, he had the heartbreaking beauty of an angel in a prayer book; the strange loveliness of something becoming extinct.

Once, in the summer of her seventeenth birthday, they had gone for a walk together in the sprucewoods up by Glendollagh Lake. As usual he was talking about his school. He was explaining that the name for a shag who had attended Winchester College was 'an old Wykehamist'; but you didn't have to be old or from Wycombe to be one. (Depending on certain mysterious circumstances, being from Wycombe might in fact rule you out.) You could be an old Wykehamist at the age of eighteen, and you could be an old Wykehamist if you came from Connemara. David Merridith's father was an old Wykehamist, for example, and soon David Merridith would be one himself.

It sounded to Mary Duane like a terrible insult. 'Shutup out of that, you auld Wykehamist, before I puck you.' But she thought she'd better not say that. Saying it might be ghastly.

Some of the shags at school had sweethearts. They would write letters to their sweethearts and send them little poems. A fellow called Millington Minor often wrote the poems. No, he wasn't actually a miner (though funnily enough his father did own a mine). If you gave Millickers Minimus a smoke or a sixpence, or ordered your fag to polish his galoshes, he'd compose you a poem that would cross your eyes.

'I suppose you've a rake of sweethearts yourself then, do you?'

'I don't know, quite,' he quietly answered.

'You don't know much, so. Do you, mister?'

'There's a girl I like a lot. I don't know if she knows it.'

'Is she pretty, so? Your little sweetheart.'

'She's the prettiest girl from here to Dublin.'

'Is she indeed? That must be nice for her.'

'Prettiest in the whole of the world, I dare say.'

'You'd be as well to tell her how you feel then, wouldn't you, mister?'

He chuckled lightly, as though conceding something. 'Probably. Sh-shouldn't wonder.'

They walked on for a while, going deeper into the woods. Everything was quiet, dark as a cathedral: dark with the incense of meadowsweet and pine. 'To pine' was an English verb for worrying or mourning; but here was a refuge where no one could pine. The syrupings of sap lay glazed on the bark. The carpeting of spruce needles and ferns underfoot. Reverence hung over the Glendollagh woods and it seemed a blasphemy to break it by speaking. She could hear the sound of his breathing beside her, the chirrup of a starling in the branches above. They wandered the otherworld, afraid to awaken it. And suddenly he had tripped on a mossy log and tumbled down a bank into a tangle of briars and foxgloves, slicing open his lip and the back of one wrist. Trying to come back up he had slipped again, and thrust out his hand to grab for help. She had taken him by the elbow and hauled him up hard; his muddied fingers gripping her bare, tanned forearm. It was the first time since childhood that they had touched each other.

He had clambered from the ditch, panting with effort and staggered forward clumsily into her arms, a deep blush colouring his mortified face. Green eyes like his mother's. Like beautiful marble. You could catch the fever from somebody's eyes.

Somehow they had ended up holding hands. They walked on through the wood, now intertwining their fingers. He started talking about drawing, but she wasn't really listening, even though she was managing to talk back sometimes. *Draw: to represent; to tie; to suck; to be in a stalemate; to attract as though by magnetism.* Soon they came to a clearing which poachers used for setting their snares. A small brook was gurgling over the white granite rocks. She let go his hand and went to the water; cupped her fingers and took a drink. When she rose again and turned, he was looking at the Twelve Bens in the middle distance, as though he had never seen them before.

Nothing had been said for a few long moments. The rules were complicated. But then nobody had ever written them down.

Winchester.

Hampshire.

Winchshire.

Hampchester.

He bowed his head and began toeing a loose stone, sometimes glancing up at her through his long tousled fringe, uneasy as a hart in a wood full of huntsmen. His fall had left a smear of blood on his upper lip, the saffron of a wild lily streaked across his cheek. He put his hand in his pocket and absent-mindedly pulled out the lining, pretending suddenly that he was looking for something. The birds stopped their twittering. He shifted his weight from one foot to the other. The sun came out from behind the trees. A filigree of gold seemed to shine around him.

'Could I k-kiss you, Mary?'

They had kissed for a few minutes and then begun to touch. After a while they had loosened their clothes. Mary Duane realised that she would always remember what was happening now. The deepness of the cleft where his collarbone was. The smell of his sweat like new-mown grass. The extraordinary feel of his Adam's apple between her lips. The shocking prickle of stubble against her neck and uncovered shoulders. She would remember his nervous hands touching her abdomen and navel, and then meeting the stonish hardness of her ribs. Then the wetness of his mouth on her small bared breasts, the heel of his wrist against her thigh; the astonishing softness of the mounds of his palm causing her to shake with gentle pleasure and grasp his wrist. His hand was like air. She could nearly feel the corrugations of his fingerprints. How he kissed her mouth while he touched and caressed her. The sounds of pleasure coming from her mouth and into his. His tongue like a marshmallow. The grind of their teeth. The knead of their lips. Her hands on his face. The down of blond when she kissed his chest. And the strangeness of the things she wanted to do. To bite his shoulder. To suck his nipples. The aromas of their bodies and the aroma of crushed ferns. The tang of dandelion milk on his sunburnt skin. He had not wanted to be touched himself – at least, he hadn't asked to be. But when she had touched him tentatively through his half-opened britches – the anguish in his eyes, their lock on her own – he had begun to softly weep, then begged her in a whisper not to stop. He had clasped to her like an ivy as his pleasure overcame him, measured her neck and breasts with kisses.

Afterwards they lay in each other's arms. Grey light was dappling through the dark green leaves. The air smelt loamy, of turfsmoke and rain. A corncrake gave its peculiar cry. She felt no shame, no remorse of any kind. Really she felt nothing, but a new kind of nothing: the kind that gave her joy to feel it. It had started to rain but had stopped just as suddenly. After a while she had fallen asleep.

When she awoke he was lying beside her and muttering some words. *Tá grá agam duit, a Mhuire. Tá grá agam duit.* A zizzing of bees could be heard in the glade. She had pretended for a while not to realise what he was saying. 'I love you, Mary,' spoken in Irish.

They had buttoned their clothes – he had turned away discreetly as she fastened her skirt – and walked back together through the fields to Kingscourt. In the distance the trawlers were heading out towards Inisheer for the night. A calf was running after its mother. Another calf was blowing; swinging his head. The cow came stately down to the shallows and started to drink from the rushy water. Two tiny figures were tedding hay on the hillside. Weary men trudging towards home from the bogland, loys and shovels over their shoulders like rifles. Very unusually, he wasn't talking.

She wondered if he was embarrassed, or shocked by her willingness. Perhaps he might think a bit less of her now. The girls in the village said it was best to hold back with a boy, even if you had feelings for him: even if you loved him. A decent boy would respect you for holding back.

He had stopped at one point and picked her a handful of purple loosestrife. They had moved into each other's arms and kissed again: less urgently now, more courteously than before, with the knowing tenderness of adults.

'Suppose you hate me now,' he quietly said.

'I could no more hate you than hate myself.'

'You promise it, Mary? I couldn't bear it if you did.'

'Of course I do, you great daw.' She kissed his beautiful mouth and moved his fringe out of his eyes. Being allowed to touch him seemed a kind of blessing. 'Don't worry. Everything is all right.'

'I – just couldn't stop. I'm sorry. Please don't think badly of me, Mary.'

'I didn't want you to stop. I couldn't stop either.'

'Is there a word?' he asked. 'For what happened today?'

'Winchester College Football,' she said. Mainly because she did not know what else she might say.

Every day that summer they went walking in the woods by Glendollagh Lake. Winchester College Football was often played. She would think about playing it when she woke up in the mornings and last thing at night before going to bed. One day in late July he went to Athlone with his father. Lord Kingscourt was buying a new brood mare. She missed him as though he had gone to America. She tried to envision all the things he would see on the journey: to look at the world through David Merridith's eyes.

At moments of the day when she wasn't near him, she found herself imagining what he might be doing. She pictured him dressing, having his breakfast; undressing again to take his bath. What a beautiful sight, to see him fully naked; but that had never happened; he was shy about his body. At Winchester College, he had explained to Mary, a boy was never allowed to be completely undressed. Even in the bath he had to wear his underdrawers. When she asked him why, he had become more embarrassed. Certain Hunnish practices had sometimes gone on at Winchester College, which it would be better if she did not know about.

His protectiveness about the secrets of Winchester touched her. She took it as a sign of wider things, a confirmation of her womanliness in David Merridith's view. She had seen her father act in a similar manner towards her mother when the subject of England in general had come up. He had witnessed carry-on as a young man in England the like of which no married woman should want to discuss. Her mother would laugh at him and shake her head. He would chuckle back archly and grab her and kiss her. And Mary Duane knew that this was love. The thing not said.

The matter of silence.

CHAPTER IX

THE MAP OF IRELAND

One afternoon while they were strolling the wheatfields at Kilkerrin, a squall had rushed in from the bay and caught them by surprise. They had taken shelter in an abandoned house near the edge of a glade; the cabin of a family who had emigrated to Liverpool. They had looked for a while around the sad little rooms, at the mouldering crockery, the pictures on the walls. The Sacred Heart of Jesus. Patrick banishing the snakes. A calendar torn from a Stockman's Almanac. A chipped enamel plate was sitting on the table, a knife and spoon placed on it like the hands of a clock, as though someone was expected home at any minute. But nobody would be coming home again.

He had managed to light a fire in the deadened ashes of the hearth and they had lain down in front of it to be together. The room was cold as a tomb but his body was warm. After they had kissed and embraced for a while, he had made to touch her thigh but she had gently moved his hand away.

'I can't today, my kitten. Let's just kiss.'

His smile had melted like snow off a rope.

'Are you all right, Mary?'

'Fossiliferous. Honestly.'

'I've not offended you? I didn't mean to take liberties.'

'You didn't, you daw.' She kissed him again. 'It's my time.'

He beamed benignly. 'How do you mean?'

'Do you not know what happens to a girl once every month?'

'No.'

'Think.'

He shrugged. 'Pocket money?'

She looked at his confused face. 'Are you serious?'

'What do you mean?'

'It happens once in the month. It's to do with the moon.'

'The moon?'

'She gets a visitor. That's the guest I have now.'

He stared at the space around her as though looking for a Guardian Angel.

'They never mentioned this at Winchester College Hampshire?'

'I don't think so, Mary. Not that I heard.'

'Maybe you should ask one of your sisters about it.'

'They do it too, do you think?'

'Every woman does.'

'Aunt Eddie?'

'Jesus. Would you stop it.'

'Does it have a name?'

'Some call it "The Curse". It has other names, too.'

'Sounds dashed inconvenient, whatever it is.'

'Not nearly so inconvenient as not doing it, I can tell you.'

'How do you mean, M–Mary?'

'Ask one of your sisters.'

✳

In late September he went back to school in England. Sometimes he had written her what she knew must be love-letters only because he had drawn hearts and Cupids in their margins. She had been too ashamed to tell him she did not know how to read. The Presbyterians ran a hedge college near Toombeola Bridge, an informal school for the children of tenants; but her father said he didn't want her mixing with Presbyterians. She didn't know why Presbyterians were reckoned to be dangerous; the great Wolfe Tone had been a Presbyterian; he had fought and died for Ireland as captain of the revolutionaries in '98. But she didn't want to vex her father. So she had taught herself the skill of reading that autumn and winter, with a primer she borrowed from the parish priest; the black stains of ink on the blue-lined leaves of copybook slowly revealing themselves as declarations of fidelity and love.

Winchester. Hampshire. England. Great Britain. He had not disappeared; you could see it on the atlas. His co-ordinates were measurable and so were her own, but the distance between them seemed vaster than degree.

She pined, Mary Duane; she understood the word now. Her boy sent her drawings of England's wildflowers: forget-me-not, lad's-love, love-lies-bleeding. She sent him back meadowsweet, heathers from the mountain. Ferns from their grove in the Glendollagh wood. She missed him so much that she became mopy and argumentative. Connemara seemed barren as a withered nest without him. At night she lay in the bed she shared with two of her sisters, waiting for them to stop whispering and finally fall asleep, so her fingertips could begin their delicious imitation of David Merridith's caresses. She wondered if he ever did the same. Boys often did, she had sometimes heard it whispered. She imagined her hands were David Merridith's hands. And she sent the thought towards him that his own hands were hers. She pictured her thought flying over the sea to England, a thought like a tiny golden star, soaring over Ireland, across the dark sea, down through Wales, trailing sparks in its wake, over the glimmering cities of the English night, the chimneystacks and factories, the palaces and slums, into his room at Winchester College where he slept in a bed with heather-dusted sheets. Her dreams about him became wilder and stranger. Soon they had a fieriness she began to find frightening. She told them – some of them – to the priest in confession. He was a happy young priest, the kind who sings at weddings. All the girls fancied him. He'd go easy on you in confession. But he hadn't gone easy on Mary Duane.

He had said such imaginings were the worst kind of evil, a poisonous affront to the Virgin Mary. 'That sin causes Our Lady to weep,' he had insisted. 'Every time it is committed Our Mother's heart is pierced with a burning sword. For a young woman to defile her own God-given body is a tremendous victory for Satan.'

There was another important matter for young women to consider. Young men couldn't control themselves. They had feelings which young women didn't have. A woman was a glacier, melting slowly, but a man was a volcano of boiling passions. Every man on earth had to carry that cross; even Pope Pius himself in Rome. That was how Almighty God had designed it, but the devil could step into the picture if invited. To ensnare some young man in an occasion of mortal sin could have disastrous consequences for his soul and his body. The asylums of every city in England were howling with men who had been ruined by women. Better a millstone were tied around a girl's neck and she be flung into Dog's Bay than to coax a young man to a lustful temptation which he lacked the mental apparatus to resist. As for his physical apparatus, the less said the better. When Satan stood up it was time to run.

She had found the priest's words, if anything, quite exciting. She knew that was wrong, and probably sinful; and she didn't want to make Our Lady weep, at least no more often than was absolutely necessary. But it was hard to push out of her head for any length of time the picture of David Merridith in the grip of demonic arousal.

But she tried. She tried to put David Merridith out of her mind completely. She agreed to go blackberrying with Noel Hilliard, a boy of her own class from Commander Blake's estate, but felt nothing at all for him despite his pleasantness and strength, his eejity jokes and his skill with mimicry. He was broken-hearted the night she told him their only future was as friends. He had pleaded with Mary Duane to be given another chance: a chance to make her happy. So many kinds of love existed in the world; surely she had one kind for him. There was simply no point, she had said to Noel Hilliard. It wouldn't be fair on him. He deserved a girl who could love him truly. Her own heart belonged to another.

One morning that autumn she had gone with her father to buy a slaughtering knife at Ballyconneely Fair. Along the road they had happened upon a group of men watching Lord Kingscourt's stallion covering a mare in a meadow, its sinewed haunches bucking and nostrils flaring. Strange laughter between the men as they watched. They were passing a pipe from one to the other. Strange laughter and few words.

That night she dreamed of the molten sword, burning as it pierced the bared heart of Christ's mother. When she woke up at dawn she was trembling and wet.

Her eldest sister, Eliza, was courting by now: a nice boy from Cushatrough who worked a conacre out by Barnahallia Lake. Mary Duane asked if she had been intimate with her fiancé.

'No,' said her sister. 'We look at the flowers.'

How would a girl avoid getting pregnant, Mary Duane asked.

'Why?'

'Just wondering.'

'That's all you better be doing, you rip. You're not so big that Mammy won't redden your arse for you.'

'What does that mean?'

'You know fine well what it means. Little holy innocent.'

'So. What's the answer?'

'You get off the horse at Chapelizod.'

'What?'

'You know the way, if you were riding from Galway to Dublin?'

'Yes.'

'Chapelizod is just before Dublin.'

'Is it?'

'Well you make him hop off the horse at Chapelizod.'

'Oh.'

'Or you hop off the horse yourself. It depends.'

Geography, it seemed, was also a language: its syntax more complicated than English.

Sometimes she caught sight of her brothers' bare bodies. One evening she saw her father's too, when he was washing himself in the brook after a day clearing stones on the mountain. She wondered if David Merridith would have that pallid pouchy look, like a gawky gannet plucked of its feathers, that seaweedy cluster between his legs. Would his belly be pudgy or taut as a drum? Would his rear be saggy or like two onyx eggs? The other realms of his body, where it pleasured him to be touched: what were they called? Did they even have words? The places of her own body where his hands had brought her such bliss as to make her tremble and cry out his name: what were the names of those? The helpless kisses and sighs shared at such moments, were they some kind of secret, unspeakable language? Did all lovers cry out each other's names? Eliza and her fiancé? Her mother and father? The mother of Jesus and her carpenter husband: had they cried each other's holy names as Mary Duane had done with her boy?

The smell of cut grass brought his body to mind; the buzzing of bees began to make her feel weak. In church she found herself staring up the crucifix, as though a new sun had arisen in the sky over Connemara and was bathing the land in a stained-glass light. The naked Christ wasn't just holy: he was beautiful, too. His alabaster thighs and powerful shoulders. The tendons of muscle tautening his forearms. If you saw him in Clifden Market instead of hanging off a tree, you'd fancy the drawers off him. You mightn't be able to stop at Chapelizod. You'd have to keep going. Till you ended up in Holyhead. She glimpsed hidden meanings in the rubrics and the prayers. This is my body. The word was made flesh. With my body I thee worship. Was it sinful to think that way? Probably it was. Poor Virgin Mary would be practically hysterical. But then again, she'd had plenty of practice over the years.

One day David Merridith would be old and tired. Would he be so beautiful then? Or ugly like his aunt? Would he grow into his father, a crabby auld bastard eaten up with bitterness and guilt? That was what her own father said about David Merridith's. A bully devoured by his rancour.

She remembered the last time she saw him before he went away to New College, Oxford. (New College, needless to say, was very old.) His father and Tommy Joyce had gone to Clifden for the day. The house was empty. They had it to themselves. She had bathed and put on fresh clothes and tied a ribbon in her hair. As she walked up the drive to Kingscourt Manor, her longings seemed to whirr before her like a congregation of birds. She was thinking carefully about the map of Ireland; the road which led from Galway to Dublin; the detours, excursions and notable delights which might be enjoyed along the way.

David Merridith himself had opened the front door. He had just returned from the tailor's in Galway and was dressed in a manner that made him hard to recognise. A mortarboard hat and long black gown, a smart black frock coat and a creamy coloured bow tie, an emerald green waistcoat with porcelain buttons. 'Subfusc' was the name for the clothes he was wearing. Everything in his life seemed to need a name.

'I don't really feel like a walk today, Mary.'

'Do you want to kiss me again so?'

'That would be nice. But to be honest, I'd better not.'

'Wouldn't be able to control yourself, no?'

'I'm sorry?'

'You're a volcano of boiling passions. I know.'

He had touched her face; the curve of her cheekbone. 'I'd never want to do anything bad to you, Mary.'

She had kissed his fingertips. She could see he was nervous. 'Would it be so bad when there's love between us? We could be careful.'

'Careful?'

She kissed the side of his mouth in the lingering way she knew he liked. 'I know a way of being careful. It will be all right. Don't worry.'

But he had pulled away, his features bleached with anxiety, and walked slowly across the room as though in a daze. He opened the piano lid. Closed it again. Began shifting around the ornaments on top of the sideboard.

'Is something the matter, David?'

A bee was circling around his head. He flicked it away with the back of his hand.

'We've known each other a long t-time, haven't we, Mary.'

'Since 1382,' she said. But he didn't laugh.

'What's wrong, David? Is something after happening?'

'My f-father has told me not to be seen with you in future.'

'Why not?'

'He says it's a question of duty, Mary.'

'What duty is it would interfere with our friendship?'

'You don't understand. He says it's my duty. And if I don't agree, he'll send you and your family away.'

'He couldn't send us away,' she said angrily. 'We're the Duanes.'

'What does that mean?'

'My father's people are on this land a thousand years. It's himself'll be sent away if he starts that kind of talk.'

'He could send you away if he wanted,' David Merridith said quietly. 'He could send you away tomorrow morning. And anyway, Mary – there's something else.'

'What's that?'

'It was your f-father who asked him to tell me this.'

She had been too shocked to say anything at all for a while.

'He seems to feel – it's unfair in some way. When you look at the whole picture. Mary, are you listening?'

'You said it was what you and I wanted that mattered.'

'I know. I know. But honestly, Mary.'

'You've changed your mind? You didn't mean what you said? All those dozens of times that you said it?'

'I just think, Mary – when one looks at the whole picture.'

She thought about the bee, sinking its sting into your flesh. They died when they stung you. They could only do it once.

'Take this, Mary. Please.'

He had reached into the pocket of his porcelain-buttoned waistcoat and offered her a handful of blackish half-crown coins. Tears were running down his face as he held them towards her.

That was the only time she had ever struck him; maybe the only time she had ever struck anyone. He had stood like a statue while she slapped his face, bearing her blows without saying a word. She didn't know how many times she must have slapped him. If she'd had a knife, she would have murdered him then. Gashed him in the throat like a slaughterman felling an ox.

It still shocked her to think about it. The violence of that moment.

Not the way she had slapped him. But the way he had let her.

Even under attack, there were rules.

CHAPTER X

THE ANGELS

The EIGHTH day of our Voyage: in which
the Good-hearted Captain makes a DANGEROUS
ACQUAINTANCE (though he did not Know it
at the time, nor until it was too Late).

Monday, 15 November, 1847
Eighteen days at sea remaining

Long: 26°53.11′W. Lat: 50°31.32′N. Actual Greenwich
Standard Time: 00.57 a.m. (16 November). Adjusted
Ship Time: 11.09 p.m. (15 November). Wind Dir. & Speed:
N.E. 47°. Force 5. Seas: Tumultuous. Heading: S.W. 225°.
Precipitation & Remarks: Big weather. Intermittent
severe showers of sleet since dawn. This day we start into our
second week out of Cove.

This dreadful day fourteen steerage passengers died, making a total
of thirty-six since commenced this voyage, and were buried
according to the rite of the sea. Four of those who expired today
were infants; one of those had lived only twenty-one days on this
earth. A fifteenth passenger, a poor fisherman of Leenaun whose
brother fell asleep in Jesus yesterday, lost his reason and took his own
life by drowning.

May God in His forgiveness have mercy upon their souls.

Eight suspected of Typhus in the hold this night. One suspected
of Cholera.

A piglet was today stolen from the cages on the upperdeck. No
doubt the First-Class passengers shall somehow survive the deprivation
of his flesh. I have ordered all the beasts to be guarded from now on.

This evening I was walking near the fo'c'sle at dusk, oppressed by a heavy mood of melancholy. The deaths of any are hard to bear, but the deaths of the young, the little children especially, seem almost a ridicule of our lives. I confess it is difficult at such painful moments to believe that Evil does not govern the world.

I was attempting my prayers in contemplative silence, as is my preferred custom of years, when I came upon one of the steerage passengers, on his hands and knees by the First-Class gates, and most violently ill from the sea. This is a curious and noteworthy character, his behaviour oftentimes odd. Though badly afflicted with a deformed foot, he is fond of walking the ship by night, and is known among the men by the sobriquet of 'The Ghost'.

On seeing me approach, the poor polliwog rose quickly and went to the rail, where he leaned over very far, and was soon in a state of substantial misery, saying good morning and good day again to his supper. I gave him a pint of freshwater I happened to have about me in a flask, and an observer might have imagined it were vintage champagne from his gratitude. A more pleasant fellow I never met in my life, though a little strange in his appearance, his hair particularly.

He said he was finding the voyage vexatious to his economy, never having been into open seas previously. His father had been a fisherman in County Galloway in Ireland but had never ventured far out from the land, the waters in that part being so abundant with fishes and crustaceans that he never had need. His father, said this amusing little fellow, was known in the locality as '*the fisherman who never went to sea*'. At that I gave a laugh. And as I laughed myself, he laughed too, and began to look more relieved in his countenance.

He and I conversed for a time about matters of the weather and such and such and he was agreeable, not taciturn at all, despite what the men say about him; speaking English in a most melodious and charming way. I asked if he would teach to me a couple of examples of his own language; for example 'good morning, sir', 'I bid you good day, madam', 'land' or 'sea' and various other ordinary things. And I would note them down in a phonetical way; for I had oftentimes wished to have a few phrases of that tongue, so as to be able to speak them to passengers as a little sign of friendship and thereby put them at more of their ease. 'Awbashe' and 'murra' are

the words for the sea. 'Glumree' means 'the waves'. 'Jee-ah gwitch'
is 'good-day'. But they have two score and upward of words for
land, depending on what sort of land is being spoken of.* 'Tear' is
one of them (pronounced in a fashion so as to rhyme with 'year').
'Tear mahurr' is 'my father's land'. He took from the pocket of his
greatcoat a handful of soil which he shewed me. It was a handful of
his father's land at Connermara. 'Tear mahurr Connermawra' I
ventured, and he smiled. It was a matter of good luck to have carried
it along with him. I said I thought it a pleasant custom and indeed
hoped it might bring him fortune (though it were better he trusted
to prayer than to fetish).

He then said that he had seen me before, on the decks at night,
and had sometimes thought to approach and to greet me, but that I
often seemed preoccupied by cumbersome thoughts. I explained
that I was in the habit of walking the deck in the evening to say my
prayers in a private manner, that we brethren of the Society of
Friends place a weight on silent reflection and scriptural reading
rather than ritual or ceremony. At that, he took from his greatcoat
pocket a small leather-bound book which he shewd to me. Imagine
my humility when I saw it was a little bible, so perfect and neat.

---

*Aibéis: the sea (archaic, from English, 'an abyss'). Muir or Mora: Old Irish: the
sea. Glumraidh: hunger, devouring, powerful sea-waves. Dia Duit: a greeting,
'May God be with you'. Mulvey was speaking the truth about words meaning
'land'. Gaelic is a language of lapidarian precision. (Rodach, for example, is the
Irish word for 'sea-weed growth on timber under water'.) For the following list
of words for land, by no means exhaustive, we are indebted to the graciousness
of Mr James Clarence Mangan of the Ordnance Survey office at Dublin, and
to the scholarship of his associates, Messers O'Curry, O'Daly and O'Donovan.
(Occasionally they disagree about spelling or accents.) Abar: marshy land. Ar:
ploughed land. Banb: land unploughed for a year. Banba: mythical name for
Ireland. Bárd: enclosed pasture land. Brug: land, a holding. Ceapach: a tillage
plot, fallow land. Dabach: a measure of land. Fonn: land. Ithla: an area. Iomaire:
a ridge. Lann: an enclosure of land. Leanna: a lea. Macha: arable land, a field.
Murmhagh: land liable to flooding by the sea. Oitír: a low promontory. Rói: a
plain. Riasg: a moor or fen. Sescenn: marshy land. Srath: a meadow or holm
along banks of a river or lake. Tír: land, dry land (as opposed to sea), a country
(as in Tír na nÓg, the mythical land of youth; a Paradise). Fiadhair is the Scots-
Gaelic word for lay or fallow land. Fiadháir is the Irish adjective for 'a wild or
uncultivated person'. – GGD

'Perhaps Your Honour and meself might read together for a moment,' he said.

At those words I own I was taken aback, in the first place that he was able to read at all, and in the second that he wished to read with myself; but how could I disagree? We sat down in a nook together and he quietly commenced to share with me from the First of Paul to the Corinthians, on the theme of Christian charity to our fellows. I was moved almost unto tears, he read so simply, and yet with such sincere devotion to the Word. Truly I felt the Spirit of Light come down. For those few moments there was such blessed peace between this stranger and I, with no shallow and worldly sense of myself being Captain and he frightened passenger; rather of both trusting to that same Admiral of Ages whose providence shall pilot all good pilgrims through the tempests of doubt. How preciously remarkable are the ways of the Saviour, that an unfortunate man so down on his luck might find nourishment and sustenance in the immutable verities of the scriptures. When we who have so much for which to be thankful so often want in gratitude to Our Father which gave it. How ashamed I was now of my weakness and self-pity, traits which in men are disgraceful.

'William Swales' is the name of this poor distorted man, so I discerned, for there it was inscribed, on the frontispiece of his bible.

I said I had never heard that surname on an Irishman before and enquired if it was characteristic of Connermara, his impoverished homeland now left far behind. He smiled gently and sadly and replied that it was not. The most frequently occurring names among the people there were 'Costilloe', 'Flaherty', 'Halloran' or 'Keeley'. The name 'Nee' was well known in a place called Cashel; the name 'Joyce' in a townland called the Recess. 'Tis Cashel for Nees and Recess for Joyces' was a thing often said in that locality. Indeed, he smiled again, one could truthfully say that everyone in that little corner of the world had been a Nee or a Joyce at some time in his past. (All those appellations I had heard many times before, and have uttered the words of burial over scores of their bearers, alas.)

He told me an interesting thing: that the surname 'Costilloe' is derived from the Spanish noun 'Castillo', a castle. And that in the time of the Armada a great ship of Spain was lost and wrecked on the coast of Galloway County, many of the sailors remaining in

Ireland thereafter, but I do not know if it is true. In fact I think it is probably not, but a captivating yarn whether yea or nay. (Nevertheless it is conspicuous that a portion of those in steerage do indeed have the dusky features of the Iberian peoples and in their mode of thinking are as remote from our own English race as the Hottentot, Watutsi, Mohammedan or Chinee.)

The more we talked, the better friends we became; and at length he asked if he might speak to me candidly about a certain matter. I said I would be happy to assist him if I could. He said his aged father was extremely indisposed back at home in Galloway, and he hoped soon to raise the necessary to convey him from that place of destitution and into America. I said that was an admirable and Christian plan; respect for the aged conferring dignity on giver and receiver, the both. He then expressed a great interest in any paid work that might be available on board, such as cleaning the First-Class cabins or staterooms or any other duties of that nature. I said regretfully we had no need at present but would bear him in mind should any such opportunity arise.

At that he looked most crestfallen and said he truly was in need of an opportunity. He was loath to ask for charity and vowed he never should. He realised he had the shameful aspect of a beggar at this present hour, but he had been a proud man in former times (before his injury). He was accustomed to the company of fine people, he said, having once been a manservant to a baron in Dublin (a gentleman named Lord Nimmo, of whom I had not heard). No, he had not a testimonial on his person at present, his papers and pocketbook having been stolen by vagabonds at Liverpool, but he was sure his skills must be of use still. And now he came to the meat of his point.

If, for example, our esteemed passenger Lord David Merridith were to need assistance of that kind (or any other kind) on the voyage, perhaps I might be pleased to recommend him as an honest sort. No fine gentleman such as Lord Merridith should be without his personal man, he averred. Perhaps I might accentuate that he, Swales, was a scion of Connermara like Lord David himself; one who had always esteemed Lord Merridith's family, particularly his late mother, a saint amongst women and greatly revered among the impoverished of that country. Would I please say to His Lordship, poor Swales asked me, that he was a man who had fallen on hard times through injury, but was neither afraid of labour nor loyalty. Even that impairment which had disfigured his body had served only to strengthen his valuation for the gift of life. And now, by the grace of Almighty God, he had almost succeeded in overcoming it compleatly, and could walk and work like a luckier man. It would be the greatest privilege to assist Lord Merridith, he said. He believed he could do him very good service if only permitted that honour and boon. Merely to be close to him he would consider a blessing.

I said Lord Kingscourt was fortunate indeed to enkindle such a devotion as this, particularly in one who had not met him, and should certainly recommend him, should need or opportunity arise. He said he intended no offence but would I possibly oblige him by swearing to that. I replied that we Quakers resile from the taking of oaths, as such, but I would promise it to him as man to man.

At that point tears of gratitude arose in the poor fellow's eyes and soon threatened to overcome him quite utterly.

'God and Holy Mary bless Your Honour's kindness,' he said humbly, and clasped me by the hand. 'I will say an Ave for you tonight, and every other in my life, as true as God is my witness.'

Then he asked me to give him counsel as to what work he might turn his hand to in America. I said America was a grand land, a country of the largest liberty, the only nation of equality and federative self-government on the face of the earth at present. Any young fellow who would be industrious and put away national peculiarities might find happiness there, so I told my new friend, and make a success of himself and end as smug as a schoolmarm. The best farmland in the world could there be had for a few dollars an acre; the soil so fertile it was told by a Cherokee Indian I once encountered at Charlestown, Sth. Carolina that a stick placed into the ground would grow into a mighty tree. At this he was amazed as a seraph who had awoken in Manchester. But then he said he had no wherewithal to buy land, having sold all he possessed in the world to sustain his ailing parent, and various little orphaned nephews and nieces, the residue being taken up by the price of his passage. (Such is the desperation of the wretched people to escape their condition.)

I said I had heard that there were good opportunities for a man who would work at ordinary labouring, such as on the railroad building or swamp clearing or mining for silver or gold, where rudimentary food and lodgings were also provided. Canal digging, ditching, laying stone walls and the like. Here I mentioned by ensample the splendid Great Eyrie Canal which runs 353 miles from Albany to Buffalo, its 83 locks and 18 aqueducts being built in the main by his own Irish countrymen; a magnificent adornment to civilisation and Free Trade. Also that tree-fellers were always required, whole territories of that continent being heavily wooded with forests even larger than the entire isle of Ireland. He was very attentive as I spoke about such matters and seemed to regard America as like unto another planet and not part of the Earth. Was it true, he desired to know, that in America at the present moment it was not night-time but afternoon? And on the Pacific coast of that continent it was now morning-time?

I explained that for every degree of Longitude west we are four minutes earlier than Greenwich, and for each one minute of distance four seconds are gained. So it was already tomorrow in London, he said, and I confirmed that it was. 'Arrah, what a miracle,' he sighed. 'They say that "tomorrow never comes" but it is already here, God and Mary bless us.' And so it must follow, he further said, that if a man spent a year travelling westwards around the world he would arrive home in Ireland the day before he left. And if he kept at this for the rest of his life he would grow up into a newborn babe instead of a crooked old fellow. How happy to be able to turn back time, he remarked, and thereby undo the impieties of boyhood folly.

At first I thought the poor simpleton had misunderstood my meaning in his childish innocence but then he clarified that he was making a witticism and we laughed together jollily until I bade him good-night. He was still laughing away as I left him. And not one minute ago he walked past my cabin and peeped in through the porthole, still happily laughing and waving. 'The scriptures instruct that we are to become as children,' he exclaimed. 'And now we know how, sir: it is to keep travelling westerly.' I laughed back to my professor: 'Tear mahurr!' And he bade me a peaceful rest and shuffled on humbly by himself.

What an example that man is. Truly the angels are come among us every day. Our difficulty is so often that in our vanity and worldliness we so utterly fail to recognise them for what they are.

. . . the Irish in America are particularly well recvd. and looked upon as Patriotic republicans, and if you were to tell an American you had flyd your country or you would have been hung for treason against the Government, they would think ten times more of you and it would be the highest trumpet sounded in your praise.

Letter from James Richey, Ulster immigrant to Kentucky

CHAPTER XI

THE BALLAD-MAKER

Pius Mulvey's parents were dirt-poor smallholders, his father a local, Michael Dennis Mulvey, born on the estate of the Blakes of Tully. A large-headed, bony-featured shaft-horse of a man who had hammered his cabin's foundations out of the tombstones of his ancestors, he married Elizabeth Costello, a one-time scullery maid in the convent at Loughglinn in County Roscommon.

Mulvey's mother, a foundling child of Catholic refugees driven from Ulster, had been taught to read by the nuns who had raised her, and she thought the skill a useful one. Indeed she saw it as more than that; as a sign you regarded the world as fundamentally knowable, your place in it definable and open to change. Reading, to Elizabeth Costello, was an indication of decency. Her husband considered it a waste of time.

You couldn't eat a book, as Mulvey's father would point out. Nor could you wear one, or use one to thatch your cabin. He had nothing against reading when practised by others. (In fact he took a certain pride in his wife's ability to do it and often let it slip to their neighbours that she could, in the forgivable way that lovers brag about each other's competencies.) It was merely that he saw it as objectively useless, like quadrille dancing or archery or playing croquet, a fatuous amusement for the children of the gentry. His wife disagreed. She ignored her husband. As soon as they were old enough to walk and speak she began to teach her sons the skill of reading.

Pius, though younger, was the better reader of the two. His mind was quick and it worked by a logic that was almost as impressive as it was eerily unchildlike. By the time he was four he could read the simpler paragraphs of the missal; aged six, he could decipher the terms of a rental receipt. Reading became his party-piece. At a family gathering, a wake or a Christmas hooley, other children would step forward to sing a rhyme or dance a hornpipe. Mulvey would open the battered English dictionary his father had scavenged from a midden heap at the back of his landlord's house and recite from its mouldering pages to the astonished grown-ups. 'My son, the scholar,' his father would chuckle. And Pius would explain how to spell the word 'scholar'. And his mother would quietly weep for joy as he did.

His brother's reactions were more complicated. Nicholas Mulvey was a year older than Pius; stronger, better looking and far more likeable. Not quite as blessed with his mother's intelligence, he was sufficiently intelligent to apprehend the loss of his power, and possessed of enough of his father's determination to fight that loss when he saw it threaten him. It took him many hours to learn what Pius could learn in minutes, but he wasn't afraid to put in the hours. He was a serious, methodical, religiously inclined boy, with an eldest child's sense of fussy protectiveness, which waged constant war with his eldest child's dread of being quietly superseded. He battled with his sibling for the greater part of their mother's love, and the principal weapon was the ability to read.

Slowly, persistently, with the doggedness of the untalented, Nicholas Mulvey gained on his gifted brother. In time he began to pass him by. His vocabulary grew, his pronunciation improved, his knowledge of the subtleties of grammar became impressive. Perhaps it was simply that Pius wasn't bothered any more, was sufficiently confident of having already won the honours to display a jaded contempt for the game. By then Nicholas Mulvey could read like a bishop. He needed no dictionary to explain how words were spelled.

Their father died from a horse kick when Nicholas was seventeen, their mother a year later, many said of grief. Returning to their cabin from their mother's funeral the brothers had wept in each other's arms and sworn on her memory to make the decent life she had struggled all her own life to give them. For a year they had tilled the stony patch of their father's tenancy, through a back-breaking winter of work and panic. There was little money. There was never enough money. The few sticks of furniture comprising their entire property were quickly pawned to cover the rent; all except for their parents' bed. To sell your parents' bed would invite bad luck, or so it was attested by the local people. The brothers needed no more of that commodity than had already come into their inheritance.

Often enough they went without food. Their rags turned to ribbons on their aching backs. They tried for a while to keep the cabin clean; but it was the bachelor cleanliness of young single Irish-men, raised by a mother who had been their handmaiden. Sheets were turned over instead of being laundered, cups only washed when no clean ones were left. They slept together in their parents' bed; the bed in whose warmth they had been conceived and born, suckled as babies, soothed as toddlers, worried for as children, prayed for as young men, and in which their father and mother had died.

Pius Mulvey began to think he might die in it, too.

It frightened him even more than having become what he was; that figure unimaginable to the young: an orphan. More than poverty and hunger it began to claw at him: the picture of himself and his heartbreakingly courageous brother growing old and then dying in that mountainside cabin. Nobody to mourn them or even to notice they were gone. No bedmate, ever, except for each other. The hills of Connemara abounded with such men. Bent, dead-eyed, ancient brothers who shuffled through life with the cross of loneliness on their backs. They limped into Clifden, laughed at by girls, to Midnight Mass on a Christmas Eve. Virgin old donkey-men with womanly faces. They reeked of their isolation, of stale piss and lost chances. Pius Mulvey did not find them comical. He could scarcely bear to picture their lives.

Never to feel what it was to hold a child who needed them; to tell a wife she was looking beautiful today, that her hair was pretty or her eyes an amazement; to argue with a wife and then make it up. To hold no other in your loving embrace and feel what it was to be loved in return. Mulvey was too young to have known those things himself, but he had seen them and been brought up in the warm light they shed. The fact that such a radiance might not shine on him again plunged him into a darkness he found terrifying.

He grew restless with Connemara and its bleak possibilities, its blasted bogscape and lunar rockiness, the grey desolation of everything around him, the rainy, acidulous smell of the air. The wind lashed in like a whip from the Atlantic and the trees grew at every angle to the ground except the perpendicular. He sat for hours at his cracked, filthy window watching them bend and warp in a gale; wondering when the fury might get too much and they would break in two or be torn from the earth. But they never broke. They just groaned and bowed low, and remained bowed after the storm had raged away. Stooped. Hunched. Twisted. Deformed: the servants of a master who detested their devotion.

His father had bowed low all his life. So had his mother and everyone Mulvey knew; but fate had returned no dividend on their loyalty. His brother spoke often of the mysteries of God. How God could never do anything wrong; God never tested you more than your abilities; the moment of crucifixion was the moment of triumph if only arrogant man had the clarity to see it. But Pius Mulvey did not see it. What he saw in his brother was a slave on his knees, adoring the truth of his own destitution, translating that fact into a sententious fiction because he lacked the courage to read it in the original. That it might take courage and not cowardice to believe in any God was a view to which Mulvey never gave countenance. To think like that was a waste of time: like washing the few dishes you still had among your possessions when you knew they would only be dirtied again the following day. If you were lucky enough to have anything to dirty them with, and that was by no means certain any more.

Their mother's absence was so sharp that it felt like a presence, no less palpable for never being mentioned. But it flowed between the brothers like underground water. They worked together on their father's patch; desperately, hungrily, from dawn to nightfall; dragging up dulse from the shore to nourish the stones; mulching in their own bloodied excrement as fertiliser; lacerating the rocks with the force of their efforts, but nothing much grew except their own sense of separation. There was no violence between them, there were no angry words. They had little at all to say to each other now.

Nicholas spent his evenings reading by candlelight when a candle could be afforded or begged from a neighbour; when it couldn't, he would kneel and pray in the darkness, Latin adjurations which Mulvey did not know. The sound of his brother's piety became an irritation; it kept Mulvey awake or away from his private thoughts.

One violently bitter day the previous January when the frost had hardened the ground to corpse-white marble, a Liverpudlian recruiting sergeant had happened along the boreen telling stories of the adventurous life of the soldier. Mulvey had been spellbound by what he had to say. The humblest private in the King's Irish Rangers could expect his days to be filled with marvels. He might find himself in Egypt, India or Beirut, where the sun sparkled down on the vines and the pineapples and the women were made like fantastical goddesses. The wine of those places was sweet and refreshing. All the scran you could eat and the pick of the girls. The uniform gave a lad a better sense of himself. 'You grow up six inches when you put on the red, boys!'

Soldiering was the profession for a spunky young buck who wanted a bite at the wonders of the world, and who required handsome payment for such an experience. As for the danger, of course it existed. But danger was merely another word for excitement; the thrill that added salt to the gruel of life. And dangers existed in every place. The sergeant had looked around at the arctic wilderness as though it saddened him to see it, as though it was immoral. As though to see the Mulvey brothers so profoundly implicated in it was a matter of embarrassment or even disgrace. At least in the army you were trained to survive danger. No Crown soldier would ever know starvation.

'Ten guineas a year in your hand,' said the sergeant, as though he couldn't believe such munificence was possible. 'And a shilling this minute to spit on the bargain.'

His breath was coming in wisps of steam. He held out his palm in its black leather glove, the small coin glittering like the eye of a saint.

'That buys you nothing here,' Mulvey's brother said quietly.

'How do you mean, cock? That's the King's money.'

'Then he's welcome to keep it for it's not wanted here. No King rules ourselves but the King of Heaven. And he'll burn in Hell with his blessed mother before a Mulvey deserts the land he was born on.'

The sergeant looked across at him with a perplexed frown.

'I – don't understand the way you're talking.'

'What I'm talking is the English language,' Nicholas Mulvey replied. 'But I wouldn't doubt that you don't understand. Ye understand nothing of this place. Ye never will.'

A slither of jagged snow fell from a nearby bough. Two rats scurried out of a broken tree trunk and into a ditch.

'No,' said the sergeant sombrely, 'I think I never will,' and he shrugged and walked back down the way he had come, his smooth boots skidding on the frozen rutted earth, his beautiful scarlet coat like the breast of a robin. Nicholas went into the cabin without saying another word. His brother stood on the boreen for a long time afterwards, watching his future walk slowly away: the whiteness of everything smarting his eyes. Watching until the sergeant had disappeared from view, back into the blankness out of which he had come.

For weeks afterwards, Mulvey was restless. Thoughts buzzed around his mind like wasps in a jam jar. He had dreams in which he would see himself dozing beneath the Pyramids, his belly full and his boots warm, as happy and snug as the grinning Sphinx. Delilahs pirouetting by golden firelight, their long limbs tanned and moistened with myrrh. Meat roasting in its own juices. Grapes exploding on his tongue like the vowels of a new language. He would awaken, shivering, beside his brother, in the preternatural darkness of another Connemara morning, with the stench of the chamberpot rising around the bed; a day of hurt and labour stretching before him like a road in a nightmare brought on by famishment.

Like a woman in a song awaiting the return of her lover from the sea, he would watch on the boreen for the sergeant to come back; but as also in a song, that never happened, and somehow he knew it never would now.

His brother was becoming ill, Mulvey could see it. His skin had a pallid yellowish tinge; his eyes were often bloodshot and rheumy in the mornings. A sort of changing weather could be seen in those eyes, a drifting of cloud across a pale, dead sky. Mulvey would watch him in the distant tussocked fields as he foraged through the bushes and swallowed leaves by the mouthful. The crows would watch, too, as though they found him strange.

Though himself half starved, Mulvey began to feign lack of appetite, hoping Nicholas would take what he left, but he never did. Gluttony was a sin, Nicholas Mulvey would say. The man with no grip on his appetites was no man at all, but a greedy beast that would end in Hell. Our Lord himself had shown fasting to be a necessary thing; an act which would bring you much closer to God. He would take away the leftovers and put them in the press and serve them again the following day, and keep on serving them again and again until Pius finally ate them or they began to rot. It became a kind of competition between them: who could stand the most starvation.

Soon it grew too much for Mulvey to be around him all the time. He began to rove the country at night, trudging out to shebeens or crossroads dances, to the ceilidhs and poteen sessions that sometimes followed Fair Days in the small towns of Connemara. If you waited till a certain point in the evening you could sometimes pick up a half-drained mug, or a bottle with a few dribbles left in the end, and make it last you the rest of the night. Often a passing gypsy woman or a roaming balladeer would sing for a few pennies and that was something Mulvey liked. It thawed the ice of loneliness like a glass of hot punch. Singing reminded him of happier times in his childhood; the warm family times before everything had changed.

The songs intersected like springs through the lowland. You saw shadows of some of them flit across others; lines borrowed, phrases improved, verses polished and moved around; events edited or left intact but told from a different point of view. As though once there had been only one great song from which the songmakers kept drawing; a hidden holy well.

Rarely did he speak to anyone at these congregations of singers; but he grew to know the people who wandered through the songs like characters in a saga that was still being written. The feeble old fool who married the girl he couldn't satisfy. The maiden expelled from her father's home all for her love of the false young man. The woman who was a vision met by a lake. The former lover encountered again, when time and experience have revealed the depth of lost love. The rambling boys of pleasure and the ladies of easy leisure. The cruel, scourging landlord and the tenant that took his wife. The fishermen, farmers, peasants and shepherds who played tricks on the tax collectors who came to harass them.

Often it felt to Mulvey as if the songs were a secret language: a means of saying things that could otherwise not be said in a frightened and occupied country. At least they seemed a way of covertly acknowledging that what was unsayable was important: that it might be said more explicitly at another time. Facts seemed to press at their camouflaging surfaces, like the ancient trees found beneath a layering of bogland, their bark still alive after five hundred years. If you looked at them collectively they seemed a kind of scripture, a repository for buried truths: the sacred testament of Connemara. What after all was the Bible itself? A clutch of tattered allegories and half-remembered stories peopled by fisherfolk, farmers and taxmen. His rambles came to seem an observance of something, but what exactly he could not name.

It was at one such event, a gathering of fiddlers and singers in Maam Cross, that Pius Mulvey began to steal. A drunken farmer had fallen down unconscious in the jakes of a public house, and Mulvey, light-headed with the hunger of several days, had relieved him of his boots and hat. It had only taken a moment to cross the border between victimhood and oppression and he felt no guilt for making the step. He hocked the boots and hat in a pawnshop down the street and returned to the inn to spend his windfall. The music sounded sweeter with a whiskey in your hand, a dish of stew before you and a dudeen of tobacco. He had even bought the humiliated farmer a drink when finally he staggered from the latrine in his wet bare feet. He felt he owed him a great debt of gratitude and he paid it in porter and fervent commiseration.

That was the first night Mulvey sang in public himself. The innkeeper had been singing a ballad of broken love to which he knew the lyrics of only two verses. He would give a full shilling to learn the rest, he said, for the piece had been loved by his lately deceased mother, a woman from Estersnowe in the County Roscommon. Mulvey quietly said that he knew the words; that his own mother had hailed from Roscommon too. 'Let's hear them so,' the publican had delightedly commanded, and Mulvey had stepped into the ragged circle and opened his mouth to sing.

Twas in the cruel of winter time, the hills being white with snow;
When o'er the hills and valleys dark, my true love he did go.
It was there I spied the fairest maid, with salt tears in her eye;
She had a baby in her arms, and bitterly did cry.

How cruel was my father, love, that barred the door on me;
And cruel was my mother, love; this dreadful crime to see;
But crueller was my sweetheart, who changed his mind for gold;
And cruel was the wintry wind that pierced my heart with cold.

Mulvey's voice was mediocre but his memory was excellent. He recalled every verse of the long, complicated love-song, a very old piece his mother used to sing, with classical allusions and multiple narrators. 'Macaronic' was the word for a song like that, its lyric alternating between Irish and English. But more than merely remembering the words, he remembered how the song was supposed to be sung: the places where you stretched out the lines just a little, the places where you fell silent and allowed the words to fall like leaves. It was a strange dark story about the seduction of a serving girl by a nobleman who had promised to make her his wife. His mother used to say it was a kind of spell; if you sang it while thinking of an enemy who had wronged you, he would fall down dead by the time you had finished. Even as a child Mulvey had not believed that. (He had tested it often and his brother had not died.) But there was an ambivalence about it which he had always liked. Sometimes it was difficult to know from the lyrics which of the lovers was speaking and which had been betrayed.

The following morning before Nicholas awoke, Mulvey walked all the way to the village of Letterfrack, returning with a basket of cabbages and a flitch of bacon, two loaves of fresh bread and a plump broiling chicken. Asked how he had come by the money to purchase such a banquet, Mulvey told his brother he had found a purse on the roadside. Nicholas disapproved of grog-shops and their frequenters, and had pleaded with Pius to stay clear of both.

'Then you should have taken it up to the constables. It's after being lost by some unfortunate person. Imagine how he must be feeling now.'

'I did take it up to them, Nicholas. Isn't that what I'm after telling you? The gentleman who lost it left a reward with the constables.'

'Is that the truth? Look at me, Pius.'

'As I'm standing here it is. May I choke if it isn't.'

'Do you swear to it, Pius? On Mammo and Daddo's eternal souls?'

'I do,' said Pius Mulvey. 'On their souls, it's true.'

'Then God is good, Pius,' his brother had said. 'We'd better not question His mercy or it won't come again. I was after praying for a miracle and here it is.'

And Mulvey had agreed. God was good. The Lord helped those who helped themselves.

CHAPTER XII

THE SECRET

Mulvey roved out the following night, to a gathering of musicians at a crossroads dance near Glassillaun. Again he had sung, and had enjoyed the experience, though now for a different set of reasons. Girls seemed to find him attractive when he sang, though he didn't know why and found such a fact inexplicable. He knew he was ugly, scrawny and feeble, entirely lacking his brother's muscularity. But they still found him attractive when he stopped singing, and such a development was not to be disregarded.

He never knew what to say to them, these laughing pretty girls. They would crowd around him or ask him to dance. The less he danced, the more they seemed to like him. Having no sister and no woman friend, he had never spoken to a girl for more than two minutes, and was entirely unprepared for having to do so now. And yet they were so beautiful when they talked and laughed, so different to men; so full of lightness. He found some of their thinking strange as the stars, and often they said things for which he simply had no answer. But they seemed to regard his silence as one of mystery rather than reserve. Silence, he learned quickly, was a thing that could work for you, a card that might be played to useful effect, particularly when combined with the willingness to sing. He had the idea they liked gentleness, courtesy, kindness; all the things which men reckoned unmanly. His ugliness was not mentioned, nor his poverty. They did not want to be swept off their feet. They just wanted to be talked to, and listened to when *they* talked. It wasn't very hard, especially if you were interested, and if you didn't want to talk, that sometimes didn't matter either. In a world of bragging chancers and roaring boys and athletes, there was a certain kind of girl who found reticence restful, and thankfully, that was the kind he liked himself.

He never spent an evening with Nicholas now. As soon as darkness began to fall he would trudge down the boreen and make for freedom. It didn't really matter which town you went to; someone would be singing or playing for dancers. There would be warmth, light, music and company; something to belong to when you felt so alone.

One night in a shebeen in Tully Cross a little one-eyed troubadour from some kip of a place in Limerick had given a piece of his own devising, a ballad on the cruelty of a local landowner, Lord Merridith, who had stretched a poor spalpeen for stealing a lamb. The song was crude and poorly sung; the singer a runt with no arse to his britches, but the people had howled with appreciation at the end of it and the singer had nodded like an emperor receiving his kowtow. 'My soul on you, boy,' one man had wept, approaching the singer and kissing his gnarled hand. 'That's the greatest living song was ever composed in Ireland. Usquebaugh Liquor! The purest drop in the house!'

Mulvey began to ponder something that would come to obsess him. Singers were admired by almost everyone; they were annalists, chroniclers, custodians, biographers. In a place where reading was almost unknown they carried the local memory like walking books. Many of them claimed to know five hundred songs; a smaller number knew upwards of a thousand. Without them, Mulvey sometimes felt, nobody would remember anything, and if it wasn't remembered it hadn't truly happened. A singer was in the same category as a faith healer or a dowser, as a midwife who could soothe the pain of labour with secret herbs, or a gypsy who could tame ponies merely by talking to them. But those who made their own songs were absolutely revered.

People fell silent when they came into a room, those shabby men and women granted the awesome gift of songmaking; the magistrates of what had happened and what had not. They didn't even have to sing particularly well. Others would sing the works they made. Neither did it matter that they rarely devised fresh melodies, that they simply used the ancient ones that everyone knew; wine-makers pouring this year's blessings into the beautiful bottles of the past. If anything such an approach made them even more admirable. Their wine tasted richer when infused with the spice of antiquity.

It was as though they had been touched by the hand of the Almighty, as though something of God's own power to conjure perfection out of nothingness had been breathed into their mortal mouths. Merely to be in their presence was regarded all over Connemara as an honour. A new song was greeted like the flowering of a crop; if it was unusually good, like the birth of a child. Often enough they derided each other's abilities, but nobody else dared to blackguard them. To insult a songmaker was considered evil luck. There was fear in the way these magicians were regarded; if you crossed one you might end up in a song yourself and be left there for ever to have your folly mocked, long after it had ceased to matter.

In his frayed, spineless dictionary Mulvey looked up the English verb 'to compose' – *to calm, to produce, to set up printer's type, to decide what is printed, to write or create, to adjust or settle, to put together*. The man who put together could also take apart. There was nothing such a wizard could not do.

He began to wonder in a quietly excited way if somehow he might include himself in this venerated priesthood, if one day he might fashion a song of his own. Always he had felt that he must have some purpose, that his life must mean something other than vassalage and frostbite. Soon he felt the need start to fume in him like a fever. Rhymes occurred to him often, and always had; he could fit words to melodies as well as the next man. His problem was the great limitation of his experience. He had never been in love or fallen out of it, never fought in a battle, never met a heavenly woman. Nor had he married or courted or killed or spent all his money on whiskey and beer or had *any* of the adventures which people worked into songs. Pius Mulvey had never made anything happen. Knowing what to write about was the hardest thing about writing.

At night while his brother was praying in the back room Mulvey would squat by the meagre fireside and try to compose. But to break open that part of him proved harder than breaking the land. He hungered to do it but it was so hard to do. Nothing came. For months nothing came.

He felt like a fisherman on a lake of shadows; just about able to glimpse the flit in the depths but able to net nothing no matter how he tried. Ideas darted past him, pictures and similes; he could almost feel them slither through his desperate fingers. In his mind he reached out to the spirit of his mother, the woman who had bequeathed him his love of singing. *'Help me'*, he prayed. *'If you can hear me, help me.'* Never since her death had he felt so painfully close to her as on the long, taunting nights when he tried to compose. But nothing came. Nothing ever came. Only the skittering of the rats in the thatch and the low fretted whisperings of his brother at prayer.

And then, one morning, everything changed. He awoke from a dream of leaves in a breeze with a couplet forming in his fuddled mind. It had happened just as strangely and as simply as that; like being roused to find a gift on your pillow. As though the leaves of the dream had suddenly fallen away to reveal it sitting there like a drowsy moth.

> *Myself and my brother were tilling the land,*
> *When up came a sergeant with coins in his hand.*

That he had heard the lyric before was his first conscious thought about it. It was good. He must have heard it before. Quickly he rose from the bed and crossed the cold earth floor to the table. A butterfly of words that might escape. He scribbled them down on the back of an old sugar bag, as though they would fly out the window if he didn't. He looked at the lines. Really they were very good. They obeyed the first principle of the architecture of balladry: each line moved the story forward.

> *Myself and my brother were tilling the land,*
> *When up came a sergeant with coins in his hand.*

A loin of steak with not an ounce of fat. Nothing at all about the lines was a waste. All the characters were introduced, their professions noted, their relationship to each other defined. Even the fact that the sergeant was said to have coinage implied that the narrator and his hard-working brother must not. Suddenly he saw that if you changed 'tilling' to 'scratching', and the dull noun 'coins' to the more sparkling 'gold', the fact of their relative poverty might be apprehended more clearly. And if you promoted the lowly sergeant to 'Corporal' or 'Captain' you would have a pleasing piece of alliteration with the flat verb 'came'. Hastily he made the alterations and read the result. The lines seemed to burst into life like a fruit.

> *Myself and my brother were scratching the land,*
> *When up came a captain with gold in his hand.*

Mulvey's elation felt almost indecent, like the giddiness of a child for remembered joys during a solemn benediction. Already you had an idea of how the song might turn out, but there was drama there too, for you couldn't be certain. Like all good stories it had choice at its heart. Would they go with the captain or stay where they were? What would you do yourself if you were in their position? Who would be the hero and who the villain? Now it occurred to him that 'my brother' might be a little too vague. But 'Nicholas' was too long to be made to fit. As though riffling the pages of a brick-thick book, he allowed himself to scan the names of all the men he knew. Who had a name that would fit the same space as 'my brother'? What about John Furey, the farmer from Rosaveel? Mulvey had only met him twice, and had certainly never scratched or scraped alongside him, but his name had the requisite trio of syllables. He scribbled it down and diedled the new line to himself.

> *Myself and John Furey were scratching the land.*

No. It wasn't as good as 'my brother'. He crossed out the name and returned the line to its original form; and the fleeting candidature for immortality of John Furey from Rosaveel was thereby cancelled for ever.

He walked out to work on the bog that morning as though carrying the light of the world in his head; a flame that might go out if left untended. *Mother, I beg you: don't take it away.* Silently he prayed the Rosary for the first time in years. He would never sin again; would never steal, would commit no impurity in private or with another. The Stations would be done every day of his life if only his flame did not flutter out. And later that day while digging with his brother, two more lines had loomed up at him out of nowhere.

And stories of soldiers all fearless and grand;
Oh, the day being cheerful and charming.

Again he was terrified he might forget them. He scratched them into the blade of his loy in case they slipped back into the nothingness later. He knelt by the roots of a fallen bog oak and wept for his mother and the kindness of God. He wept as he had never wept in his life, not at her deathbed, nor even at her graveside. For her loss; for his own; for all the things he had never told her. When his brother approached to see what was the matter, Mulvey took him in his embrace and cried like a child and told him no man ever had a better brother, and he was sorry for the distance which had come to separate them. His brother stared back at him as though he was mad. Mulvey laughed. He roared with laughter. Danced across the bogland like a mountain goat.

That night Pius Mulvey did not go roving. He hunkered on the floor of his parents' cabin with a pen in his hand and a wildness in his heart. The facts of what had happened on that wintry day were hard to meld into the lines of the ballad; if you could even say clearly what the facts actually were. So he changed them a little to fit the rhyme scheme. It didn't really matter. Nobody would ever know the facts anyway; if they somehow found them out, they wouldn't find them worth singing. The main thing in balladry was to make a singable song. The facts did not matter: *that was the secret.* He wrote and scratched out; rewrote, refined. The effect you wanted was a kind of easiness. Strong forward motion and easily remembered words. People needed to feel that the words had written themselves, that the balladeer now possessing them was only their medium. He wasn't singing the song. He was being sung.

And says he, my fine farmers, if you will sign up,
It's a handful of sovereigns I'll give you to sup.

Away with you, Captain, you redbacked auld pup.
For your words are most deeply alarming.

We have no desire for to take your fool's gold;
Your bloody auld coat is a fright to behold;
We'd rather go naked and shiver with cold
Than to put on slave's rags in the morning.

The last verse took the most time to compose. In a song like this it was a matter of custom to put something about Ireland into the climax. Mulvey didn't give a sparrow's fart for Ireland and he suspected many of his audience would give even less, but people liked a bit of a shout at a hooley. To leave it out would be not to finish the job; like building a cabin with no roof.

And if ever we take up the musket or sword,
It won't be for England, we swear to the Lord.
For the freedom of Erin, we'll rise up our blade,
And cut off your head in the morning!

The first time he sang it, at Claddaghduff Horse Fair on Hallowe'en night, there was a roar of applause afterwards that almost frightened him. And as the shower of pennies fell at his feet, Pius Mulvey's body began to fill up with light. He had discovered the alchemy that turns fact into fiction, poverty into plenty, history into art. Bread was flesh and wine was blood. He had found his true vocation.

Late in the night he met a girl with pitch-dark eyes and when they lay down together in a ditch by the roadside he felt something of what his brother talked about when he talked of the mysteries of God. A passion that would make you want to bleed out your life, then the peace which passeth all understanding. He was nineteen years old, a man, and a prince. The girl told him she loved him and Mulvey believed her. He knew he was worthy of love at last.

When he came home at dawn his brother was walking the field, his bare feet bleeding as they trampled the stones. He was gaily singing a hymn which wasn't meant to be sung gaily and at first Mulvey wondered if it was some kind of game. Though the morning was cold his brother was shirtless, his pallid chest speckled with goosepimples and dew. He was scourging himself, he quietly explained. Punishing his body for the good of his soul. He deserved punishment; he was sickeningly evil. If people only knew the lusts that festered in his heart they would burn him or drown him, he said and he grinned. When he turned away to resume his penance Mulvey saw something that stuck him to the soil. The stripes of a horse-flail across his brother's bloodied back.

He went into the cabin and found the still encrimsoned flail lying like a question mark on the packed earth floor. Tendrils of his brother's flesh were attached to its thongs, and he shakingly threw it into the fire. The smell of it burning was like cooking meat, and shamefully, as though finding himself aroused by a sister, Mulvey realised the aroma was moistening his starved palate. As he watched the whip shrivel away to a twist of molten blackness, it occurred to him that he had indeed exchanged places with his brother now; had won the unspoken contest for seniority. And he cursed himself for having ever wanted it at all, for it carried accountabilities of which he was afraid.

He brought his gulping brother into the house and settled him as best he could by the fire. *Where were you, Pius? I looked and you were gone.* Nicholas Mulvey was quietly ranting still, like a man who was dreaming with his eyes wide open, and shaking in his limbs like a calf with the staggers. *For you, Pius. I did it for you.* After a time he began to calm and he fell into a restless and muttering sleep. Mulvey went out and stood on the boreen. All sorts of thoughts were going through his mind. Where could he go? What kind of help? A priest? A doctor? A neighbourman? Who?

It was then that he saw the paper left to rest beneath the stone. He picked it up. Opened its folds. 'Final Warning of Eviction' was the opening line, but it was no brave ballad or song of resistance. The Mulvey brothers had been given four months' notice. If the back rent remained unpaid, they would have to go.

A fearful moan came from the cabin behind him, the anguished bellow of a beast in a snare. His brother was stumbling over the mossed, black rocks with his left hand outstretched and pumping with blood, and his right hand clenching a blacksmith's hammer. By the time Mulvey got to him Nicholas had collapsed into the ash-pit, a beatific smile on his hollowed face: through the grizzled wrist of his emaciated left hand protruded the stub of a six-inch nail.

Nicholas Mulvey was taken away to the asylum in Galway but returned after two months, claiming to be cured. He did not want to speak about what had happened that morning; it was a matter of hunger and exhaustion, nothing more. But Pius Mulvey was not convinced. A new lustre now shone from his brother's eyes; a light that seemed somehow the opposite of light, though you couldn't have called it darkness either. It was as if someone else had slipped into his skin. A man more rational and evidently at ease; but not the brother whose irrationality and unease Mulvey knew as intimately as he knew his own, and which, in his own way, he had come to love.

A sparse, cold Christmas was had at Ardnagreevagh. The day itself was spent in bed with nothing to eat but a couple of withered apples. Mulvey said nothing about the Warning of Eviction, fearing to madden his brother again. Time enough to share such terrors when Nicholas was fit to hear them shared. Mulvey did not know that such a conversation would never happen. It was already too late for the apportionment of dread.

Nicholas had made a decision. He was joining the priesthood. For a time he had considered an enclosed order of monks but had opted instead to go into the seminary. There was a shortage of priests in Connaught now. It was causing terrible suffering among the poor. All the signs were of famine the following year. An army of priests would be needed then. If it didn't come next year, famine would come soon. But it *would* come; Nicholas had been assured. A dreadful punishment would be visited on Ireland. Thousands would starve. Millions, maybe. The people would be scourged until they could bear no more and only when they repented would the harrowing cease. He had thought about it carefully and made up his mind. At times he had considered priesthood a waste of a life but now he could see – since his illness he could see – that the real waste would be for him to do anything else. No other calling could bring him relief. His madness had been sent as a kind of revelation.

'Stay for a while. Please, Nicholas.'

'I've been studying the scriptures this many a year now. Father Fagan up above says they'll take me in early. I'm to be ordained as soon as possible.'

'Is it that drunken craw-thumper Micky Fagan of Derryclare who wouldn't know his arse from a hole in the bog?'

'He's one of God's anointed, Pius.'

'Who says it's a sin to think of a woman? And the Jews must be damned for killing Christ?'

'He says hard things sometimes. He's an old man now.'

'What about the land? Your father's land.'

'It's my father's land I'm going off to till.'

'I'm speaking literally,' Mulvey said.

'So am I,' his brother replied.

'Don't leave me here, Nicholas. I can't stick it here alone. At least wait till the spring comes, for Jesus's sake.'

'Why?'

'We're in a hames of shite. They're going to put us out.'

'Trust in God, Pius. You'll not be alone.'

'Will you listen to me, man? I'm not talking about God!'

'Neither am I, Pius. Though maybe we should.' His brother smiled his shy and beautiful smile. 'There's a girl, isn't there? I can tell by the go of you. You're like a lamb in April lately.'

'A lamb in April is mutton by Easter.'

'You know what I mean.'

'There's someone, right enough. I don't know if it's anything.'

'Well if this one isn't right, another'll happen along soon enough. That's only nature. Your own vocation. Saint Paul says: "it is better to marry than to burn".'

'You'd not want to be married yourself one day? There's land enough here if we divided it up.'

'Half a rood? For two families?'

'There's many in Galway living on worse. We could manage it, Nicholas. Please don't go.'

Nicholas Mulvey laughed quietly as though what had been said was absurd. 'That life isn't given to everyone, Pius. I wouldn't have the courage for it.'

'Do you not see girls around that you like?'

His brother sighed strangely and gazed into his eyes. 'There's nights I've wanted someone so bad I'd weep with the lust. The devil is clever. But that isn't love; it's only the body. I couldn't love a woman in the way you could yourself. You're the better man of the two of us; you always have been. No man ever had a truer friend.'

A black weed of hatred seemed to sprout in Mulvey's heart. Even the claim of inferiority was somehow to lord it over him.

It was the fifth of January, 1832, the eve of the feast of the holy Epiphany when the lords of the East came following the star. The last night the Mulvey brothers sat down and ate together, the last time they slept in the same broken bed. Nicholas left at dawn for the seminary in Galway with his mother's prayer book under his arm and a handful of earth in his pocket for luck; his parting gift the breakfast he refused to eat before leaving and the pair of rotting workboots he said he wouldn't need any more.

That was the day Pius Mulvey's dark-eyed girl, Mary Duane from Carna village, a small place on the estate of Lord Merridith of Kingscourt, told him she was expecting his child in the summer. She was crying with what he thought must be happiness. They would have to be married now, she said. And that was a good thing because she loved him after all, and he had often told her that he loved her too. They would live here, of course: on his people's land. They wouldn't have much but they would always be here. No matter what was coming, they would face it together. They would live here and die here, like his people before him.

They went to his parents' bed and undressed and lay down, and made love long into the afternoon. Wind screeched across the boglands. Sleet beat the windows like the clatter of drums. There was a wildness in the way they made love that day. It was as though they knew it would never happen again.

He waited until she had set off on the road back to Carna, then he made a small bundle of his few shabby clothes. And as night came down over the silent stony fields, Pius Mulvey walked off his father's land, down the boreen and out of Connemara, resolved that never as long as he lived would he set eyes on any of it again.

I went up to [a prospective employer in New York] with my hat in my hand as humble as any Irishman, and asked him if he wanted a person of my description. 'Put on yr hat,' said he, 'we are all a free people here, we all enjoy equal freedom and privilages.'

Letter from James Richey

CHAPTER XIII

THE BEQUEST

WE RETURN TO OUR BRAVE VESSEL ON THE TENTH
EVENING OF HER VOYAGE; ON WHICH LORD KINGSCOURT
WRITES A FOND LETTER TO HIS BELOVED SISTER AT
LONDON, THEREIN REFLECTING ON HIS PRESENT
PREDICAMENT AND INTENTIONS; NOT KNOWING HIMSELF
TO BE UNDER A MOST GRAVE SENTENCE.

The *Star of the Sea*
Wednesday, 17 November 1847

My dearest little blister, Rashers,*

Forgive the large and disgraceful scrawl but I only have one little
tallow candle by me at present and in any case my eyesight seems
of late to be not what it was. (I have of late, but wherefore I know
not, lost all my mirth, Willie S. Yuk yuk.) Like every other deuced
bit of me for that matter.

It is said by our trusty and perspicacious Captain (who studies
charts and shipping schedules like a mystical maji and uses rather
lonnnnggg words in his caawwnversation) that we may meet
in a week or soon thereafter the steamer *Morning Dew* coming
from New Orleans and making for Sligo with a cargo of India
Meal; and so I scribble down these disorganised thoughts and

*Letter bequeathed to G. G. Dixon by Professor Natasha Merridith of Girton
College, Cambridge (the noted suffragist), September 1882. 'Rashers' was a
family nickname for Lady Natasha. Lord Kingscourt was in the habit of
referring to both Lady Natasha and Lady Emily as his 'little sisters' (or, as here,
'little blisters') presumably as a mark of affection; but in fact both were older.
(Lady E. by two years, Lady N. by thirteen months.) – GGD

greetings in the hope that they may reach you before too long. (Only larking about the Cap. Stout cove in every way. Explained me the voyage on the charts the other evening.)

It is an odd thing; but sometimes I do not know what I think about anything, quite, until I write it down, more or less. Do you ever find that, at all, dear silly little Rashers? What a very strange brother you have. Lackaday

How are you and Emily and of course Aunt Eddie? Has that daft beggar Millington popped the question to Emily yet? Do wish he'd beastly get on with it, don't you? (We Old Wykehamists are not normally so backward in coming forward. Tell him the honour of Old Tutors House is at stake.) If she doesn't look out sharpish you shall beat her up the aisle.★ And how stands dear old London? I wonder when I shall see it again.

[A passage has been struck out here.]

We feel very cut off here in the middle of the great ocean, I may tell you. Wars and revolutions could have happened back home and we should not know the first thing about them. Mark you that is not an entirely unpleasant sensation, particularly after the last several years and all that has happened since Papa passed. There is a certain seductive peacefulness out here, at night especially. The sea gets *into* one somehow, like a sort of drug. Find myself speaking (and even thinking) in wavy kind of rhythms. Queerest thing. Everyone on board seems to do it after a while. At night, especially, the ocean is quite melancholy. The sound of the waves on the hull and so on. The sky is so dark that the stars seem brighter; even more brilliant and beautiful than they are in Galway. Sometimes I think I should like to stay out here for ever.

It was very sad to have to lock up the house, even sadder than to see it quite emptied of its furniture and all forlorn like a kind of

---

★Following a very long courtship which was often 'broken-off', Lady Emily did indeed marry Sir John Millington, ninth Marquess of Hull, but the marriage was dissolved after four years. There were no children. Professor Merridith did not marry. Her many publications include *Essays on the Rights of Women* (1863), *The Cause of Learning* (1871), *Education and the Poor* (1872) and several volumes of writings on pure mathematics. She co-edited *The Higher Education of Women* by Emily Davies (1866) of whom she was a close friend. – GGD

robbed Egyptian tomb. It seemed so large and so very bare as I walked around it. Hordes of the former tenants came to say goodbye, as you can imagine, and they were extremely sad, too, with many in tears. Took me quite an hour to get down the drive and hand was sore from shaking. (All of them asked after you and Em, of course.)

But they quite understand what we have had to do and wished us all the best for the future. They gave 'three huzzahs for the name of Merridith' as I left. There seemed to be no hard feelings at all, so please do not worry. Many pleaded with me to stay in contact and to think of them as our friends, always, despite what has happened. So please put your mind at ease about this, honestly. I hate to think of you fretting.

Vickers, the valuer from the mortgage company, assured me he would do his very best to sell the lands as one parcel and not break them up any further. So that is something. Tommy Martin at Ballynahinch has said no, I'm afraid. Seems his own situation is precarious just now and he is thinking of selling up and removing to Londinium. Pity, because he's not such a bad egg and though mad as snakes the Martins have not been the worst to their tenants. But there is talk of that drunken old fraud Henry Blake being possibly interested in adding to his fiefdom. This wretched famine is driving down land prices of course, and Blake, being in funds, is taking great advantage. Seems bent on buying up Connemara field by field. The Commander of Tully may soon command Kingscourt too, or what is left of it. I said to Vickers I should rather eat my own head than allow that vulgar jumped-up bully to bid, but as he said himself it is a Free Market and we are hardly in any position to be selective. Isn't it queer, dear Nat, how things come out? But there it is. If only we knew what was down the road.

Most of poor Papa's babies had to be destroyed, which was awful. I had tried several museums and zoological societies, also the Palaeological Institute in Dublin, and had managed to find homes for some of the more valuable pieces, the skeletons and some of the rarer eggs and fossils. But most of them nobody wanted to take, being in very poor condition because of the damp in the house, and some badly infested with maggots and silverfish, and anyway there being little enough interest in taxidermy now. A Romany from one of those travelling carnivals happened past the morning I was leaving and said he would like the sabre-tooth tiger, which he had noticed on the dumpheap in the front stableyard by the ice house. He offered me a shilling but I gave it him for nothing. Frankly, I would have paid him to take it away, the stench of the thing was so bad, like rotten horse-meat. Johnnyjoe Burke and his brother dug a great pit by the shore and we filled it up with all the remainder, then set the lot on fire and covered it in again. It was like something dreadful out of Hieronymus Bosch. This shag Darwin would have a dark puzzle indeed if ever he came with his geological cronies to dig up Kingscourt.

As for the house itself, who knows what shall happen now. It is almost unbearable to picture it being demolished, but after two long centuries of Galway storms the poor old girl is a little past her best. Best not to dwell on such horrid thoughts, I suppose.

Went to visit Papa's grave afterwards at Clifden. It looked very well; Mama's too. Fresh flowers had been placed on each of their stones that morning: bog asphodels on his, wild sundew on hers. A simple little gesture but I admit I was touched by it.

Forgive me for not getting around to answering your last, which I received at Dublin not an hour before we boarded. As you can imagine, things were madly busy, with packing and fetching and the devil knows what. One would not have imagined that two small children and their weary parents would need more luggage and general paraphernalia than an entire infantry division about to invade enemy territory.

Mary Duane, whom I know you will remember of old, is accompanying us to America, and Laura has been very pleased to have her help. And I have been pleased to have her, too. It sort of feels we are taking something of Kingscourt days along with us.

You ask, in your letter, about my business scheme. You are quite correct; I have kept it under my hat until now. (Not even Laura knows about it quite, and often gives me a merciless teasing for my reticence.) But if I can't tell my own dear little Rashers then whom can I tell, I hear you say.

My secret plan is to become involved in the building of fine houses of the style now becoming fashionable among the nouveau riche of New York. Not a word to anyone, mind. I do not want to be beaten to the ball. (Or is it 'the punch' to which one is beaten? Methinks it is.)

I know I do not have an actual degree in architecture, but I flatter myself that I can draw a little and in any case I believe I have something better and more useful: personal experience. I have taken the plans of Kingscourt along with me, which I found among Papa's papers the night before I closed up the old place. I had been searching for them for years and hadn't managed to find them – you know the state of those rum old papers, stacked up to the library ceiling like the Colossus of Rhodes – so I think it must have been meant to be, that finally I turned them up at the last. It was like receiving an unexpected bequest from Papa.

I have also brought sketches and copies of the plans of several other larger Irish country houses – Powerscourt, Roxborough, Kilruddery, [*illegible*] and many more – and hope that soon many Kingscourts and Powerscourts may be an adornment to that new city and its environs. I am completely convinced that I will not fail.

I know some say the fashion at New York in the coming decades will be to build upwards into the clouds, but having studied the whole matter at considerable length I am absolutely certain that this is fanciful nonsense. If there is one thing they have in America, it is land. Nor are they attached to it in the ridiculously sentimental old way we are in Ireland. They will always build outward and never up. Why should they do anything else, when you consider it?

In any case, when one gives even a cursory look at the science involved, one can see that any building which is much taller than it is wider and deeper may simply not be made to stand up for very long. Particularly in cities like New York or Boston which are positioned on the Atlantic. It is a matter of simple physics, nothing more. You and I know, from direct experience, how strong the Atlantic gales can be. (Remember how the slates used to be ripped from the creamery roof every winter? Not to mention all the hatpins you and Em had to use. Ha ha.) A tree with deep roots can barely stand up in Connemara, so how would ten storeys stand erect on America's windblown shore? Even if they did, why on earth would any non-monkey want to live so high above the ground? And if such a folly were hypothetically possible, one might reasonably have thought that by now it would have occurred to someone in England and that London would be a forest of dozen-floored monstrosities.

No, I am quite determined not to wobble in my scheme. In the past, I think, I have made the mistake of not carrying through my instincts, and have listened too readily to the opinions of others. This time I shall screw my courage to the sticking-place. And damn'd be him that first cries *Hold enough!*

As for finances, I have a little put by, but it is a very little, so we must hope that providence favours the brave. I do hope you and Emily don't mind, but I sold a few old knick-knacks that remained in Kingscourt. I mean a painting or two, nothing very much. The piano you asked about had already been taken away by the auctioneer's gillies, I'm afraid. A few costume jewels of Mama's I sent on to you.

I suppose we shall put up at an hotel when we arrive at New York, but never having been there before I do not know which one as yet. We have taken a smallish house on Washington Square – number 22 – but it will not be vacant until March. I say a house, but actually a new kind of thing called an apartment suite, so we are truly entering into the modern spirit. It is fiendishly expensive but I think of it as a worthwhile investment, a stylish place to entertain clients. (Clients – my God, if Papa could hear that.) Laura will be seeing about servants when we get there. I should think we shall probably restrict ourselves to a butler, a maid-of-all-work, a valet and of course a cook. No sense in going mad.

In the meantime I am told by a queer sort of Indian prince who is on board that New York has one half-way decent restaurant, Delmonico's on Williams Street; so we shan't starve at any rate. (The décor is Louis quatorze, I am told.)

Our accommodation here on the ship is not so stylish, but we are rather enjoying having to 'rough it' a bit. We have four good enough rooms in a sectioned-off part of the upperdeck slightly away from the other passengers. Laura's and my cabin is pleasantly furnished, though small. Jonathan and Robert have a little palace each, with much egregious tussling about whose bathroom is the grander. Mary's quarters are at the end of the corridor and up some stairs; and we also have the use of a large unoccupied stateroom in which the Captain has kindly arranged for a rather wonderful sort of folding-up table to be placed so we may all breakfast and dine together. So it is quite the cosy nest, even if we all must shove up in the bed, as it were. The frequent presence of stewards and servants trotting about like Yahoos makes privacy difficult and irritates Laura sometimes but I suppose it must be tolerated. (I suppose Houyhnhnms would actually trot more, but you know what I mean.)*

The grub is a little unexciting but we don't kick up.

Boredom is a bit of a bore, to say the least. Very little to do on a tub I'm afraid. Poor company generally. Sometimes wander down to the Smoking Saloon in the evenings to lose a few shillings to the Maharajah at cards. But can't seem to find a single decent book on board, no matter where I hunt. Turned up a stack of old copies of the *Times* in the saloon, however, and am attempting to hullify† the editorials in a sort of chronological way. It is rather fun work though DASHED taxing, specially now I'm going blind as a bbbbbbbbboat. (ha ha).

The boys are well, and send you all their love. They are mightily pleased with themselves being little mariners but the old trouble persists with Jonathan. I think it is only a matter of

---

*Lord Kingscourt's mention of 'Yahoos' and 'Houyhnhnms' is an allusion to *Gulliver's Travels* by Jonathan Swift. The Yahoos are an ape-like race of degraded savages found on a rural island which is a colony of Houyhnhnm Land. The Houyhnhnms are rational horse-like beings who have enslaved the Yahoos as beasts of burden. Interestingly, Gulliver remarks: 'the *Houyhnhnms* have no Word in their Language to express any thing that is *Evil*, except what they borrow from the Deformities or ill Qualities of the *Yahoos*' (IV: 9; 11). – GGD

†'Hullify' is a reference to 'doohulla', a game with impenetrably complicated rules and scoring system devised by the Merridith siblings in childhood. It involved cutting out words from newspapers or other unwanted documents and forming a diamond-shaped grid of interlocking anagrams from their letters. Remarkably similar to the modern day 'crossword puzzle', an amusement as yet unknown in the 1840s. 'Doohulla' is the English name of a district in Connemara. *Dumhaigh Shalach* in Gaelic. 'Mound of Willows'. – GGD

nervousness and unsettlement and hope that when he is safely lodged in New York he can rest more properly. And stop running up the laundry bill for clean sheets! Poor old sausage, he is quite the water-clock lately. But he is looking forward to spending his birthday on ship. As for Robert he is in fine twig and scoffing like a cart-horse. (Our Captain would say he surpasseth edaciousness.) I simply don't know where he puts all the tuck. As Johnnyjoe used to remark from time to time: 'that little Lordship must have a hollow leg, be the hokey.'

There is something of a distance between Laura and myself at present, but this I put down to her not wanting to be away from London at Christmas, her favourite time of year, as you know, with the parties and the balls and all the rest of it. But no doubt it is nothing to worry about anyway. She is, as ever, a blooming brick.

The weather has been changeable in the extreme (very stormy this morning) and has brought back memories to your silly brother of his heroical navy days – when he got repeatedly, astonishingly and rather embarrassingly saesick [*sic*!] on his first and only proper voyage: a training run down to the Canaries and back on a three-masted clipper which had been kicked about the Med by one N. Bonaparte Esquire and was now approximately as waterproof as an antique bath sponge. I recall an old gunner from Longford discreetly confiding a traditional remedy, *id est:* to swallow a lump of pork fat tied to a string, then quickly yank the string back up. BEJAYZIS! I almost choked myself to death in the process and had to be given mouth-to-mouth resuscitation by a Spaniard. Not an experience I should care to repeat.

'Kiss me, Hardy,' the other chaps used to say to me afterwards, as a ballyrag. I don't think they knew your bleary brother was the son-and-heir of 'Battlin'' Lord Merridith who had scrapped alongside Nelson at Trafalgar. Of course I attempted never to trade on that. Perhaps I should have done. Might be an Admiral now if I had!

I was sorry to hear about the creditors. What ghastly bores they are. Tell them your big brother said he would come around if they bothered you again and punch 'em in the chops. Seriously, I will see what may be done directly we get to New York. I think there is a branch of Coutts over there, but if not there will be some other bank which will be able to help. No matter where you go, there is always a bank.

Speaking of bores, you can't imagine how many of that species are roaming about First-Class: rather like wildebeest wandering the backstreets of Timbuktu, only twice as ugly and thrice as forlorn. You would simply die with hilarity if you had to endure them. Laura and myself have a great laugh about it every night together. I must say I should be lost without her.

That American gobshite Dixon whom you met at one of Laura's evenings is on board and proving every degree as tiresome as ever. (You met him the night Dickens came. Remember he was prattling on about the novel he was doing?) I believe Aunt Eddie described him as 'debonair' – Dixon, I mean, certainly not Dickens – but there is no accounting for taste.

I should like to write more but it is getting stormy (*Heigh-ho*, the wind and the rain) and I shall have to get into bed and reach for the pork fat. Ah, me.

Don't worry, old thing. Everything will be fine. I know it doesn't always look it at the moment but all shall be well and all shall be well and all manner of thing shall be well.

Gaudeamus igitur.

I miss you so.

Your loving bruvving,

Davey

PS: I heard an old tar whistling this the other evening. Didn't Johnnyjoe Burke used to lilt it sometimes?

★

*Lord Kingscourt might have been disconcerted to learn that the tune is a traditional Irish march entitled 'Bonaparte Crossing the Alps'. – GGD

To whatever part of the world the Englishman goes, the condition of Ireland is thrown in his face; by every worthless prig of a philosopher, by every stupid bigot of a priest.

The Times, March 1847

CHAPTER XIV

THE STORY-TELLER

THE ELEVENTH EVENING OF THE VOYAGE; THEN SOME
PARTICULARS OF THE TENTH; AND RETURNING TO THE
ELEVENTH BY WAY OF CONCLUSION. A SEQUENCE
WHICH MAY BE SAID TO HAVE THE PATTERN OF A CIRCLE;
IN WHICH TWO ENCOUNTERS BETWEEN THE AUTHOR
AND HIS ADVERSARY ARE DESCRIBED.

32°31′W; 51°09′N
— 10 P.M. —

Grantley Dixon paused by the door to the Smoking Saloon. A strange piercing sound like the screech of a gull had stopped him just as he had reached for the handle. But above him he could see no bird of any kind. It came again; a faint but mordant shriek that twisted its way right into you somehow. He walked to the gunwale and looked over the side. The ocean churned up at him, black and frothing.

It wasn't coming from steerage or from anywhere on the ship, but Dixon had been hearing the sound for two days. He had asked others about it and everyone seemed to have noticed, but nobody could say just what it might be. A spirit, some of the sailors laughed, seeming to enjoy his lubber's unease. The ghost of a witch-doctor, 'John Conqueroo', who had died of a fever down in the lock-up back in the times when the *Star* was a slaver. A mermaid moaning to entice them to doom. A siren riding the tail winds and waiting to pounce. The Captain's Mate had expressed a more rational view. Air in the 'tween-decks of the weary old ship. A trick of the air, sir. Breeze in the gully-holes. An old bucket the age of the *Star* had been refitted many times, usually quickly and not very well. Behind every panel was a tangle of ancient fittings, rusted pipes, split timbers, rotted spars burrowed hollow by woodworm and rats. Sometimes, when the wind caught, you would swear the ship was singing. You could think of the ship as a floating flute, sir: the wrecked organ of a once great cathedral. That was how the Mate liked to think of it himself.

The little man with the club-foot was watching from behind the gates. He was always watching; that poor limping tramp. Waiting to beg, Dixon supposed. The hobo looked up at the sky and uttered a small cough. Turned. Sneezed. Shuffled back into the shadows. Curious fellow in many ways. Seemed to have no friend; no need for any company. Appeared to find the ship a place of curiosities. Dixon had seen him earlier, at dusk that evening, staring at the portside wall of the wheelhouse. Someone had daubed it with a strange graffito. A capital H enclosed in a heart.

Dixon wondered what Merridith wanted to speak to him about, but already he felt he had some idea. Perhaps this would be the night when the truth might come out. It was time it did. The lies had gone on too long. The sneakings and petty deceptions of adultery, the aliases and skulkings and railway station hotels. Perhaps last night's altercation between himself and his rival had brought matters to a head, or were about to do so now. Really it was time for such arguments to stop. They had become an almost nightly occurrence and were causing embarrassment to Laura and to others. These things could be discussed in a civilised way. He only wished he were feeling less exhausted and depressed.

A fortnight before boarding the *Star of the Sea*, Dixon had spent a whole day doing the rounds of the London publishers. Hurst and Blackett. Chapman and Hall. Bradbury and Evans. Derby and Dean. They sounded like teams of music-hall comedians and for all they had offered him, they might as well have been.

Three months earlier, at considerable cost, he had employed a secretary to make multiple copies of his collection of short stories. They were based on his recent tour of Ireland and Grantley Dixon had worked hard on them.

Late at night in his rooms at the Albany he had honed the manuscript over and over. He had tried to make his style a degree less constricted, to put away the objectivity required of the journalist; to allow his feelings to show a little more. And when he had finished, he had read one of them aloud to Laura, one afternoon just after they had been to bed, assuring her that he would appreciate an honest appraisal of his efforts.

'Your efforts?' she smiled.

'Of the story,' he said.

But she hadn't liked it.

They had argued about it.

She had accused him of being blinded by the desire to record facts. Art was about the creation of beauty. An important painter, a truly interesting writer – he took the stuff of ordinary life and turned it into something else. Mr Ruskin had recently said as much in a lecture she had attended in Dublin.

'You're saying I'm not an artist?'

'You have a wonderful talent for journalistic narration, of course. Your descriptions of landscape, for example – they're accurate. And your polemical stuff is really very strong. But an artist is somehow in a higher league. I don't know. He comes at reality from a sort of angle.'

'Like your husband, you mean.'

'I don't say that. But yes, he draws well.'

'Better than I write, I suppose?'

'I don't think that's fair, Grantley.'

'So what's fair? Our having to meet like thieves?'

'Just – why can't you be happy with what you have? Come back to bed, you silly boy.'

But he hadn't wanted to go back to bed. Somehow her critique had emasculated him. Perhaps it was simply that he had revealed a need to be appreciated and nobody since his childhood had ever made him do that. The spat had coloured the rest of their evening. Little had been said in the restaurant or at the recital. Even as he saw her off for the midnight Kingstown boat train, it had hung between them like an unspoken sin. They had bade farewell with a careful handshake as they always did in public; but it had seemed to Dixon a little more careful than was necessary. It was only after the train had pulled away that he had felt he should have apologised.

He had been determined to prove her wrong about his work. She would never love a man who wasn't an artist; anyone who knew her would know that fact. She mightn't know it herself, but one day she would discover it. Dixon couldn't bear to think about what might happen then.

Everywhere he went, his book was refused. Too long, too short, too serious, too sketchy. Stories not believable. Characters not real. As if to mock him, on his way to his last appointment, he had seen that idiot Dickens strolling along Oxford Street doffing his topper like a victorious general among the plebeians. People were rushing up to him and shaking his hand, as though he was a hero instead of a charlatan; that saddle-sniffing ringmaster of Bozo beadles, of Harrow-toned orphans and vulture-nosed Jews. God, it was dismal how they lapped it up. *Please, sir. We want some more.*

Dixon had met the publisher Thomas Newby at one of Laura's literary evenings. He had seemed a reasonable, intelligent man and was known for getting out his editions with speed when he wanted to. But his firm was small and couldn't pay much. Still, Dixon thought, at least it would be a start. Little did he know he was to be disappointed again.

'I'm not saying it's bad or anything like that, dear Grantley. It's strikingly written in its own sort of way. I just found it a bit preaching. Morbid type of thing. All that stuff about poor Pat and his donkey, you see. Fine for the newspapers. You'd *expect* it in the newspapers. But the reader of fiction wants something else. Horse of a different colour entirely.'

'And what is that?'

'A good old thumping yarn to sink his tusks into. Kind of thing you've done here gets him down in the dumps. You want to read some of this cove of mine, Trollope. You've seen his *Macdermots of Ballycloran*, have you? Now *he* does the poor but he sort of smuggles them in.'

'We're not all Trollopes,' Dixon said bitterly.

'I'm a businessman,' said Newby. 'I have to be.'

Dixon picked up a book that was lying on the desk and read the words from its gilded spine. '*Sixteen Years in the West Indies* by Lieutenant-Colonel Capadose. Volume Two.'

'What's wrong with that?'

'That's the best you can do, Tom, is it?'

'Damned interesting little read as a matter of fact. Kind of thing you should take a crack at yourself, if you want my tuppence worth. Swear off the fiction and blaze away with the facts.'

'The facts?'

'Collection of impressions of the Emerald Isle. Mist on the lakes. Jolly swineherds with queer wisdom. Pepper it up with a few pretty colleens. Do it in your sleep. Don't know why you won't.'

'You do know there's a famine in Ireland now, do you?'

'I'd be happy to send your royalties to a fund, if you like.'

Dixon plucked another volume from the escritoire and witheringly read its title: '*The Grand Pacha's Cruise on the Nile in the Viceroy of Egypt's Yacht.*'

'People like escapism,' Newby said quietly. 'Don't be so hard on them, old lad. It's only a book.'

Dixon knew he was right. He was almost always right. It was one of the more annoying things about him.

'Speaking of fleeing to happier climes, a little bird tells me you're returning to the colonies presently.'

'I'm going to Dublin for a few days first.'

'Ah. You'll be seeing La Belle Dame Sans Merci.'

He wondered what knowledge or gossip might lie behind the phrasing. Newby was a man who tended to know what was going on.

'I may do. I may not.'

'I heard she was in town the other week.'

'Was she?'

'Saying farewell to her Papa, I believe. Before setting out to break the hearts of America. Another little injection of funds required, one doesn't doubt.'

'How do you mean?'

''Tis whispered about the town that the Noble Merridith is busted. Famine's ruined him. Warrants out for his committal. Without her daddy's lucre My Lord might be in the debtors' clink by now.' He gave a profound sigh and rubbed his large nose. 'Bloody shame for Laura. One in a million. Must say I miss her a lot now she's gone.'

'If I run into her in Dublin I'll pass on your best.'

The publisher nodded and tossed him a package of books. 'Give her those, would you? Tales of passion among the ruins.' He peered at Dixon and gave an arch smile. 'Laura enjoys a touch of romance, I'm told.'

Dixon could feel a blush warming his neck. He looked at the book on top of the parcel. 'He any good? I might be able to place a review.'

'For the ladies, dear boy. Vicar from up north. As for his merits, not so convinced as I was. Only getting up 250 copies.'

Two hundred and fifty copies, he sourly said. Dixon would have given one of his limbs for that.

'You really can't take the stories? Not even if I do another edit?'

Newby shook his head.

'What about the novel? You've had it for a year.'

'Can't do it. Like to. Just honestly can't. Simply not my variety of thing. Wish you luck with it elsewhere. Try Chapman and Hall.'

'Tom.' Dixon attempted a man-to-man laugh. 'The fact is, Tom, I've been a bit stupid about all this. Made a few errors of judgement, if you like.'

'In what sense?'

'I've sort of said it to people already. That it's to be published early in the new year.'

'Oh that. Yes. I'd heard you'd been saying that.'

Dixon looked at him.

'Apparently Laura mentioned it to someone when she was over the other week. "Glowing with pride" for your achievement, so I'm told.'

The window of the office gave a rattle in the breeze. Dixon found himself staring at the rug on the floor; its frayed motif of crowns and unicorns. A girl came and went with a tray of coffee. When he glanced up again, Newby was avoiding his eyes. 'Grantley – I hope I can speak as your friend. I beg you to be careful. Merridith is no fool. He puts it on when it suits him but I wouldn't make assumptions.'

Newby gave a quiet and oddly sour laugh.

'They teach it to them, you know; in the public schools. How to put on like a cheerful idiot while all the time they've got their hands sliding around your neck. "Old chum" this. "Jolly jolly" that. But they'd butcher half of India to keep themselves in tea.'

'I wish I'd never met her sometimes. Life would be easier.'

The older man rose from behind the desk and offered his hand. 'And I wish I could do your novel. But really I mustn't.'

'Can you give me some kind of direction?'

'Just – many are called, brother, but few are chosen. Scribble me up the old observations some time and I'll certainly take a peep. "An American in Ireland". Something like that. Here. Look. Take this one, too.'

It was *Evenings of a Working Man* by John Overs, with a preface by his friend and mentor, Charles Dickens.

'No, thanks.'

'You really should. Now, that is a book. Bloody marvellous thing, Dickens's prologue especially. The way that rascal writes – it makes one want to sing.'

'I thought you didn't like anything about the poor.'

'Ah,' said Newby seriously. '*He* puts in jokes.'

*

Dixon had wasted all of yesterday on the northern vicar's dreary novel. The wind was high and the sea choppy and Laura had said she wanted time to be alone. She was acting very strangely since they had boarded the ship, making excuses to avoid speaking to him or being in his company. Perhaps she was right to want to be alone. The skulking was making him irritable; tattering his nerves.

The morning had begun with reasonable calm: a glitter of cold sunlight on a greygreen of water. He had sat outside the Breakfast Room intending to kill a few hours in reading. A single drop of rain had smacked the title page as he opened the cover. Within five minutes the sky had darkened to the colour of lead.

'Put up the lifelines. And get the passengers below.'

Sailors were already running. Lightning flickered in the bulbous thickness of the clouds; it lit them up in a crackling explosion. A powerful gust buffeted the mainmast, sending reverberations down to the maindeck and shattering crockery and glasses in the Breakfast Room behind him. The ship gave a nauseating undulation; a lurch; a sway. The shutters were being wound down, the canopy chained up. A steward hurrying past with a stack of chairs had shouted at him to get below but Grantley Dixon had not moved.

The music of the ship was howling around him. The low whistlings; the tortured rumbles; the wheezy sputters of breeze flowing through it. The clatter of loose wainscoting. The clank of chains. The groaning of boards. The blare of wind. Never before had he felt rain quite like it. It seemed to spew from the clouds, not merely to fall. He watched the wave rise up from a quarter of a mile away. Rolling. Foaming. Rushing. Surging. Beginning to thicken and swell in strength. Now it was a battlement of ink-black water, almost crumpling under its own weight; but still rising, and now roaring. It smashed into the side of the bucking *Star*, like a punch thrown by an invisible god. He was aware of being flung backwards into the edge of a bench, the dull crack of metal against the base of his spine. The ship creaked violently and pitched into a tilt, downing slowly, almost on to beam ends. A clamour of terrified screams rose up from steerage. A hail of cups and splintering plates. A man's bellow: 'Knockdown! Knockdown!' One of the starboard lifeboats snapped from its bow-chain and swung loose like a mace, shattering through the wall of the wheelhouse.

The boom of the billows striking the prow a second time. A blind of salt lashed him; drenched him through. Waves churning over his body. The slip of his body down the boards towards the water. A shredding *skreek* of metal on metal. The grind of the engine ripped from the ocean. The ship began to right itself. Snappings of wood filled the air like gunshots. The wail of the klaxon being sounded for clear-all-decks. The man with the club-foot was helping a sailor to grab a woman who was being swept on her back towards the broken rail. She was screaming in terror; grasping; clutching. Somehow they seized her and dragged her below. Hand by hand, gripping the slimy life-rope like a mountaineer, Dixon made it back to the First-Class deckhouse.

Two stewards were in the passageway distributing canisters of soup. Passengers were to retire to their quarters immediately. There was no need for concern. The storm would pass. It was entirely to be expected. A matter of the season. The ship could not capsize; it never had in eighty years. The lifebelts were merely a matter of precaution. But the Captain had ordered everyone to remain below. Laura looking pleadingly at him from the end of the corridor, her terrified sons bawling into her skirts. The three of them being grabbed by an angry-faced Merridith and dragged into her cabin like sacks.

'Inside, sir. Inside! Don't come out until you're called.'

He had found dry clothes and eaten all his soup. After an hour, the storm had levelled down a little. The Chief Steward had knocked on his door with a message from the Captain. All passengers were strictly confined for the rest of the day. No exceptions whatsoever were permitted. The hatches were about to be battened down.

He had tried to settle, to read again, as the pitch of the ocean flung breakers against the porthole and the shrill of the wind surged up and down the roof. But the novel had not done much to improve his spirits.

Yes, it had passion or passion of a sort: the usual tiresome show-off gushiness. Here and there it managed to stagger into weary life, only to be crushed by the weight of the prose style. Like most first novels, like Dixon's own, it was an attempt at a story of physical love. But it was wildly over-ambitious, peopled by puppets. The way it so flagrantly strained for its effects let it down. Reading it was like trudging through a peatbog in Connemara. A few startling flowers among a wilderness of sog.

I have no pity! I have no pity! The more the worms writhe, the more I yearn to crush out their entrails!

Sweet Christ.

How could yet more of this sludge be pumped into the world when his own carefully constructed pieces had been rejected? Newby had been correct to think it would fail. No critic in his right mind would give this eructation a good notice. It was confused, improbable, disjointed, vague. Precisely the quality for which he had striven in his own writing – a respect for the actual meanings of words – was entirely and woefully missing from this.

And yet, he knew, Laura would love it. She who had damned with the faintest of praise would adore this florid and juvenile monstrosity; this compendium of adjectives and schoolboy neuroses. She would think it 'aesthetic', high-minded, moving. It was laughable, sometimes, the way she prattled on. If he didn't love her so much, he often thought he would detest her.

The book sat on his desk: a silent accusation. The man who had committed this little crime against beauty had succeeded where Grantley Dixon had failed. It didn't matter that the critics, if they noticed it at all, would give it the beating it plainly deserved; nor even that nobody would buy it except lonely old spinsters. His novel was a fact. It could not be cancelled.

Like that bloodsucker Merridith and his so-called drawings. Those prettified daubs of his family's victims, hanging in his hallway like a huntsman's stuffed heads. And the leeches of London would pause and admire them. How elfin, the Irish. How utterly enchanting. Really he captures them terribly well.

In a hundred years' time those drawings would exist. So would *The Grand Pacha's Cruise in the Viceroy's Yacht*. Dickens's absurdities. Trollope's stupid lies. Nobody would be reading them but that wasn't the point. Long after Dixon and his ambitions were dust, aeons after Laura had shunned him as a flop, those books would still exist to deride his memory. They would still be facts when he had become a fiction.

He had taken down the box containing the manuscript of his story collection. Opened it, half wishing it might have disappeared. Removed the block-like slab of paper. Read the first line aloud to himself.

Galway is a place in love with sorrow.

Now he saw that beside the phrase Newby had inked three small red question marks. Perhaps he had a point. The sentence wasn't a good one. It was unlikely that any place could actually be 'in love' with sorrow. He knew what he had meant but those words did not say it. Indeed, a place couldn't be described as having any emotions at all. Newby was right. It was lazy and vapid.

He scratched it out and made a couple of fresh attempts.

Galway should properly be re-named 'Sorrow'.

'Sorrow' might well be a better name for Galway.

Galway. Death. Sorrow. Connemara.

He ripped out the page and threw it away. Opened his notebook and tried to write.

All afternoon he had sat at the desk, drinking Bourbon County whiskey and trying to write. He drank until his bottle was drained to the dregs, until evening darkened down like a stain on the porthole. When his candle started to flicker, he lit another on the end. But his metaphors were useless: stale and insulting. Nothing had come. Words as mud. The harder he tried, the more hopeless the task. Dixon was facing an undefeatable reality. The Famine could not be turned into a simile. The best word for death was death.

And the fact was symptomatic of a wider problem. He knew what it was and had known for months; ever since the shattering moment he had walked into Clifden Workhouse and looked at the sight before him.

He had no clear recollection of the next half-hour. Only the voice of the elderly constable who had led him up through the landings and corridors. Through the mist of pestilence and disinfectant, the darkened rooms where people were brought to die. The men died in one ward, the women in another. To allow them to die together was a breach of the rules. There was no ward as such for the children to die in, so they died in an outhouse near the bank of the river. Babies were allowed to die with their mothers, and then they were taken away to be dumped. And when their mothers died, if it could possibly be managed, they were dumped in the same pit as their newborn babies. The constable explained how the system worked; but his voice was fearful, as though he did not want to speak. And Dixon remembered not being able to speak himself, and thinking: *this has never happened before; many things have happened but never this.* He had tried to hold on to that one graspable thought, his very dumbness a tiny rock in a hurricane. Everything else came in disconnected pictures: thrown out of sequence, jumbled and split. A hand. An elbow. The twig of a human limb. An old man's naked back. Blood on the flagstones. A gutter in the flagstones. A rack of shrouds. A girl's shorn hair in a metal sink. A boy rocking in a corner with his hands to his face.

Sounds, too, were part of the memory; but he did not like to remember the sounds. Only the constant of the constable's voice, a gently spoken man, like Dixon's grandfather, but the gentleness diseased with dread and shame. In one doorway an artist had been seated at an easel, trying to draw whatever was happening inside. A middle-aged Corkman, he had been commissioned by a London newspaper to go to Connemara and make pictures of the Famine. He was weeping very quietly as he tried to draw. Wet smears of charcoal had darkened his eyes, as though he was weeping oil, not tears. His hands were trembling as they attempted to form shapes. And Dixon had been afraid to look at whatever was happening in the room. In the end he had not; he had simply walked away.

Now he looked at some of the sketches he had torn from the London journals in the half-thought he might somehow arrange for their publication in America. The emaciated faces and twisted mouths. The tormented eyes and outstretched hands. This was not happening in Africa or India but in the wealthiest kingdom on the face of the earth. Shocking the images: but nothing to what he had seen. They were not even close to what he had seen.

Nothing had prepared him for it: the fact of famine. The trench-graves and screams. The hillocks of corpses. The stench of death on the tiny roads. The sunlit, frosted morning he had walked alone from the inn at Cashel to the village of Carna – the sun shone, still, in this place of extinguished chances – and found three old women fighting over the remains of a dog. The man arrested on the outskirts of Clifden accused of devouring the body of his child. The blankness on his face as he was carried into the courtroom, not being able to walk with hunger. The blankness when he was found guilty and carried away. The blankness of a man who had become an un-touchable. Dixon had no words for it. Nobody did.

And yet could there be silence? What did silence mean? Could you allow yourself to say nothing at all to such things? To remain silent, in fact, was to say something powerful: that it never happened: that these people did not matter. They were not rich. They were not cultivated. They spoke no lines of elegant dialogue; many, in fact, did not speak at all. They died very quietly. They died in the dark. And the materials of fiction – bequests of fortunes, grand tours in Italy, balls at the palace – these people would not even know what those were. They had paid their betters' accounts with the sweat of their servitude but that was the point where their purpose had ended. Their lives, their courtships, their families, their struggles;

even their deaths, their terrible deaths – none of it mattered in even the tiniest way. They deserved no place in printed pages, in finely wrought novels intended for the civilised. They were simply not worth saying anything about.

He had slept for a few hours through a fervency of nightmares. He saw himself clinging to the up-ended deck of the *Star*. Suddenly up to his waist in blood. A hand had clutched him hard by the hair, pulling him back. He grabbed at the sodden sleeve. An aged Negro in a ragged greatcoat, a tattered scarf around his neck. In his arms an ashen child with paper-white eyes. The insistent pointing of the black man's finger. The cell at the end of the cold stone corridor: the room into which he could not bear to look.

At eleven o'clock he had decided to go to the Smoking Saloon, thinking another drink might do a little to ease his nerves.

Since his visit to Connemara, it usually did.

Merridith had been sitting alone in the dimly lit saloon, leafing through a pile of crumpled old newspapers. He seemed to be scissoring out the headlines and arranging them into some kind of order. The alcove in which he was slouched was illuminated by a candle; he was squinting closely to make out the smaller letters. A bottle of port was sitting on the table beside him. To judge from his dishevelled state he had drunk most of it already. Seeing Dixon nearby, he gave a snuffle of contempt.

'The lofty bard has descended among the mortals.'

'I won't be among you very long, don't worry.'

'Back to the old Muse,' he quietly slurred. 'Rather insatiable lady, is she not?'

'Feel like a battle of wits tonight, do you, Merridith?'

'Oh I wouldn't fight a battle with an unarmed man. That's not how we do things in England.'

'You've done it in Ireland often enough. '

He gave a smile of inebriated loathing. 'Ah, the bard's beloved Erin. The only place on God's earth best understood by foreigners.'

'And what the Hell are you? A loyal native?'

'Well my family has lived there since about 1650. A while before the white man stole America from the Indians. I wonder whether you feel *you* should go home, too. I assume you must. Only logical, really.'

Dixon looked down at him. Lord Kingscourt stared back blearily.

'Whither then, pilgrim? When you repatriate yourself?'

'Your argument is as ridiculous as everything you say.'

'Speak their own language at any rate. Sort of think it's important to any true understanding. Must have learned a smattering before going there, did you? Matter of professional pride, I expect. Not to go unarmed into the field and so on.'

The candlelight was throwing inky shadows across his face, deepening his cheekbones and the sockets of his eyes. Dixon said nothing. Suddenly he felt badly drunk himself. Shaky. Queasy. Afraid he would vomit. A scorch of whiskey acid came burning at his throat. Merridith grinned up at him like a hanging judge.

'*Ar mhaith leat Gaeilge a labhairt, a chara? Cad é do mheas ar an teanga?*'

'And what is the Irish for starvation, Your Lordship?'

'*Gorta.* A hunger. You don't even know that much?'

'I don't speak Swahili either but I know cruelty when I see it.'

'So do I, sir. I was brought up seeing it.'

'I notice you didn't die of it all the same.'

'*Is that my latest crime, sir? That I didn't die? Is that to be added to everything else?*'

The roar made the stewards turn and stare. A spume of saliva was running down his chin. His face was purple with wrath and hatred.

'You're drunk, Merridith. And even more pitiful than usual.'

'Would you like me to die? Why don't you kill me? Damned convenient, wouldn't it be?'

'What does that mean?'

'My own mother died of famine fever, Dixon. Your beautiful Muse ever bring that small fact to your attention? Caught it while feeding our tenants in '22. So I don't need your pompous lectures on cruelty.'

The ship tilted and gave a lugubrious sound, as though the force of some impact had made it rock. The door of the saloon flung itself open and slammed closed again.

'Saved a good many others in Galway, too. Mostly from the estate of a true-blue Irishman who would pimp Saint Bridget for two bob an hour. Well, it's not very important of course. Means nothing really.'

'I meant no offence to your mother. Now I'll bid you good-night.'

'No, don't let it bother you.' He kicked a chair towards him, but Dixon did not sit down. 'Let us discourse on literature. Tell me a story.'

'Merridith – '

'So the famous novel is to be set in Swahili-Land now, is it? How utterly marvellous. How fabulously *outré*. When we were all expecting the *magnum opus* to put an end to hunger in Ireland, it now seems to have transmogrified into something else.'

At that point the Maharajah had entered the saloon, accompanied by the Reverend and Wellesley the Mail Agent. Their eyes were shining with the particular excitement of land-men who have survived a storm at sea. They nodded at Merridith but he didn't nod back. Again the violence in his voice was rising, as though spewing from some animus he could not control.

'I wonder what is the Swahili word for a spoiled *poseur*. A coddled fool who prattles of literature while others have the guts to make it. Who mocks the efforts of others to end people's sufferings but does damn all to actually end them himself. That is a word you might know, I think.'

'Merridith, I'm warning you – '

'You'll warn me of nothing, you nauseating hypocrite! Put your hand on me again and I'll shoot you like a dog!'

By now the Reverend had nervously approached.

'Lord Kingscourt, sir, you're a little upset. Can I – '

'You can take your pieties and your pity and stick them up your scriptural arse. Do you hear me, sir? Get out of my sight!'

'Quite the hero,' said Dixon, when the Minister had gone. 'Courageously taking on a man twice your age.'

'Tell me, old thing – do you know the word "nigger"?'

'Shut your mouth. This instant. You drunken scum.'

'A word you would have heard in your boyhood, I imagine. "Come over here, Nigger. Little Grantley wants his gumbo."'

'I said shut your mouth.'

'Were *many* of the slaves on your family's plantation Swahili? I imagine they must have been. Didn't they teach you any? Or perhaps Bwana felt it rather below himself to mix with them, did he?'

'My grandfather was an opponent of slavery all his life. *Do you hear me?*'

'*Did he rid himself of the lands which slavery purchased for his ancestors?* Give back his inheritance to the children of those who made it? Live as a pauper to ease his conscience or the coffee-house pretensions of his mewling grandson? Who is so deeply ashamed of what pays for his vittles that he *aches* to find greater atrocities in the accounts of others.'

'Merridith – '

'*My* father fought in the wars that ended slavery throughout the empire. Risked his life. Wounded twice. Proudest thing he ever did. Didn't ponce on about it, just bloody did it. My mother saved thousands from starvation and death. While your servants were calling you "Little White Massa". Write one of your imaginary novels about that, old thing.'

'What the Hell do you mean – imaginary novels?'

'You know very well what I mean.'

'Are you calling me a fake, sir?'

'Fake is a rather coarse American barbarism. More of a sickening liar, really.'

'Is that right?'

'Is it wrong? If it is, let me see it, why don't you?'

'See what?'

'Your famous novel. Your great work of art. Or perhaps it simply does not exist. Like your right to lecture others on the crimes they have committed *in order to mask the guilt of your disgusting own.*'

Dixon became aware of the Chief Steward hauling him back. The powerful grip of a man trained in trouble. Two sailors had also come in and were standing behind him. Rain was running down their ragged oilskins. The lights were turned up to a stinging white dazzle. Merridith's look of repulsion faded to a haughty smirk.

'Caressed your little nerve, have I Grantley, old thing?'

'Lord Kingscourt, sir,' said the steward firmly, 'I shall have to request that you enjoy yourself in a more peaceful manner.'

'Of course, Taylor, of course. No difficulty at all. Just a little friendly discussion among fellow oppressors.'

'We conduct ourselves in a certain manner in the saloon. The Captain feels strongly about standards and such.'

'I dare say you're right.' He slumped back into the alcove and refilled his glass untidily, spilling a slop of port down the crystal stem. 'Speaking of which, would you be good enough to ask Massa Dixon to vacate the premises immediately?'

The steward looked at him.

'He is in breach of the rules. A tie is compulsory in the saloon in the evening. As any gentleman would already have known.'

Lord Kingscourt raised his glass and shakily drank, his free hand touching the table as though he thought it might disappear. Perhaps it was merely a trick of the light, but Dixon could have sworn there were tears in his eyes.

✳

When the man with the club-foot had shambled away, Dixon entered the saloon and pushed closed the door to the gusting gale. Merridith was at the gaming table, cutting the cards; sharing a joke with the unsmiling Chief Steward. He was sitting on a stool with his back to the door but when he saw Dixon enter he beckoned in the mirror, still going at the steward like a bore on a train.

'Do you see,' he was saying, as Dixon approached, 'with a very good word-puzzle, it is all in the way the material is composed. To me, the inventor of a pastime is a national treasure. I venerate him as I esteem Victoria Regina Magnifica.'

His face was haggard and he had not shaved. A taint of stale perspiration hung heavily around him, commingling with the odour of rotting meat. A speckling of dandruff lay on the shoulders of his evening jacket. But he was wearing a tie, as was Dixon himself.

'Good-night, Mr Dixon, sir,' the Chief Steward said. 'Your usual bourbon?'

Lord Kingscourt touched Dixon's arm to prevent reply and said, 'Fetch up a bottle of Bolly, would you, Taylor old thing? The '39 if there's any left.' He turned to Dixon. 'The '24 is preferable but there's a bit of a drought on. Still, we shall make do as best we can.'

Dixon sat down beside him and looked at the gaming table. He noticed that Merridith had set out the cards not in hands nor in suits; and yet there was clearly a careful system to their arrangement.

'I'm sort of designing a new set of rules for poker. Little hobby. Played under alphabetical values rather than numerical ones. Bit of fun. Don't expect it will catch on terribly widely.'

Silence settled. He fanned out the cards.

'You received my note all right?'

'Yes.'

'Decent of you to come. Rather expected you mightn't. Thought we should sort matters out man to man, as 'twere.' He gave a strained sigh and peered at the ceiling. 'Bit out of hand last night, old thing. Surfeit of the demon jungle juice, I expect. I should like to apologise for being such a barbarian. No offence intended to your honourable relative. Quite unnecessary. I am very ashamed.'

'I'd had a few drinks myself as a matter of fact.'

'Rather thought you had. Looked positively whey-faced. You colonial sissies simply can't take it, of course.'

'You saw the Reverend?'

'Rather saw me, I'm afraid. And scuttled the other way. Tell you the truth, few enough regrets on that score. Can't abide them. Any of the crew. For Christ's sake, where's that bloody grog?'

'You're not a believer?'

His face cricked into a jaded yawn. 'Might be something all right. Just don't care for their activities in the unmentionable Famine. Prods capering about the countryside offering tenants tuck if they'll convert. The other team saying they'll burn if they take it. I say a plague on both their houses for a confederacy of omadhauns.' He shot a bleak grin. 'Irish word. Sorry.'

The steward brought the champagne, opened it and poured two glasses. Merridith clinked Dixon's – 'here's to confession' – and took a long, luxuriating mouthful.

'What think'st thou of this poison?' he asked, raising the glass to his eyes and staring into it suspiciously.

'I prefer bourbon.'

'Mm. Do you know – I sometimes wonder if they don't just slap a vintage label on any old muck. Kind of confidence trick. Half the time we wouldn't know the difference, I expect. Be sold a pup, I mean.'

'Tastes all right to me.'

'Mm. Good. Though I'm not so sure myself.' He gave a small apologetic belch. 'Still. Beggars can't be choosers, after all.'

He refilled both glasses, produced a cigar from his breast pocket; tapped it firmly on the pea-green baize of the table. For a while it seemed to Dixon that he was going to say nothing more. He wondered if he was supposed to bring up the subject himself. Perhaps that was the way these matters were approached in England; the adulterer being expected to open the conversation with the husband. England was a place of many mysterious rules. Even its cuckoldries were choreographed.

'Merridith, you said in your note that there was a reason you wished to see me. A certain important matter you wanted to discuss.'

Lord Kingscourt turned to him and smiled placidly, though his eyes were weary and streaked with redness. 'Hm?'

'Your note.'

'Ah. Sorry. Miles away.'

He reached into his pocket and placed a book on the table.

'You left it on the bar. Last night. When you departed. Thought you'd rather like to have it back.'

He flipped open the cover and removed from the frontispiece a folded-up banknote that had been serving as bookmark.

WUTHERING HEIGHTS
by Ellis Bell
T.C. NEWBY & CO.
1847

'The prodigal returns to his master,' he grunted, through a dense mouthful of deep grey smoke.

'That's all you wanted? To give me a book?'

Merridith shrugged listlessly. 'Whatever else did you think?'

'Keep it.'

'Wouldn't want to deprive you of aesthetic pleasure, old thing.'

'I've read it already.'

'Mm. Me too.' Kingscourt nodded gravely as he pocketed the volume. 'Half-way through in one sitting. Last night. Damn near made me weep at times. And then it put the willies up me so much I couldn't sleep. Sat up till nearly dawn this morning devouring the rest. Gifted bloody blighter, this Bell cove, ain't he. The darkness and so on. It's quite preternatural. Rubs the words together till the sparks quite fly.'

'How do you mean?'

He gave a stare of bemused curiosity.

'Well you know – just that it's magnificent. Didn't you find? Work of bloody genius, if you want an illiterate's view.' He took a long drink and wiped his mouth with his sleeve. 'My God, I found it simply – I don't say that all the critics will care for it. Probably they won't, jealous little peasants. One or two of them fuelled by their own failure, of course. You know the type I mean, I expect. But they shan't ignore it, not one of them in London. New York either, if it comes to that.'

Merridith's eyes stared at him from above the rim of the glass: unblinking. He put it down slowly and pulled on his cigar. Again he picked up the cards and began to shuffle them.

'Christ the *stoniness*, do you know. The nothingness. Well it's so clearly Connemara despite the clever way it's disguised. Connemara, Yorkshire, all poor places. And yet it's something else again. A kind of universal philosophical state. Keatsian in a sense. Didn't you feel? The recurring motif of landscape as almost sentient; the way he's *characterised* it, I mean. Where a second-team man would merely describe, like some Grub Street lush with the ability to raid a thesaurus.'

'Merridith – '

'Know him at all? The talented Mr Bell?'

'No.'

'If you ever bump up against him, you must tell him he has a devotee. You might do, mightn't you? In your literary ramblings?'

'I'm given to understand it's a pseudonym, actually.'

'Aha. I thought so. *In vino veritas*.' He chuckled and brushed the cigar ash from the sleeves of his jacket. 'Just waiting to see if you'd own up to your baby.'

'Own up?'

'I know when I'm licked. I take it all back.' Lord Kingscourt put down his glass and grasped Dixon's right hand – 'You're a better man than I had you down for, Mr Bell. Many congratulations. You're an artist. At last.'

'Merridith – '

He gave a curt laugh and shook his head. 'And do you know, I always thought you were simply an idiot, Dixon. You know, one of those amateurs just out to impress with mediocre short stories and cliché-ridden hackery. A dabbler who would stoop to any depth to be admired, even to using the agonies of the dying to set yourself up. But now – well, now I see the full truth of exactly what you are. The clouds have entirely lifted from my eyes.'

'Look, Merridith – '

'Such an extraordinary insight into the female psyche, too. And of course – we both know whom your heroine is based on. A remarkably loving portrait; I thought so anyway. You've captured her quite uncannily. You don't mind if I give it to her, do you? Or perhaps you'd rather give it to her yourself. She'd enjoy that even more, I dare say.'

'Merridith, for God's sake, I am not Ellis Bell.'

'No,' smiled Lord Kingscourt icily. 'You're not, old thing, are you?'

Dixon felt the splatter of champagne in his face before he had even seen him lift the glass. By the time he had managed to wipe his smarting eyes Merridith was standing behind him and drying his cuffs with a napkin. He was trying not to shake, but his rage was making it difficult. When finally he spoke, his voice came hoarsely.

'Come near my children's mother again and I'll cut your throat. You understand me?'

'Go to Hell. If they'll have you there.'

'Go where, old love?'

'You heard me, you bastard.'

The punch smashed Dixon clean to the floor, spattering blood and saliva down the front of his jacket. The Chief Steward came running over and Merridith shoved him away. Picked up Dixon's glass and drained it dry. Tremblingly placed it back on the bar.

'Nugget of advice if one might, Little Bwana. Next time you play with the devil, try to have a good hand.'

And he spat; the Earl. He spat on his enemy. And his enemy wiped the spit from his face.

Dear son, I loved my native home with energy and pride,
Till a blight came over all my crops; my sheep and cattle died.
My rent and taxes were too high, I could not them redeem;
It's not the only reason why I left old Skibbereen.

For it's well I do remember that bleak December day,
When the landlord and his sheriff came to drive us all away.
They set our house on fire, with their cruel, foreign spleen;
And that's another reason why I left old Skibbereen.

Oh father dear, the day will come in answer to the call,
When Irishmen both brave and bold will rally one and all;
I'd be the man to lead the band beneath that flag of green;
And loud and high we'll raise the cry –

'Revenge for Skibbereen'.

CHAPTER XV

THE FATHER AND HIS SON

33°01′W; 50°05′N
— 7.45 A.M. —

— Stammer again and I shall whip you again. The choice is entirely your own to make. What is the definition of a gentle breeze?

Grinning snarl of pianokeys candleflame mirrored in black gloss lowly burning twisting translating from gold to pearl dancing with cast-back brother pianoblack reflection; a copy. Fake? Skeleton of the magnificent and once common *Megaloceros Hibernicus* Irish Elk hollowed sockets of antlers gryphonwings.

— Mmwone in which a w-well-conditioned man-of-w-war, under all s-sail and clean full, mmwould go in s-smooth w-water from one to two knots, s-s-sir.

The magnificent and once common Daniel Hareton Erard O'Connell grooves cold as a graven raven. Was it? Mama?

— Correct David. And a fresh gale.

— Mmmmwone in which the same sh-ship could kak-carry close hauled, sir.

*— A hurricane? Quickly. And do NOT stammer.

*— Please Papa. I'm afraid, Papa.

The magnificent jawbone in common hand, firebelch spew from skullish mouth. Piano lid slams. Thunder of fists inside it. The candleflame putters and hissingly dies.

David Merridith flailed awake, his face drizzled with rivulets of sweat, the pulse in his jugular driving like a steam-pump.

'Papa. Papa. I'm afraid. Wake up.'

His son and heir was shaking him hard by the arm. Milkwhite sailor suit and crumpled nightcap. Mouth messily bloodened with the juice of a plum. That body in the Lowerlock. Deathboy.

Merridith elbowed up painfully, stupefied with sleep, his mouth sourly slickened by last night's tobacco. The clock on his locker read ten to eight. A glass of water had overturned alongside it, spilling its contents over the pages of a novel.

No pity.

Grind their entrails.

The wind wuthered and the ship rolled. Somewhere outside, a bell was clanging. Merridith had the strange sensation of being underground. He stretched his chin, massaged his aching neck. He felt as though his brain had come loose from its moorings.

The cabin smelt warmly of his offspring's hair, his lineny personal odour mingled with the reek of carbolic. Laura was never done washing his hair. Fearful of lice. Maggots in the fur.

'How is my little captain?'

'Woke up early.'

'You wet in the bed?'

The boy shook his head seriously and wiped his nose.

'Good man,' said Merridith. 'See, I told you it would stop.'

'Had a nightmare, though. Men were coming.'

'Well it's all right now. Are you all right?'

He nodded glumly. 'Maze I come in the tent?'

'Just for a minute, mind. And speak properly.'

The child clambered up on to the bunk and stuck his head beneath the sheets. He gave his father's forearm a soft, fond bite. Merridith chuckled wearily and pushed him away. Soon he was gnawing the pillow like a puppy, giving strangled little yaps and barks as he chewed.

'What are you doing, you bloodified lunatic?'

'Hunting for rats.'

'No rats here, my Captain.'

'Why not?'

'Too expensive for them, I expect.'

'Bobby saw one yesterday, the size of a wolfhound. Running up a rope where the poor people are.'

'Don't call them that, Jons.'

'That's what they are, isn't it?'

'I have told you before, Jonathan, don't bloody *call* them that.'

His tone was sharper than he'd meant it to be. The child gave a confused and long-suffering look at the injustice of being punished for truthfulness. He was right to feel affronted; Merridith knew it. Of course they were poor, and euphemism wouldn't change that. Probably nothing would change it now.

Lately he'd been snapping at the boys and at Laura. The strain, he supposed. But it wasn't fair. He reached out and tousled his son's already slovenly fringe.

'What did he do with it?'

'With what?'

'The rat, you cluck.'

'Shot it and gobbled it on a piece of crunchy toast.'

The child flung himself on his back and performed a boisterous yawn. The ceiling of the cabin was low enough for him to be able to touch it with his feet. For a while he did that and not much else; stretching and pedalling like an upside-down unicyclist. Then he flopped down again heavily and pulled a pouting scowl.

'I am bored. When shall we be in America?'

'Couple of weeks.'

'That's not soon. That's forever.'

'Isn't.'

'Is.'

'Ain't.'

'Is. And anyway Mummy says *ain't* is common.'

Merridith said nothing. He was feeling very thirsty.

'Is that right, Pops?'

'Everything any squaw says is always right. Now come on, old scout, let's have a doze.'

The boy lay reluctantly down on his side and Merridith curled behind him, feeling his animal warmth. Sleep rolled up gently: a wave on wet sand. Spindrift frothing in the salted air. A picture of his mother was trying to form; he saw her as though from a very great distance, walking Spiddal beach with her back turned away from him. Pausing to throw a bundle into the shallows. Gulls ascended from the seaweed and cheeped around her. And now she was drifting the orchard in spring; a confetti of apple blossom decorating her hair. A catch in his chest made him stir and drove her away. He could feel the boy's heartbeat coming faintly through the sheet. From somewhere on the deck he heard the shouting of a sailor.

'Pops?'

'Mmn?'

'Bobs has been telling fibs again.'

'It isn't cricket to peach on your brother, old thing. A shag's brother is his greatest chum in the world.'

'He says a man came into his cabin early yesterday morning.'

'Good.'

'He had a big knife like a hunter's. And a funny sort of black mask on his face. With holes cut away for his eyes and his mouth. He made a funny clomping sound when he walked.'

'I expect he had horns and a long tail also.'

The child chuckled ludicrously. '*Nooh*, Pops.'

'You shall have to instruct Bobs to look more closely next time, shan't you. All good monsters have horns and a tail.'

'He says he woke up and the man was standing there looking down at him. All in black. He said – "what room does your daddo sleep in?"'

'That was polite of him. What did Bobs say?'

'Said he didn't know, but he'd better cut along or he'd biff him one in the head. Then he heard someone coming and bolted out the window, see.'

'Good for him. Now go to sleep.'

'Can't.'

'Then scuttle down to Mary and she'll make it all better.'

'May I have some stinking poxlate for breakfast?'

'Speak properly, Jons. Don't be a bloody ninny.'

The child uttered a groan of mock impatience, as though dealing with an imbecile who had approached him for alms; the kind of sigh Merridith had often heard Laura give in Athens when contending with a waiter who pretended not to know any English. 'Drinking chocolate, Pops. May I have some of *that*?'

'If Mary says so, you can have a double whiskey.'

His son dropped to the boards and picked up a shirt. He placed it over his head and flapped his arms: a ghost of boyhood in a temperance illustration. When his father didn't react, he clicked his tongue and tossed the shirt on the back of an armchair.

'Pops?'

'What?'

'Did you feel sad when you were small? That you didn't have a brother?'

He looked at his boy. His beautiful guilelessness. It reminded him of how Laura used to look around the time that they met.

'Well I did have, old thing. In a way, that is. Before the old stork brought me along he'd brought another little tyke. My big bruv, he would have been.'

'What was his name?'

'Actually it was David. Like my own name, you see.'

The boy gave a soft laugh at the strangeness of the revelation.

'Yes,' his father chuckled. 'It is rather funny, isn't it?'

'Where is he now?'

'Well he got sick for a bit and went up to live in Heaven.'

'He got sick?'

The child knew he was lying, Merridith could see it. There was a piercing quality in his gaze sometimes: a look that was hard to ignore.

'Your mama feels you're a little too young to know.'

'I shan't tell her, Pops. Dob's honour I shan't.'

'Well there was an accident in the house. Very sad thing. My grandpapa was supposed to be sort of standing sentry one day. Only the little chap escaped, you see. Got at the fire.'

'He was burned?'

'Yes, my love. I'm afraid he was.'

'Was he sad? Your grandpapa?'

'He was very sad, yes. My papa and mama too.'

'Were you?'

'Well, I wasn't here, then, of course. But I was sad later. Surrounded by bloody girls, you see. You know what they're like. Beastly old things. Would have been fun to have another chap about. Kick a bit of ball with. Things like that.'

His son approached awkwardly and kissed his forehead.

'I am sorry, Pops.'

He ruffled the boy's hair. 'Yes,' he said quietly. 'I am, too.'

'I shall draw a picture of him later. So you can see him in Heaven.'

'Good scout.'

'Are you crying, Pops?'

'No, no. Bloody eyelash, that's all.'

'I shall be your brother if you like.'

Merridith kissed his son's grubby hand. 'I should like that very much. Now pop down to Mary.'

'May I get in her bed?'

'No.'

'Why not?'

'Because.'

'Why not because?'

'Because because.'

'Pops?'

'What?'

'Do ladies make water sitting down?'

'Ask your mother. Now bugger along.'

He watched his son slouch unwillingly from the cabin. It was too late now to go back to sleep. An ache of pity clutched at his heart. His boys had inherited his own propensity for night terrors. That might well be all they would inherit.

Rising from his bunk Merridith put on a dressing gown and padded gloomily to the shuttered porthole, opening it creakily on to the day. The vast sky was the colour of day-old gruel, but streaked with violet and orange clouds; some pallid and ragged and tinged with black, others mottled like ancient leopardskin. Down on the maindeck, two Negro sailors were huddled up to a brazier and sharing a mug. The Maharajah was walking near the forecastle with his butler. That poor little fellow with the wooden foot was hobbling up and down, slapping his arms against himself to keep warm. A kind of solace, the normality of everything. Odd, the things from which we take our consolations.

He found himself wondering about the two sailors. They looked so close; like brothers perhaps. There were other varieties of closeness between men; Merridith knew that and knew it from experience. Once or twice in his fleeting spell in the navy he had been propositioned by other officers, but had always declined. It wasn't that he found the idea disgusting. At Oxford he had experimented, contentedly and not infrequently. Rather that he'd have found it disgusting with any of the ones who asked.

He left his cabin and walked down the steel-cold passageway, pausing to knock on his wife's door. No answer came. He knocked a second time. He tried the handle but the door was locked. The smell of fresh bread drifted from the galley like an undeserved blessing. He was badly in need of one of his injections.

Yesterday afternoon she had come to his cabin and told him her decision. Her mind was made up. At first he had laughed, certain she was joking; experimenting with some new tactic to make the rat squirm harder. No, she had said, she had thought about it carefully. She had considered the whole picture. She wanted a divorce.

There was a frightening tenderness in the way she said it. She was unhappy, she said; had been unhappy for some time. She felt he must be terribly unhappy, too, but she was finding his indifference impossible to tolerate. Indifference was poison in a troubled marriage. Anything could be survived in a marriage but that. She said the word 'anything' as though it was significant to her, a cloaked invitation for Merridith to confess.

'I'm not indifferent,' he had said instead.

'David, my love,' his wife had mildly answered. 'We have not spent a night together in almost six years.'

'Christ, this again. Do you never tire?'

'David, we are married. Not brother and sister.'

'I have had things on my mind. You might have noticed that.'

'I have had more opportunity than I ever needed to notice. And to wonder and be frightened about what they might be.'

'What does that mean, Laura?'

When she spoke again, her voice was quiet. 'You're not an old man, or a little boy, after all. I assume you must still have all the normal feelings you once had for me.'

'What does *that* mean?'

'Has some other person come into your life? Please tell me if that has happened.' She took his hand in hers and held it. Even to himself his hand felt dead. 'If mistakes have been made, they can be forgiven, David. Forgiveness can be possible with love and truthfulness. None of us is a saint; certainly not myself.'

'Don't be ridiculous.'

'Is that an answer or another evasion?'

There were only two ways he could think of to react: a shout of bogus anger or a mask of placidity. 'Of course there's nobody else,' he calmly said, though he didn't feel calm, he felt like running from the room. He was afraid that if he stayed he might tell her everything.

'Then I don't understand. Can you help me understand?'

Whenever she approached him as a woman to a man, he had brushed her away or made some excuse. He had made her feel ashamed to want what was beautiful, the small, shared intimacies of married life: the closenesses which had once brought them such happiness and friendship. He had made her feel a whore for wanting to love him. He had become private, secretive; completely unattainable. It had started long before the death of his father, but ever since then he had been much worse. It was as though he himself had died, she said, or perhaps had become afraid to live.

Something was terribly wrong with him; she could see that clearly. Often she had tried to help him, but had obviously failed. Being married to him required a passivity she didn't have any more; like standing on a pier and watching a ship sink in the bay, knowing you were entirely powerless to save it. But she wouldn't wade in further and risk being drowned herself.

There were practical matters to consider, too. Her trust fund had been exhausted by what had happened at Kingscourt. To pay the fares to Quebec of seven thousand tenants had cost more than would have maintained the family for two years. There had also been the cost of evicting them: the driver-men's fees. Her father had said he was extremely worried about her situation and could not continue bailing them out. If he discovered she had also gone into her capital he would be absolutely furious and cut off all her funds. He would find out soon enough that she had sold the children's stocks and shares. There was simply no telling what he might do then.

'David, I may as well tell you: he has advised me to leave you.'

'What the Hell business is it of his?'

'It is none of his business, of course. But he worries. He says he has heard things which do not make him happy.'

'These riddles you talk in. What am I expected to say? Perhaps if you gave me the crimes I am charged with, I might be able to enter a defence.'

'He has not been specific. He merely says I am to be careful. Sometimes he says you are not what you seem.'

'Well he seems like an ass and he brays like an ass. You can tell him from me, I shall see him in the libel courts if he doesn't learn to shut his braying mouth.'

'David. Please. We need to be courageous. We have made our best efforts. We must know when to stop.'

It had taken every bit of Merridith's persuasiveness to convince her to give him one last chance. America would be good for them, the fresh start they needed; a means of putting all that had happened behind them. Jonathan and Robert needed tranquillity now. They had been through enough; they deserved to have both their parents.

'If you think they have had both their parents in recent times, you are sorely mistaken, David.'

'Please, Laura. One last chance.'

Now it was morning the conversation seemed absurd: as though it had never happened or had happened to someone else. He wondered would she mention it. Would she pretend they hadn't spoken? Perhaps he should fetch her a warming cup of tea. He'd go down to the galley and organise it with the cook.

As he passed the open door of his son Robert's cabin he saw Jonathan was in there: and he wished he had not. He was hauling a yellow-stained sheet like the folds of an old wedding dress and trying to cover his sleeping brother with it.

'What are you doing in Bobby's room, Jons?'

The boy froze and gaped up at him, his face brightening with shame. His mouth opened and closed. He dropped the sheet.

'Nothing,' he said. He sucked his gums.

'What kind of nothing? Answer me this minute.'

'I was just . . .' He shrugged and pushed his hands into the pockets of his britches. 'I wasn't doing anything. I was . . .'

He fell guiltily silent and looked at the floor. Merridith gave a sigh. It wasn't fair to set a trap for him. He could see what the child was doing; he didn't need to keep asking him. He came slowly into the cabin and picked up the ruined sheet.

'Told me you hadn't wet in the bed, old thing. There's no need to go fibbing about it. Let alone planting the evidence on Bobs.'

'I know, Pops. I didn't mean to.'

'Very disappointed, Jonathan. I thought we didn't tell each other fibs, you and me.'

'I'm sorry, Pops. Please don't tell.'

Probably he should start into a lecture now, but for some reason he didn't have the stomach for it. This early in the morning seemed a poor time for superiority, and anyway the child had had enough lectures already. 'Run along and fetch some hot water, then, like a good scout. We'll wash it out together. What about that?'

His son looked up at him with a wrenching hopefulness. 'You won't peach on me, Pops? You promise?'

'Of course I won't.' He rubbed the boy's cheek. 'We chaps don't go tattling like girls on each other, do we? But no more porky-pies in future or it's into the stocks.'

The boy hugged his leg and tottered gratefully from the cabin. And at that moment something depressing caught Merridith's attention. By the porthole, the imprint of a single dirty palm; a smallish hand, but maybe a man's; the kind of mark that might have been made by a greasy glove.

He would ask Laura to speak to Mary Duane about it. Really, things were difficult enough just now, but there was no reason at all for the place not to be kept clean.

Ireland's famine was the punishment of her imprudence and idleness, but it has given her prosperity and progress.

Anthony Trollope, *North America*

CHAPTER XVI

THE POWER OF DARK THINGS

The THIRTEENTH or MIDDLING day of the Voyage;
in which the Captain records certain
CURIOUS SUPERSTITIONS (notably common among
Sea-faring men) and comes to the protection
of the WOMEN of Ireland.

Saturday, 20 November, 1847
Thirteen days at sea remaining

Long: 36°49.11′W. Lat: 51°01.37′N. Actual Greenwich Standard Time: 11.59 p.m. Adjusted Ship Time: 9.32 p.m. Wind Dir. & Speed: N.N.W. (342°). Force 4. Seas: Restless. Many large whitecaps. Heading: S.S.E. 201° Precipitation and Remarks: Extremely heavy fog. Visibility diminished to 400 yards. We have slowed to two knots.

Last night nine of our brothers and sisters were gathered, and this morning were committed to rest in the deep. Carmody, Coggen, Desmond (x2), Dolan, Murnihan, O'Brien, Rourke and Whelehan.

A great 'growler' iceberg was sighted this afternoon at a distance of approximately half a mile; the size of a large London house, more or less. A multitude of the steerage passengers came up to look and marvel, never having seen such a sight before.

The cook, Henry Li, has come to me with a scheme by which we might relieve the sufferings of some in steerage without incurring expense to the company. (Heaven forfend.) A quantity oftentimes remains uneaten on the plates after supper and luncheon in the First-Class Dining Saloon. Bones, gristle, rinds and suchlike but sometimes fats or the skins of fish. He proposes, rather than to throw these leftovers away, or to make of them pigswill (as is usually the practice), that he stew them down to a soup to be given to the hungry, which would be in the nature of an assistance to them. I think it a compassionate notion and have agreed that he should do it. (Indeed, it ought make any Christian man feel rueful that a pagan displays more fellowship than many of the saved.)

There is a very strange and horrible smell about the ship tonight. I do not mean the usual odour emanating from steerage where the poor people must contend as well as they can; but something much worse and quite pestilential. It beggars description.

I have ordered the whole vessel swabbed down with brine and vinegar but the abominable stink continues even as I write. I never experienced anything like it before; an overpowering reek of utter putrefaction such as one might expect to encounter from the sink-holes of an ill-kept shambles. Nothing was found rotting in the front hold or cargo hold. I am quite at a loss as to know what to do; it is greatly distressing the passengers and some of the men. For such a phenomenon to come upon us on this day of all others is a very unfortunate circumstance which will only bring alarm.

The middling day of any voyage is regarded as unlucky, as on its own is the thirteenth day. For both to fall together, as they do this day, is regarded as particularly ill-fated by seamen. One sailor, Thierry-Luc Duffy of Port au Prince, refused to leave his quarters and come on to his watch this morning, insisting that the com-bination of forces indicated 'voodoo'. (Today is also Saturday, the day of 'the black sabbath' in that eerie superstition.) He said to Leeson that he had been hearing a queer catlike or birdlike scream in the night. He is a very agreeable man usually, of near my own age, and we have sailed many voyages together; there is a good and long established friendship between us; so I went down to the men's berths to see what might be done. He said this day was unholy and he would not work. I said it were sacrilege to prattle in this manner and next he would be broiling his mother to be eaten for supper by himself and Baron Samedi. (That aristocratic gentleman seems to be the voodoo-men's devil; but he wears a top hat to conceal his horns, like half the House of Commons.) At that he laughed but still would not work.

He said if it were sacrilege to believe in life after death, the existence of the devil and the power of dark things, then all the Christian world were sacrilegious and near enough to every last soul on the ship. Each man must believe what he liked, he said; but he did not know what kind of God it was who could send his own boy to be murdered on a tree. And as for cannibalism, the Roman Catholics would happily tell you they gobbled flesh and quaffed gore so maybe Pope Pius himself was a voodoo-man zombie. I said it was not meet to speak so disrespectfully when so many of the passengers are of that great and majestic (if doctrinally errant) faith. He apologised and said it was only a jape, adding that his own wife was a Catholic (of Eleuthera Island in the Bahamas) and his youngest daughter a postulant nun. He was quite beyond persuasion of any variety; saying he would contentedly surrender all rations and go to the lock-up in chains rather than work out his watch this day. I allowed him the day but said I would have to dock it from his wages. He quite understood and seemed content.

As I left, he was uttering some words I did not understand.

Tonight I had necessity to punish one of the men, Joseph Cartigan of Liverpool*, who had been importuning some of the women in steerage and making shameful suggestions by which he meant to gain advantage from their present unhappy state. Apparently he had been offering food in return. I do not like at all to punish the men, but they know I will not have decent girls ruined on my ship. Summoning him to my quarters, I asked if he had wife or daughter and he said neither. Then I asked if he had a mother; and how would he care for her to be translated to a whore? He said she was one already, the busiest in Liverpool. (I swear his ears quite wriggle with insolence.)

Chaucer asserts, in his Prologue of the Reeve: 'Til we be roten kan we not be rype.' If that be the case, then this Mersey-mud placket-hound is so ripe as to be practically intoxicating.

His appeal was that he had attempted nothing save what was

---

*Unusually, Captain Lockwood here makes a mistake. About a dozen of the *Star*'s crew were Liverpudlians but none was called 'Cartigan'. A 'Joseph Carrigan' is included in the Register of Crew, also a 'Joseph Hartigan'. From enquiries made much later among the surviving crew, it seems Hartigan was the sailor whose punishment the Captain records here. – GGD

natural, given the length of the voyage & cetera. At that I ordered the wretch's rations halved for three days, the moiety to be given to some poor girl in steerage. I have oftentimes observed the veracity of the late Admrl. Wm. Bligh's remark (first captain under whom I myself served as boy, on the charting and fathoming of Dublin Bay) that when a man claims in mitigation that his actions be 'natural' he is invariably behaving much worse than a beast, without exception to one much weaker than himself.

The stench now become very evil indeed. As though the ship itself were beginning to rot, or traversing a very real sewer.

If you were to see old Denis Danihy, he never was in as good health and looks better than ever he did at home. And you may be sure he can have plenty of tobacco and told me to mention it to Tim Murphy. If you were to see Denis Reen when Daniel Danihy dressed him with clothes suitable for this country, you would think him to be a boss or a steward, so that we have scarcely words to state to you how happy we felt at present. And as to the girls that used to be trotting on the bogs at home, to hear them talk English would be of great astonishment to you.

Letter from Daniel Guiney in Buffalo, New York

CHAPTER XVII

THE SUITOR

In which a True and unadorned History of certain
DIFFICULT EVENTS in the earlier life of David
Merridith is given.

At home for Christmas furlough, 1836, a respite from which he was
never to return to the navy, David Merridith had been pushed into
an engagement with the only daughter of Henry Blake, the
neighbouring landlord of Tully and Tully Cross. He was now
twenty-three, his father pointed out; a good age for a chap to put his
head in the sack. You didn't want to leave it very much later or you
might end up having to take whatever donkey you could get. This
wasn't London. Supplies were limited. The Blake lands bordered
Kingscourt in several places. Blake was in funds; Kingscourt needed
heavy investment. A happy coincidence, Merridith's father had said,
and of course not the main thing or anything like it. But the two
estates combined would be a force to be reckoned with. Even the
Martins of Ballynahinch would be put in their place; not to mention
those posing puff adders, the D'Arcys of Clifden. And Miss Amelia,
after all, was the beauty of the county.

It simply hadn't occurred to David Merridith to marry; but in a
way, he supposed, his father was right. Amelia Blake wasn't the
worst prospect. Granted, they were cousins, but extremely distant
cousins, not the sort who produced web-toed, cross-eyed children.
He had known her for years and danced with her sometimes at
weddings. She was pleasant to look at. They had a shared interest in
horses. If you couldn't exactly call her intelligent, neither could she
be fairly described as an idiot.

David Merridith and Amelia Blake. Their names had an
inevitable, satisfactory rhythm. She was a soft-featured, coltish, fidgety

girl with a remarkably derisory sense of humour, which came flicker-ing occasionally through her habitual insouciance like a fire-cracker through a foggy night. Often he found her humour unsettling. Her way of forging an alliance was to find out who you didn't like and then to demean them as often and as vigorously as possible. This was diffi-cult for David Merridith; there were very few people he truly disliked. She was also quite fond of hitting you as a sign of affection. Her response to a joke was a raffish slap across the shoulder. If she'd had a glass of sherry she could start flailing at you. Soon, Merridith realised, he was avoiding making jokes in her presence (not to mention giving her sherry) because he found being cuffed by his fiancée confusing.

Two weeks after their engagement was announced, he went alone to Viscount Powerscourt's annual shooting weekend in County Wicklow. He didn't care for shooting, not being much of a shot; but he liked to try to understand exactly how the guns worked; the reek of gunpowder in the apple-crisp air. At dinner he had been seated across from a boyishly beautiful English girl whose carefree laughter made him want to keep looking at her. It was the first time she had been to Ireland and she found it bewitching. Her best friend, a girl with whom she had schooled in Switzerland, was the second eldest daughter of the house: one of the celebrated Wingfields of Powerscourt. He and the English girl had danced a little. She had teased him for his gaucherie at dancing the Lancers, for making a botch of the convoluted figures. They had strolled for a while on the torchlit terrace, admired the rococo fountain which decorated the ornamental lake. It had been purchased by her friend's father in Italy, she told him, and was a copy of a piece by the great Bernini. Everyone thought it was an original but she knew it was a copy. She had a talent for spotting fakes, she said. She would like to go to Italy one day. She was sure she would get around to it.

An attractive efficiency underlined her conversation, an assured-ness he wasn't accustomed to in the women he knew. She wasn't like his sisters, certainly not like his aunt, and she wasn't a giggler like Amelia Blake. There was a confidence about her that was almost brazen; it reminded him of someone he rarely thought about now. The night he met Laura Markham he had not had much sleep. Somehow he sensed that he would always know her, though in precisely which way he could not be sure.

The next day he had found himself watching her through his field binoculars when he should have been shooting, or watching other people shoot. She and the other young women spent the morning on the terrace, wrapped in blankets, sipping coffee. Some played chess and others plucked at guitars but Laura Markham spent the morning reading *The Times.* Merridith found that completely intriguing. He didn't think he had ever seen a woman reading a newspaper. He kept hoping she would find some reason to come down to the meadow, but she never did; she just sat there reading.

Luncheon was noisy and slightly drunken. The parlour games that followed were noisy, too: a cacophony of flirtations and excuses for touching. That evening, everyone had gone holly hunting before early supper. He and Laura Markham had formed one of the teams. Daringly she had linked his arm as they crunched the gravelled pathways, as they crossed the carpet-like upper lawn, as they inspected the ranks of stately foreign trees that needed battalions of gardeners to keep them alive in Wicklow. Little interest was shown in finding holly, or in finding anything except a place to be quiet. In the lengthening shadows the plucked shrubs and primped hedges (pruned into hippogriffs and otherworldly birds) appeared slightly macabre to Viscount Kingscourt. But he felt easy in her presence; quietly companionable. Glancing back at one point, he had seen their footprints traversing the frosted lawn in untidy parallel. The sight had seemed to Merridith a signal of something peaceful. Soon they had found themselves in the Lower Pet Cemetery, where the Wingfields gave their animals the touchingly respectful burial they did not give to many of their tenants.

She was looking at the elegant gardens in a way he found unreadable. The lights of the house in the misting distance were like those of a ship in a magnificent dream.

'Is it like this in Galway?'

'No, it's wilder in Galway.'

'I think I should rather like that. I like wildness.'

She sat back onto one of the ornate porphyry slabs, the tomb-stone of a colt that had twice been placed in the Derby, and folded her arms with an amused sigh. A screech-owl rose from the rhododendrons with a startled clatter.

'Yorkshire and Brittany and places like that. These prettified gardens make me feel slightly sad, I'm afraid. A bit like seeing a pixie forced into a corset. Don't you agree?'

Merridith was a little taken aback. The restrained women of his acquaintance didn't say words like 'corset' in public. He suspected Amelia Blake wouldn't even say it in private.

'Perhaps you'll come and visit us one day. In Galway.'

'Yes. Perhaps you shall invite me to your wedding,' she smiled. 'I should like to come and observe you in your natural habitat.'

He hadn't realised she knew he was engaged and he wondered silently how she might have found out. It thrilled him that she might have been interested enough to ask someone. 'Would you dance with me if I did?' was the best response he could manage.

'I might do,' she said, gazing out at the lake. A gondola with flaming torches was gliding across it. 'But I think you'd need more lessons first. Don't you?'

He remembered the first time his hand had touched her waist. She'd been wearing a white dress that Sunday night, with a sky-blue sash that emphasised the small curve of her hips. A crucifix glittered near the hollow of her neck. The dance was a waltz and his arms had ached with stiffness as he held her. 'I suppose they don't waltz much in Galway,' she said. 'Will you get me a small brandy? We'll drink it together.'

Brandy made him nauseous, and always had, and its popularity among sailors had helped to ruin his days in the navy. But he fetched her one anyway and watched her sip it. She hummed along quietly with the elegant music, sometimes whispering a joke as a graceless dancer passed: sometimes touching the back of his wrist.

They had admired the ancestral portraits on the third-floor landing; the grave gazings of the long-gone Wingfields. Outside her room she had shaken his hand. A kiss to his cheek was awarded like a medal. Before he knew what was happening the door had closed and he was alone beneath those gazes with the empty brandy glass.

She was the only daughter of a Sussex industrialist family; her father's home was near the coast. He owned several large manu-factories of pottery and delftware. She was three years younger than David Merridith but twice had been engaged before: once to a cavalry lieutenant who had died of consumption, the second time to a businessman her father knew. It was she who had ended the second engagement. She had no regrets about making the decision.

When the weekend was over and the guests had wearily departed to prepare themselves to be wearied at the next weekend, the Viscount of Carna had remained at Powerscourt. In later years he was often to think of that time as having a carapace around it; the happiest period in a less than happy life. Certainly the happiest if you shaded Mary Duane from the picture, as by then he tended to do.

He and Laura Markham had gone with the Wingfields up to Dublin, attending the theatre and several concerts; going to a masked ball at the Duke of Leinster's. Seeing them waltz, their sodden old host had tottered up and congratulated them on their excellent news. 'Nobody informed me your new fiancée was such a corker, Merridith. I dare say I should have nabbed her for myself if they had. Thoroughbred in a roomful of trotting ponies.'

After he had staggered away in a fog of halitosis and gin fumes they laughed together at what he had said. But there was a new quality to their dancing after that. It was as though what was happening between them had finally been spoken. The closeness which dancing permitted became a way of acknowledging it.

Merridith had accompanied her to the Italian circus; had ridden out with her in Phoenix Park in the early mornings. There they would watch the troopers parading to the screeches of the monkeys awakening in the zoo. By the end of the fortnight they were almost inseparable. On the afternoon she was leaving for Sussex, he had gone to see her off at the ferry at Kingstown. Snow was falling. Emigrants were queuing along the pier. When he tried to kiss her at the gangway she had drawn away silently, though the look in her eyes had given him hope. He tried again, but she drew away again. Yes, she said gently, of course she had feelings for him; but she wouldn't act unfairly towards another girl.

She didn't envy Merridith the choice he faced now, but she wouldn't push him or ask him to do anything. Only he could know what his true feelings were. He must do what he thought was correct and nothing else. The happiness of several people was at stake. To cause hurt to a person to whom you had given your word was a serious thing and could not be done lightly. He was to think about it calmly and carefully, she said. Every choice involved a rejection.

She would understand his decision whatever it might be and would always respect it and remember him fondly. But she would only contact him again if he contacted her first. That was not to happen unless his engagement to Amelia Blake were broken off.

On the mail-coach back to Galway, Merridith had known what would happen. There was a nobility behind Laura's reluctance which had only made him want her more; a decency which he knew he probably lacked himself. He, a man who was promised, after all, had thought nothing of speaking of love to another woman. He would have gone further if going further had been possible. What that implied would not be easy to confront but it would have to be confronted or he would always regret it.

Dusk was descending as the coach crossed the Shannon. A blizzard had swelled the river to breaking; farmers in drenched oilskins were banking up sandbags. Soon the landscape began to change, the prosperous meadows of the lush midlands giving way to the stonewalled scrubs of Galway. The cold air smelt of peatsmoke and the sea. He would never forget the fear that had clutched him when he saw the lights of Kingscourt Manor in the distance.

His father was seated at the table in the library, examining a fist-sized yellow egg with a magnifying glass, making notes in a leather-bound accountancy ledger. Though it was only three weeks since Merridith had seen him, he seemed to have aged by several years. It was not long after his second stroke; the attack had left him with a tremor and greatly reduced sight. The black leather glove he usually wore on his right hand was twisted on the blotter like a poisonous spider.

Merridith gave a knock. Without looking up, his father murmured: 'Enter.'

He took one anxious pace but he didn't really enter. 'I wondered if we might have a short talk, sir.'

'I am quite well, David. Thank you for asking.'

'Forgive me, sir. I should of course have asked.'

His father nodded grimly but still did not look up. 'This – short talk – which you would like to have. Does it concern your use of my house as an hotel to which to repair between social gatherings?'

'No, sir. I apologise for the length of my absence, sir.'

'I see. Then what does it concern? This short talk you would like to have.'

'Well – concerning matters with Miss Blake and myself, sir.'

'What about them?'

'I have. I seem to have. That is to say.' He gathered himself and began again. 'I have formed an attachment to another person, sir.'

Calmly the Earl took a tiny paintbrush from a drawer and started dusting the egg with an unsteady motion. 'Well,' he said, quietly, as though to himself, 'you had better unform it in double-quick time then. Hadn't you?' He held the object up to the pale gold firelight; ran a finger along its circumference as though coaxing it to hatch.

'I seem to recall,' he almost whispered, 'that certain of the "attachments" you formed in the past were not wise either. They, too, had to be unformed.'

'I believe this is different, sir. In fact I am certain of it.'

Now his father looked up at him. His eyes were like stones. After a while he rose from the table and pulled on his glove.

'Come closer,' he murmured. 'Into the light.'

Merridith was trembling as he moved towards his father.

'Is something the matter with your shoulders, David?'

'How – do you mean, sir?'

Lord Kingscourt blinked slowly, like a sleepy cow. 'Perhaps you would do me the inestimable honour of standing up straight when you speak to me, if you please.'

He did as he was told. His father stared. Wind clattered the windowpanes; moaned in the chimneybreast. Slates were clacking on the creamery roof.

'Are you afraid, David? Answer me honestly.'

'A little, sir.'

A long moment passed before Lord Kingscourt gave a nod. 'Do not be ashamed. I know what it is to be afraid.' He shuffled slowly and heavily to the mahogany sideboard where he felt for a stone decanter and awkwardly unstoppered it. Carefully he poured out a goblet of brandy, though the quake in his grip made it difficult to pour. Without turning, he asked: 'Will you have a drink with me, David?'

'No sir, thank you.'

His hand with the decanter was hovering over a second glass, as though about to make a judgement that might have lasting implications. 'Mayn't a man have a drink with his own son now, without having to go up to Dublin for the privilege?'

The grandfather clock gave a click and a whirr. The time it was telling was wrong by many hours. Somewhere in the room a lighter timepiece was ticking, as though in rattish argument with its solemn forebear.

'F-forgive me, sir. I will, please. Thank you. Perhaps a small glass of wine.'

'Wine,' said Lord Kingscourt, 'is not a drink. It is a kidney-flush for Frenchmen and prancing fops.'

He poured the second glass of brandy to the brim and placed it on a side table beside the piano. Merridith went and took it. It felt cold to the touch.

'Your health, David.' Lord Kingscourt drained half his glass in one swallow.

'And your own, sir.'

'I see you do not drink. Perhaps your toast is insincere.'

Merridith took a small sip. His gorge rose.

'More,' said his father. 'I want to be healthy.'

He swallowed down a mouthful: eyes moistening with disgust.

'All of it,' Lord Kingscourt said. 'You know I am very ill.'

He finished the glass. His father refilled it.

'You may be seated now, David. Over there if you please.'

Merridith crossed to the overstuffed sofa and sat down, and his father inched painfully into a dark leather armchair, his face distended with the effort of moving. He was wearing unmatching slippers and no stockings. The eczema from which he suffered had blistered on his bony ankles, its livid scars raked with the ragged trace of fingernails.

Again he said nothing. Merridith wondered what would happen. From somewhere in the distance a donkey gave a ludicrous bawl. When finally his father began to speak again, it was in the exaggeratedly deliberate and enunciated way he had employed to conceal his slur since the seizures had struck him. A drunk man trying to disguise his drunkenness.

'I was sometimes quite afraid of your grandfather when I was your age. He and I did not enjoy the close relationship which you and I enjoy. He could be a portion of a tyrant as a matter of fact. Old-fashioned and so on. Or I felt so, at any rate. It is only in recent years that I see he meant well. That what I perceived as strictness was actually loving kindness.' He gulped hard; glottal, as though swallowing a piece of gristle. 'But when one is young, one always feels that about one's father. Natural for a boy to feel like that.'

Uneasily Merridith wondered how he was supposed to respond.

'And in battle, too; I have often been afraid.' He pursed his pallid lips and gave a soberly rueful nod. 'Yes. You appear surprised but it is true. At the battle of Baltimore I was certain I should die, David. We were cut off at one point. And I was afraid then.'

'Afraid of dying, sir?'

His father peered absently into his glass as though he could see strange pictures in the vapours rising from it. Though the room was cold, his beard looked matted with sweat. 'Yes. I expect so. Of the pain, I expect. When a young man has seen other young men die – when he has had the duty of sending them out to certain death – he will know that death is not a glorious thing at all, but a loathsome one.' He gave a small shudder and brushed the dust from his sleeve in a desultory way. 'All the lies we spout about dying for one's country. That is all they are, you know, David. Barbarities and lies.'

'Sir?

'I have formed the view that these absurdities are a way of stopping us being afraid. Crush the fear that might otherwise drive us together. Religions. Philosophies. Even countries themselves – they are a kind of lie, too. As I see it.'

Merridith was confused. 'In which sense, sir?'

'I mean we are all comparable under the outward appearance. Human, I suppose. If you prick us, et cetera.' He nodded again and took a long sip of brandy. 'Except the French, obviously. Garlic-eating savages.'

'Yes, sir.'

His father frowned. 'That was a joke.'

'Sorry, sir.'

'Yes. I am sorry, too. More than you know.'

He gave a short, sour laugh. 'Matter of fact, I sometimes think the old Frog had it right. Liberty, equality, fraternity, et cetera.' He gaped around the dismally cold room as though he despised it. 'Wouldn't say no to a slice of liberty. Would you?' His words had a shading of irony which David Merridith couldn't understand.

'Well – no, sir. I shouldn't think so.'

'No indeed. No indeed. And neither should I.'

The grandfather clock gonged from deep in its chest: a sad sound, spent, a cough of chronometry. Shadows moved. The fire fizzed. The ratchet of windings readjusting to their drudgery. The father looked up at the warped brown ceiling; then at the clock; and then at his son.

'What was I saying to you, David?'

'You were talking about death, sir.'

'Was I?'

'Yes, sir. About the battle of Baltimore.'

Slowly his father began to speak again. 'What I feared. Even more. Than that possibility' – and Lord Kingscourt's eyes seemed to dissolve with tears.

Merridith was as horrified as if his father had lost control of his bowels. For a moment he sat still, his head bowed very low, his left hand clenching at the length of silvered braiding which attempted to decorate the arm of the chair. Then his shoulders began convulsing as he quietly wept. Sobs racked his chest and still he tried not to move. Small sounds of resistance. A shake of the head. His breath came in gasps that seemed to stab into him.

'Are you – quite all right, sir?'

Lord Kingscourt nodded but did not look up.

'May I fetch you a glass of water?'

No answer was made. A dog was heard barking; an insistent, repeated two-tone yelp, and the whistle of a sheepman calling it to heel. Lord Kingscourt's quivering fingers went to his forehead; shielded his eyes like a man in shame.

'You must forgive me, David. I am a little out of sorts this evening.'

'It's quite all right, father. Is there anything I can do?'

'Your mother . . . was the finest person who ever lived.'

'Yes, sir.'

'Her compassion for people. Capacity to forgive. Not an hour goes by without my feeling her loss. As a crippled man would miss a limb.'

Tears were seeping down his face again and Merridith was by now afraid to speak. He thought he might cry himself if he did.

'You will be aware that we had our good days and our bad ones, David. God knows I was very far from what she deserved. I failed her so often. Through anger and stupidity. I have wasted so much that I cannot bear to think of it. But you must never think there was no love between us.'

'I never would, sir.'

'Because. What I feared that night at Baltimore, David. Was not just the pain – the physical pain. But that I should never. See you and your mother again. Particularly you. Not to embrace. My only son. Most terrifying feeling I have ever known.'

'Sir, I beg you not to torture yourself with thoughts of the past.'

His father's mouth was twisted with grief. 'It is I – who beg. Please – never be afraid to come to me with any little difficulty you might be experiencing in life. Never, David. Everything can be overcome. Never feel you are alone. Will you make me that promise?'

'Of course I shall, sir.'

'Will you shake my hand on it?'

Merridith had gone to his father and taken his outstretched, lifeless hand. Never in his life had he felt more close to him; a visceral animal closeness he could not remember feeling for anyone. His father had wept like an orphaned child and David Merridith had clutched his hand. He had wanted to enfold him, to wrap him like armour, but the moment had passed while he was still trying to imagine it. Perhaps it was just as well. His father had never liked to be touched.

Lord Kingscourt dried his eyes and gave a small, brave grin. 'So you've fallen in bloody love, then. Turn-up for the books.'

'Yes, sir. Seems to look that way.'

'And you're sure?'

'Yes, sir.'

His father suddenly chuckled and clapped him on the shoulder. 'Think your old ogre of a guv'nor never caught that little ailment, do you?'

'Of course not, sir.'

'I bloody did. Often. Wasn't always the broken-down wreck I am now. Gave a few little Judies a good fright in my time, I may tell you. So I think I understand your predicament, my boy.'

'Thank you, sir. I truly felt you would do when I put the situation.'

'Yes. It's all perfectly understandable. Natural thing in fact. '

He poured himself another balloon of brandy.

'Pretty face. Sparkle in the eye. Nice bit of upholstery, I don't doubt.' He gave a strained cough and turned away to wipe his mouth. 'Now that's all very well, you see. None of us here without it. But there's more to a marriage than that, after all.'

'Oh yes, sir, I know.'

'There's one's duty to consider. Marriage is a contract.'

'Yes, sir.'

'Lot of gush and blather about love these days. Know what the definition of love is?'

'What is it, sir?'

'Resolve to keep one's word, David. Nothing more, nothing less. To do one's duty, always; whether one feels like it or no.'

'Yes, sir.'

'The animals do as they feel. And an animal can be beautiful. That, in fact, is the nature of its beauty. But we men have morality. That is the only difference. The only thing which makes human life worth continuing.'

'I certainly intend to keep my word to Miss Markham, sir. I should think keeping my word will be a great p-pleasure. When you meet her I'm certain you'll agree.'

His father's dying smile made David Merridith think of a fading coal. When he spoke again his voice was shrivellingly cold and quiet.

'I was speaking of your word to Miss Blake and her father.'

The fire gave a spit and belched in the hearth. A red log fell out and sizzled on the floor of the grate.

'You also have obligations to the people of this estate. Does that occur to you for even one moment?'

'Sir – '

'I have given my word that the lands are to be improved when funds become available from your marital settlement. Am I now to tell them that my word means nothing? As your own has meant less to your fiancée and her father.'

'S-sir – I have written today to Miss Blake to explain the situation, and also to the Commander. As for the tenants – '

'I see,' his father interrupted. 'You have written. How very courageous. So this entire conversation has in fact been academic.'

'I felt it was best to apprise the Commander of the new situation, sir.'

His father grinned mirthlessly. 'And is the Commander the fool who has raised you, mister? Is the Commander the fool who puts bread in your mouth?'

'I . . . have done my best to explain it to you, too, sir.'

'You're saying you'll countermand me? That is your last word? Think carefully, Mister. Your actions have consequences.' Lord Kingscourt had crossed to the bell-pull and was holding it in his gloved hand. 'Your life has come to a crossroads now, David. The choice is your own. You must choose like a man.'

'I'm sa-saying my situation has altered, sir. My feelings.'

Lord Kingscourt nodded abruptly and tugged on the bell-pull. The chime jangled somewhere far away. 'All right then. So be it.' He turned and limped heavily back towards the table.

'Father?'

'Be gone from this house by the time I rise tomorrow morning. Do not return.'

'F-f-fah – '

'Your allowance will be stopped with immediate effect. Now go.'

'Father, please –'

'*Please what, sir?* Please continue to indulge my every latest whim? Please subsidise me to flounce about the country like a dancing-master? Do you think I hear nothing, sir, is that it? I have few friends left but I have some still, to carry me news of the latest embarrassment. Well, you'll idle no more on any money of mine, Mister. I swear you that on the grave of your mother.'

'It isn't a question of money, sir, surely – '

'Oh, "it isn't a question of money, sir." Is that so, you insolent brat? And how did you mean to support this so-called wife of yours? On a junior lieutenant's wages?'

'No, sir.'

'*Yes,* sir! Stand up when I speak to you! From what I am told of your bloody miserable efforts you are unlikely even to progress to Commander.'

'Actually I thought I might resign my commission, sir.'

His father scoffed. 'I presume you do not refer to the commission which my hard-earned money had to purchase for you.'

'Miss Markham has means of her own, sir. Her family has made a success in business.'

Lord Kingscourt stopped pacing. A glower of repugnance widened his eyes. 'Now you are joking.'

'No, sir.'

'Do you hate me so much? Do you want to kill me?'

'Sir, I beg you – '

'Did I raise you and educate you and sponsor your uselessness for you to live like a shopkeeper on the proceeds of trade?'

'I – didn't see the matter in those kind of terms, sir.'

'Oh you didn't. How convenient. How touchingly modern. And you don't consider it unseemly? For a man to be maintained by a bloody woman?'

'Sir.'

Lord Kingscourt pointed vaguely in the direction of the window. His face seemed almost dirty with rage. *Salach* was the Irish adjective for dirty: a word that sounded like its own meaning. 'Not a man on that land, not the poorest among them, would dream of allowing his wife to keep him.' He slammed down his glass on the lid of the piano, so hard that the contents slopped over his glove. 'Did you ever hear of responsibility or duty or loyalty? Do you have even a modicum of manliness in you, mister?'

David Merridith said nothing. The piano strings were reverberating. Absurdly the metronome had clicked into life but Lord Kingscourt did not seem to notice its awakening.

'I suppose you'll suckle and wipe arses too, will you? While your bawd is out busily minding the shop.'

'Sir, I know you are a little upset at the moment but you compel me to say that I resent your choice of – '

His father lunged and struck him hard across the face.

'Resent me, will you, you contemptuous wastrel?' He clutched his own hand, the blow had been so violent. 'By Christ that day hasn't dawned yet, nor ever will. I'll beat you from here to Clifden in a minute, you libertine God-blasted dog. *Do you mind me now? Do you mind me, sir?*'

David Merridith was weeping with shock.

'*Stand up when I address you, Mister! Or you'll go through that wall!*'

'I ap-pologise, father.'

'Cry one more tear in front of me and you'll cry like a kicked bitch, you stuttering imbecile.'

'Yes, father.'

'I have done it before and I'll do it again. Your life has been too damned easy by far. Everything you needed without the slightest condition. As my only son I had natural feelings, but I see to my shame that I have quite spoiled you.'

At that point Tommy Joyce, his father's valet, had come in. He stopped near the doorway with an apprehensive mien. It was clear that he had overheard some of the argument.

'Your Lordship rang, sir.'

'Pack the Viscount's clothes and other belongings. He will be leaving in the morning at first light. He will give you whatever address he would like them sent on to.'

The servant nodded slowly and turned to leave.

'On second thoughts, rein up the pony and get out the phaeton. He will be leaving us tonight, my so-called son. Just as soon as his effects are packed.'

'Begging Your Lordship's pardon,' Tommy Joyce attempted tentatively, 'but it's the devil's icy night to be going the roads.'

'Are you deaf?'

'Sir, I only thought – '

'Are you deaf as well as brazen, you pig-ignorant lout?'

'Sir.'

'Obey your bloody orders and obey them fast if you wish to remain in my employment one minute longer.'

'Father, I beg you – '

'*Do not dare use the word "father" to me.* You failed at Oxford. You have failed in the navy. In every small test which life has presented, you have failed. And now you mean to fail once more and to drag my name in the shit of this county as you do.'

'Father, please calm down. You'll make yourself unwell.'

'Get out of this house before I whip you out. You disgust me.'

'Father – '

'*Out!*'

David Merridith had left the room. Closed the door behind him as quietly as possible. Vomited in the hallway as the phaeton appeared in the yard. Vomited as his bags were trundled down the stairs. 'Out' was bellowed once again from the study.

The last word either Merridith would ever speak to the other.

Gaelic Mental Characteristics. – Quick in perception, but deficient in depth of reasoning power; headstrong and excitable; tendency to oppose; *strong in love and hate;* at one time lively, soon after sad; vivid in imagination; extremely social, with a *propensity for crowding together;* forward and self-confident; deficient in application to deep study, but possessed of *great concentration in monotonous or purely mechanical occupations,* such as hop-picking, reaping, weaving, etc.; want of prudence and foresight; antipathy to seafaring pursuits.

'Comparative Anthropology' by Daniel Macintosh,
The Anthropological Review, January 1866

CHAPTER XVIII

THE TRANSLATOR

───────

───────

Monday, 22 November, 1847
Eleven days at sea remaining

LONG: 41°12.13′W. LAT: 50°07.42′N. ACTUAL GREENWICH STANDARD TIME: 02.10 a.m. (23 November). ADJUSTED SHIP TIME: 11.26 p.m. (22 November). WIND DIR. & SPEED: E. (88°). Force 5. SEAS: Turbulent. HEADING: W. (271°). PRECIPITATION & REMARKS: Heavy fall of snow in the afternoon. Sky leaden all day. A human body was sighted in the water at a quarter to five, 300 yds to starboard. Sex indeterminate. Very decomposed and lower limbs missing. Reverend Deedes and some others said a prayer as we passed.

Seven passengers died last night and were committed this morning to the mercies of the deep. Their names have been duly struck off the Manifest.

The queer stench about the vessel continues most over-poweringly and distressingly. Have ordered the boards scrubbed down thrice daily until it diminishes. Leeson reports that an unusual thing is happening in the holds. It seems they have been quite deserted by rats; but a great number of those vermin have been observed scuttling about the decks as though in a state of utmost frenzy. One child of steerage was bitten today and all have been warned not to approach if they see them. Surgeon Mangan is extremely concerned about the increasing infestation in public areas. I have ordered the laying down of poisons.

Several reports of mysterious cries from about the ship at night; or weeping or 'yowling'. Doubtless the usual hubbub and racket we shellback Methuselahs of the *Star* know well by now: 'John Conqueroo's shanty': but louder and even more eerie than before, it is said. Apparently the Reverend Deedes was approached by some of the steerage passengers and asked if he would perform a rite of exorcism. He said he felt such a course to be rather unnecessary but conducted a service on the quarterdeck tonight. Very large attendance.

It can only be that we have struck some great sea creature, possibly a very large shark or cetacean, and killed it; portion of the fluids or membrane of same having somehow adhered to the body of the vessel. For the stench is clearly that of some dead and decomposing beast. (Needless to say, King Duffy of Haiti has his own macabre theories but a rational man had rather look to the rational world.)

For some time I have allotted one half an hour of every day for any passenger who wishes to see me – but obviously only on matters of deepest urgency. (Leeson weeds out the wheat from the chaff, a separation most necessary given more pressing demands.) This afternoon a couple from steerage presented themselves at my quarters during that period, and announced that they desired to be married. Speaking no English, they had brought with them Wm. Swales the cripple whom I have mentioned previously, as interceder. And it is a mighty good thing they thought to do so; for otherwise I would have possessed no notion whatsoever of what they were saying in their strange but not entirely unpleasant language. He wished me good afternoon and pronounced it a pleasant coincidence to see me again. And I attempted to greet the young people in their own Gaelic vernacular – 'Jee-ah gwitch' – with some success, I am delighted to report, for they nodded back happily and repeated it to me. 'God be praised this day,' Swales laughed mildly and we all looked at each other like partners waiting for a dance to start; but it did not, sadly.

Through my ragged pedagogue the young people explained they had heard it reported by many before that a Captain may perform a marriage at sea. I advised them (again through Swales) that in actuality this is not the position (despite the romantic stuff of ladies' fiction). Indeed I may discharge no legal ceremony of any kind (with the exception of a funeral or the execution of a prisoner in time of war); and I advised them they must needs wait until we reach New York and there seek a Credential of License from the city authorities. (As Captain Bligh used to put it, 'a sea-wedding is only legal until the ship returns to port'.) Whatever the fashion in which Swales explained it, they looked most crestfallen to learn it. An approximation of the words he uttered to them is this: 'Shay dear on budduck knock will bresh beah lefoyle.'★

I enquired as to the matter of how long they had known each other. They answered but a fortnight, having met on the ship. (He is of the Blasket Islands, she of the Arans.) I then asked if they had heard of the wise old adage: 'He who weds in haste shall repent at his leisure'; and they said they had, so Swales attested, but had fallen helplessly in love. The youth is eighteen yrs, the girl a year younger; a dark-headed 'colleen' with the comeliest eyes I ever saw. One could conjecture how easily the poor lad must have been set to swooning; she reminded me of my own wife, in fact, at a tender age.

Again I advised that I had no authority to perform such a ceremony and said they must be patient another eleven days; adding that it was not very long to wait, especially for a happy couple who wished to spend all of eternity together. They went away, looking mighty downcast, but Swales requesting to remain behind for a moment.

We shared a little joke about the silliness of youthful ardour. Had I a guinea, I remarked, for every pretty girl I ever wished to wed after two weeks of kissing and boyhood foolery, I should be the richest man in Great Britain now. He gave a mighty laugh and clapped me about the back in a rather familiar way, which I did not

---

★A curious remark. Possibly, according to a number of scholars of Gaelic, including Samuel Ferguson Q.C. of Belfast, *'Sé deir an bodach nach bhfuil breis bia le fáil.'* In English: 'The churl [or old fool] is saying that no extra food is to be had.' The word *'bodach'* (pronounced 'buddock') may be related to *'bod'*, a low Irish colloquialism for the male genitalia. The usage is not unknown in Connemara. – GGD.

like. And he then said he had hoped to see me on deck over the last few days or nights and had waited for a long time but had not succeeded in seeing me until the fortuitous coincidence arose this morning of the young couple & cetera. I explained that I was rather occupied with matters below, my happy pastime of managing the ship by times interfering with my paid employment as chief barterer of falderols with the passengers, but I hoped we might soon have an agreeable little talk.

Swales said he truly was most anxious to find a position with Lord Kingscourt if possibly he could; and there was not all that long a time remaining of the voyage. His fear, he explained, was that as soon as we arrived at New York, Lord Kingscourt and his family would commence their further travels and he might lose his opportunity.

I said I had mentioned the matter a couple of nights previously but Lord Kingscourt had no need, the family already possessing a maidservant. But he had given me five shillings to give to Swales, with his blessings. This I duly handed to him. But the ingrate did not seem very happy to receive it. When I asked him what the deuce could be the matter now, he replied that he could not eat five shillings, nor even ten thousand. At that I bade him good-day. Many and great are the obligations of captaincy, but to procure employment for presumptuous dolts does not lie among them (as yet).

As he went away (and others came in), Leeson told me that he had been pestering him for several days to come in; announcing he and I to be bosum friends & cetera. I said it were a pity I could not divide myself into replicas, so that every last waffler on the ship could have one of me. Like a worm, Leeson said. (But I think he meant no offence.)

Later, in the evening, whilst taking the readings on the foredeck, I observed the young man who had wished to marry, now tenderly canoodling with a quite different goddess; a pretty little Helen with a halo of golden tresses. So Paris of the Blaskets would appear to have recuperated from whatever disappointment he felt! Yet such are the ways of younger love. Hot as the sirocco when first it blows up; but it cools just as quickly, or alters direction.

Thought he had heer'd speak of Bonaparte; didn't know what he was; thought he had heer'd of Shakespeare, but didn't know whether he was alive or dead, and didn't care. A man with something like that name kept a dolly [a prostitute] and did stunning; but he was such a hard cove that if he was dead it wouldn't matter. Had seen the Queen but didn't recollec' her name just at the minute; Yes, he had 'eered of God, who made the world. Couldn't exactly recollect when he'd heer'd on him. Had never heer'd of France, but had heer'd of Frenchmen; Had heer'd of Ireland. Didn't know where it was, but it couldn't be very far, or such lots wouldn't come from there to London. Should say they walked it, aye, every bit of the way.

East London street trader to the journalist Henry Mayhew
Name unknown

CHAPTER XIX

THE THIEF

The night Pius Mulvey walked out of Connemara, a hurricane struck the west coast of Ireland, felling twenty thousand trees in under six hours (according to the London *Times* for the following day). The winds were fearful but the trees did the damage. They blocked the roads and tumbled into rivers; pulverised farmhouses, cottages, churches. The tornado raged up and down the western littoral, from the Skellig Islands off the coast of Kerry in the south to the northernmost tip of County Donegal. Scores of bridges collapsed or were swept away. Two men in Sligo were killed by a landslide, a woman in Clare by lightning. An aristocrat from Cashel, up at New College, Oxford, wrote in an edition of the student newspaper that the country might never look the same again.

Mulvey walked the two hundred miles from his home to the great city of Belfast in the County of Antrim, a journey which took him the best part of a month. He had never set foot in any city before, let alone one as stately and commodious as this. So prosperous, so gracious, so large was Belfast that people sometimes argued about exactly where it was; part of it in Antrim, another part in Down, everyone wanting to claim his piece. The river was so beautiful they wrote songs in its praise: the lovable old Lagan that severed the town in two. The vast granite alcazars which sentried the square seemed as wonders in Mulvey's eyes, fortresses of marble and imperial columns; the innumerable rows of redstone houses specially built for the labouring classes no less a matter of jaw-dropping awe. They gave you a house. They gave you *neighbours*. If Connemara was Antarctica, Belfast was Athens. So it seemed to Pius Mulvey. The vast flag of empire on the Town Hall turret was the size of his father's field back home.

He made his way down to the bustling docklands where he found employment on a labouring gang for a time, widening and deepening the harbour. It was work he liked, uncomplicated and healthy; unlike Connemara farming, you could see the results of it. Your back might be aching by the time you knocked off; your muscles pulped, skin peeling with cold, hands blistered as those of a stigmatised hermit; but at the end of the week you got a fistful of shillings and they seemed a sweet balm to the pain. Food was plentiful and cheap in the city. If you wanted drink it was easily had; not the toxicant poteen of northern Galway, but smooth mellow ales and warming malts.

Nobody in the port cared if you came or went. Mostly they were coming or going themselves. Raised in the practically incestuous closeness of Connemara, Mulvey found the anonymity of the city a bliss. The freedom of conversation with an affable stranger: the chap who was only talking to you to kill a little time. A companion who wanted nothing and offered nothing in return. You might never set eyes on each other again and that meant you could parley without fear of a comeback. Or the freedom to engage in no conversation at all, but at least to be faced with a choice on the matter, which usually you weren't on a mountainside in Galway. The exquisite silence of the city late at night. To saunter the ways of the sleeping metropolis; to hear your echoed footsteps on black, wet stone; to catch sight of the distant moonlit hills through a gap at the end of a terraced street, before heading back to your dockside hut with a bottle. It seemed to Pius Mulvey the life of a god.

His mother had spent a fortnight in Dublin as a girl. Any time she spoke of the customs of the city she remarked disapprovingly and deeply suspiciously that it was a place where you could truly be yourself. But it seemed to Pius Mulvey that you could be anyone you chose: that the city was a blank folio on which your past might be redrawn. 'Palimpsest' was the English for a document written in the place created by the erasure of another. He came to think of

Belfast as Palimpsestia, County Antrim. There was no reason to confine yourself to being yourself. And soon enough, he discovered in Palimpsestia, there were plenty of reasons to be someone else.

It was there that he began to go by an assumed name. A kindly Protestant comrade with whom he shared lodgings had discreetly confided a few of the rules. Belfast was changing. People were talking 'auld nonsense'. He'd have no truck with bigotry and never had. A man's own religion was business of his own; the world would be a deal happier if it stayed that way. But it was important for a Roman Catholic to be careful now. Certain territories of the city were not to be walked by the bearer of a name as richly suggestive as Pius.

For a while, he became his own brother; but being Nicholas Mulvey seemed a kind of indecency; too severe an act of colonisation. And anyway 'Mulvey' was still a little too Papish for most employers to be able to stomach. To settle on the right name proved difficult in the extreme. As John Adams he was a stevedore for almost four months; as Ivan Holland a cattleman's helper; as Billy Ruttledge a deck-hand on a pilot's tug. Waterfront life was various enough to allow such frequent christenings.

As William Cook he was mate to a longshoreman who loved the Lord, and who persistently encouraged Mulvey to love him too. Mulvey had as little interest in finding Jesus as he hoped Jesus had in finding Mulvey, but he loved to listen to the extraordinary poetry his superior spoke. Dancing was 'back-legs fornication'; whiskey or porter 'the devil's buttermilk'. People didn't die, they 'fell asleep'. Pope Pius was 'Captain Redhat' or 'Johnny Longstockings'.

He was a Justified Bible Protestant, the longshoreman would say, separated unto the gospel by Holy Ghost Power. Mulvey didn't know what 'justified' or 'separated' might mean in such a spiritual context; why justification was a necessary aim, nor from which heavy impositions separation might be required. But to be able to talk like that about your religion seemed a thing that could give you a reachier punch. He was baptised an Evangelical in a tent in Lisburn and went to Mass in Derriaghy on his way home the same night, his clothes still sodden from the earlier immersion. Neither rite had revealed much of Holy Ghost Power to him; but as his father used to say when he had a few drinks taken, you couldn't expect bloody miracles when you were talking about God.

In time Mulvey began to grow weary with port life, its new mistrusts, the mutual suspicion now growing among the men, and he decided to try his luck in some other place. It was Daniel Monaghan who signed on the cattleboat that plied across to Glasgow. It was Gabriel Elliot who came back the following month, having found no work whatsoever in that impoverished city, and many of the same tensions which quietly throbbed in Belfast.

Physical labour bored him now and he wondered how else he might procure a living. He began to go about the pubs of the dockside at night, singing to the drinkers the ballad he had composed. He learned to adjust it to the requirements of his audience, to tread carefully within the multiple borders of Belfast. If the drunks were Protestant he would make the insulted sergeant a lazy Irish Catholic begging for a hand-out; if they were Catholic he would cast him as a bible-thumping vicar prowling for converts among the reverently starving. When it was finally discovered, as he knew it must be some time, that essentially he had been singing the same song to the two opposing sides, both came together in fleeting coalition to have him beaten unconscious and slung from the city.

He woke up under a tarpaulin on the deck of a coalboat with his pockets empty and his clothes in shreds. Men were talking a language he did not know; a curious vowelly tongue he took to be German. It took him a while to realise that actually it was English but spoken in an accent he had never heard. They dropped their aitches and exaggerated their consonants. 'Ed' was a head. 'Gored' was God. Norsemen, maybe. Latter-day Vikings. Or perhaps they were Americans, Mulvey thought. Americans were known for such swagger and braggadocio. It was only when their Captain proposed a toast 'to the very good elf of King Willum' (Gored blissim) that Mulvey understood who the strange creatures were. The beings after whom the language was named.

He remained in his hiding place for one more day, only venturing out when land became visible. The natives greeted his appearance with wails of cheerful surprise, but did not beat him or kick him or fling him into the water, at least one of which courses he had expected them to take. Instead they fed him and gave him to drink, bucked him up and pronounced him a good'un. He was addressed as 'my covey', 'my chum' or 'my china', all terms seeming to connote fellowship among them. It was explained to the traveller exactly where he was, the names of the undiscovered lands he could discern in the distance. Foulness Island. Southend-on-Sea. The settlement of Rochford whose peoples were warlike. The ancient, tribal homelands of Basildon, Essex.

Fabled Sheerness. The Isle of Sheppey. They sailed up the Thames estuary, past Purfleet and Dagenham, Woolwich and Greenwich, the Isle of Dogs, Deptford and Limehouse, Stepney and Shadwell, through the fallow swirling fog that lay on the docks. Until the fallow fog parted like the curtains of some gargantuan theatre, and there stood London, city of cities. Majestic in the dusk, biblically colossal, for all her millions of twinkling lights, forlorn as a faded prima donna in borrowed jewellery. Stupefied Mulvey could not even speak. The diva might have dubious origins, but already he was conquered.

Into the docklands the slow ship wended, by Wapping and Pennington to St-George-in-the-East; the surface of the river like a sheet of beaten gold; the dome of St Paul's a Croagh Patrick of copper. His rescuers wished him good fortune as they tied up at the dock. He stepped off the steamer and tottered away. The sailors chuckled with their waiting wives and put his gait down to a case of poor sea-legs. But the diagnosis was wrong. The voyager was love-drunk. He hoped he would never be sober again.

Two urchins, little mudlarks, were dicing on the quayside, warbling a ballad of dauntless highwaymen.

> *Oh, my name is Fred'rick Hall,*
> *And I rob both great and small;*
> *But my neck shall pay for all,*
> *When I die, when I die.*

Pius Mulvey made the sign of the cross. Never again would he have to be baptised.

For two years Frederick Hall lived in the East End of the city, earning his bread by swindling and robbing. It was simpler than singing, and much more profitable, and much less likely to result in a beating, at least if you used your common sense. Gentlemen came into the quarter late at night to find girls, and they were such easy prey that Mulvey could scarcely believe his luck. If you appeared in an alleyway and said you had a pistol, the mark would hand over his pocketbook with scarcely a word. If you took out a cudgel he would do anything you asked. And if you sidled up behind him just as he was leaving a brothel – just as he was buttoning up his flies and thinking to himself that he had got away with it again – and if you gently said at that precise moment: 'I know where you live and I will tell your wife,' he would practically beg you to take everything he had and thank you afterwards for having taken it.

Soon Mulvey discovered an interesting thing: that the easiest way to acquire money was simply to ask for it. He would single out a gentleman who looked a little uneasy in the street – a novice, perhaps, in the etiquette of the East End; some poor old duffer who had the horn so bad you could practically see it twitching through his Savile Row britches. Mulvey would amble up to him with the most empathetic smile he could muster and hold out his arm like a welcoming *maître d*. 'I've a nice little Judy just around the corner, sir. Beautiful thing she is; breasts like peaches. Shall I go and fetch her for you, sir? Her rooms are nearby. Nice and discreet. She'll do anything you want.' Sometimes there would be a moment of nervous hesitance and Mulvey would quietly repeat the word 'anything'. The gentleman would hand over a couple of hot coins and Mulvey would thank him and walk directly into the nearest pub, certain of not being followed into it by the toff. And certain, in the event he might ever be wrong, that no man would publicly ask for the whore he had been promised. No gentleman, anyway. They had to live by the rules. You could turn their rules to your own advantage; that was the secret on which London's existence was predicated. Immigrants lived or died by their knowledge of that secret and Frederick Hall understood it better than most.

He loved the city of London like most people love a spouse. Its inhabitants he found decent, fair-minded, tolerant; conversational when sober and wildly generous when drunk; far more hospitable to outsiders than he had been led to believe. What helped was that most of them were outsiders too; many living with the knowledge that they might be again. To walk the streets of Whitechapel was to walk around the world. Jews with black ringlets and skullcaps and beards; sloe-eyed women in fabulous saris; Chinamen with pigtails or conical hats; navvies with skin so richly black that in a certain light it appeared blue as the Atlantic at dawn. Often it struck him as profoundly correct that the Irish term for a black man was *fear gorm*: a blue man.

Beneath the sagged beams of the loft in which he dossed, he would count the stars through the holes in the slating and listen to the clashing musics coming up from the street. If he couldn't sleep – and often he couldn't – he would sit at the window in his tattered underwear and watch the sailors wandering up from the docks; filtering into the bawdy-houses and grog-shops, to the freak shows and peepshows and streetside burlesques. Some nights he went down and strolled among them, for no other reason than to be among people. To be jostled; crowded; not to be alone.

Moroccans in turbans; teak-faced Indians; handsome Texans with suntans so vividly orange that when Mulvey first saw one he thought the poor Jack was jaundiced. Frenchmen; Dutchmen; Spaniards who smelt of spices. Wine merchants from Burgundy. Acrobats from Rome. One evening he had watched from his seventh-storey perch as a party of opera singers from somewhere in Germany came processing up from Tobacco Wharf, up through the East End like a pageant of judges. They were chorusing 'Messiah' as they majestically went, bestowing mock blessings on the cheering passers-by. Gazing down in wonder from his head-spinning rookery, Mulvey sang it back to them like a liberated slave.

King of Kings!
And Lord of Lords!
And He shall reign for ever and ever!

Most of all he loved the languages of London, the clamorous fanfare of the city in conversation with itself. To hear Italian or even Arabic was nothing unusual; Portuguese and Russian, Shelta and Romany; the mournfully beautiful entreaties and praisings that drifted from the synagogues on a Friday at sunset. Sometimes he heard tongues he could not even name; languages so strange and resistant to penetration that it was hard to believe they were languages at all; that any two speakers in the world could know them. 'Pig Latin' Carny; traveller Pidgin; the rhyme-slang of stall-boys; the 'flash-code' of criminals; the patter of bookies and three-card-tricksters; the drawling patois of graceful Jamaicans and the singsong lilt of Welshmen and Creoles. They borrowed from one another like children trading streamers; a bold lingua franca which anyone could own. It was as though the Tower of Babel had emptied its multitudes into the reeking streets of Whitechapel. Mulvey came from a place where silence was constant as the rain, but never again would he know such an awfulness.

And the cockneys talked as though talking in colours. Brash, blowsy banners of words. He listened for hours as they nattered in the markets, as they dandered through the carnival in Paternoster Square. How he wished he could talk with such brio and bite. He practised in the evenings, over and over; made reverent translations into their tongue.

> *Our old guv'nor,*
> *which dosses in Lewisham,*
> *swelléd be thy moniker.*
> *Thy racket be come;*
> *thy crack-job be done,*
> *in Bow as it is in Lewisham.*
> *Scalp us this day our lump of lead*
> *and let us be bailed for our dodges;*
> *as we backslaps the pox-hounds and Berkshire Hunts*
> *what dodges agin us. (The bumsuckers.)*
> *And jemmy us not into lushery or lurks*
> *but send us skedaddling from blaggery.*
> *For thine is the manor, the flash and the bovver.*
> *Till mother breaks out of the clink. Amen.*

The lexicon of crime became his favourite contemplation. The English possessed as many words for stealing as the Irish had for seaweed or guilt. With rigour, with precision, and most of all with poetry, they had *categorised* the language of thievery into sub-species, like fossilised old deacons baptising butterflies. Every kind of robbery had a verb of its own. Breeds of embezzlement he never knew existed came to him first as beautiful words. Beak-hunting; bit-faking; blagging; bonneting; broading; bug-hunting; buttoning;

buzzing; capering; playing the crooked cross; dipping; dragging; fawney-dropping; fine-wiring; flimping; flying the blue pigeon; gammoning; grifting; half-inching; hoisting; doing the kinchen-lay; legging; lifting; lurking; macing; minning; mizzling; mug-hunting; nailing; outsidering; palming; prigging; rollering; screwing; sharping; shuffling; smatter-hauling; sniding; toolering; vamping; yack-snatching and doing the ream flash pull. Stealing in London sounded like dancing, and Mulvey danced his way through the town like a duke.

In the beginning was the Word and the Word was God. He loved those verbs, their fizzling magnificence: the majesty of their music in his Connemara accent. He stole a notebook and began to collect them. When that one was full, he stole a bigger one. Like the dictionary of his childhood he studied it constantly. It was Bible, cyclopaedia, passport and pillow.

He walked the noisy city like Adam in Eden, reaching out his grateful hand to pluck the fruits. But he wouldn't commit the predictable sin, the cupidity that would cast you out of Paradise and into Newgate Gaol. He stole what he needed – never anything more. There was no point in being greedy, nor any need to be.

And he loved to steal. It made him happy. It gave him what he had never experienced except when singing: a dizzying sense of his own mastery. To live by thievery was to go by your wits, a Free Trade entrepreneur of the alleyway and marketplace.

He dressed himself in the princely togs of the East End flash-boy; the scarlet waistcoats, the spats and cravats, the velvet-collared frock coats and button-down britches; the uniform which announced your thievery to the world and told the world it had better take note of your arrival. The one thing he never stole was his clothes. You couldn't be sure they'd be good enough if you stole them. The account at his little Jewish tailor's was more than a half-year's rent in Connemara. '*Schmatta*' was the Yiddish for fine-cut clothes; '*schmuck*' (literally, 'a penis') for the man who would wear anything less. Pius Mulvey's days of schmuckery were over. To be a robber in the East End was not to be ashamed or cast down, but to be held up to youngsters as an example of possibility. In London it was the criminals who appeared in the songs; the highwaymen and muggers and cutpurses and cracksmen who ran through the city like a seam of gold through a dunghill. Their names were reverently uttered like a communion of saints. Swindling Sal. Joe the Magsman. The fence Ikey Solomons who escaped from Newgate in '31. They dressed as though to parody the class who ruled them. *Beware*, their appearance seemed to say. One day we might take your clothes and put them on. One day the emperor will have no clothes. We will be you. And you will be us. And if you were us, could you last five minutes?

Even in defeat, nobility clung to them. They paraded to the gallows in silvered coaches drawn by teams of sixteen stallions, retinued by fleets of liveried servants and weeping women in gem-studded gowns. The important thing was not that you were about to die, but were about to 'die game', unbroken and disdainful. Such a departure required the sense of the moment which most of them had trained for years to affect. The first time Pius Mulvey went to a hanging he came away envying the dangling victim, who had flung an armful of roses into the crowd as he stalked up the steps of the scaffoldage like an actor. One hand on his hip, the other to his ear – as though he couldn't quite make out the manic applause and would cancel the performance if it didn't increase.

As he dipped into the pockets of the roaring throng around him, Frederick Hall told himself that one fine day he would be every bit as loved as that pouting, glamorous corpse.

Whenever he grew bored with the easiness of stealing he would venture his luck as a pavement balladeer. He tried singing some of the old Galway songs, but the people of London didn't seem to like them. They appeared to find them wearisome or faintly disturbing, and they didn't need to pay to be wearied or disturbed. Dark songs did not play so well in Whitechapel. Perhaps it had darkness enough of its own.

He began to try out the song he had written himself; the ballad of the recruiting sergeant spurned in Connemara. You couldn't possibly sing it in its original form, but if you changed its uniform or clad it in camouflage it might be pressed into earning its maker a supper. He stitched at the text for a couple of nights, affixing ribbons of street names and crests of London slang; unpicking anything too disquieting or too noticeably Irish. Not a jot did it bother him to alter the ensemble. It was tailoring Galway remnants into East End swell-duds. The morning he finished the tacking and tucking, he hurried down to Bethnal Green Market and sang it fourteen times in a row, in the East End inflection he had now begun to master. 'Cockney toe-rag', a constable muttered as he passed. Frederick Hall took it as moment of apotheosis.

> Me and my chum dodgin' down in the Strand,
> When up marches Major wiv sword in one 'and,
> And yarns of his soldierboys fearless and grand;
> Oh, the day bein' cheerful and charming.

> And says 'e, my gay cockerels, now sign up wiv me,
> And it's ten sparklin sovereigns you'll suddenly see,
> Wiv a crown in the bargain I'll toss in for free,
> For to drink the king's elf in the morning.

> Cut along with you, Major, we boldly did say,
> For we loves Piccadilly and 'ere we shall stay;
> To dodge all the night and to dally all day
> Is to live life most cheerful and charming.

> Oh the nancies we chases are free as the air;
> The doxies of Dean Street and sweet Leicester Square,
> And you'd lug us to Ireland with nary a care;
> Where we could get plugged without warning.

> So we'll stay 'ere and play 'ere, flash-lads in the know,
> Where the sweet Thames flows slowly from Richmond to Bow;
> And with said benediction, we bowed very low;
> And bade him be buggered this morning.

One evening in Limehouse, just as he had finished singing it, an alarmingly bearded gentleman in tails and a topper approached him politely and asked if they might speak. Mulvey had noticed him before in the neighbourhood, creeping the midnight alleyways like a burglar. Once or twice he had even considered trying to rob him, for he always seemed ill at ease in Whitechapel. His name was Dickens, the gentleman explained, but he preferred his friends to call him either Charlie or Chaz. Immediately Mulvey felt he was being told a lie. This milksop toff had never been called Chaz, except maybe in his dreams or his mickey-pulling fantasies.

Charlie or Chaz or Charles or Dickens was a writer of stories in literary magazines. He had a great curiosity for the culture of the working man, he said, for the songs and sayings of the labouring classes of London. Anything authentic interested him greatly and he had found Mulvey's song fantastically interesting. Was it terribly old, he wanted to know? How had Mulvey come to learn it? There was a hopefulness in the way he put his questions and Mulvey discerned that an opportunity might lie here; an opening which honesty might well close down.

He had confided to Charlie that he was feeling too hungry to speak and the author had led him into a chop-house across the street and ordered up a dinner which would have satisfied a convocation of bishops. As they ate and drank, Mulvey spoke to him about the song. He had learned it from an aged pickpocket who lived in Holborn, he lied, a Jew who ran a school for young thieves and runaways. It was indeed very old and extremely authentic. Charlie was fascinated; he kept writing down Mulvey's answers, and the faster he wrote them, the faster flowed the lies. Mulvey's ability to lie amazed even himself. Before long he almost believed he was telling the truth, so vivid was the picture of the chuckling, sagacious Israelite, his artful little disciples and the voluble tarts who befriended them. When he ran out of inspiration he started stirring in details from Connemara ballads: the maiden betrayed by the false-hearted aristocrat, the girl of easy virtue murdered by her lover, the poor little waif sent into the workhouse. It was as though he had lived among these imaginary people; as though he had become one of his own fictional characters. Soon Charlie asked if he might copy down the lyric. Mulvey said he would happily sing it again, if only his throat were not so confoundedly dry. A pitcher of ale was hastily ordered and Mulvey sang it two more times. Charlie was trying to scalp him, but that was fine. Charlie was being thoroughly scalped himself. The song was an act of mutual robbery. There was a living to be made from manufacturing the authentic.

'And his name?' asked Dickens, 'the name of the Jew?'

An ugly face arose in Mulvey's memory: the hideous visage of a living gargoyle. The most evil old Jew-hater he had ever met. The parish priest of Derryclare. The thief who had stolen his brother away. Here was an opportunity for small but blissful revenge; to magic the old bastard into what he most detested.

'Fagan,' he said.

Charles Dickens smiled.

'I think you have given me enough,' he said.

CHAPTER XX

THE HARD-LUCK MAN

On a mercilessly hot night in July of 1837, the tenement in which he squatted was set ablaze (by its owner), and Frederick Hall decided to ramble south of the river, to test his luck in another quarter. He tried Southwark for a while but without much success; the natives were careful and had nothing worth robbing anyway. Greenwich proved also a waste of his time. There were too many soldiers and prowling policemen. In Lambeth he fell in with a Glaswegian pickpocket and blackguard called Right McKnight (or so he improbably claimed) who had stolen a vicar's cassock from a laundry in Ealing and was looking for a partner with whom to put it to good use.

'Prating' was the term for what he proposed: the misappropriation carried out by a bogus preacher usually with the aid of a disguised accomplice. It was a useful addition to Mulvey's dictionary and a matter that swelled his admiration for the peoples of Britain once again. How could any language worthy of speech not have a word for that?

Mulvey would smear his visible portions with boot blacking and put on a tunic of coal sacks. Thus made up as 'the convertite African', and accompanied by his converter, the Reverend McKnight, he would roll his eyes and caper at the captivated onlookers, babbling a ceaseless stream of Connemara Irish. McKnight would bellow and point at the heavens, brandishing a crucifix and thunderously rolling his Rs: '*Oh, hearr the pagan parrlance, brrothers and sisterrs. The verry verrnacularr of Luciferr himself. Won't you imparrt a few farrthings forr the converrsion of his trribesmen, who luxurriate this morning in the sewerr of idolatrry.'* Little did they know that what the gibbering infidel was usually reciting was either the Sorrowful Mystery of the Rosary or a random list of villages in the county of Limerick; a region whose indigenes he had always found bothersome.

At the climax of the performance, barbarian Mulvey would be made to sink to his knees in heart-rending reverence and copiously spit upon 'a pagan idol'. (Actually a souvenir statuette of King Leopold of the Belgians, robbed from a junk shop in the Charing Cross Road and beheaded by the Scotsman with a spoon.) A kiss to the crucifix and another menacing blast of full-throated Irish would persuade the last of the doubters to reach for their purses. They knew very well that he wasn't a black man. But whatever he was, it was savage.

From this dodge could be garnered five or even ten pounds a day, as much as a labourer might earn in six months. The Scotsman spent most of his share on gin and whoring, but Mulvey spent most of his own on clothes. Gin didn't interest him and whoring never had. Nothing much interested him except survival and clothes, and collecting new words for stealing.

Sometimes when he had a little money to spare – which happened quite often, for his needs were few – he would send a couple of pounds back to Mary Duane in Carna. But he never wrote. There was nothing to write. He simply couldn't think of anything to say.

McKnight eventually drank himself into Bethlehem madhouse so Mulvey was forced to go out on his own. He didn't mind. It was time for a change. He had always found the Scottish an appealing people, bookish and deliberative as he was himself, but McKnight was not one of their finer ambassadors: a dullard when sober and violently unpredictable when drunk. Mulvey often suspected he had been swindling him on the quiet.

He became a solo performer, the pavement his theatre, with a new drama for each new day. He prided himself on his scope and limitless energy, his lack of requirement for partners or props. Into the street he would saunter every morning, a gambler in a land of heavily stacked odds, outfitted with nothing except his imagination. Sometimes he was an impoverished mariner who had fought against the French; a distressed widower with seven hungry children; a miner who had survived a terrible explosion; a man who had once owned a flower shop in Chelsea before being mercilessly cheated by his unscrupulous partner. Women would weep as he told his tales. Men would beseech him to take their last pennies. Often his stories were so completely convincing that he would even weep himself.

The other hard-luck men who worked the area accused him of being greedy and not giving them a chance. When he refused to accept their proposals for regulating the market, one of them 'ratted him in' to the police. The judge proved a less receptive audience than some Mulvey had known. Frederick Hall was found guilty of obtaining with deceptions and sentenced to seven years' hard labour in Newgate. He was stripped in the Gate-House and carefully searched, being forced to bend low so they could investigate his rectum, then shorn of his hair and blasted with a fire hose and examined by a doctor who passed him as healthy. He was dusted with a powder that was said to kill lice; then invited to swallow a measure of saltpetre, which the guards said would quell your natural desires. Declining to swallow it, he was strapped to a chair and had it pumped down his gullet with the aid of a funnel. Naked except for a bloodstained towel, he was chained to a leash and led into the prison; through cast-iron gates, along whitewashed landings, up the metal staircase to the Governor's office. There Prisoner Hall and two other newcomers were given a talk by the Governor's assistant, a man with the gentle smile of a paedophile uncle. There was a plaque on his desk inscribed with the debatable words: WE MUST CEASE TO DO EVIL & LEARN TO DO WELL. They had probably heard many things about Newgate, he said, but they were not to believe these exaggerated tales. The institution only existed to help them. Punishment could be an act of deepest love.

The cell in which they lodged him was a seven-foot cube with an opaque leaded window the size of a handkerchief. Moonlight was vaguely discernible through the greasy grating. Mulvey sat on the floor and began to count the black bricks. By the time he got to a hundred 'lights-out' was called and what he had thought was the moonlight was briskly extinguished. He heard the slam of cell doors receding down his landing like the doors of a train preparing to leave a station. Something small with a tail scurried across his bare feet. It was quite a short time afterwards when the screaming started; he heard it echoing up from the landings below. Mulvey didn't understand it; there was little point in screaming. It was only the next day that he learned what lay behind it. The prisoners had more to contend with than mere incarceration. The Governor of Newgate had progressive ideas.

The loneliness of the cell at night was something for which Mulvey had had time to prepare. Solitude was part of the condition of Connemara. What stunned him was that isolation was also enforced by day. Companionship was bad for men in prison, so went the Governor's idealistic policy; the evil of the hardened would infect the merely misguided. Association of any kind was not allowed: not even with the guards or the Visiting Committee. Any human relationship was the enemy of reform, an act of unchristian cruelty to the already unfortunate prisoner and by extension to the civilisation he might hope one day to rejoin. When he was taken from his cell for his exercise or his work detail each inmate was clamped into a black leather hood before being allowed to enter the yard. The mask had minuscule slits through which you might see and an arrangement of pinpricks through which you might breathe and it was bolted around your neck with a padlock and choke-chain that would strangle you if you raised your arms above your head. More to the point, it made each man equally unrecognisable; absolutely identical to all his fellows, as they broke the stones or turned the treadmill and ceased to do evil and learned to do well.

It was put about by the more enthusiastically progressive of the guards that they, too, sometimes donned the masks; so you could never tell exactly who was working beside you, who was screaming and clawing at the air. Were his agonies real or a matter of performance? If you were being reformed, that wouldn't matter. You would be aware that conversation was forbidden under pain of the scourge. If an inmate was heard by a warder to have spoken to another, he would receive fifty lashes of the bullwhip for every word he had said. If he was unreformed or unwise enough to do it again, he was put into solitary confinement for the remainder of his sentence. There were men in the windowless depths of Newgate who had not seen another life-form for fifteen years. Not a prisoner, nor a guard, nor even a rat: for their cells were so thick that nothing could penetrate them and in any case were kept in darkness every hour of every day. Even at chapel, isolation was maintained. Each inmate knelt in his own partitioned booth from which nothing was visible except the cross above the altar. But they were allowed to sing and to respond to the prayers; so attendance at chapel, though voluntary, was widespread.

Mulvey was regarded as an excellent prisoner. He gave no trouble and made no complaints and the only time he had to be punished – two hundred lashes for saying 'I didn't hear you' – he had taken his scourging like a man. Alone in his cell he had wept that night, his back and buttocks flaming with pain, the base of his spine a nub of pure agony; but he discerned a small victory in what had happened. As soon as they opened his handcuffs and ordered him to rise, he had pulled on his britches and his sackcloth shirt and walked straight to the warder who had flailed the flesh off him and held out his hand in a gesture of thanks. He was so dazzled with pain that he could barely see his torturer. He could hardly even stand. But he made himself do it.

The warder, a Scottish sadist who had often raped insane prisoners, and had twice raped Mulvey and threatened to castrate him, had seemed astonished as he accepted his victim's outstretched hand. Mulvey had put on a penitent face and given a series of small, humble nods. He knew the Governor and the Visiting Committee were watching from the gallery and he wanted to make an enduring impression. As he left the Correction Hall he passed directly beneath them, performing the sign of the cross as he did so. One of the visiting ladies was quietly weeping at the scene, as though the reformation she had just observed was somehow too much for her. Frederick Hall paused and bowed to the lady. As she sobbed and collapsed into the arms of the Governor, Mulvey knew he had won this battle. To allow yourself to be flogged without getting something in return was not just unmanly; it was stupid.

Never again was he whipped or punished. On the contrary, he began to be given small privileges. He noticed that the guards were opening his door before anyone else's; leaving it ajar after lights-out was called. One night they failed to close it at all so he closed it himself as a warder was passing, making sure that the officer could see what he was doing. Learning that he could read, the Governor arranged for him to be given some books. A bible at first, then a *Complete Works of Shakespeare*. Prisoner Hall wrote to the Governor to express his thanks, being careful to say he was undeserving of such luxuries and to ask for nothing else. A week later more books arrived, along with a tilly-lamp by which he might read at night. By now he had learned something important about English authority. The less you asked for, the more you got.

He read the bible completely, then all of Shakespeare, then the fables of Aesop and the lives of the poets. Milton quickly became his favourite; he read all twelve volumes of *Paradise Lost*. The description of Hell in the opening book – where 'hope never comes that comes to all' – reminded him strongly of tormented Newgate. *O how unlike the place from whence they fell.* But the thunder of the language utterly thrilled him: the fiery march of the imperial rhythms. It became his secret amusement to baptise the warders with the weird names of Milton's devils. Moloch and Belial, Asmadai and Baalim. The Governor he silently thought of as Mulciber, the architect of Pandemonium.

He grew fitter and stronger than he had ever been. The regime meant regular food and regular sleep, both enforced by the dread of punishment. (Prisoner Refused Supper: thirty lashes. Awake After Lights-Out: a week in solitary.) Tobacco, snuff and alcohol were forbidden, so his lungs grew cleaner and his thinking more clear. Work had hardened his muscles to rocklike bulges. By the end of Mulvey's second year in Newgate he was able to lift his own body-weight in broken stones. Even the solitude rarely bothered him any more. 'The mind is its own place,' Milton contended, 'and in itself can make a Heaven of Hell.' If that wasn't quite true, it was certainly worth the effort. Mulvey came to think of the door of his cell as keeping out the crazies rather than keeping him in.

In time he was moved to a larger cell, the window of which looked down over the Gate-House. At night he could see the guards chatting and joking with the small army of beggars who congregated outside, pleading to be given shelter for the night. It was widely known among the poor of London that the Newgate screws would sometimes let you in for a penny; permit you to sleep in an unoccupied cell.

It took him a while to reckon how he might turn the view to

his advantage, but before too long the answer came to him. If you kept watch through the window early in the morning you could see prisoners being released at the end of their sentence. Their names were read aloud by the Sergeant-at-Arms in the gateway, and if you earwigged very carefully you might just make them out. Even if you didn't, you could notice on your way to the yard which cells had been emptied that morning and were now in the process of being de-loused. If you put these facts together and waited for your moment you were in a situation of considerable power without danger.

No man in Newgate could inform on another and hope to live to the end of that week. But you could say what you liked about those who were no longer inside without any fear of retribution. Mulvey began a careful programme of reporting to the Governor, always snitching on a prisoner whom he knew had just been released. You couldn't do it often or it would look too suspicious; but once in a while it could make you appear zealous, particularly if you did it in tones of regret. 'Inmate C34 talked last night, sir.' 'B92 proposed an indecency to me, sir.' 'F71 told me his name, sir. I'm concerned he might be interfering with my being reformed, sir.' Mulvey's co-operative attitude to authority was noted; it began to gain him rich returns.

He sensed the other prisoners turn against him. In the yard they stopped looking at him, or handing him tools. Mulvey didn't care. If anything, he was glad. The more he was ostracised, the more the authorities regarded him as one of their successes. He was asked to attend before the Visiting Committee where he gave a powerful speech in favour of the separation system. Mouse-droppings began to appear in his gruel; a shard of glass secreted in a cake of soap sliced open his forearm. He thought of these tribulations as forms of promotion, rites of passage to a higher state. He started slashing his own skin whenever that was possible, reporting attacks on his person that had never happened. Every time he did it he was moved to a more comfortable cell, until finally he was moved to the Governor's own house, where only the very richest of criminals were lodged and the cells had feather beds and wallpaper.

Half-way through the fortieth month of his sentence he was given a special duty as a reward for his progress. One prisoner was needed to tidy the lower yard at night, to grease the gears and clean the chain of the treadmill, to scrape the pigeon mess from the flagstones and bollards. Such a man, said the Governor, was a lucky man indeed, for he would be required to perform this important work alone and thus would be excused the wearing of his mask. He would also be permitted to speak to the warder-on-duty, but purely about matters of work. The official minutes of the meeting record that Prisoner Hall was seen to weep with gratitude. 'God bless you, sir, for I don't deserve it.'

The lower yard was bounded on three sides by the guardhouse and cellblocks. The fourth side was enclosed by a twenty-foot wall, mortared into the top of which was a barrier of rotating spikes; a *cheval-de-frise* in the English dictionary, 'the death-horse' in Newgate's implacable vernacular. In the angle where the wall abutted on the guardhouse, about five feet below the iron-thorned summit, a small metal cistern was poorly secured; and in a tight space above it there were no spikes.

It seemed curious to Mulvey that such a space had been left unprotected. It was as though the cheval-de-frise had been made nine inches too narrow, or perhaps the wall had been built too wide. Respectfully he pointed out the oversight to one of the warders. Surely it was a temptation to the more ruthless of Newgate; to those unfortunates less reformed than Mulvey himself. The guard laughed quietly and looked up at the death-horse. The last wretch who had tried to escape had impaled himself so thoroughly that the only way to get him down was to cut away that section. He had died in such atrocious agony that nobody had attempted it again. His screams had been heard fully half a mile away.

The wall and its possibilities began to interest Mulvey.

As he worked, he would position himself in such a way that he could always see it; could note its cracks and small protrusions, the jags where the grout had fallen away. It became his habit to study that wall with the attentiveness of a detective scrutinising a forged banknote. Mentally he divided it into sixteen sections and he made it his task to memorise the details of each. With breadcrumbs and threads and flakes of loose plaster he sketched it out on the floor of his cell. A crumb was a stub-end of brick to which a hand might grasp; a thread was a tiny cleft where a toe could be inserted. With powderings of mortar he attempted to join them, to trace a climbable course from flagstones to cistern. But no matter how you plotted it, it couldn't be done: not unless you were to sprout an extra hand.

He began to present for his duties earlier than was required of him, to stay in the yard as long as the warder would allow. Often as he worked he would think about his mother, an old saying she would come out with when times were hard at home. No mountain exists which may not be defeated. Jesus will show you the way across.

For two months he considered the problem of the wall, without realising that already he had the means of solving it in his hands. And then it occurred to him. Quietly; simply. Like the click of a key in a complicated lock.

It was a Sunday night in February of 1841. Most of the empire was at peace. Its Queen was celebrating the first anniversary of her marriage, for which instance of happy incest the Padre was conducting a service of thanksgiving. Almost every guilty soul in Newgate attended. The chapel was resounding with gratitude to God.

> *There is a fountain filled with blood,*
> *Drawn from Emmanuel's veins;*
> *And sinners plunged beneath that flood*
> *Lose all their guilty stains.*

He waited, the thief, and he listened to the singing: the prisoners murdering the hymn. The duty guard that night was the flogging Scotsman. It was a blessing Prisoner Hall had truly not expected.

Moloch opened the gate with a key on a chain and Mulvey followed him into the yard. Dusk was falling; everything was golden. The windows of the cells were glimmering with fire. A blackbird was drinking from a puddle in the cobblestones and he cocked a head at the invaders as though he resented them.

The previous morning the treadmill had jammed, as Pius Mulvey knew it would. A nail dropped into its workings had seen to that. Carefully he opened the maple-wood panel that housed the cog-works and pulleys at the base. He unhooked the filthy drive-chain from the teeth of the gears. It was heavier than he had imagined. About twelve feet long.

'What do you think you're at?'

Mulvey looked up at his saggy-jowled abuser. An odd thought came into his mind. He wondered if the man might somehow know what was going to happen to him, if perhaps he had awoken early that morning with a vague premonition of pain and doom. Had he wondered, as he bade farewell to his wife, if this were the last time he would say goodbye to anyone? Had he felt as he walked into Newgate Gaol, as his hundreds of broken victims must have felt, and as Mulvey had felt on numberless occasions, that the sun was already going down on his life: that the moment had come for hope to be abandoned?

'Sir, the Governor asked me to oil the chain, sir.'

With that single lie Mulvey's escape was effected. His shadow had already broken free from his body and flapped away over the long-studied wall. Lying to a guard was punishable by two months in the basement, in a cell little bigger than a coffin. The one thing he knew was that he would never see that cell. He would go over the wall or they would unskiver his corpse from it. But he would not wake up in Newgate tomorrow.

'Oil, you say?'

'Sir, yes, sir. Has to be oiled, sir. Or it won't work, sir.'

'He didn't say nothin about oiling to me.'

'Sir – I won't do it if you say so, sir. If you clear it with the Governor, sir. I don't want to get into no trouble, sir. He seemed very adamant, sir.'

'Adamant?'

'Sir, yes, sir.'

'What's that mean?'

'Sir, it means keen, sir. That he wanted it done, sir.'

'Sharp, aren't you, Mulvey?'

'Sir, I don't know, sir. If you say so, sir.'

'Sharp for the grovelling bastard of a diseased Irish bitch. What are you?'

'Sir, a grovelling bastard, sir.'

'What was your mother?'

'Sir, a diseased Irish bitch, sir.'

'Well stop lazing, you pimple of mange, if he's so bloodied adamant. We all know you're never done annointing his arse.'

Moloch walked away and looked up at the sky. Mulvey quickly slipped off his boots. The blackbird ascended with a flutter to a ledge. The men in the chapel were singing a new song.

> *O God, our help in ages past,*
> *Our hope for years to come,*
> *Our shelter from the stormy blast,*
> *And our eternal home.*

He picked up a rock and walked quietly up to the Scottish warder and struck him hard in the back of the skull. As he slumped to the ground like a ripped sack of shit, Mulvey began beating him hard with the rock, pummelling him in the face until his cheekbones collapsed and his left eye burst open like a shattered egg. He tried to call out and Mulvey stepped on his neck, grinding his foot as though crushing a snake. He began to gurgle and whisper for mercy. It was tempting not to give it to him, to let him suffer before death, but Mulvey told himself that would be needlessly indecent. He sank to his hunkers, murmured an Act of Contrition in his dying rapist's ear and bashed in what was left of his face with the rock.

He dipped a finger in his victim's blood and scrawled two lines from Milton on a dusted flagstone.

> *To do aught good never will be our task,*
> *But ever to do ill our sole delight.*

He unbuckled the guard's belt and took it off him; tied it in a loop through the end link of the drive-chain. Flung it with every splinter of his strength. It sailed heftily upwards, clunking on the wall. Fell back down with a nauseating clangour. The second throw sent the belted link drifting over the summit. Mulvey yanked on it. It began to slide. Stuck in the prongs of the cheval-de-frise.

He took a hard run, somehow clambered up as far as the end of the chain. Climbed its thick links, his naked toes clinging. Grabbed a tight hold on the stanchions of the death-horse. A breeze caught the spikes and spun them slowly. Immediately his hands were flittered with cuts, but he hung on, moving himself – swinging himself – around the upper walls of the yard, until he came to the leaking, corroded cistern. Planted his foot on the ashy rim. It gave a skreeking lurch as it took his weight. His arms were shaking. His hands felt like anvils. A lunge gained him the summit as the cistern crashed into the yard. He clambered over and dropped to the ground, his whole body sopping with blood and rusty water.

Trailing gore like a stuck pig, he began to totter in the direction of the river. By the time he was in sight of it, he was almost fainting. It was no use. He would never make it this way. As the trill of police whistles rose up from the distance he slipped back through the alleyways and coach-lanes in the direction of Newgate, crossing the back gardens and stealing clothes from a line. A workman's overalls. A soldier's old greatcoat. He wrapped his hands tightly to staunch the bleeding and staggered onwards, light-headed with fear. It occurred to him now that there still was a way. If he could stay on his feet for another five minutes, he would not be caught. He would never be caught. Onwards he lurched, back towards the prison. Its blackness loomed up at him like a ghost-hulk in a story. Back to the prison. Only the prison. When he was close enough to see the bars on its windows, Frederick Hall knew he was a free man now.

He spent the night in the gateway huddled with the beggars, occasionally banging on the door and pleading to be allowed in. He stayed there for a week, until his wounds had begun to heal.

The harder he banged on the door, the more they told him to go away.

CHAPTER XXI

THE SCHOOLMASTER

The further WICKED DEEDS of Pius Mulvey, also
known as THE MONSTER OF NEWGATE; his Mockery
of Lawfulness and other Dark Matters.

Accounts of the atrocity were published in the newspapers. Most
were edited or heavily censored, the details shaded over as being far
too gruesome to be placed where women and children might read
them. Some articles described his victim as 'a married man with a
family'; others as 'an officer of great experience' or 'a devout
Wesleyan and abstainer from alcohol who had entered public service
to succour the unfortunate'. No doubt, Mulvey thought, he had
been all those things, as well as many others at the same time. The
numerous mentions of his charitable work were hardly surprising.
There were plenty of leering curs who would throw you a penny
mainly because they liked to watch you bow.

His own description was printed too, and just like the dead
man's it was accurate, if incomplete: *A cold cunning thug; irreversibly
corrupted; a 'lone-wolf' who will gorge on the unsuspecting.* It did not
offend him to be described in such terms. It was nothing he hadn't
thought about himself at some point, and anyway, every story
needed its villain and its hero. It was just that this story had two
villains, not one. The description applied both to killer and victim.

Posters materialised on the streets of London offering twenty
pounds' reward for his capture or shooting. The sketch which
appeared on them showed the face of a murderer, a narrow-eyed,
ape-chinned, sneering Beelzebub, but Mulvey could see in it the
ghost of his own. The artist had merely done what the ballad-maker
does; what is done by the historian, the General and politician, and
by everyone who wants to sleep with an easy conscience. He had

embellished some details and understated others. You couldn't really blame him for doing his job.

Sightings of 'Frederick Hall, the Monster of Newgate' began to be reported all over the country – in every conurbation except the East End, where the bludgeoning of a prison officer would have won you the Freedom of Whitechapel. It was to his rowdy old quarter that the murderer returned, slipping back into its labyrinths and catacombs. Pius Mulvey of Ardnagreevagh was his pseudonym now.

Every day he stole the newspapers to learn of the Monster's latest appearance. It was rumoured that he had been seen in the northern wilds of Scotland; in the ghettos of Liverpool; in a graveyard near Dover, trying to smash off his manacles with a blacksmith's chisel. Six of the poor were arrested for his crime, and embarrassingly for the police, who were already hated by the poor, five of them confessed to it under vigorous questioning (the sixth notoriously escaping from Manchester Prison disguised as the chaplain's mistress).

Gradually the details of what had happened that night came to be 'leaked' to the gutter press. In the guise of condemning their widely read competitors, the quality dailies published them too. The frightful particular of the lines of poetry inscribed in the victim's blood encouraged frenzied speculation, as their inscriber had carefully calculated they should. What half-way normal man, escaping from prison, would take the time to do such a thing? What could the eerie couplet mean? Was that part of the story true or invented? It began to be whispered around the East End that 'Frederick Hall' must be a *nom de guerre*. The crime had been done by somebody else. The guard had been murdered by a colleague he had cuckolded. The murderer was a member of the Royal Family on a visit, a syphilitic minor Duke who had suddenly gone insane. The slaying was the work of a bizarre Masonic cult to which the slaughtered officer had once belonged. (The latter piece of hearsay garnered even more currency when his widow appeared to confirm in a newspaper interview that her husband had indeed been a member of a Masonic lodge. When denied by the Lodge's captain in a subsequent interview, it came to be regarded as gospel truth.)

'Freddie Hall' was an *agent provocateur* for the Crown. A religious fanatic. A secret agent of the Chartists. 'Freddie Hall' had been billeted in the Governor's house. Permitted to work without his mask. Given books. Allowed to speak. Moved around Newgate like a guest in an hotel. Darker rumours began to circulate. The popular papers stoked up the coals. The prison was now said to be a nest of Satanists. If you gave each letter of the monster's name its corresponding numerical value and added together the resulting digits, you would come up with a total of 66. And if you appended the 6 you got from the capital F, you would be left with the number of the biblical beast. It was the *Tomahawk* magazine which first pointed out that 'Freddie Hall' was an anagram of Hellfire Dad!

Emboldened by the fact of his own escape, Mulvey began using the now infamous name as a verb; as a schoolboy might scratch his initials into a penny to see how long it takes before it comes back to him. Before too long, it did come back. To freddie a person was to beat him senseless. Men were being freddied all over the country. Oxford had freddied Cambridge in the annual boat race. One of these days those ungrateful bastard Irish would get the bloody freddying they so thoroughly deserved.*

Every time he heard a rumour concerning the monster, Mulvey tried his absolute hardest to scotch it, knowing that would encourage the rumour-monger to tell it again, and to tell it even more imaginatively the next time he did so. Men in grog-shops would quietly confide to him that they knew *for a fact* who had done the awful crime. They had met him, or were related to him, or had once had a drink with him. The wife had a brother who had a chum a screw in Newgate, and *he* said the whole affair was a cover-up by the Jews, and if you didn't believe it you could *ask him yourself.*

When finally it was suggested in the liberal *Morning Chronicle*, by a scrupulous young reporter who had interviewed many of the prison's former inmates, that Frederick Hall, the Monster of Newgate, was in fact a cunning Irishman called Murphy or Malvey,

---

*See Henry Mayhew's monograph 'The Speech and Language of the London Poor' (1856). '"*Freddie*"' (*n*): *a fatally violent assault. "To Freddy" (vb): to attack or to murder. "Freddying" (adj.): an expletive common among criminals and women of a certain character.'* Soon the term entered the lexicon of literature. To freddie an author was to give him an unnecessarily harsh review. – GGD

who had contrived his crime to look like the work of a madman, Pius Mulvey left the city and quickly headed north. *Punch* magazine picked up on the item and scoffed at it. No Paddy would be intelligent enough to think of such a plan. Most of them had only recently swung down from the trees.

Eighteen months were spent rambling the north of England and the borderlands of Scotland from Berwick to Gretna Green; then the midlands and the eastern part of Wales; then down to western Devon and into Cornwall, where Lancelot and Merlin once walked with the elect. Often the fugitive found work at the harvest: the planting time, too, sometimes was good to him. Picking apples or sowing corn was a pleasant disguise; easy to blend with the hordes of migrant Irishmen who filled England's meadows at those times of the year. Their accents stirred memories he tried hard to put away. The old nights of singing. The nights with Mary Duane. To think about her brought a guilt he found difficult to bear. He could not endure their company when they started into singing.

For a month he was a gang-man, digging foundations for railway tracks. One entire winter he spent on the outskirts of Sheffield, where a grain merchant was building a Gothic castle, an enormous roofless barn of a place, the size of Westport church. The merchant and his family slept in their current mansion, Mulvey and the other workers in a wigwam on the site. At the first stirring of spring, he quietly moved on. He never stayed in one spot for too long.

For a while he fell in with Lord Johnny Danger's Travelling Circus and worked at setting up and taking down the tent. It was work he liked, it was simple and pleasing, and yet it required a rational mind. The tent was a three-dimensional theorem from geometry, a vast conglomeration of ropes and hooks, of poles and couplings and bolts and rivets, with only one correct way to put them all together. Mulvey could see a way of doing it more quickly and was given charge of the tentboys by the grateful ringmaster. Under his direction, this little Irish tinkerman, they learned to fling up the entire framing in less than two hours. He loved to sit looking at the naked tent; the skeleton of the dragon King Arthur might have speared.

He felt oddly at home among the freaks and bearded ladies, the homunculus clowns and pig-faced wrestlers. To make a living out of perceived inadequacy seemed a brave thing to Mulvey; an effort requiring a measure of true adaptability, which by now was the quality he most esteemed. After a show there were plenty of girls; sometimes a drinking session that went on until dawn. But the happy times were not to last. One day while dismantling a cage he was bitten by a lion and lost the greater part of his left foot. His wound was cauterised by the harlequin who doctored the animals, and a wooden clog carved for him by one of the trapeze-boys, from a broken piece of signboard that had once been made to read THE UGLIEST BEAST IN THE WORLD. The upside-down W seemed like a capital M. 'M is for Mulvey,' the trapeze-boy smiled.

They kept him on for a couple of months but he knew he had become a liability. He wasn't able to manage the tent work any more, nor was he truly needed to direct it. Others had learned from him how it was done and in fact had found ways to improve on it. Neither could he shovel or sweep or scrub: and he was afraid to go near the shabby old furbag that had mauled him. A Piedmontese acrobat helped him learn to walk again, showed him how to shift his balance and change his centre of gravity. They gave him the position of advance-man for a while; his task was to go ahead of the caravan into the next town and pass out handbills or complimentary tickets. One day in York he had performed his duties and sat on a bridge looking down on the Ouse, waiting for the others to trundle into view. By nightfall they hadn't, and he knew they wouldn't now. They hadn't had the heart to tell him he wasn't wanted, and for that much at least he felt something like gratitude. But it wouldn't help him much, and he knew that, too. Once again he was alone in a world of strangers.

The winter of '42 was devastatingly harsh, by far the worst in living memory. Snow began to fall in early November, followed by multiple freezing frosts that left the few leaves on the trees like steel-hard blades. The roads of rural England became ramparts of slush, buried under yards of ice and frozen mud. Mulvey tried begging, but it didn't come easily to him; and country people were unimpressed by his poverty and lameness. Lameness was nothing in the winter of '42. Half-beggared themselves, they had nothing to steal.

The new year came but the weather did not change. Soon came February. The weather grew worse. One day near Stoke he happened upon an amiable Welshman, a frighteningly emaciated scarecrow of a man whose legs looked as if you could snap them with a twist of your hand. William Swales was a poor schoolmaster of Mulvey's own age, on his way to seek a position at the village of Kirkstall near Leeds. He had little in the way of food or refreshment but what morsels he had he was surprisingly willing to share. He was fond of the Irish, he let Mulvey know, because his mother had run a boarding house on Holy Island near Anglesey, a port directly across from Dublin, and she had always found Irishmen scrupulously clean. Swales himself was not so convinced, but the Irishmen had paid for his grub and his tutelage, so he felt he owed their countrymen something of a debt regardless of their hygiene or deportment.

They spent nineteen days together walking the road towards the north and nineteen cold nights in barns or byres. Often as they trudged the slush-filled byways, they would talk about matters of scholarship. Mulvey found such conversations a surprising pleasure. Though his newfound associate was erudite and eloquent, Mulvey could keep up in general discourse and sometimes even best him.

Swales was a classicist, an old-school man. He knew music and geography, poetry and history: all manner of legends and ancient tales. But his greatest love was mathematics. Numbers were so mysterious and yet so simple and beautiful. 'For instance,' he would say, 'where would we be without Nine? When you think about it, Mulvey, where would we be? The neatness, man. The utter perfection. It isn't quite Ten, I'll grant you that. Ten, after all, is the emperor of numbers. But it's so much more than poor old Eight; a darling little number in its own right of course, and a pleasant sort of number, but not Nine. You'd go to bed with Eight but you'd marry Nine. The sheer, cunning, marvellously bumsucking, miraculously bloody *nineness* of it.'

Mulvey found this variety of patter intriguing but often tried to undermine it purely to while away the hours. Nine was a number much like any other, he would maintain, but not quite as useful as most. You couldn't use it to count the days of the week, the months of the year, the deadly sins, the decades of the rosary, the counties of Ireland or even the teeth in your dense Welsh head. Swales would scoff and roll his eyes. Nine was magical. Nine was *Godly*. You could multiply Nine by any other number, and the digits of your answer, if you kept adding them together, would always add up to Nine. (A whole day was passed, from Woodhouse to Doncaster, in Mulvey fruitlessly trying to disprove this contention without having recourse to fractions or percentages, entities Swales regarded as actually evil. 'Fractions are illegitimate,' he often averred. 'The bastards of Outer Mathematica.')

He had a more than middling bass singing voice, a thing Mulvey found startling in such a thin man; when he sang he seemed to rumble like an antique cello. He taught Pius Mulvey his favourite song, a nonsensical sea-shanty you could chant as a march, and together they would sing it as they crunched the snowy lanes, the scholar's sonority putting much-needed gravitas beneath Mulvey's uncertain and piping tenor.

> *One night betimes he went to bed, for he had caught a fever,*
> *Said he, I am a handsome man, and I'm the gay deceiver.*
> *His candle just at twelve o'clock, began to burn quite palely,*
> *A ghost stepped up to his bed-head and said,*
> *'BEHOLD! MISS BAILEY!'*

They would bellow the last three words as loud as they could. It became a contest to see which of them could roar the most ferociously. Often Pius Mulvey let the other man win, simply because he liked him and wanted to please him. He had no ferocity at all, the skinny little schoolmaster. He had never won anything in his life.

Singing was a way to keep up the spirits, but Mulvey was finding it harder to maintain his composure. His ravaged foot pulsated with agony. The pains in his back were growing worse by the day. One morning he woke up soaked with dew, fingertips numb; nose and eyes streaming. A strange itching sensation was irritating his scalp. When he scratched it, his fingernails came back bloodied. An arrow of horror stabbed through Pius Mulvey. His hair was crawling with lice.

He wept with shame and loathing as Swales shaved him bald, as he plunged his head into the icy stream by the roadside. Had there been an easy way of dying he would have taken it, then. He did not speak a single word for the next two days.

'We're nearing Leeds,' Swales would smile. Everything would be fine when they got to Leeds, as though they were walking the golden highway to Paradise. The Yorkshireman was the decentest cully in England; he would always give a fellow a fair crack of the whip. He was a man of his word, the Yorkshireman was, not a twister or a bounder like some Swales could mention. There would be work for Mulvey when they got to Leeds.

'Maybe find ourselves a couple of good girls, eh, Mulvey, my flower? Settle down. We'll live like princes. Wine and sweet cake and a pork chop for breakfast. And Queen of Puddings for lunch, by Christ!'

In the meantime they ate anything edible they could find along the road: roots, leaves, wild herbs and cresses, the few berries not picked off the blackened shrubs by the birds. Sometimes they ate the bony birds themselves; occasionally they were fortunate enough to happen upon a starving grouse. One morning near Ackworth they found a dead cat in the lane and had a fire built and lit in a nettled ditch before each man said what the other had been thinking: he would rather go hungry than eat a cat.

It was a marvel to Mulvey that to talk about food seemed almost the same thing for Swales as to eat it. It appeared to give him genuine sustenance, and oddly Mulvey never found it an irritation. In time he even began to anticipate today's feast; the banquet of words his companion would cook up as they tramped the frosted fields and slithery canal paths. 'A roast swan, Mulvey, and a platter of oozing steaks. Sticks of celery and boiled asparagus. Potatoes the size of your Irish head. Cheeses, by Jesus, and Tuscany Muscadee and a flagon of hot cider to wash it all down.'

'That's only a titbit,' Mulvey would say. 'What about the main dish?'

'Coming to it, coming to it. Hold your horses, man. A wild bugger of a boar with a Bramley in his chops. A bathful of gravy and another one of claret. Oranges from Seville in brandy sauce. Served up by Helen of Troy. In her drawers!'

'Well that'd do for myself well enough, I suppose. But are you not having anything for yourself, Willie, no?'

And so it went, from day to starving day. 'To eat one's words' was an English slang expression; to withdraw some foolish or unwise thing you had said. But poor William Swales seemed to eat his words literally. His student learned to do it, too.

There were times when Mulvey suspected the master was so ill that he wouldn't last the night, never mind see Leeds. He coughed up spumes of watery blood. Shivers racked him so badly that he couldn't hold a cup. Through all of it he kept up a stream of quips and ventriloquism, as though he knew he would die if he stopped laughing for even an instant.

On the first of March, 1843, they left the town of Gildersome at five in the morning. Three hours later the dawn came up, and as the cold sun yellowed the snowy fields, William Swales began to sing a Hosanna. He nudged at trudging Mulvey and pointed up ahead of them, to the smokestacks and black steeples of Leeds in the distance. It was the Feast of Saint David, Master Swales pointed out. The holy hero of Welshmen everywhere.

All day they hiked like weary soldiers, but the road was hard and progress slow. At some point they got lost and appeared to be doubling back; by four o'clock the dusk was beginning to shadow the land. A hobo with the curious name of Bramble Prunty met them near Castleford and counselled them to be careful. The local constabulary were hard sons-of-bitches, he said. They would fling you in the bridewell for vagrancy just as soon as look at you; maybe give you a kicking simply for the fun of it. The best option for a doss was to go deep into the woods. The trees were thick and the forest floor dry and the constables never bothered to look in there. Two lads with a mutchkin of gin might have themselves a good carouse, with no uninvited callers to cause any distress. Assuming the man was looking for drink, Mulvey said he regretted that they had none to offer. The tramp gave a grin and produced an earthen flask from his coat. 'Ten shillings,' he said with a greedy stare. It was nine shillings and sixpence more than the market rate but they bargained him down to a pair of shoes.

Night had fallen by the time they found a place to camp. The wood on the ground was too damp to burn so Swales lit a fire with a few of his shirts and Mulvey went off in search of water. The air was so cold that the trees were cracking. When he got back to the camp, his shuddering companion was tossing his philosophy texts into the flames.

'Heraclitus said every bloody thing in the world is made of fire. Now he knows, the daft Greek sodomite.'

'Willie – that's terrible. You'll need your books.'

'Doctor Faustus burnt his. Didn't do him no good. Least you and me get a little warmth in our sainted arses out of mine, eh?' He looked into his knapsack and gave a small laugh. 'What say'st thou, liege? Shakespeare or Chaucer?'

'Shakespeare'd burn longer,' Mulvey said.

'Ah, nuncle,' sighed Swales, 'but Chaucer'd burn *sweeter*.' And he tossed *The Canterbury Tales* into the snapping flames. 'Burn thy soul, thou whoreson zed.'

The rotgut they had bartered from the vagabond was evenly shared, though Mulvey handed over an extra swig of his own. It had been Swales's Sunday shoes that had helped to procure it. Apart from that and a handful of tea and a small loaf stolen by Mulvey in Dewsbury, there was nothing to keep out the blasting cold.

They burnt their way through the history of English literature, from *The Dream of the Rood* up to Keats's *Endymion*, sparing only Shakespeare from execution by fire. (Though Act III of *King Lear* was put to a purpose its author had not intended when the gin met the lining of Swales's famished stomach. 'Blow winds blow,' he chuckled miserably as he squatted. 'And crack your cheeks,' cackled Mulvey in return.)

By midnight all the drink was gone, but it hadn't had the effect for which Mulvey had hoped. He was still sober enough to be able to think and his thoughts became black, as he knew they would. It was the last night he and William Swales would spend together. For all the brave talk of the glories of Leeds, Mulvey knew the place would have nothing to offer him. He had been up this end of England before; had observed what was needed to survive in such cities. Mill work or labouring required physical strength, a stamina he simply didn't have any more. He had seen the battalions of grim-faced men who assembled at the gates of the factories in the mornings, hoping to be picked by the gangers for a shift. Strong men with hungry families at home. Men who would labour for twelve straight hours without even pausing for a sup of water. The foremen would saunter up and down the line like corporals, selecting the beefier candidates with a nod, rejecting the pitiful implorings of the rest. They weren't all brutes;

they were merely realistic. There wasn't a bossman from Brighton to Newcastle who would give a hobbling cripple a start.

Leeds would mean nothing but another clutch of tribulations, in a colder and rainier climate than London. Swales would go on to his situation in Kirkstall; Mulvey would be thrown back on his jaded wits in a city whose workings he did not know. To revise the life of thievery seemed an insurmountable thing to him now; a wall he had no heart left to climb. It occurred to him darkly as he gazed into the spitting campfire that he would be better off at this moment had he remained in Newgate.

'Penny for 'em, nuncle,' Swales enquired.

'Zero,' said Mulvey.

The scholar looked up, his face reddened by the flames.

'Nine times zero,' Mulvey said. 'It gives you zero.'

Swales nodded sorrowfully, as though admitting to something. 'So it does, my old gallowglass. Pity, that.'

'I should say goodbye to you tomorrow, Willie. You know that, I think.'

'Don't be a lummox, man. We're off to make our fortunes.'

'There's no fortune for myself in Leeds, Master Swales.'

'Friendship is a fortune. We're friends now, ain't we?'

'We're friends, but – I don't know. I feel awful low in myself now, Willie.'

'Things'll seem jollier after a good night's kip. You see if they don't.'

They curled up together under the shelter of an ash, Swales in his blanket, Mulvey in his greatcoat, and sang themselves quietly to sleep in the rain.

Mulvey awoke at dawn to find William Swales brewing the dregs of last night's tea. The morning was still: a little misty and cold. He limped down to a brook that was trickling over the black rocks and knelt and washed his face and hands. Snow had begun to fall by the time he had finished; fat, wet clumps of woolly whiteness. *No other choice* was the phrase in his mind. He had been close to death before but not as close as this. He would die if he attempted the walk back to London. The snow descended; milk-white crystals. There were no stones in the brook, or none he could carry, so he used the broken branch of an oak.

Nine was multiplied by zero.

He buried William Swales in a pit he scraped out of the forest floor; covered him with branches and broken bracken; filled in the grave as respectfully as possible and wept for the only man in England who had ever shown him a kindness that was totally uncomplicated. Not knowing what faith his victim had belonged to, if any, he said an Ave Maria and a decade of the Rosary and sang the one verse he could remember of the Tantum Ergo. When it came time to erect the little wooden cross, he carved the words PIUS MULVEY, GALWAYMAN AND THIEF. Then he drank the tea, packed up his bundle and took the road for Leeds.

For eighteen months, Mulvey lived in another man's clothes. He found schoolmastering a peaceful and satisfying life. The children were aged from five to eleven, so no Doctorhood of Divinity was required to instruct them. Provided you acted with understated certainty, nobody would notice the gaps in your knowledge. Anyway he was teaching them important lessons: the facility to read, to figure and write; the proficiencies which had brightened his gloomiest days. Mulvey was learning an important lesson, too. People see only what they want to see. The best place to hide is in the open.

It was the happiest time of his adult life, so he often thought; perhaps the only time he had ever truly been happy. The little cut-stone house that went with the position was warm in winter and cool in summer. He had a bed, a roof, five shillings a week and all the food he could possibly want, for the people of the area would bring him endless gifts of food. The sympathy so often felt for the single man.

Sometimes at night he would look around his neat cottage. Only one thing was missing and it could have been a paradise. But the thing that was missing he did not like to name.

The murderer discovered that he liked the company of children. He found their curiosity and artlessness affecting, their earnest wonderment at ordinary things. A stone, a feather, a fragment of torn sailcloth – these were the makings of a marvellous story. The poorest among them he liked the most, the little snotty boys and ragged girls who shuffled into school in their siblings' cast-offs. They had little interest in learning and Mulvey was loath to blame them for that, but always he insisted they take part in the lessons. All they truly wanted was a place to be warm for a while, a respite from the tribulations and hungers of home, the cup of hot milk they received in the mornings; perhaps a kindly word from their bogus master. It seemed to Mulvey as useful a lesson as any other that sometimes you had to dissemble to get what you needed out of authority; that all masters were in some objective sense bogus, but they needed their mastery confirmed from time to time. In this he felt no superiority whatsoever to the children. Being poor himself, he had learned it from experience and merely wanted to pass it on.

They could be unruly and demanding when they wanted to be, and some of them took a mischievous pleasure in goading him. But he never used the cane that hung on the schoolhouse wall and one night he snapped it and threw it into the little pot-bellied stove. To beat a child seemed a grotesque kind of evil to Mulvey, an admission of your utter spinelessness and inadequacy. He *was* inadequate, he knew that already; but certain limits existed which should never be transgressed. A child was not capable of hurting you deliberately. To respond to that reality with the infliction of hurt was a statement that adulthood had no meaning.

It began to eat at the killer that he was a father himself, that his blood coursed through the veins of another living creature he had not had the courage to love. Such thoughts had haunted him before in England but always he had managed to put them away. Surrounded by children, it was harder to do. Every child in his care seemed the ghost of his own.

The child would be thirteen at its next birthday: a terrible age, a time when you needed your father to guide you. Every life contained moments when your true nature was tested. When that moment had presented itself to Pius Mulvey he had fled from it like a vampire from light. Thoughts of his own father's fortitude tormented his dreams, of his mother's loyalty and endless work for her sons. Blights had come and gone and his parents had never left him. How had he repaid their memory for all their love? Deserted the only grandchild who would ever bear their name. How had he repaid Mary Duane for hers? No mere betrayal, his abandonment was also condemnation. He knew how it worked; had seen it often enough; the shame of the unwed mother a variety of widowhood.

No man in Ireland would be father to another's child. ('Who'd buy a cracked egg?' he had once heard a priest say.) He had ruined for ever her chances of marriage or companionship. Disgraceful what he had done: beyond forgiveness. And yet such a guilt was also a cowardly lie, and he knew it. The thought of her being married to anyone else was unbearable.

Why had he left? What was he fleeing? Was it the fear of starvation, or had he wanted to hurt her? Did something lurk in his soul that was truly that monstrous? He wondered if he was father to a girl or a boy. The thought she might be a girl made his spine prickle with dread. A girl with no father to advise and protect her. A young woman in a world of Pius Mulveys. 'Bastard,' they would mutter, when they saw her in the streets of Clifden. The bastard created by Pius Mulvey. Daughter of the whore he also made.

Often he would dream about the night he had walked out of Connemara, that terrible night of the wrecking hurricane. So many times he had wanted to turn back, but somehow every step had made it less possible. He could not starve. He could not die. He loved Mary Duane but he had been so afraid. Some selfishness in his being had beaten down his love but he had allowed it to happen; from that shameful fact no flight was possible. He saw himself running through the tumbling forests, through crashing elders and a snowstorm of leaves. Bridges crumbling; being swept away. He had done a grave thing to the child and her mother. Was there any way back from a sin of such magnitude? Could a bridge, once collapsed, be shored up again? Were the rubbles still there, just below the cold surface? Could even those ruins serve duty as stepping stones?

On the first of September, 1844, he sat at his table and wrote her a letter. It was the longest document he had ever written, twenty-one pages of apologies and pleadings, and he was determined not to pollute it by the inclusion of a single lie. As a young man he had loved her and hoped they had a future; in all his years in England he had loved no other woman. He had no excuse for the cruelty of what he had done. Simply that he had panicked and succumbed to his cowardice. If she would only take him back he would never hurt her again. Things had happened to him in England: terrible things. He himself had done terrible things in England. The worst horrors he had ever been forced to face had been bearable only because he knew she had loved him once. He had thought about her every day for almost thirteen years: at his darkest moments he had remembered how once he had been loved.

At midnight he stopped writing and read over the letter. But he knew it was wrong; it was all completely wrong. Words could not disguise the truth of what had happened. He had deserted the only woman he had ever wanted, for no other reason than his own sickening weakness. He ripped up his letter and watched it burn.

One morning the next week, the Chairman of the Board of Management was waiting in the porch when Mulvey came across from his cottage to unlock the school. He said that a delicate little matter had arisen. He had received a letter from William Swales's mother to ask why her son never answered her correspondence. Was her son quite well? Had anything happened to him? Somehow the monster had managed to remain silent as he scanned the widow's anxious pages. A piece of maternal over-enthusiasm, he finally agreed. The tears in his eyes were interpreted as filial love.

'Send her a line like a good thing, William, won't you? We only have one mother, after all.'

'I certainly shall, sir. Thank you, sir.'

That night he packed a carpet-bag and walked out of Kirkstall, making for Liverpool, which he reached in four days. There he sold the books he had stolen from the school and the horse he had stolen from outside the inn at Manchester.

His days of rambling were over now. He would head back to Carna, to Mary Duane and the child. He would tell her what had happened; he had been afraid to stay. If he said it to her face, forgiveness might be possible. If it wasn't possible now, it might become so in time. He would work; he would *slave* for her and the child. To be near the child was all he wanted now. To prove he was not a beast, just a man who had been afraid.

He boarded a steam-packet at Wellington Dock, filched a pocketbook from a sleepy Duke; arrived in Dublin the following morning. A mail-stage was leaving the wharf for Galway and he paid the driver to take him along. He walked from the city into southern Connemara and before nightfall he had come to the village of Carna.

For a while he thought he must have made a mistake; must

somehow have come to the wrong place. He looked at the blackened and crumpled cabin. The broken-down walls. The thatch overgrown with lousewort. Bits of dismembered furniture lay on the floor as though they had been trying to form themselves into some instrument of torture.

Mounds of soggy ashes. Scorch marks on the flagstones. A shovel handle thrust through a lichened windowpane.

The breeze off the lake was surprisingly warm and it brought the faint redolence of rushes and summertime. But now he saw something that made him feel cold. The door of the cabin had been sawn in two. He knew what it meant. The eviction gang.

Nobody was nearby. The fields were deserted. A fisherman's currach was mouldering near the gateposts, its cross-ribs bleaching where the canvas had rotted away.

He left the wrecked cottage, intending to go up to the manor. He would ask what had happened. Where had everyone gone? As he walked, he became aware that he was stumbling in panic. Another broken bothy. A burnt-down pigsty. Barbed wire across the bogland. A goat's crusted shinbone. A smashed, rusting bedstead upended in a boundary ditch. A daubed table-top as a signboard, hammered into a midden.

> THESE LANDS ARE THE PROPERTY OF
> HENRY BLAKE OF TULLY.
> TRESPASSERS WILL BE SHOT
> WITHOUT FURTHER WARNING

An old man appeared on the boreen leading an unkempt pony.

'God be with you,' said Mulvey in Irish.

'And Mary with yourself,' the old man replied.

'Are you a local man, sir, if you don't mind me asking?'

'Johnny deBurca. I worked above at the manor one time.'

'I'm seeking Mary Duane that lived down by the bayside.'

'There's no Duanes here no more, sir. There's nobody here.'

It swam up at him like a nausea that she might have emigrated with the child. But the old man said no, she was still living in Galway. At least he thought as much, if they were speaking of the same woman.

'Mary Duane,' said Mulvey. 'Her people are from Carna.'

'You mean Mary Mulvey as lives up near Ardnagreevagh.'

'What's that?'

'Mary Mulvey that married the priest, sir. Twelve year ago now, I believe it is.'

'— The priest?'

'Nicholas Mulvey, aye. That used to be the priest. Brother of him that got her in pup and scuttled off to America.'

How the prisoner and the immigrant are treated by the government, how the poor are treated and those without influence: this is secretly how the government would like to treat all of us.

David Merridith

From notes for a pamphlet on penal reform. 1840. Unfinished

CHAPTER XXII

THE LAW

The SEVENTEENTH day of the Voyage: in which
the Captain records the DELIVERANCE of Mulvey
from a precarious encounter with RETRIBUTION.

Wednesday, 24 November, 1847
Nine days at sea remaining.

LONG: 47°04.21′W. LAT: 48°52.13′N. ACTUAL GREENWICH
STANDARD TIME: 02.12 a.m. (25 November). ADJUSTED
SHIP TIME: 11.04 p.m. (24 November). WIND DIR. & SPEED:
N.N.E. (38°) Force 5. SEAS: Turbulent. HEADING: S.S.W.
(211°). PRECIPITATION & REMARKS: Shower of very large
hailstones in the afternoon. Raw, severe wind. The bad smell
recently reported about the ship would appear to be diminishing.

Last night two steerage passengers died: Paudrig Foley, farmhand of
Roscommon, and Bridget Shouldice, neé Coombes, aged serving
woman, latterly inmate at Birr Workhouse in King's County.
(Insane.) Their remains were committed to the sea.

The total who have died on this voyage is now forty-one.
Seventeen isolated for cholera in the hold.

I am compelled to relate a series of troubling incidents, which
arose this day and greatly disturbed the peace of those in steerage,
with distressing and almost calamitous results.

At three o'clock approximately I was in my quarters studying
the charts and attending to some engrossing matters of calculation
when Leeson came in. He said he had been told by a young woman
of steerage that there was considerable unrest among the ordinary
passengers and if I did not hasten with him there might be murder

before we were done. This was no innocuous donnybrook but a veritable carnival of thuggee. He insisted we take two pieces from the lockbox, for the passengers were in a very frenzy of anger. We then set out.

Making our way along the maindeck we came upon the Reverend Henry Deedes at meditation, and I prevailed upon him to accompany us below. For although most of those in steerage are of the Roman faith, they regard all men of the cloth with respect and approbation and I considered it might be advantageous to have him with us.

When we went down the ladders to the hatch (Deedes and Leeson and self) a dreadful scene was being enacted. The unfortunate crippled man, William Swales, was cowering on the floor near the water closets. His appearance was most pitiful. By the marks upon his person it were easily deducible that he had been victim of an assault, or several prolonged assaults. His clothes were pulled apart and he was shaking in fear, his face a pulp of blood and unspeakable filth and ordure.

At first the passengers refused to say how this had happened, and even the wretched man himself was greatly reluctant to speak of it, insisting that he had fallen down while inebriated and would soon be happy again. It must be noted that among the common class of Irish exists the general and curious custom of not informing to any person they perceive to be in authority of the shortcomings and crimes of their fellows, be they ever so dastardly. And until I promised that the rations would be halved forthwith, and the company's rules relating to on-board drinking more strictly enforced than had been the case hitherto, silence was maintained. It was only at the issuing of these latter threats that the full concatenation of events began to be disclosed.

It was revealed that there had been a theft from a passenger called Foley of a cup of Indian meal and this crippled man was suspected. This was adduced as the cause of his punishment. I said the ship sailed under the law of England and in the eyes of that law was *part of England's territory;* and under that same benign law a man was innocent until he be proven otherwise, be he ever so great or ever so small. And if any man dared to raise up trouble on my vessel or take the law in his own hands, he would be confined and fettered for the remainder of the voyage the better to ponder his philosophies. The good Minister then spoke up, saying it was not Christian to abuse an unfortunate man without so much as knowing him and he a cripple and did Our Redeemer not take pity on such & cetera.

'I know him,' then issued a retort from the back.

The crowd parted to reveal one Shaymus Meadowes, a violent passenger much given to thieving and foolery of the lowest kind and exposing himself. He is quite given over to drinking and its attendant train of ruffianly debasement and has a face like a robber's dog. Only this morning had he himself been released from the lock-up and then only at the great intervention of Minister Deedes who had befriended him and made kindly intercession on his behalf.

'Your name is Pius Mulvey,' said he. 'You took a neighbour-man's land off him when he was down on his luck.'

(Among these Irish of the villein class there is no man lower than he who has taken the holding of another in such a circumstance. They had rather the land were left idle and barren than it be husbanded by one who was not born on it.)

'You are after confusing me with somebody else,' said the cripple. 'My name is not Mulvey.'

At this he began to limp away, his appearance most greatly alarmed.

'I believe and know it is,' said the other. 'For I seen you often with that leg of yeers.'

'No,' said the cripple.

'Your neighbour was put out – evicted I say – by that "shoneen" b★★★★★d Blake of Tully, may he die choking in his own sh★t.' (Other remarks which may be imagined were then made, concerning one Commander Henry Blake, a personage not at all popular among the Connermara poor.) And he went on: 'Stead of shunning that filthy b★★★★★d of a landlord, you got the lease of your neighbour's land off him and got it cheap, too.'

At this a great clamour of insults and spitting arose. 'I'd crack the head of him if I had the strength,' said one. 'A worse man never faced the sun,' said another, a woman, and she called for a noose to be made. (It is distressing to note in these situations that the women are sometimes the worse offenders than the men.)

'His name is William Swales,' said I.

'The "divil" goes by many names,' cried Meadowes. 'He is Pius Mulvey of Ardnagreevagh as I live and breathe. Who done another man to death through his cruel robbery.'

Some began to roar again. Once more the Reverend Deedes attempted an intervention but was himself now abused and called horrid names that touched upon his religious persuasion. I did have to assert that judicious and sincere holiness is the inheritance of no particular faction, but that the banner of true religion while it contains an assemblage of distinct threads affords decoration and pride to the whole world by their intimate coalescence. I was myself mocked at this point.

By now Meadowes had the floor and was enjoying fully his celebrity and determined on that (as such men will be who are always unproductive in any sphere save bragging and bullying).

'Will I tell them the best part?' said he.

No rejoinder came from the cripple. He was so afraid.

'Beg me not to,' said the first, a horrid smile on his lips.

'I beg you not to,' the cripple pleaded.

'On your knees, beg me not to,' said Meadowes.

The poor cripple sank to the boards and commenced to weep quietly.

'Call me God,' said Meadowes. 'You crown-shawning c**t.'

'You are my God,' exclaimed the cripple through his tears.

'That's right now,' said Meadowes, the low scoundrel. 'And you will do all I command.'

'I will,' said the cripple. 'Only have mercy on me, I beg you.'

'Lick the filth off my boots,' Meadowes ordered, and his wretched victim commenced to do so. At this performance of disgraceful cruelty many of the passengers laughed in mockery; though many again, kinder among them, called for it to stop.

'Please,' said the cripple, 'do not tell on me, I beg it.'

Meadowes bent low and spat into his face.

'The neighbourman you did was your own brother,' said he.

'Lies!' cried the cripple.

'Nicholas Mulvey that was once the priest up in Maam Cross. I knew him well. A good decent man, Christ give his soul rest. And his blood is on your hands for certain sure. You murdered him! You murdered your brother!'

'That never happened,' cried the cripple, and then: 'Do I look like a man with a farm of land?'

'You were put off the land you stole by your decent neighbours and the Liable Boys of Galway, more luck to them,' insisted the first. 'And it did happen. For I used to sell kale with my "oldfellow" in Clifden. So didn't I hear all about it in the town! Land robber! Murderer! Priest hater! Judas!'

'That is not me. You have the wrong man, I swear it.'

It was only by dint of self and Leeson producing our firearms that utter calamity was avoided and even then I had occasion to fear for my own life as we contrived to take the miserable cripple out of that place.

He is at present lodged in the lock-up by reason of the threats against him. And whatever transgressions may lie in his past – as do lie in the pasts of all men and women, or at least in their hearts and the profundities of their consciences – I pray none will put their hand on that poor man again; for his life will be ended on this ship if they do.

I believe that is all I have to say.

This day I met with Evil's footman, whose name is Shaymus Meadowes.

If I seed my gal talking to another chap I'd fetch her sich a punch of the nose as should plaguy* quick stop the whole business. The gals – it was a rum thing now [I] come to think on it – axully liked a feller for walloping them. As long as the bruises hurted, she was always thinking on the cove as gived 'em her . . . When the gal is in the family way, the lads mostly sends them to the workhouse to lay in, and only goes sometimes to take them a bit of tea and shugger. I've often heerd the boys boasting of having ruined gals – for all the world as if they was the finest noblemen in the land.

London street trader to the journalist Henry Mayhew
Name unknown

*'Plaguy': a slang abbreviation of 'plaguily'; i.e., as quickly and violently as a plague. – GGD

CHAPTER XXIII

THE MARRIED MAN

Containing frankest and NEVER BEFORE
PUBLISHED Revelations of Lord Kingscourt's
SECRET Times; certain of his Habits and hidden
Aspects; his Nightly visits to certain
Establishments which were better
not frequented by Gentlemen.

'Those whose ambitions exceed their abilities are fated for disappointment, at least until they grow up. Those without ambition are also sentenced. A man with no enterprise is lost . . .

David Merridith, letter to the *Spectator* (7 July 1840)
on the subject of 'Crime in London'.

Emily and Natasha Merridith had risked their father's rage by travelling to London for their brother's wedding. Lord Kingscourt's absence had been explained away by a fortuitous coincidence. The coronation of Queen Victoria was taking place the same morning and every member of the House of Lords had been commanded to attend the ceremony. Laura's parents had quite understood. In fact they had seemed rather proud of the fact and her father made a point of mentioning it in his speech. 'The Earl, you will all know, is detained elsewhere.'

John Markham proved a most generous benefactor. His wedding gift was a five-and-a-half-year lease on a townhouse on Tite Street in the fashionable borough of Chelsea. Nothing less than the very best was good enough for his beloved only daughter and her husband. For all the time the newly-weds spent in London they did not need eighteen rooms and a coach-house in Chelsea, but Mr Markham insisted that was not the point. Their home would be ready when they wanted it.

For two years they travelled, the Viscount and his bride, to Paris, Rome, Greece, Florence, further afield to Turkey and Egypt, collecting bibelots and works of art wherever they went. Venice became a home away from home; they lived there in a suite at the Palazzo Gritti through the bitter winter of 1839, and it was there that their first son was born, in December of that year. Friends from London came out to visit. There were trips down to Amalfi and north to the lakes. Lady Kingscourt had a tasteful eye and an expert's knowledge, an imperturbable eye for a bargain. She knew about paintings, sculptures, books. She had eleven thousand guineas per annum from her family. She bought a lot of books.

Morocco, Tangier and Constantinople were visited; Athens again; a summer in Biarritz. When they ran out of destinations they drifted back to London, moved into their large and comfortable house. It was immediately remodelled to Her Ladyship's design, with the latest fine wallpapers and gilded mouldings. Paintings were hung; objects put on display; a Renaissance fresco she had purchased in Fiesole was installed on the ceiling of their bedroom for a time, and then dismantled and moved to the study. (Its leering devils and writhing sinners tended to worsen her husband's nightmares.) A regiment of servants was soon employed to attend to the Merridiths and their treasures. Experts from the National Gallery came to make sketches. The Keeper of the Queen's Paintings wrote an article on the collection. Laura began to host her celebrated evenings.

Poets and essayists and novelists and critics would turn up in gangs on a Wednesday night: usually hungry and always late. They stood around the buffet like gnu at a waterhole. Money, or the lack of it, was their favoured theme, not beauty or art or mysterious lakes. The guest list was a roll call of belletristic London. To be invited to the Merridiths' was to know you had arrived. G. H. Lewes of *Fraser's Magazine*, Thomas Carlyle, the journalist Mayhew, Tennyson, Boucicault, the publisher Newby; even the famous and envied Mr Dickens who sat in a corner looking morbidly depressed, biting his fingernails when he thought nobody was looking. A cartoon was published in *Punch* magazine of two writerly gentlemen in turbans and smoking jackets stabbing each other with bloodstained pens. The caption said a lot about Laura's careful efforts: 'By Jove or by Allah! Only one invitation to Lady Kingscourt's "evening" has come. Enough to make an Etonian behave as an Afghani.'

Laura bought the original and had it mounted and framed. She hung it beside the mirror in the downstairs guest lavatory, which carefully chosen location offered several benefits. Most callers would see it at least once in the course of any evening, but they would think her too fashionable to care about it much. If you cared you would have hung it in the hall or the drawing room: the places where the Viscount's Connemara drawings were hung. The Viscountess understood the nature of style.

For a while they enjoyed a certain quiet happiness, an everyday contentment which was not often questioned. Their son was a beautiful baby, pink and strong; the kind who causes policemen to stop on the pavement and coo into perambulators like elderly nuns. But quite soon after the new family returned to London from Italy, something strange had begun to happen to David Merridith.

A clawing unease crept into his days; the restlessness and anxiety he had known as a child. Marrying Laura Markham had driven it away, but *being* married was somehow allowing it to return. He began to feel dissatisfied, was prone to depressions. People gradually noticed he was losing weight. The sleeplessness that had plagued him since boyhood worsened. The greater the congratulations for his enviable existence, the more obscurely discontented the Viscount became.

Part of it was boredom, the sheer lack of purpose. The life of a gentleman of leisure did not suit him, it made him feel useless and vaguely ungrateful: the ingratitude making the uselessness sharper. His days were entirely empty of anything important. He would fill them up with plans to improve himself: to read all of Pliny in chronological order, to learn ancient Greek or take up some pastime; to do something good for the poor, perhaps. He visited infirmaries, joined philanthropic committees, wrote a lot of letters to newspaper editors. But the committees never seemed to get anything done and neither did the endless and repetitious letters. The making of plans consumed much of his time, but there never seemed to be time to follow any of them through. His journals for those years reveal innumerable beginnings: long walks in the park; unfinished books; abandoned projects; unrealised designs. A life of wishing the days away. Waiting, perhaps, for his future to start.

His wife was a good woman; beautiful, gentle, with a gift for joy which he had often found inspiring. Given the choice she would rather be happy, and with a childhood like Merridith's that was something attractive. Their house was elegant, their son happy and healthy. Neat as a uniform laid out on a bed, the life of David Kingscourt of Carna; but often he felt their marriage was a kind of masquerade. They didn't converse as much as they used to; when they did, the subject was always their child. The boy's father became contentious, more ardent than before. He found himself becoming a man he disliked: correcting the servants on matters of grammar, picking fights with waiters, with guests at the house. Views he had never held he began to assert furiously. Soon no evening was complete without a disagreement.

They broke with some of their long-time friends. He was advised by his physician to stop drinking, and did so for a while.

The couples comprising their innermost circle were also new parents; crazed by parenting. As happily, devotedly besotted by their children as Laura was by Jonathan, and as Merridith was not. At dinner tables and in opera boxes he would find himself grinning at the latest citation of neonate genius, the heartiness of appetites, the firmness of stools, while secretly wishing he was anywhere else. He did not feel superior: rather more of a failure. How marvellous to be a father as befuddled as that; drunk on the wine of paternal love. To scrutinise the contents of your progeny's diapers like a Roman soothsayer pronouncing on the runes. He loved his boy but he could not love him that much. Often, in shameful fact, he found fatherhood a millstone. The noise of nannies clattering through the beautiful house had an irritating tendency to interfere with his plans.

He came to have an image of Laura and himself as actors in a play somebody else had written. There was courtesy in the text, it was mannered and restrained. A critic might have given an admiring notice. She spoke her lines; he spoke his own; rarely did either player interrupt or fluff the script. But it didn't feel like an actual marriage. Rather it came to seem like living on a stage set and wondering whether the audience was really out there past the limelight; and if it wasn't, exactly whom the performance was for.

The literary evenings continued but Merridith found them a trial and eventually commanded that he wanted them to stop. He was surprised by the intensity of Laura's defiance. He could make his own decision as to whether to attend them, but they would certainly not stop: it was wrong of him to ask it. She was not some lifeless chattel to decorate his existence. She had married a husband and would not have a master.

'Is a man to be gainsaid in his own house?'

'It is my house too.'

'They are a waste of time and a waste of money.'

'My time is my own. And so is my money. I shall waste them or spend them precisely as I see fit.'

'What does that mean, Laura?'

'You know very well.'

'I certainly do not. Please enlighten me.'

'When you can say the same things about yourself, you may give lectures. In the meantime I shall do exactly as I please.'

Sometimes when they argued, and they began to argue often, she would say she did not know why he had married at all. Neither of them uttered it, but they both knew the reason. It was little enough to do with Laura Markham.

Often at night, in the middle of one of the soirées, or after his wife had retired to her bedroom, he would slip from the house and walk down Tite Street; those few hundred yards which led to the river. To stand quietly alone on the bank of the Thames – it brought the relief which only water brings. London at that time could still be tranquil at night; the certain blissful peace found at moments in cities when all around seems nothing but fiery noise. There were moorhens in the shallows on the long summer evenings, swans gliding past on their progress up to Richmond. The water, and the moorhens, would remind him of Ireland, the place of his boyhood: perhaps his only home.

And often as he stood at that muddy, peaceful river, he would find himself remembering a girl he had once known. The sound of flowing water seemed to raise her like a spirit. He wondered if she thought of him. Probably she didn't. For God's sake, why would she? Better things to do.

As youngsters they had gone walking in the meadows of Kingscourt, through the woods and the boglands, up the reefs of Cashel Hill. He would bring along the chart made by one of his ancestors, an exquisite delineation of 'The Propertie of Merridith'. For all its fine detail and beautiful draughtsmanship, the maker, a seaman, had done it as a kind of joke. The estate lands of Kingscourt were drawn as water; the seas at its edge were rendered as dry land. It showed courses for yachting in the Maumturk Mountains, the safest paths for marching over Roundstone Bay. A madman, she said, as she laughed at the subverted perfection. And she had shown him things he owned which appeared on no chart. A yew tree whose berries were said to heal fevers. A rock where a saint left the imprints of his knees. A well at Tubberconnell often visited by pilgrims. The few times she pointed to some feature he knew already, he would pretend not to know it, because he liked to hear her explain it.

She had loved that strange chart. In the end he'd had to give it to her. And he loved her exegeses of boulders and crags. They had strolled the fathomed slopes, the contours and flatnesses, the wheatfields that led to the sea at Kilkerrin. Cruelty and bloodshed have walked with cartographies; with gods, too, and their soldierly saints. Such plottings seemed distant from the cliffs of Kilkerrin. That was the place where he pictured her now: gazing out towards Inishtravin Island – 'Inishtravin Lake' on his forefather's chart – as though it had appeared in the night. She seemed to find beauty in ordinary things: the coconut smell of a gorse bush, the spiral of a cockleshell, the glint of the lighthouse on Eeragh Point. Her laughter skimmed the billows of Ballyconneely Bay, bouncing towards the horizon like a slate-stone. The whole world seemed fresh to her, as it would to a child. She wasn't a child, and neither was she a saint. But he had never once seen her do an act of deliberate cruelty.

She would be twenty-eight now. Her appearance would have changed. Already she might be grey and her face might be wrinkled, for they aged early, the women of Connemara: the rain and the salt wind leathered their skin. Or she might be like her mother, more beautiful in age; turf-dark, stonish, strong with self-possession and strong with the possession of all she had survived. He wondered if she had married; whether she had even remained at Kingscourt. Born a poorer man, he might have married her himself. All he had owned had come to disown him; but that was to judge himself lightly, and he knew it. He had not had the mettle to break out of his prison. He was too young to do it, and too afraid. He had murdered her trust for no other reason than obedience: his crippling and crippled desire to please. Out of hunger for love he had thrown love away. In a way he had used her as bait.

And when the bait didn't work, when his father didn't bite, he had used Laura Markham as weapon. He had married her mainly because he could not be stopped from marrying her. He was not a cowed boy, he was beyond control; would pay any price to prove his manhood. Marriage, for Merridith, had been a feat of vengeance, but an act that had only imprisoned its kicked-down perpetrator even as it seemed to have given him liberation. What had made him a freeman had also enslaved him: the slavery all the worse for being self-imposed.

The laudanum he was prescribed for sleeplessness rarely did its job; when it did, it gave him dreams almost as unbearable as his nightmares. Blizzards of shimmering opalescent colour that made him feel as though swimming through tar. Opiate tinctures and lozenges were suggested by his apothecary, but still the dreams were fearful dazzlings; exhaustions of images he did not understand. Finally the family physician showed him how to inject: how to use a tourniquet to bulge out the vein, how precisely to hold the syringe and exert the correct degree of pressure on the plunger. Injecting, said the doctor, was the better remedy for insomnia, as well as a safer way to use the medicine. It was well known that you couldn't become addicted to opium if you injected. Injecting was the procedure of the gentleman, he advised; the method the doctor himself always used.

In February 1841, Queen Victoria celebrated the first anniversary of her marriage. A thief escaped from prison, having battered a guard to death. A journalist from Louisiana began to appear at London soirées. An aristocrat from Galway had just become the father of a baby whose parents had exchanged barely a word in months. Born six weeks early, he was nevertheless healthy;

but the marriage he was born in was by now at death's door. On one occasion constables came calling at his home, alerted by the neighbours to the sound of a furious argument. The night of his christening, no entry appears. The choices made by diarists as to what will be included tell us much, so we think, about contemporary times. Perhaps what is excluded tells us more.

Merridith's journals record that it was in February 1841 that he began to roam the East End of London at night. He would leave his fine house and walk eastwards down the riverbank and into a world which imagination could not have fashioned. And sometimes as he drifted the deafening streets he would think of a song he had known as a child; a ballad often sung him by Mary Duane's mother, about the girl who puts on the clothes of a soldier and goes among soldiers to find her love.

The diaries become difficult, even chaotic at this point, often written in a fantastically meticulous code, a combination of Connemara Gaelic and 'mirrored writing'. Whole weeks are left blank or filled in with false details, which must have taken hours to contrive. Other entries abound with violent self-loathing; fevered charcoal sketches of the quarter that was to become his haunt.★ The flavour arising from those terrible pages is fearsome indeed: unforgettably so. The scribbled pictures are haunting: the work of a man in torment. One thinks of the fresco of *The Punishments of Hell* which once looked down on their creator's marriage bed.

Freak shows, carnivals, rat-killing dogs; gin palaces, hock-shops, 'suicide saloons'; bookies' stalls and faith healers' fit-ups; evangelicals' booths and revival meeting teepees; mediums' nooks and fortune tellers' bunkers, where people who had little future of any

---

★At the time of revising the present edition of this book (1915) Lord Kingscourt's executors still insist that the drawings may never be published, and that only selected quotations from the journals may be used. (Mysteriously, one of his drawings appeared in a pornographic work published anonymously in London in the late 1870s. In fact it is not one of his 'Whitechapel' sketches but a copy of 'The Three Graces' from the book of symbols *Emblematum Liber* (1531) by Andrea Alcation, which Lord Kingscourt made while honeymooning in Italy.) The daybooks in which the Whitechapel drawings were made are kept under lock and key at the 'Secretum' or Secret Museum for Obscene Works at The Department of Antiquities, British Library, London. – GGD

kind would pay what they couldn't afford to be assured that they did. The local myth was of life's predictability, the commodity most enduringly sought after by the poor. Healing, salvation, an unforgettable experience might be yours. Deliverance was for sale, or certainly winnable, if only you had the gumption to buy a ticket for the draw. The one tiny gamble you didn't want to take might well be the miracle that would make you rich. 'Who knows?' said the parasites. It could be you.

Everything in the East End was deferrable, for a price. Boredom; poverty; thirst; hunger; disappointment; lust; loneliness; loss, even death itself and death's finality. Here was the mirrorland where your loved ones never died but merely slipped into the unseen room. From there they could assure you of continuing tenderness if you'd only cross the palm of the seer.

Deliverance was shouted from the doorways and the shadows, a cry that drew him like gravity. Here in the alleyways of Cheapside and Whitechapel were the fancy houses of late-night whispers at his club. Often he had wondered about those basements and back rooms where women pleasured men or gave them pain. Some men liked pain, Merridith knew that; to be beaten, spat upon, whipped, degraded. And others elected to administer degradation. He had encountered such brutes in his navy career; had once risked a court-martial for daring to intervene.★ Violence was an aphrodisiac for certain men: they found the infliction of torture arousing. How terrible the fall before resorting to that: how bestial and severed the man from his emotions. Merridith was thankful he was no such monster, that his own frantic hungerings were at least so ordinary.

For a handful of coins they would do anything that was asked.

★'Towards the end of the run occurred an unsavoury incident, recollection of which has never quite left me. A Negro cabin-lad, formerly a slave, was being cruelly set-upon by a drunken Commodore when a young Irish Lieutenant, Viscount Kingscourt of Carna, happened upon the scene. Contrary to every rule, the Commodore had stripped the boy. A brawl ensued during which the Viscount struck his superior officer. The former had been Middle-Weight champion at Oxford University, a matter the latter discovered ere long. It was only at the intervention of the Viscount's father that profounder unpleasantness was avoided.' From *Four Bells For the Dog-Watch: A Life at Sea* by Vice-Admiral Henry Hollings K.C.M.G. (Hudson and Hall, London, 1863.)

Not that he would dream of asking them to touch him. He was too much the gentleman to ask for that, and anyway, as ever, he could scarcely bear to be touched. To watch them undress was what he preferred, and there were establishments to cater for that desire, as for all others. To sit in the shadows with his eye to a spy-hole and watch that happening, again and again. A normal man at his normal leisure. A man with an eye for beauty.

In some of the establishments, they were too young: they were children. The children he would always send away. Then the madams would send in more, or send in old women dressed like children. He stopped going to places like that.

But there were other places. There were always others. He found a place that suited him better and soon he was going there almost every night. It was a place for men, the madam said. Normal, manly, civilised men. There were no frightened children and no old women: no lashes, no debasements, just beautiful ladies. Fresh and natural, hand picked like orchids: the kind you would see in a painting by a Master. There was really no difference, the madam contended, between her own refined establishment and the National Gallery.

He would shake with desire as he watched from the darkness, his breath misting the glass which separated watcher from watched. Sometimes he would inject himself while he observed the undressing women. A bee-sting of pain. A small convulsion in the flesh, like an attack of pins and needles but much more sudden, and then relief oozing his marrowbones; crushed ice in a desert.

If his wife enquired as to where he was going at night, which by now she rarely bothered to do, he would say there was a game of cards at the club. Other invented alibis are included in the journals, almost always with minutiae of times and venues: often with long accounts of entirely fictional conversations. A gathering of the Friends of the Bethlehem Asylum. A committee meeting of a charity for 'Fallen Girls'.* A dinner for Old Wykehamists which never took

*Though he was never a committee member of any such body, he appears to have made regular financial contributions to one: a society established by Dickens and his friend Angela Burdett-Coutts (of the banking family) 'to rescue betrayed and unfortunate girls'. – GGD

place. Early in the autumn of 1843 she said she would like to take the boys to Sussex for a few weeks. He raised no objection and that was just as well for she had already packed their bags and ordered up the coach. Viscount Kingscourt told a friend he was unsure if she would return, adding, perhaps truthfully, that he did not care any more.

One night the girl was Irish who stripped in the booth: dark-eyed, from Sligo, with black hair that shone, and when she quietly enquired if he wanted anything else from her, David Merridith found himself saying he did. She opened the lock and pulled back the partition. 'There now, alannah,' she whispered as she kissed him. 'Come in to me, sweetheart, and show me how you love me.' What happened was over in even less time than it had taken to think of a lie when she asked him his name. Afterwards the girl had risen from the divan and quickly washed at a metal bowl in the corner and left the compartment without uttering a word. Returning to Tite Street just before dawn, her client looked down from Chelsea Bridge and contemplated throwing himself into the Thames. It was only the thought of his children that stopped him.

As the sunrise reddened his solitary bedroom he forced so much laudanum into his biceps that he slept for almost all of the day. The servants did not intrude. They knew better by now. He dreamed he was his father as a newly married man: the morning he had found his own father's body hanging from the Faerie Tree in the Lower Lock meadow. When finally he awoke he injected again, so agonisingly deep that his needle touched bone; then he rose and dressed and went to his club to dine and returned to Cheapside just as night was falling on the East End. (Though as he puts it himself in one of the journals: '[T]he night does not fall there. Rather it lifts up; raising the stone of daylight under which Whitechapel crawls.') The establishment he preferred had been raided by the police; its madam arrested and sent into Tothill Prison. But there were other establishments. There were always others.

He came to know every sidestreet and back lane of Whitechapel as a prisoner would know every brick of his cell. He carried a map of it around in his mind and he walked it like a pilgrim in a back-to-front fable, condemned to know less the more he walks. Somewhere in the labyrinth was waiting what he needed. The Irish girl. Another girl. Two girls together. A man and a girl. Two men, maybe. Often he would enter an establishment at random; always he found quickly that he could not stay. The moment whatever he suggested became available, he immediately stopped wanting it and would have to leave.

What precisely he was seeking can never be known; and if a striking remark from the diaries contains any clue, it is possible he had little enough idea himself. He had heard it said often in his navy career that a hanged man experiences erection at the moment of death. It was how David Merridith had come to feel now. 'Choked, strangled; a deathly stiff.'

He began to take more and greater risks. Soon even White-chapel was not enough for him. Spitalfields. Shoreditch. Mile End Road. He drifted down to Stepney where the entertainments were darker; eastward into Limehouse where children carried weapons; down towards the riverfront, around Shadwell and Wapping, where even the police were afraid to venture at night. At least once he described himself as a journalist from Ireland; another time an Oxford professor of criminology; the owner of a brigantine; a manager of boxers; a man on the search for his runaway fiancée. Many years later he was still remembered on the docks; the wolfish aristocrat known as 'Lord Lies'.

A city skulked in the shadows of a city. In the culverts and warehouses, boys would fight dogs; drugged women could be hired for the price of a newspaper. But women were not the interest of the prowler any more. 'Woman delights me not, nor man either,' he wrote, paraphrasing Hamlet in the masquerade of madness. The opium you could find there was strong and raw, straight off the ship from China or Afghanistan, illegal to buy without government licence but thrown around the wharfage like rice at a wedding. A single half-grain caused the stars to explode; a pod of grains made you think your heart was bursting. David Merridith chewed it by the juicy mouthful, until his tongue blistered up, and his gums and palate bled, and he flew like a death angel through the clouds over London. He came to like the tang of his own mouth's blood. Sometimes he thought he had no heart left to burst.

Between Sutton Dock and Lucas Street was Hangman's Quarter, a plot of rubbled and rat-swarming wasteland where the girls were half dead with hunger and disease. Often he tried to speak to them, to give them money or food, but they did not understand that by now he only wanted conversation. Some of their images appear in his manic drawings; their faces like grave-cloths hanging on fists, blackened by the cudgels and boots of their pimps. It became his place of final resort. Every night ended in Hangman's Quarter. He never went near the women now; he watched from the ruins as they fought and touted. And he drew those mastered women like a knife draws blood.

Perhaps watching them and being there carried the risk he needed now. Risk as narcotic. It made him feel he existed.

One night a constable approached him in the Mile End Road and said this was no place for a gentleman to allow himself to be seen. Merridith tried to appear affronted at what he called the impertinence, but the officer – an Irishman – quietly persisted. The way he kept calling the aristocrat 'sir' made it abundantly clear who had the power here. 'A gentleman might even find himself blackmailed, sir.'

'I don't care for the tone of your insinuations, Constable. I merely got lost on my way home from a walk. I was dining with my father at the House of Lords.'

'That Your Honour may find his direction, so. Next time perhaps you'll accompany me to the station. I can show you a little map the Sergeant keeps in the cells.'

Through the toxified haze of his neural firings he was vaguely disappointed when the policeman walked away. What he wanted, he realised at that giddying moment, was not to be secretive but to be discovered and disgraced. To be kicked into the gutter and spat on by the respectable. Recognised for the untouchable he knew he was.

He returned to his townhouse that sweltering night shaking with an emotion he thought must be fear. We know he spent most of the following afternoon talking alone with a minister of religion; though what was discussed we do not know. Whatever it was, it appears to have changed nothing. At dusk that evening he was seen in Whitechapel.

That was the night he became aware that he was being followed. Near Christ Church Spitalfields he noticed him first: that tall, cadaverous, unusually dressed blade with the huntsman's short jacket and the mop of russet curls. His complexion apart, he might have been a gondolier. He was smoking a cheroot and staring up at the moon. Something about him took Merridith's attention. For a while he didn't quite know what it was. But then it occurred to him in a moment of fierce clarity 'like the one immediately before the opiate brings sleep or stupefaction'. It was the man's very nonchalance, his casual air. It marked him out like a pointing finger. He was the only man in the East End at midnight who did not appear to be selling or buying.

He saw him again in King David Lane, again at the bottom of Ratcliff Road, standing in the light of a gin-shop doorway and reading a newspaper that was folded in half. The sound of raucous singing was coming from the groggery: a song of the beauty of Whitechapel girls. Merridith watched for fifteen minutes. The man never turned a page of his newspaper.

Two women drifted towards the Viscount and briefly tried to tout him. A lamp-man illuminated the naphtha globes on the corner. A window opened. A window closed. A coach went past in a clatter of wheels. When he looked again, the man was gone.

Perhaps just paranoia: an hallucination of some kind; like the clack of footsteps behind him in the soot as he crossed by the match factory to find a hackney. But three mornings later he saw the man outside the house, peering down curiously into the below-stairs area. As though sensing the gaze from the drawing-room window he had looked up slowly and steadily to meet it. A foxlike face. Ginger sideburns. He smiled and tipped his hat and walked casually away, as leisurely as if he owned Tite Street and all its inhabitants and had finished making inventory of his possessions.

For weeks afterwards Merridith dreaded the arrival of the mail, certain it would bring an extortionist's missive. He sat awake at night in a chill slick of sweat, cursing himself for his weakness but mostly for his stupidity. Laura would leave him. The boys would be taken away. It would be Laura and the boys who had to bear his disgrace.

On the morning of his thirtieth birthday, he realised he had contracted an infection. A discreet consultant doctor, a former college-mate at Oxford, had taken care of matters in a briskly efficient way. He had made no accusations; asked no questions.

Probably he did not need to ask. But Merridith would have to be careful, he counselled. He had been fortunate this time but might not be again. Gonorrhoea could cause insanity. Syphilis could kill. Such dreadful diseases could be passed to his wife. Given the sleeping arrangements at Tite Street that would have been impossible, but he appears to have made up his mind to swear off the East End.

December came. Laura and the boys returned from Sussex. Christmas was peaceful enough in the Merridith household that year. He began to calm down, to take less laudanum. In April the family engaged a controversial new physician, a pioneer of hypnotism and other unorthodox methods: he prescribed the smoking of hemp to soothe the patient's nerves. It seemed to work, at least for a time. A strong swimmer since his boyhood on the shores of the Atlantic, Merridith took to bathing in the Serpentine early in the morning. The journals start to display a lighter touch: a man emerging from a long, fearful night. By summer he had become a regular at a Turkish Baths near Paddington, where he was 'thrashed about by chubbies with the branches of trees'. He exercised at the gymnasium at his Mayfair club and 'chucked about the medicine-ball like a champion bloody pugilist'. Relations with his wife evidently improved a little, though the use of separate bedrooms was always to remain. Sestinas and villanelles appear in the diaries, rather workmanlike little sonnets but not entirely unimpressive. (One, perhaps importantly, is entitled: 'Reparation'.*) That he had done harm to 'the unfortunate of the East End of London' perhaps gave him cause for a deal of careful thought; so it might appear from his numerous large donations to the church groups and charities working in that area. In October 1844, he writes in a margin: 'Certain painful events of the last several years have come to seem as those from the life of some other man; a creature with little to do with myself.'

And then one morning at breakfast what he had dreaded finally happened. His winnings from the raffle were delivered through the door.

*Permission to reproduce has not been granted by the executors. – GGD

CHAPTER XXIV

THE CRIMINALS

IN WHICH DAVID MERRIDITH EXPERIENCES
A NUMBER OF GRAVE REVERSALS.

He looked at it for a time as it lay on the salver. *Kingscourt. Tiet Street. Chelsea. London.* It was not the error in spelling that gave away the contents, but the anonymously careful print in which the envelope had been addressed. No copperplate hand that might be identified: the exaggerated neatness of the poison pen.

'Is something the matter?' the Viscountess asked.

She had not seen the letter, Merridith knew that. Easily he could have pocketed it and waited until later to read it. But he did not try to conceal it; nor his fear. Instead he ordered the servants to leave the room immediately and he waited until his wife returned to the table. His thoughts at that moment may only be guessed. His actions we know about; and they seem perhaps strange.

He told Laura Markham he had loved her always, that he always would, as long as she would have him. But what was in this letter could not bring them happiness. It would change things between them, possibly for ever. He had suspected it was coming. Now it had come. She might feel she had to leave; he would understand if she did. He would leave the house himself if that were her decision. But whatever the letter's contents, he could not hide any more. He had hidden for so long; the time had come to face things. Did she understand what he was asking? Could she bear to be asked it? She said she did – or thought she did – and would stand by him now, no matter the cost.

Opening the envelope, he sliced into his fingertip. A smear of betraying blood may still be seen across the first page.

November the elivith 1844 Martlemas
Lord David.Merridith
sun of THE MURDERER
we men ar sertin of yr Fathers tenants in the distrits of
kilekierin carna glinsk and ailencally this past sixmounth he
has bien raesing the rents by dubbal an more al around

anyman belaytd with his rent by wan weak is afterbien told
he is to be evictd no mather his sircumstans or Fambly

he is after sellin some lands alriddy

a third porshion of we his tenants ar now orderd to pay rent
to that bastard Blake at Tully a grater meazel who never livd
and he is after evicting many by now

five hunderred are put out on the roadsied many is starvd
hier with no Relief espectd

theyr is NOTHIN espectd hier only an imediat starvasion

yr Father is afterbien warnd but has not quit so i do heirby
warn yrself to advis him most surtinly to put back the rents the
way they war an help the poeple in thise desprit timse or if he
does not he an yr Fambly will fiel the displaeshuor of me an
my bretherin

i am my men will bare it no longer WE AR NOT
DOGS

y wil mayke him to quit it or els-be lybill

we are men who wuld rather to work than to fiet but by
Christ we will fiet when we have to

shuld he contineu to grind us we wil be under the nisissity
of shooting any member of yr Fambly in the open dayliet for
we may as wel loose our lifes as to loose our suport

nobody wil get no merci not yrself nor yr Wife nor yr Suns
nor any othr whiel or own wifes an childerin get only
starvasion an coldnes

i am as wel die on a Rope as by hunger

it puts no plaeshour on us to writ this words but we mean it
we swaeyr to Jaesis Chriyst Crucifiyd an vow it solem with
our bloud so help us

thier is yr doom David Merridith
so if you liyk it
let yr Father contineu in his tirany
an you wil right sune be held lybill for it
y may see from this letter that we nowhere is yr hous
Be warnd – London is not so far from connemara
Y AR WATCHD & MAYBE GOT ANNY TIME

i am

yr humbl an lyill srvnt (no more)

Cptn Moonliet of the Relybill Hibernian Defenders

Jaesis rest her but yr late Mother wuld be ASHAMD this day
of the ROTTIN name of Merridith

The smile of the foxman flamed through his mind: the picture of him walking away down the street.

He held the letter lightly, as though the paper were burning.

'How did you know?' Laura asked him tearfully.

Her husband answered quietly that it was a matter of intuition.

*

He wrote to his father immediately but the letter came back unopened. He sent it again but there was no response. Laura said he should go to Galway without further delay, but Merridith felt that might be to make things worse. Almost eight years had passed in silence between son and father. The Earl had never even responded to the news of the births of his grandchildren; had ignored Merridith's periodic attempts at reconciliation. You couldn't just amble up to the house without warning.

'Then write and say you're coming whether he likes it or no,' Laura said.

But the spurned son had not been able to do that.

Instead he wrote to the Rector of Drumcliffe, Richard Pollexfen, revealing nothing about the note he had received from the tenants, but merely asking for news of the estate. A long letter came back the following week. Merridith was thanked for the generous donation he had sent and assured that the Rector would put it to good use among the local poor. Things at Kingscourt were not at all happy lately. The north wing had been closed up; the roof had collapsed. The storms of last November, which had damaged the manor, had also torn down the piers in the bay. The fishermen had nowhere to land a catch. Many were begging. Some were in the almshouse. Since the last of the servants had resigned from his father's employment, the manor had gone to rack and ruin. Only the groom, one Burke, remained on the property, and was living in the ruins of the burnt-down gate lodge. The Earl rarely left the house any more.

The tenants' rents had been raised by a third in February and then doubled at the start of the summer. Every one of the three thousand families had received a visit from a hired agent, saying rents would have to be paid promptly from now on, or evictions would follow within a matter of weeks. Many observers had found what had happened inexplicable. Lord Kingscourt, if doing things in his own certain style, had always been regarded as fair to the tenants. But that had now changed. Some of his actions were quite beyond understanding. He, the Rector, had tried to intervene, but His Lordship had refused to meet him or even to respond to his letters.

It was true that about a third of the estate appeared to have been sold to Blake of Tully. Immediately the Commander had evicted seven hundred families for non-payment of arrears. The situation was becoming critical. A gang of agitators calling itself 'The Hibernian Defenders' or 'Else-be Liables' – you did as they ordered, or else you were liable – had been attacking the outlying fields of Connemara's estates, maiming cattle and burning crops. They ran around the country in hoods and cloaks. Their marque was an H enclosed by a heart. If a man were denounced as a collaborator by one of his neighbours he would soon receive a visit from these miscreant savages. Seven Connaught landlords had been assaulted this year. It was only a matter of time before one of them was murdered. 'Old obeisances are eroding with frightening suddenness, as the banks of the bay after November's storms.' Clichés were beginning to acquire fresh power, for it might now be said with a bitter accuracy that Connemara was edging close to the precipice. Where it all might end was anyone's guess, but open revolution must be counted a possibility. 'If Your Lordship can think of any means by which your father might be converted from his recent policies, that would be to do him and the people a very great service.'

Emily returned from her travels in Tuscany. Natasha left Cambridge where she had been studying privately in the hope of somehow gaining admission to take a degree. Both went to Galway at Easter '45 and stayed. Emily's letters to London were frightened and confused. The poverty of the people was shocking, she wrote; it seemed far worse than anything she could remember. She had been reading newspaper reports of a strange new potato murrain which had appeared in Europe; if it made its way to Ireland something dreadful would happen. Her father was refusing to discuss whatever he had done. It was nobody's business how he ran his own lands. His health was deteriorating with a speed that was appalling. He could hardly sit up and had to be helped to do everything. A woman in Clifden market had spat at Natasha's feet. A little boy had shouted: 'Landlord's bitch'. One day, while out walking, she had been followed across the fields by a trio of men in hoods and cloaks.

By September it was clear that the strange blight had come. The smell of the rotting tubers tainted the air of Connemara: a choking sickly-sweetness, like cheap perfume. The poor had nothing. Many were already starving. Lady Emily wrote to her brother and pleaded with him to help. He sent a donation of two hundred pounds.

And then his father had died. And everything had changed. He remembered the words of Emily's telegram. 'Papa's sufferings almost ended. He asks for you, Davey.'

He and Laura had travelled to Dublin that night. His father had died the following evening in the arms of the heir he had driven away. Under his pillow was a note he had left, in a spidery and almost illegible scrawl. According to its date, it had been written more than a year ago, and Merridith did not know which possibility was the more terrible: that his father had lost his understanding of time, or had indeed written it a year ago, knowing he was about to slip into the void. 'Forgive me, David. Bury me beside Mama. Do your best for the tenants, always.'

The Union colours flown on his last battleship were draped across the casket by the Lord-Lieutenant of Ireland. Atop was placed a pair of buckskin gloves which the deceased had been gifted by

Nelson at Copenhagen. On the advice of the Sergeant of the local constabulary, 'driver-men' with shotguns were hired to accompany the coffin, in case the Liables came to attack it. A riderless horse clopped ahead of the procession to Clifden; a slightly ludicrous touch, Merridith thought, and he wondered who had insisted on it.

The roads were heavy with that saccharine stench, the once green meadows now swamps of turbid grime. A cabin was burning on a stone-strewn hillside. Small clumps of clothing were lying in the fields.

Most of the resident landlords of the county were waiting in the dim and draughty chapel. Amelia Blake and her husband, the Baron of Leinster. Tommy Martin of Ballynahinch. Hyacinth D'Arcy of Clifden. The catafalque by the altar had been covered with a banner that was emerald green with a large gold harp. The late Earl's instruction, the Rector explained; the standard had been draped over his own father's casket. Not one of Kingscourt's tenants or former tenants came. Many in the streets of Clifden turned their backs as the cortège passed. One man who had been evicted was seen to spit on the ground. Another called out: 'May the bastard rot.' But the mourners pretended they did not notice.

There was a brave attempt at singing, and even at harmony, but the nineteen voices comprising the entire congregation were not quite loud enough to be heard above the organ.

> *Jesus, Saviour; pilot me,*
> *Over life's tempestuous sea.*
> *Unknown waves before me roll,*
> *Hiding rock and treach'rous shoal.*
> *Chart and compass come from thee,*
> *Jesus, Saviour; pilot me.*

The Lord-Lieutenant dropped the first clod of earth in the grave. He gave a salute as the Last Post was sounded but there was no oration and no volley of gunfire, the Earl having made clear that he wanted neither. The Rector read the verses from the opening of Genesis: the creation of the world, the naming of the animals. Captain Helpman of the Coastguard laid a wreath of white lilies. The instant the Prayers of Farewell were finished, Merridith said he needed a few moments to be alone. Everyone understood. He was told to take his time. Hard to be the mourner who disappointed the deceased.

He walked around the rear of the black stone church, opened his cuff, tugged up his sleeve. Improvised a tourniquet from his New College necktie. Took what he needed from the pocket of his overcoat.

The spike pierced his skin with a small, clean burn. A bright bead of blood appeared from the puncture and he soaked it dry with a monogrammed handkerchief of his father's. Dullness flooded him: a soporific heaviness. He turned to leave.

And that was when he saw her.

Standing in the rusted gateway with a baby in her arms.

She was wearing a black bodice and a dark green skirt; laced black boots that came up to her ankles; and it came into his mind for no good reason that he could not remember seeing her wearing anything on her feet.

A ribbon was tied around her frost-white neck; a twist of dried rushes around her fragile wrist. She was humming a ballad of broken love: quietly, coldly, with graven stillness. Crows rose up from the scrubland behind her like fragments of charred paper borne on the breeze. Her eyes had a defeated, closed-down look, but otherwise she had not changed in any way he could see. It shocked him how very little she had changed. A little thinner, that was all. A little more pale. But her hair was still beautiful: lustrous and black.

He tried to smile. She did not smile back. Unbuttoning her bodice, she put the infant to her right breast and continued lilting it the ancient tune. He knew the song. He had heard it often. It was said that if you sang it to an enemy, he died.

'Mary?'

She took a sharp step back from him but never stopped humming. He watched the tiny child as it suckled, as her fingertips stroked its downy head around the fontanelle. The child gave a stir and wearily puked. Weakness trembled the watcher's legs. He wanted to sit. He wanted to run. A hot, strong thirst was salting his mouth.

'Is everything all right, David?'

He became aware of his wife and Johnnyjoe Burke standing behind him. Without saying a word she had turned and left the

gateway, cradling the baby close as she pushed through the nettles.
He watched her walk away across the muddy, thorned morass, the
hem of her skirt knocking spores from the ragwort.

'Your Lordship? Are you sick, sir?'

He managed a laugh. 'Why would I be sick?'

'Your face is terrible white, sir. Should I get Doctor Suffield?'

'No no. Just rather gave me a start. Seeing Miss Duane after all
this time.'

His wife was giving him a curious look.

'You wouldn't want to mind that one, sir. She's gone odd as
bedamned.'

'What was her name again, Johnny? – Mary or something,
wasn't it?'

'Oh, that one twasn't Mary, sir. Tis her sister. Grace Gifford.'

Merridith turned to him slowly. 'You don't mean little Grace?'

'Married now, sir. Living over in Screeb.'

The black-plumed horses were whinnying as the hearse was led
away: down the rutted hill and towards the hungry town of Clifden.

'And her parents? Both well, I hope.'

'The mother's gone on a year now, sir. The father six months.
May they rest in peace.'

'Oh dear. I didn't know. That is very sad news.'

'Aye, sir. Old Mrs Duane, Lord have mercy on her – she had a
great fondness for you, sir. She spoke about you often, so she did.'

'I was terribly fond of her, too. She was a very natural person.'
His words sounded so trite that he hated himself. He wanted to tell
Burke that Margaret Duane had seemed a mother to him, but
somehow that seemed the wrong thing to say.

'And what's-her-name – Mary – would be married herself now,
I suppose.'

'Aye, sir, this past ten year and more. Living up near
Rusheenduff. Little babogue of her own now, too, I believe. A
girleen I think.'

'She keeps in touch with us from time to time, does she?'

'I seen her in Galway Market the other week I think.' Burke
gave a dismissive wave and looked at the stony ground. 'But she
doesn't be coming down this way much any more, sir. Not for a
good many year. She's her own little clan up there now.'

'I wonder – would it be possible to visit Mr and Mrs Duane's grave. Just to pay one's respects. Do you think we might arrange it?'

'You haven't much time, sir, I know. You'll be wanting to head back to London as soon as you can.'

'It would only take an hour. I assume it's at Carna; wouldn't it be? At the RC chapel?'

'I don't think you understand me, sir. You've been away a while now.'

'What's the matter, Johnny? How do you mean?'

Burke spoke very quietly, as though ashamed of a crime. 'Their grave – it isn't known, sir. They died in Galway workhouse.'

CHAPTER XXV

THE UNPAID ACCOUNT

The steadfast plack of the casement clock, the odour of dust and antique leather so redolent of the headmaster's study at Winchester.

He would build a new pier and a moorings for the fishermen, perhaps a model school for the smallholders' children. Get in a proper estate manager to help the tenants; some local man, a young man, who was clever and decent. Maybe send him to the Agricultural College in Scotland. Teach the people about soil and hygiene. Give them the benefit of modern ideas. Encourage them to widen their old-fashioned thinking, to change their outmoded customs and unwise ways. This reliance on the 'lumper' or 'horse potato', for example, when it was clearly so prone to infestation by blight – that could all stop now. Merridith would stop it. Kingscourt would be the best-managed estate in Ireland, or anywhere in the United Kingdom for that matter.

The heavy door opened, ending his private thoughts. The lawyer came stately into the dark panelled chamber like an executioner entering the condemned man's cell. He sat at the desk without uttering a word; broke open the seal on the scroll of vellum.

'This is the last will and testament of Thomas David Oliver Merridith, R.N., K.C.B., Admiral of the White Ensign of the Queen's Fleet, the noble Lord Kingscourt, the Viscount of Roundstone, the eighth Earl of Cashel and Carna.'

'What, all of them?' Merridith's dowager aunt chuckled feebly: to a disapproving glower from the notary public.

It commenced with a number of small bequests. Fifty guineas to a fund for indigent seamen, sixty to establish a naval bursary at Wellington College: 'for a boy of the labouring classes who would serve his country but whose family's means do not come up to his abilities'. Two hundred pounds per annum to the new workhouse at Clifden: 'to be utilised for the benefit of the women and children only, my beloved son David to be Chief Trustee, and sole executor of my entire estate'.

His assortment of rare and extinct zoologica was willed 'to some respected institution of animal scholarship, preferably open to the poor and the young; that the fruits of a lifetime of cataloguing and classification may be shared, and the seed of the pleasure of solitary learning planted'. It was stressed that the collection was to be exhibited intact, properly insured for its full value and named in memory of his late wife: 'The Verity Kingscourt Memorial Collection'. Merridith's eldest sister Emily was bequeathed her father's library, also his collection of ancient charts and maps. His other sister, Natasha, was to receive a number of paintings, her father's nautical instruments and his Erard grand piano. Small trust funds had been established for both the Earl's daughters, 'to be annulled, naturally, on the occasion of their marriages'. Twenty pounds was to go to Mrs Margaret Duane of Carna, 'in thanks for her services in the care of my children'. Lord Kingscourt's two best horses were left to his stable manager, a local tenant farmer named John Joseph Burke: 'as a mark of gratitude to a true and loyal friend'.

At that last phrase, Emily started to quietly weep. 'Poor Papa.' Merridith crossed to her quickly and took her by the hand. That only seemed to make her more upset. 'Whatever shall we do without him, Davey?'

'Shall I continue, My Lord?' the lawyer asked barely.

Merridith nodded. He put an arm around his sister.

'The demesne, dwelling house, outbuildings, fishery, creamery and sundry other lands now held in tenantry at Kingscourt in Her Majesty's County of Galway, are left in entirety to the Law Life Insurance Company of London to which said properties have been mortgaged in full.'

The solid tick of the clock: how it seemed to fill up the room. Down in the street a cart trundled past. He could hear the clop of the drayhorse's hooves, the lonesome cry of a costermonger. His aunt, his sisters did not even glance at him. They knew the moment was too shameful for direct looks. They had bowed their heads, or gazed at their hands, as the lawyer's voice continued its sombre enumeration. The Latinate cadences of England's laws. The antique French phrasings of law's own poetry. The knifely precision of Merridith's disinheritance.

When the reading was finished, the lawyer expressed his sympathies. Discreetly he asked Merridith to remain behind for a moment. There were a number of matters arising which must be discussed. The ladies need not be troubled by such trifling preoccupations at this time when their grief was so natural and fresh.

From a drawer he took a dossier the size of a family bible, stuffed with letters from banks and insurance companies, relating to the mortgaging of Kingscourt. His father had granted lien on the property fifteen years ago, to raise funds for an investment in a bauxite mine in the Transvaal. But he had been poorly advised and the venture had collapsed. It was profoundly to be hoped that the sale of the estate would cover at least the capital sum. The value of land in Ireland had been plummeting lately. But we would worry about that when the time came to worry about it. Sufficient unto the day was the evil thereof. And there were matters that would have to be worried about now.

In the food shortages of '22 and '26 and '31, His Lordship had spent considerable sums importing grains for charitable purposes. Apparently at the suggestion of the late Lady Verity, he had commissioned a brigantine, at very great expense, to fetch a cargo of India meal from South Carolina to Galway. Whether such had been an entirely judicious course (or not) was perhaps not a matter for the lawyer to adjudge. Certainly in the wake of those unhappy events, promised rental income from the estate had failed to materialise. The lands, in fact, had been allowed badly to deteriorate and had not been adequately maintained for several decades.

All of the late Earl's accounts at his bank had been overdrawn for some years. There were a number of other unpaid loans, some considerable and long overdue, secured against numerous sizeable investments, which had either not realised or been disappointing in the extreme. One hesitated to employ such an indelicate word, but the late Earl was in effect bankrupt in all but name. Large amounts were owing to vintners and horse dealers; also to bookbinders and dealers in animal curiosities. A very substantial sum had been borrowed from a certain Blake of Tully, fourteen years ago now, at moderate but still significant interest. The debt was being called in under threat of litigation. The Commander wished to extend his landholdings and was being prevented from so doing by the non-payment of the deficit. It appeared at least a *prima facie* case of nonfeasance. As sole executor, Merridith was personally liable. Court action would be expensive and highly unpleasant.

There was also the small matter of the lawyer's own account which had accrued over thirty years and never been paid. Perhaps now might be an opportune time to clear matters up, as it were. He pushed the crested parchment rather contritely across the desk, as though surrendering a piece of pornography of which he was ashamed.

The sum could have bought David Merridith a mansion on Sloane Square. 'You'll take a promissory cheque, I expect, will you?'

'Oh, I don't think there is any –' The attorney paused. 'That is to say –' He stopped and began again. 'Whenever you have time to attend to the matter will be quite sufficient, My Lord. You will have your mind on other subjects at the present.'

Merridith took out his debit book and wrote a draft for thirty-five thousand guineas, knowing he had less than two hundred pounds at his bank. The lawyer took it without looking at it and put it into a file.

'I expect Your Lordship must be feeling a little taken aback by developments.'

'In what way?'

'I mean the position regarding the lands in Ireland and so on. Your Lordship must have had certain expectations.'

'Naturally Father explained the situation some years ago. We had a good talk. I quite understood his position.'

'I had no idea Your Lordship and the Admiral were so close. I should imagine that must be a great comfort to you now.'

'It is.'

'You were with him at the end, of course?'

'Naturally.'

The lawyer nodded tactfully and lowered his eyes. 'If I may say so, sir – your father was a great man. A man who deserved better than providence allowed him. We who were destined to come into his orbit were really most fortunate. If only we knew it.'

'Indeed.'

'There it is. There it is. We know not the hour, sir.'

'Quite.'

'Still – you'll receive the most important thing, of course. The treasure which no vicissitude can ever depreciate.'

'What is that?'

The lawyer stared across at him as though the question was ridiculous. 'Well his title, of course, My Lord. What else?'

The ninth Earl's maiden address in the House of Lords was on a proposed change to the Poor Law Amendment Act (1834), which had made hard labour a condition for entry to workhouses. The speech was reported in *The Times* the following morning under the headline NEW CALLS FOR DECORUM IN THE HOUSE. Laura snipped it out and pasted it into a scrapbook.

> I thank My Noble Lord for the warmth of his remarks but I confess myself ashamed to stand in this House tonight. This place which gave its benison to one of the most ignominious manoeuvres ever to originate from a civilised parliament; this repulsive contrivance for wrenching the grief of desolate widowhood; for refusing the hand of friendship to needy age; for incarcerating the foundling in Bastilles of neglect and for sentencing to beggary the betrayed and abandoned poor.

Three hundred miles north-west of the point where he was standing, a woman was passing a milestone for Chapelizod. She was hungry, this idle tramp: this fodder for the workhouse. Her feet were bleeding badly and her legs were very weak. Not so long beforehand, she had given birth in a field; but the ratepayer would not be burdened by having to keep the child alive. She walked easterly, quite slowly, in the direction of Dublin, and beside her flowed the Liffey on its way to the sea. On the sea must be a ship that could take her to Liverpool. Glasgow or Liverpool. It did not really matter. All that mattered now was to stay on her mangled feet: to somehow keep walking through the town of Chapelizod. Her name would not be mentioned in the House that sunny evening; nor in *The Times* for the following day.

As she came to a brow and saw the sea in the distance, those debating her across that sea were remarking on something curious. The extraordinary passion with which the new peer was speaking; how odd was his ardour, his clear sense of outrage, when the gallery was almost as empty as the chamber itself. *Hansard* records the making of a genteel intervention.

> MISTER SPEAKER: Might I respectfully counsel His Noble Lordship that although some Noble Lords may be a trifle hard of hearing, and although his Hibernian tones are pleasant in the extreme, there is really no need to raise them to quite such an operatic degree. (Laughter from the House. Cries of 'hear hear'.)*

It was as though he was not making a speech at all, many said. As though he was shouting at someone in the room, some enemy he had long been waiting to attack. All the more strange when you looked up the records and saw that the man who had seconded the original bill was Thomas David Kingscourt of Carna, the Viscount of Roundstone: the maiden Earl's father.

✳

The Chief Director of the company agreed to a compromise. Forty thousand guineas would have to be paid immediately, the remaining three hundred thousand at the end of the year. Those were the very best terms that could be offered. They had only been possible because of Lord Kingscourt's position. Nobody wished to bankrupt a peer of the realm; to auction the lands of his birthright would be utterly unthinkable. We Old Wykehamists had to stick together now.

The literary evenings stopped. The sculptures were sold, then the paintings and finally the entire library. The Renaissance fresco was purchased by a Yorkshire grain merchant who was building a Gothic mansion on the outskirts of Sheffield. The total raised was a little short of nineteen thousand. It wasn't enough, the company said.

Laura sold the jewellery she had inherited from her mother,

*Hansard, vol. 234, col. 21 (1846).

having first ordered paste copies to be made of every piece. She dreaded letting her father know what course she was taking or the circumstances that had caused her to take it. If he ever discovered either, he would be enraged to a fit. Six thousand guineas were raised at the auction at Sotheby's, a disappointing sum given their actual value. It was still not enough, said the company's banker. The instalment required was forty, or the lands would be sold.

The rent on the house at Tite Street was eight thousand a year. If they gave it up and took the children out of school, they could scrape together the forty thousand. The plan was sold to the boys as a great adventure; similarly sold to Laura's father. The family would be removing to Galway for a while. Clean air. Open fields. The ancestral lands.

They arrived at Kingscourt in August '46 to find a forest of tepees in the Lower Lock meadow, where Blake's evicted tenants had come to camp. The smoke from their fires could be seen five miles away. There was talk of an outbreak of Typhoid fever. When Merridith went among the people of Kingscourt, many refused to speak to him, or even to look at him; though some of the women raged at him that his family was a disgrace.

At night he could see the men talking angrily in the shadows. Crowds of fifty or a hundred would congregate beneath the trees. He let it be known through the police that he would tolerate no trouble. He would put nobody off the land in such difficult times but there were certain rules that must be obeyed. Anyone seen with a firearm would be arrested and evicted. He had Johnnyjoe Burke put bars on the windows.

The house was leaking badly; rotting with damp. Their advertisements for servants remained unanswered. They moved into the servants' quarters at the back of the manor where the cries of the people at night could not be heard. They would see the ravaged faces peering in through the windows. The hungry faces of weeping children. His sons became terrified to leave their quarters. Laura would not leave the house without an armed bodyguard or a pistol. Merridith came to dread opening the curtains in the morning; a dozen more tents would have appeared in the night. By September the entire meadow was filled with the landless, and their colony was spreading into the distant fields.

The police came to see him and insisted the lands must be cleared. The encampment was the size of a small town by now and presented great risks both to health and security. Three thousand people were camping on the demesne, every last one of them a Liable sympathiser. He told the constables to leave and not to return. He could not put starving families on the roadside.

He wrote letters to London and insisted there must be more aid. This talk of 'government relief works' would have to stop. The people needed food; they were too weak to be asked to work for it. It was true that this year's crop had not failed in its entirety; but it was far too small, too lacking in nutrients; grown from the rotten seed of last year's blight. And many had nowhere to grow even that. Tens of thousands were being evicted.

In October the first of the tent-people died. Four the first day; nine the next. By November, eighty were dying every week. He had Burke paint over the windows of the boys' rooms with black varnish.

They spent Christmas at the Wingfields' Dublin townhouse. The boys had begged not to be taken back to Galway on New Year's Eve. The Wingfields were going to Switzerland for a few months' holiday; when they offered to take the boys, their parents agreed. Laura was also invited, but bravely declined. She would have to remain with her husband now.

On New Year's Night they returned to Kingscourt to find a cordon of armed constables surrounding the house. An informer had told them to expect a Liable attack. Nearly two hundred tenants had died in Christmas week. The Sergeant could only allow the Merridiths entry to the manor if they agreed to station fifty troopers inside the building itself.

On the sixth of January, 1847, Merridith returned to Dublin alone. Laura was ill with suspected pneumonia and was in no condition to face the journey. She had pleaded with him not to go; the journey was dangerous. By now there was talk of landlords and their agents being attacked on the road to Dublin. But he had little choice. He had no choice at all. A document had arrived during their absence over Christmas. It was a notice of eviction from the Kingscourt Estate.

The attitude of the man from the company shocked him. He

had expected to be meeting with the Chief Director, Lord Fairbrook of Perthsire, ninth Duke of Argyle. But apologies had been conveyed by the Dublin Office manager. His Lordship had been detained by a late sitting of the House. In his place he had sent Mr Williams of the Liability Collection Office: a small, bald, furiously sweating Londoner who looked as if he would kick a dog to death if it barked.

'Have you brought what is required?'

'I beg your pardon?'

'Do you have what is required to redeem your debt, sir?'

'Not at the moment. I rather thought we might agree to a compromise. Lord Fairbrook and I have discussed the matter previously.'

Williams nodded desultorily and wrote in his ledger.

'I thought three years would be the appropriate period,' Merridith said.

Williams made no reply. He mopped his mouth with a handkerchief.

'Preferably five: but I think three may show results. My plans are laid out in the document I have given you. You will find costings and so on. I assure you it is all in order. Matter of riding out the storm for a while.'

Williams nodded again without looking up from his record book. Fingered his greasy moustache as he wrote. Finally he stamped a seal on the completed page and closed the ledger so abruptly that it gave a dusty thud.

'You have failed to repay the mortgage. The property will be sold as soon as possible. The lands still having tenants will all have to be cleared.'

'There is absolutely no question of that, I'm afraid.'

'It will be done, My Lord, whether you do it or no. Land with unpaying tenants produces no income. Moreover their continued squatting will keep driving down the value.'

'Squatting?'

'What would you call it yourself, My Lord?'

'Some have lived on those lands for five hundred years. Since long before my family ever came to Connemara.'

'That is not a matter of any interest to the company.'

'I know the company very well, thank you. The Chief Director is a long-time friend of my family.'

'Lord Fairbrook is quite aware of the situation, Lord Kingscourt. I can assure you I am acting on his direct authority. The lands will be cleared and that is an end to it.'

'How do you expect me to clear the lands? Am I to turn starving people onto the highway?'

'We understand there are professionals who do that kind of work.'

'Hired thugs, do you mean? Driver-out men?'

'Call them what you will. They enforce the law.'

'No bailiff has ever set foot on Merridith land. Not in two hundred years of my family's presence in Galway.'

'It is *not* "Merridith land", sir. It belongs to the company. You gave undertakings that payments would be made and they have not been made. You have failed in your obligations, sir. Utterly failed. One would have thought it might be a matter of honour for you to meet them, but obviously your word is not your bond.'

'How bloody dare you address me in that manner, sir. I'll take no such talk from a glorified usurer.'

'You seem happy to take when it suits you, My Lord. You are living as a guest on a property not your own.'

'I am a squatter too, then, am I?'

'*You* have been a squatter for a very long time, sir. At least they paid something to live in the place.'

'I shall never hand over the deeds of my land.'

'The titles are already in our possession, I assure you. Any other documentation can be obtained by order of the courts. The company's lawyers have the matter well in hand.'

'Surely – some compensation for the families can be arranged.'

Williams laughed bleakly. 'Are you making a joke, sir?'

'I do not understand. How do you mean?'

'It is not the company which has profited from your tenants' labours for two hundred years. So why should the company now offer compensation?'

'They have absolutely nothing. Surely you can see that.'

'You can evict them and compensate them in whatever way you wish. Or we shall evict them with no compensation. The choice is your own. You have until June the first. The evictions will begin on that date. The lands will be sold as soon as possible thereafter.'

'A brief respite is all I ask. Two years; no more.'

'The time has elapsed. Good-day, Lord Kingscourt.'

'One year, then. Please. You can manage a year.'

Williams pointed towards the door with his dripping pen. 'Good-day to you, My Lord. I have other appointments. My sailing returns to London at seven tonight.'

Dusk had descended by the time he left the office. Sleet was surging noisily into the rubbish-strewn streets. A girl who looked like a housemaid was kissing a soldier in the doorway of a shop. A trio of schoolboys was watching and laughing. He walked for a while through the crowds and the beggars, beneath the gracious colonnades of the Parliament on College Green. Down towards the river and Sackville Street next. The Liffey had a black and scabrous look. A tall ship was tied up at the south-side wharf, its three bared masts a spider web of rigging. Barrels were being unloaded by the squads of stevedores and stacked on the grey, wet flagstones.

Lightning crackled violently over the Customs House dome. He began to walk again, through the stinging blur of the hailstones. A page of a newspaper slapped against his chest. He told himself he didn't know where he was going; but that was one thing he did know. The only thing, perhaps.

Pushing now, into the slab of wind, as he crossed the slippery bridge in a flutter of coat-tails. The stern figure of Nelson glared down from his pillar: an Easter Island idol in regimentals of granite. Traders around the pedestal were packing up their stalls. A colony of gulls flapped low and scavenged their leavings, ascending in squabbles of twos and threes. Soon he was in Faithful Place; then Little Martin's Lane. The terraces became darker, their inhabitants shabbier. Skull-like the stare of the windowless tenements. The reek of wet coal and unlaundered clothes. A circlet of grime-faced urchins cringed around a brazier as he crept through the alleyways leading up to the Diamond; and the tolling of the Angelus from a score of chapels.

The shatter of thunder. The squeal of a skipping-chant. An old-soldierly cove was trudging the street with a placard on which had been painted REPENT; but the letters had begun to run in the rain.

A chancer perched on a dirty metal keg was declaiming the miraculous properties of a potion he was selling. Two sailors hurried past under a girl's pink parasol. The women were preparing to start work for the night.

Some sat on their windowsills, sipping cups of tea; others stood in the doorways of their small, dark houses, calling out softly to passers-by.

'Hello, my husband.'

'Night-night, ducks.'

'I have what you need, love. Nice and fresh.'

He crossed Mecklenburgh Street in his leaking boots and drifted down the tiny alleyway connecting Curzon and Tyrone Streets; so narrow you could touch both walls as you walked. A vagrant was crumpled in a stinking doorway, drunkenly lilting a music-hall tune. He came to a house. Stopped. Looked up. A red light was burning in the window of an attic, like the glow before the tabernacle in a Catholic church. He took off his wedding ring and slipped it into his pocket; and he knocked on the bolt-studded panel of the door.

The hatch shot back. Deadened eyes looked out at him. The hatch shot closed and the door was opened.

The doorkeeper had on a black sacking hood, a long black coat under a thick leather pea-jacket. A cudgel was clasped in the crook of his arm, through its handle a wristlet of chain.

'Five,' he murmured, jerking out his gloved palm. Merridith handed over two half-crowns. The door was slammed and locked behind him.

He was led down a flight of very steep stairs; past a door behind which a piano was jangling 'The Bucks of Oranmore'. Another door further down was slightly ajar; three cadaverous girls in corsets were sitting on troopers' knees.

The madam was a Dubliner, well dressed and muscular, and she spoke in the antique accent of the innertown Liberties. She was smoking a Turkish cigarette in an ivory holder; on her bosom a fancy necklace of bright golden coins. The visitor was greeted with professional hospitality. Would he have a cuppa tay? A nice toddy of punch? She spoke like an innkeeper with a little time to kill.

'You're not a son of Dublin, sir. To judge from your nice way of speaking. Is it English, Your Honour? Commerce or pleasure?

Well you're welcome indeed and a thousand times welcome. No strangers here, sir: only friends we haven't met. And Your Honour 'ud fancy a little sport on a cold night, I expect, sir. Banish all the cares and troubles of the day. Time enough tomorrow for sorrows, says you.'

Merridith nodded, shivering in the draught. She gave a mild chuckle, as though relishing his discomfort.

'And why not, says you? Won't we be a long time dead? Divil the jot of harm ever came from the gambol. We'll rosin up your bow for you, sir: you see if we don't.'

His hand was trembling badly as he handed over the money. The man in the mask had appeared again and was beckoning towards a corridor that Merridith hadn't noticed. Up some stairs, along a shabby landing. He entered the dark room and quickly undressed. He realised he was crying as he lay on the filthy mattress; but he dried his eyes. He did not want to cry. The air stank of sweat and putrefaction and cats, but drenched in a fug of sickly-sweet perfume. From outside in the street he could hear strident laughter, the fatigued tread of cart-horses plodding the cobbles.

A long time seemed to pass before the black door opened. The girl entered quietly, as though she was tired. She had a candle in one hand, a ragged towel in the other. Her chemise had been loosened to reveal her breasts. Her hollowed, deathly face was a grotesquerie of rouge.

'Good-night, sir,' she said. And then nothing was said.

The candle flame flickered.

It was Mary Duane.

No words can describe this peculiar appearance of the famished children. Never have I seen such bright, blue, clear eyes looking so steadfastly at nothing. I could almost fancy that the angels of God had been sent to unseal the vision of these little patient, perishing creatures, to the beatitudes of another world.

Elihu Burritt *A Journal of a Visit of Three Days to Skibbereen*
London, 1847

CHAPTER XXVI

THE SHIPPING REPORTS

Friday, 26 November, 1847
Seven days remaining at sea

LONG: 48°07.31′W. LAT: 47°04.02′N. ACTUAL GREENWICH STANDARD TIME: 02.31 a.m. (27 November): ADJUSTED SHIP TIME: 11.19 p.m. (26 November). WIND DIR. & SPEED: E. (92°). Force 6. SEAS: mountainous. HEADING: W. (267°). PRECIPITATION & REMARKS: Peak wind gust of 51 knots recorded. Tore mizzen-sail loose. Churning over easterly Grand Banks of Newfoundland.

The crippled person is lodged in the lock-up. He has slept for almost all of the past thirty-six hours. Surgeon Mangan has cleaned the wounds of his face, small lacerations and swellings. No broken bones. It seems that his name is indeed 'Mulvey' as was said; the error of calling him Swales being my own. (From the name on his bible, but he had received it from a friend.) Leeson is of the view that he is most extremely untrustworthy; but there never was a man so entirely bad that life had boiled all the goodness out of him.

Last night seven of the steerage passengers died and their mortal remains were committed to the deep. Their names were John Barrett, George Fougarty, Grace Mullins, Denis Hanrahan, Alice Clohessie, James Buckiner and Patrick Joseph Connors. God have mercy on them.

Just after dawn we made sighting of the brigantine *Morning Dew* out of New Orleans for Sligo and accordingly signalled to belay. Signal being received was returned.

We dropped anchor at 47°01.10'W, 47°54.21'N and prepared a boarding party. I went across in the launch with the Mail Agent Wellesley and some of the men (also some of the stronger passengers, and a boy) to load and receive several bags of mail. Also to put on to her Eliza Healy, seven yrs, a child whose mother and father have died on board and who has no relative to care for her in America.

I took coffee and a little brandywine for my chest with Captain Antoine Pontalba of Shreveport in his quarters. He had most worrying information to divulge.

He first enquired if we were bound for Quebec, and when I said no, he remarked that this was a mighty good thing. We discussed the horrible events which occurred there this past summer,* which were yet the talk of his ship; but I was most extremely alarmed when he said that the catastrophe has not yet run its appalling course but is still claiming hundreds of souls every week. I had thought the dreadful crisis ended but alas it is not. Indeed some say much worse may yet come.

Master Pontalba confided that his First Mate had met a man at New Orleans who had come down recently from Quebec, the latter asserting that a large section of the St Lawrence River, which course forms the main channel in to Canada, is entirely frozen over, also an enormous area on the banks, comprising many score of miles all around. This man, a Russian merchant of furs, had many stories of the sufferings now being endured by the unfortunate people in that place. Reportedly he could not speak English very well but the gist of what he said was frightful.

Forty or more ships are reported to be waiting to go in to

---

*Captain Lockwood is alluding to the tragedy at Grosse Ile in the summer of 1847, when the Quarantine Station on the St Lawrence river was overwhelmed by an enormous number of sick and hungry immigrants, many from Ireland. Thousands died; Quebec and Montreal suffered devastating fever epidemics. By the time of the *Star*'s voyage, the river was in fact closed to all shipping and the authorities had at least begun to gain control of the crisis; but clearly, from the above, terrible accounts of what had happened must still have been circulating among travellers. – GGD.

Canada, lined several miles down the river, with upwards of fifteen thousand emigrants on board, almost all from Ireland; many of these with cholera and typhus and entirely without means to be treated or even quarantined. It is accounted that on some vessels not a single man, woman or child is without affliction, neither passengers nor crew. On two vessels, it is said, all have died: every last human soul on board. Nothing less than an undiminished calamity may be expected now, with enormous loss of life.

To add to this heavy news, there had been rumours that the authorities at New York and Boston might turn back all ships deriving from Ireland, those ports being now choked with many vessels unable to go in to Canada, and the authorities at New York greatly fearful of epidemics.

I begged him not to let any of my passengers know of it but I fear it was perhaps too late, for returning in the launch I observed that several of them looked most frightened and chapfallen. I made the bosun lift the oars for a moment and said to all that we had a solemn duty not to spread alarm among our fellows, that the traveller's best friend is a cool mind. Everyone agreed to keep his counsel, even the boy, who was very afraid. But as soon as we returned to the *Star* and unfurled, I noticed that many of them were congregating on the foredeck and appearing most extremely distressed. Presently they commenced to pray aloud, in that fervently incantatory manner they have, the many strange names they give unto the Mother of Jesus.

I know from many years that this is a sign of their deepest dread.

I lay down in my quarters, intending to rest me for a moment, but fell into a deep and very troubled sleep. And I dreamed I saw the ship as from a terrible height, its body crying out for mercy to the Queen of High Heaven.

CHAPTER XXVII

Saturday, 27 November, 1847
The Twentieth Day
50°10.07′w; 43°07.01′n

O
Earth
unsown.
Ora pro nobis.
Fountain Sealed.
Ora pro nobis. Adam's
Deliverance. *Ora pro nobis.*
Advocate of Eve. *Ora pro nobis.*
Aqueduct of Grace. *Ora pro nobis.*
Bride of the Canticle. *Ora pro nobis.*
Fleece of Heaven's Rain. *Ora pro nobis.*
Eastern Gate. *Ora pro nobis.* Flower of
Jesse's Root. *Ora pro nobis.* Undug Well.
Ora pro nobis. Wedded to God. *Ora pro
nobis.* Lily Among Thorns. *Ora pro nobis.*
Rose Ever Flowering. *Ora pro nobis.* Garden
Enclosed. *Ora pro nobis.* Workshop of the
Incarnation. *Ora pro nobis.* House of Gold.
Ora pro nobis. Joseph's Wife. *Ora pro nobis.*
Unploughed Meadow. *Ora pro nobis.* Tower
of Ivory. *Ora pro nobis.* Throne of God. *Ora
pro nobis.* Undefiled. *Ora pro nobis.* Maid
Clothed in Sunlight. *Ora pro nobis.* Throne
of Redemption. *Ora pro nobis.* Surpassing
the Seraphim. *Ora pro nobis.* Treasurehouse
of Sanctity. *Ora pro nobis.* Surpassing Eden's
Meadows. *Ora pro nobis.* Mirror of Purity.
Ora pro nobis. Cathedral Unassailable. *Ora
pro nobis.* Spotless Dove. *Ora pro nobis.*
Vessel of Devotion. *Ora pro nobis.* Font
of Virginity. *Ora pro nobis.* Virgin Most
Pure. *Ora pro nobis.* Unlearned in the
Ways of Eve. *Ora pro nobis.* Victor
over the Serpent. *Ora pro nobis.*
Hope of the Exiles. *Ora pro nobis.*
Citadel of David. *Ora pro nobis.*
Queen of Africa. *Ora pro nobis.*
Sisterly Mother. *Ora pro nobis.*
Mary Immaculate Star of the Sea.
Ora pro nobis. Ora pro nobis.
Mea maxima culpa.
Ora pro nobis.

CHAPTER XXVIII

THE DENUNCIATION

IN WHICH A DOCUMENT UNCOVERED BY AGENTS
OF THE AUTHOR IS IMPARTED TO THE READER
(WHO WILL SEE WHAT IT MEANS).

HER IMPERIAL MAJESTY'S ASSIZES:
EXHIBIT 7B/A/11*

April 1847,
Galway,
to the cptn of the els-be liable men.

*my name is Mary D**** and i am of a good family. i was marrid to
N******* M***** of A'nagcraomha for near thirteen year and five
months until he destroyed his own life and the life of our infant daughter
A**** M*** M***** on christmas eve 1845 by drowning.*

---

*Document discovered five years after the voyage by detective employed in
Dublin by GGD. Fair copy. Original lost. Entered in prosecution evidence at
Galway assizes, 6 June 1849. 'Being in the matter of the trial of James O'Neill
labourer, formerly of Kilbreekan nr. Rosmuck (evicted), alias "Captain Moonlight" or "Captain Dark" of an agitational society, namely "The Hibernian

i am handing this to a certain man who i know will have knowledge of who to give it to. god send you get it for it needs to be got.

i am going to america shortly and will never come home again so i want to say what follows and hope ye and yeer men act on it. i know people in this christian county of hypocrites do be slightin about me and spreading slurry and gossip on my name and i am going away so i do not give 'that' what is said no more but here is the truth and the full of it.

when i was nineteen yrs i was promisd to one p**s M***** of A'nagcraomha, only brother of N******* M***** that was once the priest. and as i live, no man ever knew me before that time. the same p**s M***** put me in a certain way and then jaunced off with himself to my great distress. he betrayd me. i was put out of my house by my father for the shame of it and for a time had to go the roads but then i livd with my brother in law and my sister in screeb. and him that ruined me the jolly roving ploughboy.

his brother N******* was a priest in **** *****. when he heard the condition i was afterbeen put in he came down to see me and said he was very sorry over it and ashamd of his brothers low roguery and falseness to myself. he said he would leave off being a priest and wed me and rare my child if i would have him. at the first i said i would not but he insistd he would do it and did not want any lanna sired by a M***** to be a bastard itself and the mother disgracd. i said it would be wrong for him to do it an it wasnt gods will but he wouldnt be said about leavin off being a priest and he did do that anyway and kept in at me. we were lawfull marrid in the chapel at C**** (my home village) on the ninth of july 1832 and i went up to tully to live with him on his peoples land.

my child was deliverd lifeless a month after (RIP) but we were afterbeen marrid by then and nothing to be done to cancel it out neither in law nor religion.

N******* M***** was an honest and sober man but we did not live

---

Men", "Hibernian Defenders", "Liable Men" or "Else-Be-Liables"; on charges of Destruction of Property, Common Assault, Assault on a Constable, Conspiracy to Murder, Inciting or Suborning another Person to Murder and Membership of a Named and Prohibited Organisation. Document found by constables in a search of the shelter of the accused on Hayes's Island." (He was hanged in Galway Barracks on 9 August 1849. Two of his sons were later transported for life to Botany Bay for membership of 'The Irish Republican Brotherhood' or 'Fenians'.) Names excised by the Court Reporter.

as man and wife for many years. it was partly that my husband was oftentimes not well and feeble enough in himself and partly that the natural feelings were not there between us. there was sometimes unhappiness between us in the house over it but sometimes there was not. in the end of it i went to a priest Father Fagan and my sister about it and they said i was not been fair be my husband to deny him what was right and also there would be nobody for to carry on his land an we had no issue. we began to live as man and wife then. in 1843 i learnd that i was expecting an event and our child was born in janary 1844. we were quiet enough together at that time. my husband had a great longin to be a father and was the gentlest ever and loving kind. he had me destroyed with flowers and combs, the ribbons he got me would go around the world. he was like a woman itself with the child. he could not do enough for the child so he couldnt. those that call him madman or fool are not one bit fair to him. he was never that way until driven it by the cruelty of another.

in september of 1844 his brother p**s M***** came back from wherever he was and began into torturin us. though he was after abandonin me and had no right on me at all he was seethin jealous now. the first thing he done was come back onto our land and say the half of it was his own in law and custom and he couldnt be put off it or he would tell the county we were after robbing him of his homeland and blacken us. he wrote a letter to cmmndr blake and said he was entitled to be on the land and would be able to pay a better rent for it than we could ourselves. he put up a cabin for himself on the land and would not go away from it. every time i came out of the house he would be stood there and he looking at me in a certain way improper and looking hateful at his own brother and the innocent child. he would come up and look in through the window of our house at night and i undressing myself. his face would come up at the window. one time i saw him watching in at us when my husband and myself were together in a natural way. all the unhappiness came back in to the house. he killed a cow belongen to us i believe. he thrished up our potato beds and ruind them. he tore down a haggard my husband made and a wall he made to bounden our plot of the land from his own half of it. there was no piece for us. when his brother my husband was off away at his work he would come up on me and say he still desird me and loved me in soft words. he is the same coaxing liar and false deceiver he always was before with a coying tongue but a black heart. he would talk the rain out of wetting him so he would.

once and once only when my husband was away from the house and we *were not getting on well together i was weak which i will rue all my days and gave into him p**s M***** i mean to my shame. he gave me whiskey first. he said he would help me with a sup for the child if i did it and he would leave off from sneaping my husband. it is my own fault and sin what i did but also he took an advantage of the feeling that was between us before as young people. afterward he tortured me for it and said he could gain me any time he wanted. he broke my life on me, bad scran to that creepin judas.*

he was forever saying he would tell my husband about it. he spoke improperly to me about it. some things he did i cannot even say them. he would wait until he knew my husband was there and then make sighs as those which happen between a woman and her man at certain times and he lairing at me. once he took certain womans garments of mine off the gorse where they were drying and waited until my husband was coming up the boreen to pull them out his pocket. he skithered about the townland and told the neighbours my child was not the lawful breed of my husband at all but a tinkers bastard or an englishmans. as true as i live that is a lie what he said. my husband and himself had a fight over it. my husband nearly put him into his grave for himself and it is only the pity he didnt.

when the blight came on the crop the summer forelast he would not help us. he himself was all right because he had money go leór* he was after getting on his travels some way and i think he is a thieving weasel anyway who never has want of money or finery or maybe he is a landlords lackey in secret or a castle bloodhound. i would put no slyness nor trickery past that fox so i wouldnt. he is the jesus Christ of trickery. it is said by some of the people that he is a driver-out-man or a bailiff in secret. he had food in rakes when my eanling was hungry. to some he says he is a liable man and to others a friend of landlords and sheriffs. he will tell any lie. he will swear a hole in a skillet if he thinks it will put money in his way. we were evicted by cmndr blakes agent in Ottober 1845 for not paying of the rent. a driver-man came down from Galway with fifteen peelers to bate us out of it. they bet my husband in front of myself and his own child while his brother watched. they laddered him. all the while they milled him the driver-man was saying do you see this now, M*****. do you see this you dirty scullions pig. here is a bating you will never forget not so long as you live. isn't that right now. answer me pig. and they made him say yes that was right, and that he was a pig, and would not lay off of him till he did say that. he was never the same

---

*Irish: 'to sufficiency'. Origin of the English word 'galore' – GGD *after the bating he got that time. it was hag-seeds they were, not natural men. they broke him that day.*

we could pay nothing owing to the blight and to p∗∗s M∗∗∗∗∗ killing our cow. blake would not allow us credit but put us out on the road itself. it was p∗∗s M∗∗∗∗∗ took over our land then and he breakin his smig laughing at us as we were put out. we went down to rossaveel and lived in a scalp my husband dug above in the woods, myself and my husband and my infant wean in dirt while p∗∗s M∗∗∗∗∗ took our rightful land and he lording it. he is still up there now like the king of england.

he was spat on and thrun stones at by the people at his own brothers funeral and shunned but not one of them did a screed to help me.

it was hard times I had after my husband and child died. it was the workhouse for me until i coulden thole it no more. i went all the road to dublin and lost another child on the way. i had to beg in the street for nigh on a year and do what no woman should ever have to do in that place. i am now a nanny and am going to america. i am working as a nanny for the family of Lord and Lady ∗∗∗∗∗∗∗∗∗ . i will never come back to galway again an i live to a hundred. there is no use in galway for a decent woman.

everything said by the people about p∗∗s M∗∗∗∗∗ is true. i denounce him as a land robber, a seducer and a blackguard. he is after harryin his own brother and my only child into a grave and i would like something done on him by you and yeer men. <u>i know well ye have done it to others before</u>.∗ ye will know him because he has a camath† way of walking having only one foot and a wooden one marken M (for murderer, it might as well be). any fate in store for him he deserves it. while a cullion the ilk of himself is allowed to do what he will it is no wonder but the people are put down so low in these times. i do not know how so called irish men can allow it.

that the child of my womb be in hell this day if i am after telling word of a lie here. it's one foot he has and a gun-stone for his heart.

the dogs of Connamara know the truth of what i say.

i denounce him every way i can, the blackest craven cur that ever wore shoe leather and rotted the land of galway by his walking on it.

god send he die in screams of shame

Mary M∗∗∗∗∗ (nee D∗∗∗∗)

∗This phrase underlined and initialled by the Crown Prosecutor's Office, Dublin Castle.

†*'Camath'*: possibly a mis-spelling of a dialect word for limping, or a conflation of *'cam'*, Irish for 'crooked', and *'gyamyath'*, Shelta cant, meaning 'lame'. – GGD

Do not wait ingloriously for the famine to sweep you off – if you must die, die gloriously; serve your country by your death, and shed aroud your names the halo of a patriot's fame. Go; choose out in all the island two million trees, and thereupon *go and hang yourselves*.

John Mitchel, 'To the Surplus Population of Ireland' 1847

CHAPTER XXIX

THE LOST STRANGERS

TREATING OF THE TWENTY-SECOND DAY OF THE
VOYAGE; IN WHICH A GRIM DISCOVERY IS RECORDED BY
THE CAPTAIN; (WITH A SOMBRE REFLECTION ON THOSE
WHO MUST LEAVE THEIR LANDS; AND OTHER MATTERS
TOUCHING THE CHARACTER OF THE IRISH PEOPLE).

Monday, 29 November, 1847
Four days remaining at sea

LONG: 54°02.11′W. LAT: 44°10.12′N. ACTUAL GREENWICH
STANDARD TIME: 03.28 a.m. (30 November). ADJUSTED
SHIP TIME: 11.52 p.m. (29 November). WIND DIR. & SPEED:
S.S.W. Force 7 (last night Force 9). SEAS: Still heaping severely.
HEADING: N.W. (315°). PRECIPITATION & REMARKS:
Driving rain most of the day. Fogbank to north

'Is there no balm in Gilead?' Jer. 8: 22

Last night four of the steerage passengers died; and this morning they
were buried according to the rite of the sea, RIP. Their names:
Owen Hannafin, Eileen Bulger, Patrick John Nash and Sarah
Boland; all four of the county of Cork in Ireland.

This day was made a dreadful discovery.

The bowsprit mast had snapped in the storm of last night and its
rigging had become entangled in the chains at the waterline. Bosun
Abernathy had rope-climbed down the hull with some of his crew
when he saw a very large infestation of monstrous rats which had
congregated in the sewerage-gulley channel leading from the First-
Class quarters: an aperture of perhaps four feet in diameter.

Thinking to discover the source of the odour on the ship of late, he approached with some of the men to make an investigation. A piteously sorry sight was soon met.

The badly decayed remains of a youth and a girl were lying in the drainway; side by side, still enfolded in each other's embrace. Surgeon Mangan was called to pronounce death. The lad was about seventeen yrs; the girl perhaps fifteen. The girl had been several months with child.

I confess there are bitter tears in my eyes, even as I set down these words.

Nobody is unaccounted for on the Manifest of Passengers; so it must be assumed that these poor frightened people had been concealed there ever since we left Cork; or Heaven help them, even Liverpool. They must have climbed down the chains and got into the culvert, thinking to hide themselves there until we arrived at New York. As Leeson pointed up, the very many extra passengers we took on at the Cove are making us lie much deeper than is usual in the water.

A number of children were playing on the deck and I ordered them sent below.

We took them out and gave them a Christian rite as best we could; but they had nothing at all by which we might even discover their names. Many of the men were extremely distressed, even those who have seen many hard things at sea. I myself was overcome as I attempted to say the words and had to be helped by the men. Reverend Henry Deedes also assisted me and said a simple prayer. 'That these children of God; of Ireland or England; each of whom was child of a mother, and each of whom was beloved of the other, may find their safe home in the arms of the Saviour.' Afterwards the men and I sang a hymn. But it was very hard to sing anything today.

How I thought of my own dear wife and our beloved children; wishing I had them about me now. How I reflected that every little quarrel of married life may be ascribed to the very contiguity which that state brings, such as which exists between coterminous realms. And – most painful – how I thought of my own treasured grandson and wished I could embrace him for even an instant.

For me to leave my own happy situation and away to sea is such a painful thing; even after all these many years. What anguish, then, must be endured by those on board who will never again in this life see their loved ones who must remain behind? The man who will never more go walking in the evening in his home town with his brother, quietly reflecting together on the matters of the day. Or the girl who must bid farewell to respected parents whom she knows to be too poorly to countenance such an arduous voyage. The happy young couple who must part from one another and the father parted from his wife and children, to travel into America by himself where the means only exist to pay for one passage. To wander alone among strangers, they risk all.

And these, may God help us, are among the luckiest of their people. They are not the poorest of the poor of Ireland, who are almost entirely without means of any kind. 'The basest beggars are in the poorest thing superfluous,' says the bard; but not so in the tortured country of Connaught. Many of the western part of that place own almost and oftentimes literally nothing. A few manage to scrape a means across to Liverpool or London. There they become enchanted by unscrupulous 'immigration agents' who prey among them like leeches and thieves; robbing them of their very clothes by times; or a man of the tools by which he might labour in the natural and dignified way for his family; and in return spirit them on to some vessel at night, making false promises of riches in the new land.

The situations in which they sail are hideous in the extreme and would make the privations which must be endured on the *Star* seem as a Paradise. Sometimes the vessel is not even bound for America, but for any country or territory out of Great Britain; no matter how unfriendly or cold it were.

And it is all so bitterly unmerited. For as truly as the night comes down on every day, if the world were somehow turned downside-up; if Ireland were a richer land and other nations now mighty were distressed; as certain as I know that the dawn must come, the people of Ireland would welcome the frightened stranger with that gentleness and friendship which so ennobles their character.

I can write no more. There is no more to be written.

I am sorry I was ever born to see this day.

If any class deserves to be protected and assisted by the government, it is that class who are banished from their native land in search of the bare means of subsistence

Charles Dickens, *American Notes*

THE BRITISH LION AND THE IRISH MONKEY.

CHAPTER XXX

THE PRISONER

57°.01′w; 42°.54′N
— 9 p.m. —

The killer was awakened from a dream of dictionaries by the clang of the watch-bell tolling on the upperdeck; a cold, iron jangle he could almost taste. He sat up blearily in the dripping half-darkness. Stones in a canister. Stones like bullets. Looked at the ratlike grin of the bars.

A full moon was visible in the centre of the frame; around it an aureole that made it look saintly; further out again a couple of stars, but too few to be able to name them. He watched for a while. Cassiopeia, maybe. But without the whole picture the stars were anonymous. A sneeze shook him badly. Pain in the abdomen. Everything depended on how much you could see.

The squall rose up in a sudden whistled gust, racketing the loose timbers and clattering a door. It died down as suddenly. Changed its mind. It sounded to Mulvey as though another storm might be coming. He hoped he was mistaken. He could not take another storm.

From somewhere behind him through the bulk of the ship came the damped-down complaining of fiddles and pipes. The tune had several names, a reel from Leitrim, but he could not remember any of them, though he had heard it a hundred times. He tried to stand or at least to squat, but a seam of astonishing pain ran its way down his leg.

The taste of his mouth disgusted him now. Coppery, astringent:

the taint of blood. His teeth had been chipped in the beating in steerage; every time he slept they ground against his tongue. He was afraid to sleep again, the pain was so bad. He did not have nightmares any more: just physical pain. No evil dream or incubus since Nicholas died. But the whet of jagged teeth on tongue and gums.

He crawled to the corner of the small, dark cell and took a swig of greasy water from the chained-up jug. A crock of mushy pap had been shoved through the hatch. The grub was stone cold but he had eaten worse. A congealing of potato with mashed pig offal and hardtack, a concoction the sailors called 'Lobscouser Boxty'. He ate it quickly and licked the dish clean. It was better than anything available in steerage.

For a time he looked at the graffiti scratched into the seeping walls. English words and Irish words: names, obscenities. More strange the pictograms which had been etched like badges. Lions and apes. Perhaps a giraffe. A diagram that looked like a map of a forest. The characters of some language for which he had no name.

~ א # ψ ℑ Ψ Ξ Φ

Manacles and hoops had been set into the bulkheads. A cast-iron lattice in the deck planks served as latrine; thirty feet below, down a shaft of leaden tubing, was the echoed blackness of the agitated sea. And you could watch that, too: but not for long. Upsurge, downdraught. Like the boil of a cauldron. The kind of dissipation that could set you astray. Last night he had contemplated trying to escape down the hole; had considered ways in which the bolts of the lattice might be unscrewed. To hold your breath and plunge into the water: to feel the hard scrape of the keel on your back. But even as he was thinking, he knew he was only passing the time. Such days were long over. His strength was gone.

A captain bold in Halifax, who dwelt in country quarters,
Seduced a maid who hanged herself, one morning in her garters.

From down the oaken corridor he heard the Northumbrian guard singing.

His wicked conscience smited him; he lost his stomach daily,
He took to drinking turpentine, and thought upon Miss Bailey.

Queer his nickname, the neat little Northumbrian; a birdlike man who twittered when he sang. He had explained it several times to his interested prisoner. Scrimshaw: a term used by seamen for trinkets fashioned from maritime wreckage or ivory. He would talk to you sometimes if you wanted him to talk. But more to the point, he would leave you alone.

Mulvey went to the gate and shouted for Scrimshaw. When he appeared at the hatch, the prisoner told him he was parched. The guard slouched away without uttering a word and returned a minute later with a mug of cider. The captive swigged it down but it didn't slake his thirst. Crawled back to the bunk and lay down in a crumple.

Maritime wreckage. Bone and driftwood. Darker now: the wind blasting and stopping, like exchanges on a battlefield when ammunition is low. Everything had a bluish and shadowy look. He tried to curl up in the dismal coldness and shut out his thoughts as best he could. The blanket was a comfort on a night like tonight.

That nobody could kill him seemed a less measly blanket; that no killing would have to be done by himself. The ship would rock and the water would pound and he would plunge no dagger into any gulping victim. No crack of shattered ribs, no twist in the gristle. No sag of the body when you pulled out the blade.

Twelve dawns previously he could have done it easily. The target had been sleeping when Mulvey crept into the cabin. As his eyes adjusted slowly to the stale, cold darkness he could make out that the prey was lying on his back. The low, muttered uneasiness of drunken slumber. The whimper of a man trawling through his own depths. And Mulvey had stolen up like a lover to his bed, so close he could smell the victim's whiskey-tainted perspiration. The morning star would rise soon; the dreamer would not see it. Everything fell quiet. Even the sea seemed quiet. It felt to the killer as though the dilation of his pupils might be noisy enough to give him away.

He thought about the whisper of the target's son, the scarcely discernable, sleep-fuddled boy who had half woken in the blackness of Atlantic night to find a shadow shifting across from the open porthole. The boy gave a stir. Mulvey said nothing. 'Grantley?' the boy murmured. 'Are we in America now?' Mulvey did not move. The ship gave a peaceful pitch. 'Go to sleep,' he said softly. 'It is only the night steward.' The boy's breathing became drowsier; he yawned into his bolster. 'What room does your daddo sleep in?' the dream-figure whispered. And the boy had gestured vaguely and rolled back into the void.

His father was dead to the world, arms folded across his chest, as though already in a coffin or a sailcloth shroud. A corpse, David Merridith. And a killer looking down on him. The Monster of Newgate resurrected from the past – rising with the first pallid glow in the east.

Knife in hand. Knife raised to strike. But his hand was shaking. He could not bring himself to do it. No question of morality but of visceral disgust. To kill was a matter of angle and propulsion, the movement of steel from one co-ordinate to another, but he who had murdered for no other reason than survival had found it impossible to work the equation again. He did not know why, merely that it was impossible. He had known it from the moment he was given the task, from long before that: from Leeds, maybe. He had killed two men. He could never kill another. You could call it cowardice; he did not care what it was called. Here in the cell he was safe from definitions. His only imminent problem was the threat of release.

He dozed for a while but not deeply or easily. The muffled music was loudening; shrilling; through it he could hear the obscure clap of dancers. My Love is in America? Name of the tune. The docks at New York. What would they be like? Like docks in Liverpool or Dublin or Belfast. *Dock: the place where a prisoner stands.* Would his murderers be waiting? Bluster and bluff. *Bluff: a hill, a bank, a precipice. A term in poker. An empty brag. Perhaps from Middle Dutch: blaffen; to boast.* His brother was sitting in the murk with him now. The Newgate Governor. A girl he didn't know. His father by firelight. Dickens. Moloch. Michael Fagan of Derryclare. The voice came from close to him but he did not know from where. It sounded again; a red-hot blade, but plunging ferociously into the iced-over Corrib; the whispering hiss: *A friend issss here, Mulvey.*

He opened his eyes to the cavelike darkness. Looked up at the grating. A shadow was moving.

'Who's there?' he called.

No answer was given.

'Is somebody up there?'

A footstep scuffed quietly on the timberdeck by the bars. He thought he heard the heaviness of a large man breathing. A clatter of boots as he sat down on the boards.

'Come over to the window,' the voice muttered urgently. 'A friend is here and wants only to help you.'

'What's your name?'

'It is the Reverend Henry Deedes. Be quick. My time here is short.'

Mulvey rose from the putrid blanket and cautiously approached. The wind blaffened up like a boasting rage and then stopped as before; as though it had been killed by something violent. He could make out the breathing more clearly now.

'I say, owld Pius. Do come a little closah. Don't be afeared. I *am* a man of gawd, awftah awl.'

Low came the chuckle, like a sneak's while watching a caning.

'Say who you are in truth or I'll not move another inch.'

The voice came back at him, wild with anguish.

It is your brother. Nicholas Mulvey. I am in torment this night! They roast my soul, Pius! They scourge me on the hobs!

'Who in the name of Hell is this?'

No response. He took another step. Craned his neck. Climbed on to the bench. A fist thrust through the grating and grabbed at his hair. Mulvey lurched backwards and fell to the drenched floor. A lugubrious snicker came from the window. The oddly regretful laugh of a man addicted to torture.

'Fairly had you that time, Deadman. But the day's coming soon. You'll be seeing that gulpin brother of yours before too long.'

The hand pushed through the bars more slowly this time and dropped something soggy on the slimed planking.

'There's your heart, Deadman. I'm after cuttin it out for you.'

The prisoner toed it carefully: it oozed as he did. A glutinous clump of yellow-black sea-wrack.

'Can you read that, scholarboy?'

Mulvey said nothing.

'That's right, Deadman. We're closin on land. Three days now and we're in sweet New York.'

'Who is this?'

'He was given his job, boys, but he didden do it. Murra, he thought he was after escapin by gettin himself slammed.'

'Who are you?'

'You were told you'd be watched on the ship. And you are watched.' A hacking cough. The rasp of a match. 'Well maybe I'll get myself slammed, too. We'll have a royal auld spree, the two of us together. I'll teach y'a few little jigeens you won't forget.'

'How do you know me?'

'Don't you remember me, scholarboy? Think good and hard now.'

'I don't know you at all.'

No answer came back. Just the wheeze of his laughter. The rainstorm of applause from the steerage compartment.

'Give your name itself like a man.'

'You might go reportin on me then.'

'I'm no rat or informer.'

'You're both and worse, you milk-livered gallowsbird. But it don't make no matter, for there's plenty more like me. They all have your description, that's been seen to.'

'Show your face for Jesus's sake.'

'But that's no use. It had a nice little mask on it last time you saw it.'

'A mask?'

'Aye, Deadman. I was one of them came to give you the little send-off your last night in Ardnagreevagh. Me and me cumrades had you shriekin like a mule in a snare that time. But you'll make worse screams again we're finished.'

'Liar,' cried Mulvey. 'This is some antic. Go to Hell.'

The scrape of feet. A stir in the breezy dark. A face appeared in the moonlit grating; a malevolent leer the prisoner recognised.

'You're buried, Deadman. You're watched every minute. And that treacher Merridith ever laves this ship, there's five hundred in New York who'll line up to stick you. And you squeal on me to anyone, it'll only go slower for you.'

Seamus Meadowes gave a grin through the rusted bars.

'I'll raffle you, Mulvey. For who gets the first slice.'

Gaelic Physical Characteristics. – A bulging forwards of the lower part of the face, most extreme in the upper jaw; chin more or less retreating (in Ireland the chin is often absent); forehead retreating; large mouth and thick lips; *great distance between nose and mouth;* nose short, frequently concave, and turned up, with yawning nostril; cheek-bones more or less prominent; eyes generally sunk and eyebrows projecting; *skull* narrow and very much *elongated backwards; ears standing off* to a very striking extent; very acute in hearing. Especially remarkable for open projecting mouths, with prominent teeth (i.e., prognathous-jawed – the Negro type), their advancing cheek-bones, and depressed noses, etc.

'Comparative Anthropology' by Daniel Macintosh
The Anthropological Review, January 1866

CHAPTER XXXI

THE GUEST OF HONOUR

The TWENTY-FOURTH day of the Voyage
(that being WEDNESDAY the first day of
DECEMBER); in which the Reader is offered a
number of Contemporaneous documents; also the
TRUE RECOLLECTIONS of some of the Passengers
pertaining to the EXTREMELY IMPORTANT events
of that day; and the Author's own Account of a
disturbing Birthday Celebration (which latter he
will never Forget so long as he Lives).

Captain Lockwood's Quarters
— 9.38 a.m. —
An Emergency Note in the Register

CALENDS DEC. 47

I have not five minutes ago compleated a conference of myself, First
Mate Leeson, the prisoner Pius Mulvey and Lord Kingscourt. The
circumstances in which the interview occurred were as follows:

Two hours erewhile, at dawn this morning, I received word that
my presence was required in the lock-up. The prisoner Mulvey was
in a state of profound distress all night. He said he needed pressingly
to speak to myself and to Lord Kingscourt about a very dark matter
indeed. He would not reveal it then and there but intimated that he
had happened upon extremely troubling information touching the
safety of Lord Kingscourt and his family aboard this vessel.

I gave orders for him to be conveyed to my quarters. There he
refused to breathe another syllable until Lord Kingscourt was
brought to him in person. I was obviously averse to arrange for this
but he said he would say nothing (and indeed would return to the

lock-up, taking his information with him) if he could not see His Lordship and speak to him in person.

Contriving a pretext so as not to cause alarm I sent a message to Lord Kingscourt's quarters and asked if he would breakfast with me. When he came in, Mulvey became quite distraught. He fell to his knees and began to exclaim, kissing the hands and garments of Lord Kingscourt, invoking the name of his late mother as that of a holy personage. His Lordship appeared disconcerted by such an effusion and asked the other to stand up. I explained to Lord Kingscourt that this was the man of whom I had spoken previously, who had asseverated a great fidelity to the Merridith family.

Mulvey told us that last evening at approximately midnight he had been looking out the bars of the lock-up when he had perceived two men of steerage passing by on the deck. They had paused nearby and commenced to mutter and whisper.

One confided to the other that he belonged to a secret revolutionary society, namely 'The Else-Be-Liable Men' of Galway. And he revealed that he had been placed on board the ship in order to murder Lord Kingscourt and his wife and children as a revenge for evictions and other deeds carried out by the Merridith family in that unhappy district.

Lord Kingscourt was very greatly shocked; but he then said that he had indeed received threatening notes from the same hooligan gang in the past. Moreover he mentioned that he had reason to believe his father's grave to have been desecrated by these very barbarians and that he had been advised by the Irish Constabulary not to travel through his Estate without an armed bodyguard. He was exceeding concerned that his wife and children should be protected on the ship. I guaranteed to him that I would order personal guards from this on. He implored me to do so in such a way that his wife and children should remain unaware of the situation, since he did not want them to be upset. I said it were better if they remained in quarters for the rest of the voyage; and he said he would see what might be done about it.

One of the conspirators Mulvey was not able to distinguish; but the other that had spoken of dastardly murder he named as Shaymus Meadowes, lately of Clifden.

Immediately I sent Leeson and a number of men down to

steerage to arrest him. A meticulous investigation was made of his belongings and therein was found a sample of revolutionary literature, that is, the words of a hateful ballad about landlords which a number of the men have heard him singing late at night when he was drunk. He has been placed in the lock-up until we arrive at New York, at which time he will be given into the custody of the authorities.

Lord Kingscourt thanked Mulvey most sincerely for what he had done and pronounced himself greatly in the latter's debt. He said he understood that it must have been difficult, knowing very well the informer was regarded among the commoner Irish as a pariah. He offered Mulvey a reward for his courage but it was insistently refused. Mulvey said he had done nothing other than his Christian duty, that he should not have been able to sleep at night had he taken any other course. Again the memory of Lord Kingscourt's mother was mentioned, Mulvey revealing that his own parents had benefited from her kindness on one occasion and often prayed for her repose still and once a year visited her grave at Clifden. (Queer; I had thought his mother to be deceased.) That a picture of the late Countess hung to this day in their humble cottage, a devotional candle burning constantly before it. That one of his own sisters had been christened 'Verity' in veneration of the memory of Lord Kingscourt's mother. That to allow Lady Verity's son to be murdered by a reprobate such as Shaymus Meadowes would be unrealisable for him. And that the thought of the two little boys being harmed or worse was simply more than he could bear to countenance.

At that point Lord Kingscourt became very distressed. Mulvey begged him not be sad but rather to believe that the great majority of Galwaymen would feel the way which he, Mulvey, did but that there was always one rotten apple in the orchard to get all the others a bad name. He said poverty and forgetting their faith had created such a hardship among the people that violence had sadly sprouted in that barren field where before was the naturally existing friendship between humble servant and sheltering master. Lord Kingscourt thanked him again and collected himself a little.

At that point it occurred to Lord Kingscourt that Meadowes being in the lock-up, and steerage being no sort of possible haven, there was no safe place on the ship for Mulvey to go to. 'I suppose that is true,' Mulvey replied. 'I had not thought about it. But it is all in the hands of the Saviour, may His will be done always. He will protect me, I know.' And he added: 'If I am murdered for what I am after doing this day, at least I can die with my conscience unsullied. And I know I shall see your mother in Paradise this night.'

I said I could perhaps offer him a berth among the men, but Lord Kingscourt would absolutely not hear of it. He said it was not every day that a man had his life saved and he meant to show at least some variety of gratitude for it. His Lordship and Mulvey agreed with myself that he would be accommodated in the First-Class quarters for the remainder of the voyage; in a lazaretto next to Lord Kingscourt's own stateroom which is used for the storing of linens and such. A subterfuge was agreed by which such an arrangement might be cloaked.

He, Lord Kingscourt, said he would need a short time to discuss it with his wife. (Her Ladyship, it appears, is the wearer of the britches.)

*

Countess Kingscourt's Cabin
— about 10 a.m. —

'You're not serious,' Laura Merridith said.

'It is tiresome, I know. But Lockwood insists the poor chap is at death's door.'

'Precisely, David.'

'What does "precisely" mean?'

'He could have cholera or typhus: any kind of filthy infection. And you propose to allow him to sleep next to our children?'

'Hardly next to them, for pity's sake.'

'In the cabin next door, then. And across from my own. How, convenient, should he require a trio of companions for bridge.'

'Will you never understand that we have a responsibility to these people?'

'I have done nothing to "these people", David. And they have done rather a lot to me.'

'I will help an unfortunate man who is down on his luck. With or without your blessing, Laura.'

'Then do it without!' she shouted. 'As you do everything else.'

She went to the porthole and stared out hard, as though she expected she might see land from a distance of five hundred miles.

'Laura – surely we can conduct ourselves without raising our voices.'

'Oh yes. I forgot. We must never raise our voices, must we? Must never have a single human emotion about anything. Must insist on the same bloodlessness and lifelessness as one of your father's damned skeletons.'

'I had rather you did not turn these quarters into a barrack-room with your language, Laura. And what we must do is to think of the boys. You know they find it upsetting when we have words.'

'Do not presume to give me instruction on my children, David, I warn you.'

'I would never do that. But you know I am right.'

She spoke over her shoulder, as though he wasn't worth the effort of facing. 'How would you know what they find upsetting? Is it you they come to when they are upset? Their father who cares more for individuals he does not know than he does for his own wife and family.'

'That is not fair.'

'Is it not? Are you aware that today is your eldest son's birthday? It would not have hurt you very much to mention it to him if you were.'

'I'm sorry. You are right. I had momentarily forgotten.'

'You might rather say sorry to the person your thoughtlessness has hurt. When you have quite finished saving the world from itself, of course.'

'They are dying in tens of thousands, Laura. We cannot do nothing.'

She made no reply.

'Laura,' he said, and he made to touch her hair. As though sensing the gesture, she moved to avoid it.

'It will not trouble us to help a little, Laura. Surely you can agree. We shall be in New York in only three days.'

She spoke very quietly, as though it hurt her to speak. 'They'll never love you, David. Why can't you see it? Too much has already happened for that.'

He gave a blunt laugh. 'That is a strange thing to say.'

She turned. 'Is it?'

'The only love I have ever wanted is yours. Yours and that of the boys. If I have that, I have everything.'

'You must think me even blinder than I am. Do you?'

A wave doused the porthole and dribbled down the glass. Through the walls they could hear their shouting sons. A knock sounded on the door: the chirp of the cleaning-steward.

'May I have your agreement to help the man, Laura?'

'Run to them, David. Like you always do.'

The Lock-up
— 10.41 a.m. —

I ... John Lowsley ... seaman Duty-Officer, state that at ... 10.41 ... on this day a prisoner ... P. Mulvey ... was released from my charge and his belongings returned to him in full degree for which he signed; viz ... one bible six pennies and one farthing.

Pius Mulvey's Lazaretto
— about 11 a.m. —

(Extracts from a letter from George Wellesley, Agent of the Royal Mail, to G. Grantley Dixon, 11 February 1852)

On the morning of Wednesday, December the first ... a steward came to my quarters and said they needed to take back the Linen Garderobe or Glory-Hole in which I had stowed two trunks ... A supposedly sick man from steerage was to be lodged in there, it was said. I was a little irritated to hear this,

I own; but the steward said he was under orders and no more about it . . . I had some papers I needed to keep about me in one of the trunks but I could not remember which one. My clodpate of a servant, Briggs, was puking like a geyser with seasickness that morning, so I said I would fetch them myself. [. . .]

Guards had been placed in the First-Class accommodations that morning; one man at every door. The steward did not know why, but I thought little about it. My own view is that we should have been guarded from the very moment of leaving Queenstown and that it was an outrageous disgrace that this had not been done, given the moral complexion of most of our fellow travellers. [. . .]

When I arrived at the little room – perhaps six feet by eight feet, shelved all around with no porthole – Lord Kingscourt and his eldest son Jonathan Merridith were assisting a man to make up a rough cot out of cushions and blankets on the floor. I should say the man in question was about five feet and four inches in height, very slender with morose blue eyes. He was ragged and emaciated and obviously of that type who would at all times rather be idle than work. The usual unpleasant odour hung about him. One would have thought his disfigurement would be the most noticeable thing – he had a 'game' foot and limped heavily in consequence of it – but his eyes were in fact the most memorable feature. Being looked at by him was rather like being regarded by a mongrel that has been kicked out in the rain for the night.

I cannot say I saw anything violent or criminal in his facial cast. Far from it; he appeared as one in whom innocence was strong, perhaps even to the degree of mild idiocy. He was rather like a Caucasian nigger, if such a horrid centaur exists. Not evil as such but more childlike and stupid.

Nor can I remember at this remove if there was any conversation; but if there was, it was entirely inconsequential. But I do recollect that at one interval I looked up from searching my chests and became aware of a sort of strained silence in the cabin. Lord Kingscourt and the man – I am damned if I can express it – but they seemed uneasy being together in such a small space. And yet they were grinning like freakish idiots at each other. It is hard to explain. Rather like a débutante having to dance with an ugly baron, perhaps, or Mama will scold her and the family will be ruined. Nothing was being said and yet profound unease was there; and shared, indeed, by both the parties.

I went back to my search and found the documents I needed. The young lad had begun to fiddle about with the sheets on the shelves and his father told him to behave himself. It was quiet and good-humoured; nothing unusual about the scene. And it was just at that moment that the girl came in.

She stood very still in the doorway, as motionless as a plaster madonna. I never saw any woman stand quite so still in my life; not before or since. You know how they fuss and fidget like lepers. But this was stillness like that of a sentry. The girl could be decidedly odd in her manner, possessing the usual slatternly attitude of that ingrate class and nationality; entirely lacking in grace or good humour, and would look at you like devil's daggers if you paid her a simple compliment; but this appeared, at least to myself, some new kind of eccentricity or oddness. It was as though the sight of the cripple had profoundly shocked her. As for the cripple, he looked similarly aghast.

There were two pillows in her arms, which I assume she had been ordered to fetch. But she simply stood there in the doorway without putting them down. She did not grow pale or make any displays. She just did not move for a weirdly long time.

Then Merridith began to make introductions, as though some kind of queer house party was about to commence: 'Oh Mulvey. I don't know if you've met my children's nanny. Miss Duane.'

'It's yourself, Mary,' the mick said very quietly.

Kingscourt appeared mildly confused. 'You know each other?'

Again nobody said anything for a considerable period.

'You've knocked into each other going about the ship, I suppose?'

Very meekly the hopfoot said: 'Miss Duane and myself, sir, we knew each other when we were young people, sir. Our families was friends one time. Back in Galway I mean.'

'I see. Well that is nice. Isn't that nice then, Mary?'

Not one word or syllable came from the skivvy.

'Should I let you alone for a while to catch up?' asked her unfortunate master.

She put the pillows on a shelf and left without a word. Merridith gave a dissatisfied chuckle as of confusion at the performance.

'Bloody women, eh?'

'Yes, sir.'

'She was bereaved of her husband not so terribly long ago. She has been a little out of sorts. You must forgive her.'

He answered in his ugly and ridiculous accent: 'I understand, sorr. Tank you, sorr. Blessins o' God an his mudder on you, sorr.' They murder the Queen's English as well as everything else.

And that is all I have to tell you. I locked up my trunk and went away.

The girl was standing at the end of the passageway with her back to me now. The guards were looking at her but she did not seem to notice. I thought no more about it and returned to my quarters. [. . .]

One would have thought that to be in the presence of murderer and victim would have left more of an impression; but to be completely plain, it did not. I was more concerned with having had to leave my trunk in the presence of one who would have gnawed it open had he thought it contained a bottle, a pistol or a Rosary beads.

❊

Main Passageway in First-Class Quarters
— about 1 p.m. —

From a statement sworn to Officer Daniel O'Dowd and Captain James Briggs of the New York Police Department, 20 December 1847, a fortnight after the murder. John Wainwright, a Jamaican sailor on bodyguard duty in the First-Class quarters, recalled the following angry exchange from the main stateroom or sitting room, which he first assumed to be an argument between Lord and Lady Kingscourt. 'They were always feuding and quarrelling,' he explained, 'but the Captain had ordered they were to be left alone.'

WOMAN: Get out of my sight, you low bastard.

MAN: I beg you. Five minutes.

W: And I'd known you were on this ship I'd've thrown myself off of it. Get out!

M: No excuse could ever excuse it. I'm bitter ashamed of what I done.

W: You'll never be ashamed enough. Never! Do you hear me, you bitch's leavings? If you blaze in Hell for all eternity it wouldn't be a minute of what you deserve.

M: I loved you. I was maddened.

W: My own innocent child? To be drowned like a mongrel?

M [distressed]: It's not myself went doing that to her, Mary.

W: It's yourself did it and you know it, too. As certain as if you held her down in the water and squeezed the life from her body with your own murderer's hands.

M: – Mary, forgive me, for the love of Jesus –

W [screaming]: The child of your own brother? That your people's blood was running in? What kind of devil of Satan's bitch are you? What kind of crawling excuse for a vermin?

M: Mary, I never thought he'd go doing what he did. On the life of me I didn't. Sure and how could I know?

W: You knew well enough when you saw us put out on the road like dirt.

M: I didn't know it'd ever come to that. I didn't know they were going to give him the beating. If I was there that day they came, I'd've stopped it, I swear.

W: Joined in with it more like.

M: Mary, I wouldn't. As true as Jesus, I'd have stopped it. I'm after being denounced to the Else-Bes [?] over it, Mary.

W: Good enough for you, then. I hope they kill you. I will laugh.

[The male speaker "gave a very loud and piercing cry".]

M: Look, then! Look what they are after doing to me. Do you like that? Can you see it clear enough? Did I deserve that, Mary? Would you have held the knife that did it?

[The woman said nothing.]

M: I walked every inch of Connemara looking for you, Mary. Yourself and Nicholas and the little one, too. I walked every field from Spiddal [?] to Westport, till the skin was pared off my feet with the walking.

W: [shouting] You blackened, filthy sleeveen liar. I curse the living day I ever let you near me. You bitch's bastard excuse for a man.

M: It – doesn't suit you to be talking that way, Mary.

W: He cursed you before he died. I hope you know that. The curse of a priest is on your head and can never be lifted.

M: Mary, don't go saying that.

W: That you may never look at water without seeing his ghost in fire. That you may never sleep a night again in your life. That you may die in the agonies. Do you hear me? May you die!

A scuffle was heard. The woman now gave a loud scream.

At that point the sailor knocked hard on the door. No answer was made. There followed a furious exchange in a language the sailor was not able to understand. Something smashed in the room. The man now disregarded his orders and opened the door, fearful that the disturbance might end in fatal violence.

The steerage passenger, Mulvey, was in the room with Miss Mary Duane, the Merridith family servant. His shirt was open and he was in tears.

The sailor asked Miss Duane if everything was in order. She made no reply but left the stateroom, clearly in a state of great distress.

Mr Mulvey was asked to leave the cabin and return to his quarters. When he turned, the witness was horrified to see that a large scar 'shaped like a heart with a H in it' had been slashed across Mulvey's chest and upper abdominal area. The scar was suppurating badly and his skin was turning black with gangrene. 'I could get the stench of it from across in the doorway.'

He did leave the room, without saying anything else.

✱

First-Class Dining Area on the Upper-Deck
— about 2 p.m. —

'What is going on?'

'Luncheon at the moment. Though perhaps it has just finished.'

'I have been told by Captain Lockwood that the children and I are to remain behind the gates from now on. Why?'

'You shall have to ask Lockwood. I do not manage the ship.'

'Grantley says – '

'I do not give two damns what your precious *Grantley* says. Or anyone else. Do you hear me, Laura? You and your precious Grantley can drown yourselves for all I would care. As a matter of fact it would be highly convenient.'

She sat down at the table. 'David – Is it true?'

'Is what true?'

'That we are in danger?'

He turned a page of his newspaper. 'Don't be bloody ridiculous.'

'Locks? Bolts? Curfews? Bodyguards? There were seven armed men on guard in the corridor when I left just a moment ago. A private conversation of any kind in the First-Class quarters seems entirely impossible now.'

'How horribly inconvenient, Laura, the removal of your privacy.'

'It is not mine of which I speak but that of your children. They were not brought up to live in a prison.' She paused before adding: 'Nor is it fair to Mary.'

'Mary will do as she is ordered and like it.'

Two stewards came by and collected up the crockery. A splatter of dirty surf landed on the deck boards.

'I should have thought you would have a little more respect for the girl than that. In the circumstances.'

'I am sure I do not know at all what you mean.'

'You know very well indeed. As I do, also.'

'She is an old friend of the family, as I have told you previously.'

'Your conscience is your own, David. I neither expect nor require explanations. Neither do I expect hypocrisy when it comes to judging mine.'

He looked at her now. She was staring at the sea.

'Are we in danger on this ship, David? I have a right to know.'

'It's a piece of bloody ridiculous talk. A rumour; nothing more.'

She nodded calmly. 'And the boys are targets too?'

Merridith said nothing.

'How did you discover it?'

'If you really must know, we were alerted by Mulvey. The man you would not lift one precious finger to assist. But thankfully not everyone is such a screaming snob as yourself, otherwise we might all have been shot in our beds already.'

Reverend Deedes now approached and greeted the Merridiths. He had a birthday gift for Jonathan, which he gave to the Countess: a copy of John Newton's *Olney Hymns*. Perhaps noticing that a domestic dispute was in progress, he did not remain in their company but took another table, further away than the one at which he had been sitting previously. Lord Kingscourt returned to his newspaper. When he looked up again, his wife was silently weeping.

'Laura.'

Tears filled her eyes and spilled down her cheeks.

'I am very sorry,' he said. 'Forgive me, Laura. It was cruel of me to speak so harshly.'

She gave a wrenching, agonised sob that twisted her face. It was the first time in years that they deliberately touched. Her fingers twined hard around his own as she wept. She swallowed hard and gaped around the deck; a look of unspeakable incomprehension blanking her features.

'Nothing will happen, Laura. Nothing. I promise it.'

She nodded again; kissed his knuckles. Rose and walked quickly away down the deck.

✳

Pius Mulvey's Lazaretto
— about 4 p.m. —

(As recollected many years later by Jonathan Merridith; aged eight years at the time of the events.)

'Everything all right, is it?'

Mulvey jumped up as they entered the little cabin. A crust of bread and a small hunk of cheese were sitting in a fold of muslin on his bedding.

'Yes, sir. Thank you, sir.'

The poor man looked as petrified as if he was about to be arrested.

'Good man, good man. I say, good shirt you have on.'

'Her Ladyship came in with it a while ago, sir. I didn't want to take it.'

'Nonsense. Looks bloody better on yourself than ever it did on me.'

'It's too good of you, sir. Thank you, sir. It was a great honour to meet Her Ladyship, sir. She's a very kind lady indeed, sir, so she is.'

'Rustled you up a bit of tuck as well, I see, did she?'

'Thank you, sir; yes sir.'

'Good. I say, Mulvey, we wanted to have a little word. The Captain and myself.'

'Sir?'

He nudged his son. The boy stepped forward and spoke in the toneless drawl of the reluctant, a speech he had been made to learn by heart. 'Mr Mulvey, I should very much like to invite you to my birthday tea this evening if you have no previous or more pressing engagement.'

'And?' said Lord Kingscourt.

'And we shall have a cake if I and my brother are good for the rest of the day.'

'And?'

He scowled. 'And if we are naughty there shall be no cake.'

Merridith winked knowingly at his charity case. 'What do you say, Mulvey? Sound like a good sort of adventure?'

'I – wouldn't have anything proper to put on myself, sir. Only what I'm standing in.'

'Oh, the Countess can ask Mary to go through my things. Must be some old bit of schmutter we could kit you out in.'

'I'd as lief not, sir, if it's all the same to Your Honour. I'd only be in the way.'

'Nonsense. We'd be mortally offended if you didn't. Wouldn't we, Jons?'

'Would we?'

'Yes, we bloody would,' his father said.

'May we invite Mr Dixon, too?'

'I imagine he may well be busy, old thing.'

'No, he isn't busy, Pops. I asked him already. He said he'd be delighted. I thought he might tell us a story afterwards. He tells awfully good stories, Pops. Nearly as good as yours.'

Jonathan Merridith's father did not look happy. 'Don't you want to have just family and friends, old Captain? Didn't think we'd have a whole slew of outsiders along.'

'Neither did I,' his son replied. 'But then you and Mama said we must invite Mr Mulvey.'

Lord Kingscourt gave a sigh and said he supposed it would be all right.

'Your Honour,' attempted Mulvey, now pallid and appearing very anxious, 'I'd feel I was in the way. It's kind of Your Honour but it's too much.'

'Rot. It's an order from the Countess and myself. Sort of feel it's good for the boys, if you see what I mean.'

'Your Lordship?'

'Mixing with a wide variety, sort of thing. Don't want them thinking everyone's a mincing bloody aristo, do we?'

'Sir.'

'My mother, whom you were kind enough to mention before: she used to give a big shindig on her birthday every year. Tenants, workers. No airs and graces. Everyone used to trot along and muck in together. None of this bloody absurdity of master and servant. All Galwegians together, you see. Tradition we'd sort of like to keep up.'

'Sir.'

'So stagger along at seven or so; yes? Good man. Good man. Oh. There's this too.'

He handed Mulvey a cut-throat razor.

'The Countess's idea,' Lord Kingscourt said. 'You'll find it nice and sharp.'

✻

Stateroom used by the Merridith Family for Dining.
— about 7 p.m. —

Mulvey shuffled in, gruel-faced and perspiring, in an evening suit too large for him by several sizes. His hair had been plastered to his scalp with some kind of grease and his skin was gleaming like ice on a corpse.

> *For he's the jolly gay fellow*
> *For he's the jolly gay fellow*
> *For he's the jolly gay fellow*
> *Which nobody can deny.*

On one side of the table sat Robert Merridith with his mother; between them was Jonathan, the eight-year-old Viscount, in a crown roughly fashioned from a page of a newspaper. His mother and brother were also wearing paper hats. On the side Mulvey couldn't see, with their backs to the door, were Mary Duane and Grantley Dixon, both uneasy in cardboard bonnets. At the head, near the porthole, was seated Lord Kingscourt of Carna. He beckoned in greeting. He was wearing no hat.

'*Failte*,' he cried. The Irish for welcome.

'Boys?' said Laura Merridith, rising quickly. 'Here is our guest of honour. Mr Mulvey.'

'Good evening, Mr Mulvey.' Jonathan grinned, blessing him expansively with a shining dessert spoon.

'Who on earth is that?' asked Robert Merridith disdainfully.

'Mr Mulvey is a friend who has come to join us for supper.'

'It's gracious of Your Ladyship to invite me,' the interloper murmured.

'The graciousness is your own for accepting, Mr Mulvey. Won't you please be seated? We have saved your place.'

He limped to the only free setting at the table, the seat between Grantley Dixon and Mary Duane. The children before him were laughing quietly with their mother. He stared at the arsenal of gleaming silver cutlery, at the phalanx of crystal glasses and stacks of fine plates. Four stewards quickly entered carrying trestles of food. Whoops and wolf-whistles came from the children.

'Gingerbread!' one yelled.

'Cake!' proclaimed the other.

'Haven't you forgotten something, Mulvey?' Lord Kingscourt raised his right hand and sternly snapped his fingers. A newspaper skullcap was fetched to the table by the Countess and placed on the guest's head with a little show of ceremony.

She gave a soft, abashed laugh. 'You don't mind, do you?'

'Of course he doesn't bloody mind, you cluck. I never met a Galwayman who didn't care for a party.'

The stewards were still arranging the food on to serving tables. Bowls of potatoes and steaming carrots. Dishes glistening with drops of moisture. Jugs of lemonade and syllabub and custard.

'What happened to your face?'

'I cut it shaving, master.'

'You've practically sliced off your bally head.'

'Jonathan,' said his mother.

More trolleys and trays of food arrived. Mary Duane rose from the table to help the stewards unload it. Jonathan Merridith was beaming at Mulvey.

'My grandpapa fought beside Lord Nelson. He killed a lot of Froggies. Have you ever killed a Froggie, Mr Mulvey?'

'No, master.'

'A German?'

'No, master.'

'He might kill you in a minute, if you don't shut up,' Lord Kingscourt said. 'Drink, Mulvey?'

'I don't take a drink, sir, thank you.'

'Go on, have a small one. The claret or the chablis?'

'Wine – isn't something I know, sir.'

'Oh you must have a preference. Come on, spit it out.'

Sensing his embarrassment, Laura Merridith said, 'Do you know, Mr Mulvey, I don't have a preference either. I always feel time spent on such matters is utterly wasted. Don't you?'

'Lady.'

'Perhaps you would try a small sherry with me. That's what I like myself.'

'Thank you, lady. I will, then. Thank you.'

'I can't see any blasted sherry here,' Lord Kingscourt said.

'It is there, David. Right by your hand.'

'Ah. So it is. Pity the poor blind. Foostering about like an imbecile tonight.'

His drink was poured and brought to the table by Lord Kingscourt.

'I should like to kill a few Froggies when I grow up. Probably a few Germans as well, I should think. Shoot them in their ugly fat faces with a cannonball.'

'Jonathan, please,' his mother said.

'Well I shall.'

'Did you know Queen Victoria's husband is German, old thing?' said his father.

'That's a beastly lie.'

'Certainly isn't. As German as sausages.'

'Perhaps you'd like to say grace tonight, Jonathan.'

'I want Mr Mulvey to say it. His voice is nice.'

'What a capital idea,' Lord Kingscourt said. 'Would you mind, Mulvey? In your own time of course.'

He spoke the words of a prayer in a very quiet voice, which was devoid of even the slightest feeling. 'Bless us oh Lord and these thy gifts, which of thy bounty we are about to receive, through Christ our Lord.'

'Amen.'

Lady Kingscourt and Mary Duane began serving plates of salad. The birthday boy was gulping his tumbler of lemonade.

'Are you a Wesleyan, Mr Mulvey?'

'No, master.'

'A Methodist?'

'No, master.'

'You're not a bally Jew, are you?'

'Mr Mulvey is a Roman Catholic, Jonathan,' said Lord Kingscourt. 'At least I imagine so. Is that correct, Mulvey?'

'Yes, Your Honour.'

'Oh yes,' said Jonathan Merridith. 'Of course. He would be.'

'I have always thought of Catholicism as a very pleasant religion,' said Laura Merridith feebly. 'Rather a wonderful sense of drama. We have a number of very close friends who are Roman Catholics.'

'Yes, lady.'

'Mr Dixon is Jewish,' said Lord Kingscourt quietly. 'That is a pleasant religion, too.'

Jonathan Merridith appeared amazed. 'Are you, Grantlers?'

'My mother was; yes.'

'I thought Jews had beards.' He was speaking with his mouth full. 'They always do in the newspapers.'

'Perhaps you shouldn't believe everything you see in the newspapers.'

A polite laugh was shared by some of the adults at the table. 'Now that,' said Lord Kingscourt, 'is a matter on which we can all agree.'

'So what do Jews believe, Grantlers?'

'They believe many of the same things we believe ourselves,' said Lord Kingscourt. 'That we should give each other a fair crack of the whip. Not give a fellow a drubbing when he's down. They are often remarkably kind and humane people.'

'That's not what some of the masters at Winchester used to say.'

'Well that is very sad and stupid of the silly old goats.'

The boy fell quiet and looked at his plate. For a while everyone ate in restless silence, broken only by the scratch of forks on china. It was as though each diner was waiting for someone else to introduce a topic, but after several minutes nobody had.

The crystal chandeliers, the sheened, teak pillars gave the stateroom the air of a restaurant in Paris. Only the clanking of a chain outside the porthole broke the illusion.

'Oh, Dixon,' said Lord Kingscourt, forking at his food, 'I meant to say I saw that piece of yours. In the *New York Trib*. The one in which you were kind enough to mention myself. Your response to that daft old letter of mine. One of the chaps got it for me on that tub we passed the other day.'

'I may have been a little overheated when I wrote it.'

'Actually I rather thought it was food for thought. If I may so. You're quite right. We have so much. Seems unfair, somehow. Rather crystallised some of the things I think myself.'

Dixon looked across at him, expecting the customary sneer. But he wasn't sneering. He was looking exhausted and pale.

'Mm.' The Earl shook his head and crumbled a bread roll. His eyes ranged around the room and took on a strangely mystified expression, as though he was suddenly confused about how he'd got there. 'Best in the whole world, if you ask me. The Irish people, I mean. Always felt sort of at home there before it all went wrong.' He gave a melancholy smile. 'The world is an unfair old place, isn't it?'

'It's exactly what we've made it, I suppose.'

'Quite. Quite. Neatly put.' He chewed another mouthful for a long time. 'I used to think – you know – had I got my hands on old Kingscourt. Might have been able to do a little better. Than was done in the past, I mean. Given it a crack anyhow.' He poured a glass of water but for a moment did not drink. 'Ain't going to happen now at any rate. Pity.'

'Pops,' said Jonathan Merridith. 'Ain't is common.'

'Perhaps we might talk about something a little less dull,' said Lady Kingscourt meaningfully.

'Sorry. I'm being a bloody bore again.' He turned to his son. 'Six of the best for Papa for being a bore. What shall my punishment be?'

The boy held up his glass. 'More lemonade for the King!'

His father laughed easily and went to the serving table. He picked up a jug and began to pour. And what happened next to David Merridith was so shocking that it took him a moment to realise it was pain.

'David?' said his wife. 'What is the matter?'

Dixon rose quickly and got to him as he stumbled. A dish was knocked from the serving table, spilling its contents over the rug. His face was beaded with droplets of sweat. A tremor ran through him; he gave a small gasp.

'Are you all right, Merridith? You are pale.'

'Absolutely fine. No matter at all. Bloody heartburn.'

Dixon and the Countess helped him to his feet. He shuddered again; leaned his hands on the table.

'Pops?'

'Shall we fetch the Surgeon, David?'

'Don't be bloody dense. Little indigestion cramp or something.'

'Jonathan darling, will you pop down to Doctor Mangan's quarters and see if he is there?'

'Laura, really I am fine. Let us just have our supper and not make a bloody operetta. Honestly.'

He sat painfully back down and took a long drink of iced water. Made a pacifying gesture with his hands to the Countess. Mopped his forehead with a rucked napkin.

'Bloody shipboard rations,' he chuckled. 'Give a dead man the shites.'

His sons giggled with the relief and delight of hearing him swear.

'David, please.'

'Sorry. Let that remark be stricken from the record, you two.'

'May I pass you some more greens, Jonathan?' asked Grantley Dixon.

'No, thank you. I only eat pudding.'

'You certainly do not, sir,' Laura Merridith said with a frown.

The child accepted a spoonful of limp vegetation. Poked at it with his knife, wrinkling his nose.

'There shall be a double dose of lessons tomorrow for petulant gentlemen who do not eat their greens,' Lord Kingscourt said. 'Then they shall have to walk the plank.'

'I hate lessons. More than I hate girls.'

'Did you ever hear the like of that in your life, Mulvey? A boy who doesn't like his lessons.'

'No, sir.'

'What do you think would happen to a boy like that if he didn't mend his ways?'

'I don't know, sir.'

'You bloody do know; you're just being polite enough not to

say. You expect he wouldn't make the best of himself in life, don't you?'

'Sir.'

'Exactly. He might have to work as a chimney-sweep, mightn't he?'

'Sir.'

'What else might he have to work at, would you say? An idler who did not attend to his lessons.'

Everyone but Mary Duane was looking at him now. 'Perhaps a costermonger, sir.'

Lord Kingscourt gave a hearty laugh at the thought. 'Do you hear that, you indolent little loafer? A costermonger you shall be if you don't watch out. Sweet apples here, Missus! Penny the dozen bejaysus!'

The boy scowled and pulled abruptly away from his father.

'Today's lesson was astronomy,' said Lord Kingscourt, tossing his son's hair. 'But I'm afraid it didn't stick, hmm? Toffee and treacle are the only things that stick. But at least we attempt to show willing. Isn't that right?'

The child forked an egg into untidy quarters. His face was the colour of his father's wine.

'Jons,' said his mother gently. 'Papa was only playing.'

He nodded sullenly but still did not say anything. Merridith looked at his wife. She gave him a stare that was hard to read. The Earl made to speak a few times but in the end he said nothing.

'Do you have a place to go in New York, Mr Mulvey?' asked Grantley Dixon.

'No, sir.'

'You have family there, I suppose.'

'No, sir.'

'Friends, then.'

'No, sir.'

Mulvey continued eating, his head bowed low. Eating like a man who had known the life of hunger, a man for whom eating had become a matter of chance: rhythmically, determinedly, with grim concentration, as though the sands were running steady through some hourglass of providence and the plate would be taken away when the last ones disappeared. Not gorging, not gulping – that was much less efficient: in your hurry you might leave the tiniest scrap uneaten. His hands rose and sank like those of a puppet drummer-boy, from plate to mouth, from mouth to plate, and he swallowed while they sank, so that his mouth would be empty at the instant when his fork rose to astonish it once more. He chewed quickly, mechanically: taste was not the issue. *Taste* was not something that had mattered for years. His hands trembled sometimes; his face was damp with purpose. To write it down is hard; it reads as though it were ridiculous. But to witness it was harder, and not funny at all. Even those merry boys stopped laughing as they noticed; my own feeling was that none of us would ever laugh again. Had the room burst into flames, or the vessel struck an iceberg, he would have continued implacably eating as death sat down at the table.

'Perhaps . . .' said Laura Merridith, and her voice trailed off. Never before had she witnessed a starving man eat. 'Perhaps you might do us the honour of staying with ourselves for a while. Would that be a good idea, David?'

She was trying not to cry.

Lord Kingscourt looked at his wife with an expression of bewildered gratitude. 'What a very nice thought. Don't know why it didn't occur to me.'

Mulvey stopped eating and stared at the floor. There was a strange sense that the air around him was acquiring a colour. 'I couldn't do that, sir.'

'We should like it if you did. Till you get on your feet.'

The Countess touched the back of his emaciated wrist. 'We really should. You have done us such a kindness.'

Tears appeared in the guest's eyes but he pinched them away. Inclined his head lower so that his face could not be seen. His hand reached for a glass and he took a sip of cloudy water.

'What kindness is that, then?' asked Jonathan Merridith.

'Mr Mulvey has helped me with a small matter, that's all,' his father said.

'But what?'

'Mind your own business before your business minds you, sir.'

'Pardon me, lady,' said Mary Duane suddenly. 'But might I be excused from the table?'

The Countess looked at her. 'Are you unwell again?'

'Yes, lady.'

'You don't look unwell. Are you sure?'

'Lady.'

'What is the matter, then, for pity's sake? I warned you three times earlier, this is a special occasion.'

'For Christ's sake,' sighed Merridith, 'if the girl says she's unwell, she's unwell, Laura. Must her head fall off and roll about the table?'

Robert Merridith snuffled with mirth at the thought. His father leered across at him and pulled a clown's face.

'Your mama's a silly old mare sometimes, ain't she?'

'I only meant it seems a pity for Jonathan's birthday to be spoiled,' said the Countess. 'But if Mary wants to leave, then of course she must leave.'

'Can't you stay for a little time, Mary?' asked Jonathan mopily. 'I should very much rather you did.'

A long moment passed. She went back to her food.

'May I pour you a glass of water, Miss Duane?' offered Grantley Dixon.

She nodded her thanks. He filled her tumbler. The salad course was finished without another word from the diners.

The plates were removed, and a platter bearing three chickens was placed on the table. Lord Kingscourt picked up a carving knife and held it towards Mulvey.

'Little tradition,' he explained. 'We always invite the guest of honour to carve.'

'David, for Heaven's sake, let us not have all that formality.'

'Oh do shut up, can't you, woman. That is more than half of the fun. To attention at the double, Corporal Mulvey, and perform thy duty else thou be whipp'd.'

Mulvey took the knife, stood up unsteadily and began to slice the meat. The Countess and Dixon handed him plates. He cut with surprising neatness, as though he was used to doing it. Whenever anyone said 'thank you' he nodded briefly but did not speak.

The plates being loaded, they began to eat again. Dishes of vegetables and sauces were quickly passed around. Glasses refilled. More wine opened. Only the silence of Mary Duane worked against the attempt at festiveness – hers and the silence of Mulvey the killer. Their wordlessness hung over the table like an unasked question.

'Isn't this agreeable,' said Lord Kingscourt after a few minutes. 'All nosebagging together. We should arrange it more often.'

Low, vague sounds were made by the boys. None of the adults gave any response.

'How is it the Bard puts it, Dixon? Merry feast, etcetera?'

'Small cheer and great welcome makes a merry feast.'

'Indeed. And how true. Old *Othello*, that is, Jonathan.'

'Actually,' said Dixon mildly, 'it's *The Comedy of Errors*.'

'Of course; silly me. Antipholus, aint it? The shag from Ephesus.'

'Balthazar in fact. Act Three, scene one.'

'Bloody heck,' sighed Merridith to his son, 'it's the dunce's cap for your imbecile Pops tonight. Thank goodness for Mr Dixon's presence among us.'

Dixon laughed warily. 'I played the part once in my student days, that's all.'

'Oh, I'd say you were very good,' Lord Kingscourt smiled.

The ship pitched. The chandelier tinkled. The Earl broke a piece of chicken wing and began eating it with his fingers.

'Excuse me, Mr Mulvey?' said a small and timid voice that had barely spoken a syllable since the start of the supper.

The guest looked across the table at the face of Robert Merridith. A bonny little boy. The broth of his father.

'Didn't you come into my castle one morning?'

Mulvey shook his head. 'No, master. I didn't.'

'One morning you came into my castle. With a funny kind of black mask on your face and a great big knife –'

'Bobby, that's enough,' Merridith interrupted with a sigh. 'Please excuse us, Mulvey, we have a fertile imagination.'

'He's only making a crack, sir, it's all right.'

'I'm not making a crack.' The child gave an apprehensive giggle. 'It was you, Mr Mulvey, wasn't it?'

'Bobby, I told you that's quite enough. Now shut up and eat your confounded supper.'

'I think we are a little tired, David,' the Countess said gently. 'You know how we become more imaginative when we are tired.'

'We may be tired all we like. There is no need to be rude.'

'I didn't mean to be rude, Pops, I just thought it was him.'

'That's all right,' said his mother. 'We can all make mistakes.' She turned to the guest of honour. 'I am sure Mr Mulvey understands.'

Robert was staring at him now. Mulvey tried to laugh. 'A big man like myself'd never fit in through a little window like that, master.'

'But he had a funny kind of walk. Exactly like you have. He was a cripple. He –'

The next sound was the slap. It made the boy's head whip back. The ship plunged hard. Nobody said anything.

'Apologise to our guest this minute.'

'Sir, there's no need,' Mulvey said.

'There certainly is. This minute, do you hear.'

'I'm s-sorry, Mr Mulvey.'

'Now apologise to your brother for ruining his birthday.'

'David, for pity's sake – '

'Do not *dare* to interrupt me, Laura, when I am speaking to my son. Do you understand me, woman? Must I write it out in my own blood? *Must you flaunt your disrespect and contempt for me on every possible occasion?*'

She made no response. He turned back to the boy. 'I am waiting, Robert.'

'I am sorry, J-Jons.'

'*Use his name you ridiculous fool.*'

'I am sorry, J-Jonathan.'

'Do you accept his apology, Jonathan?'

'Yes, sir.'

'Shake hands.'

They did as they were ordered. Robert was quietly crying.

'Now get to your bed this minute. *You make me sick to the stomach.*'

The child slipped down from his seat and tottered from the cabin. After a moment, Mary Duane rose and followed.

Merridith filled his glass and took a long drink of wine. Went back to his food as though nothing had happened. A deadened, dazed look had invaded his face, and he cut up his meat with surgical attentiveness.

'I should like to add my own apology, Mulvey. My own and my

wife's. My wife feels that children should be indulged whatever they do. A matter of how she herself was raised, no doubt.'

'Your Honour –'

'Not another word. I don't mind a joke. But bad manners are intolerable. We are not in a swinery.'

Dixon sat very still. Jonathan Merridith was pale. The Countess went to a serving table and began to stack the dirty plates. John Conqueroo gave a groan and moved closer to America.

'Now,' smiled the Earl. 'Anyone for cake?'

CHAPTER XXXII

FROM

'THE BLIGHT'

FRAGMENT OF AN ABANDONED NOVEL
BY G. GRANTLEY DIXON

Details of the following extract drawn from notes made by
Surgeon William Mangan (coeval with the events described herein)
and from a long interview conducted with him shortly
before his death in 1851.

62°08′W; 44°13.11′N
— 11.15 P.M. —

'I'm not disturbing you, Monkton?' said Lord Thomas Davidson.

The weary-faced surgeon stepped back from the doorway and squinted in surprise.

'Lord Queensgrove. Not at all. Come in, sir, come in.'

Inside the cramped but orderly cabin sat the surgeon's sister in a

315

Japanese kimono. A teapot and porcelain cups had been placed on a card table, near a chessboard whose pieces were also Japanese. She rose to meet him with a careworn frown.

'Good-night, Mrs Darlington. Forgive my intrusion at this unconscionable hour.'

'Please, don't worry. Is everything all right?' Her loosened hair was wet. 'It's not one of the children?'

'Both sleeping like Endymion. We had a little birthday celebration earlier this evening.'

The lamp was burning low from the rafters over the card table, so that the corners of the room were lost in shadow. A dark mirror hung over the desk which was squashed into an alcove and in it could be seen the reflection of a hunting print.

'You'll join us for some tea? Or something a little stronger? I have a nice bottle of Madeira stowed away somewhere.'

'No, thank you, Monkton. Fact is, I wanted to see you professionally for a moment if I might.'

The surgeon half nodded. 'Honoured, Lord Queensgrove. Just general run-down feeling, is it?'

'Well, that – yes. And there's another small matter.'

'That's all right, that's all right. As a matter of fact, we were only saying, Mrs Darlington and I, how you seemed to be looking a little pale of late.'

'It's possibly a little delicate.'

'Ah. You'd prefer Mrs Darlington to leave us for a moment?'

'No no. Not at all. I didn't mean that.' He did mean that, but he didn't want to offend her. The surgeon appeared to understand.

He turned to his sister. 'Marion, my love – would you go and see about that little message I was mentioning before.'

She smiled. 'I was just about to, dear.'

Monkton gave a quiet and good-natured laugh as she left the cabin. 'We chaps sometimes have a difficulty looking after ourselves properly and coming out with a thing. Not like the memsahibs in that way at all. And yet, you know, we really must.'

'Quite,' said Lord Queensgrove. Already he was feeling it had been a mistake to come here. He loathed the surgeon's ingratiatingly chatty manner, the back-slappery and presumption that lay behind it.

'Would you care to tell me a little more? Oh excuse my oafish manners, please sit down, My Lord; sit down.' He beckoned to an armchair beside the small rolltop desk and sat down himself on a stool nearby.

'It's rather disconcerting to say it. I find myself a little embarrassed.'

The surgeon opened a drawer and took out a notebook. 'North or south? In a manner of speaking.'

'South.'

He nodded diplomatically and dipped his pen.

'Little digestion problem? That type of thing?'

'Not that.'

He licked his fingers to separate the pages; nodded again and began to write. 'South by south-west, then. My Lord Nebuchadnezzar.'

'I'm sorry?'

'The old waterworks, as it were.'

'I suppose one could put it that way, yes.'

'Lack of vigour?'

'Not that, no.'

'Inflammation? Pain?'

'A little of both.'

'Mm. Passing water all right lately?'

'Not really. Gets extremely painful, then.'

Again the surgeon nodded, as though he wasn't surprised. For a moment there was no sound but the scratch of the nib on the paper. 'Discharge at all?'

The word struck the patient like a slap across the mouth. A blush flared up; his face was almost smarting.

'Sometimes,' he said.

'Ah. I see.' The surgeon wrote in his notebook for what seemed a long time. Then he pursed his pale lips and gave a fatigued sigh. 'Conditions on board a ship aren't what they might be, of course. Hygienically speaking. Even here in First-Class. It's my own little bugbear, I must confess. Mine and also Mrs Darlington's. Ah, Lord Queensgrove, the predicaments we might avoid through simple cleanliness. Mrs Darlington does a lot of work among the poor.'

For a moment Davidson didn't know what to say. He wondered

if he was being invited to defend the ship's policies on hygiene, or his own; or to comment on Mrs Darlington's mysterious works among the poor. But by now the surgeon was rummaging in a small leather bag.

'You enjoy a drink, My Lord?'

'Perhaps too much sometimes.'

The physician chuckled. 'Far from alone in that regard.'

'Quite.'

'But we all need to keep an eye on our general consumption. Doesn't help anything to do with the waterworks or liver. Matter of build-up of toxins, you see. Can cause pain in the lumbar and also the private area generally. Night sweats, too.'

'I understand.'

'You bathe regularly of course, sir?' He took a stethoscope and a couple of small metal instruments from the valise.

'Twice a week, yes.'

'Mm. Good fellow. Good for you.' He went back to the notebook and resumed his writing, pronouncing aloud the last few words, like a pleased schoolmaster completing a report. 'Bathes. Twice. In every. Week.' With a flourish he made a motion of heavy underlining and then a vigorous full stop, as though trying to stab an insect with the nib of the pen.

'I'd probably bang it up to every other day. Or even daily if poss.'

'All right.'

'That's the style. Now, pop over here and let's take a look at the old site of battle, eh?'

The surgeon lit a tilly-lamp and lengthened the wick, brightening the flame to a rich golden glow. Damp clothes and bed linen had been hung around the sitting room; on the chairs, on the sofa, on a fold-up dressing screen.

Davidson opened his britches and underclothing and pulled them down to his thighs. Undid the lowest three buttons of his shirt. The surgeon took what looked like a pillowcase from a pile of pressed clothes and draped it quickly over the back of a chair.

'Lean the old stern against there if you would.'

He did as he was told. Monkton knelt and began examining him.

'Little delicate there?'

'Yes.'

'And there, I expect?'

Davidson flinched.

The surgeon clicked his tongue in fraternal sympathy. 'Just another moment or two like a good man. I believe we've got the enemy in our sights.'

One of the steel instruments was so cold that its touch made him shudder. For a while afterwards there was no sensation but the heat of the lamp on his prickling skin; the doctor's fingertips probing his scrotum and perineum. Then a glitter of pain sparkled through his loins and lower gut, a tremor that trembled his thighs.

'Mm. Thought so.' Monkton rose to his feet, wincing with the effort. 'Little parasitical chap. Mild enough sort of infection; nothing more. Painful old nuisance but he's easily vanquished. See a bit of him always in close confinement situations. Prisons. Barracks. Things like that.' He paused and snuffled. 'Workhouses.'

'Can you say how I might have got it?'

He looked into Davidson's eyes for a moment.

'Perhaps you might have some idea yourself, sir.'

Lord Queensgrove felt hot. He gave a shrug. 'No.'

The physician nodded. He crossed to a basin-stand and began carefully washing his hands and wrists. 'Clothing or towel not properly laundered. Privy seat maybe. Can be worsened by chafing of the thighs or the undergarments. But a good hot bath will set you right. Don't use soap, just very hot water. Just as hot as you can bear it. Have your wife ask that pretty serving girl of yours to get a good handful of garlic from the galley and lob that in too.' He gave an amiable smile. 'You'll smell like a Frenchman but it won't last long.'

The ship rolled gently and righted itself slowly, causing the lantern on the ceiling to sway on its hinge. Shadows danced around the airless room.

'Oh and probably best to abstain from anything too demanding for a fortnight or two. Maritally and so forth.'

'I understand.'

Monkton lowered his voice and spoke in an oddly rueful way. 'These little things can be passed to the ladies. And with the ladies, of course, it's that much more difficult. The old plumbing, you see. It's not as available.'

'Just so.'

Davidson pulled up his britches and began fastening the buttons on his shirt. A creak of complaint came up from the floorboards, as though the wood itself was somehow suffering. Now he noticed that the surgeon seemed to be staring at him. He was smiling again, but not with his eyes.

'Who's that pretty little fellow? On your abdomen there.'

'Oh that.' He glanced downwards. 'Just a pimple of some kind.'

'Sore chap, is he?'

'No no. I had forgotten about it, actually. I get them now and again.'

'May as well take a squint at him now you're here. Can you undo the shirt a little more?'

'I assure you it's nothing.'

'All the same. Now you're here. Might be prudent.'

There was an insistence in his voice that was hard to gainsay. Lord Queensgrove opened his shirt and stood with his behind resting against the chairback. The surgeon dragged over the stool and sat down in front of him.

'God blast it,' he muttered. 'Tedious dark in here.'

'Can I assist in some way?'

'Maybe you'd hold the lamp, like a stout fellow? Would you mind awfully?'

Davidson took it and held it at the level of his waist, the pungency of oil ascending to his nostrils. The surgeon was using his fingertips now, softly stretching the skin around the crusted little blister. He was close enough for the patient to feel warm breath on his navel and the thought occurred to Davidson of the extraordinary intimacies permitted to doctors. He was asked to hold still and did as he was asked. Monkton reached out and hauled over his beaten-up valise; pulled out a magnifying glass and a ream of gauze.

For several minutes he said nothing as the examination continued. When he spoke again his voice was calm. 'You've not had any other lesions? Rashes? Nothing like that?'

'A few years ago, maybe. Inheritance, I'm afraid.'

The surgeon glanced up with a quizzical expression.

'Pineapple skin,' Davidson said. 'My late father suffered from the same complaint. Of course he spent many years at sea. Usually put it down to the lack of fruit in the rations.'

'Ever had lesions on your palms or the soles of your feet?'

'Now you mention it, yes. But a good many years ago.'

'How many years?'

'Five or six, I suppose. They cleared themselves up.'

'Ever get sore throats? Spells of dizziness and such?'

'Now and again.'

'Eyesight fine, is it?'

Davidson gave an abrupt laugh. 'I've been told I need spectacles. Usually by my good lady wife. I'm afraid it's another little matter I've tended to neglect.'

Monkton smiled. 'Bless 'em, the ladies do tend to go at us, don't they?'

'Indeed.'

'But we like them all the same, the bothersome old termagents.'

He rose and rinsed his hands at the basin again, drying them carefully on a new shred of gauze. When he had finished he held the rag in the lamp-flame with a pair of tongs until it burned completely away. His carefulness disturbed Davidson. Why so careful?

'There is a kind of lotion for the blistering,' Davidson said. 'My father used it sometimes. Smithsonite, I think it was called. Pinkish in colour.'

'Yes, that's right. Zinc and ferric oxide.'

'That's the one. Damned if I didn't forget to bring any along with me like a fool. Perhaps you might have some in your bag of tricks.'

The surgeon turned and looked at him seriously. 'Lord Queensgrove, I'm going to need my sister's assistance just to make a few notes and do a small test. It's almost certainly nothing but I should like to be positive. Now I assure you there's no need at all for modesty. She's a person of the utmost discretion and very well trained.'

Davidson felt a bead of sweat trickling down his thigh. 'All right.'

Monkton quickly left the room.

Lord Queensgrove heard the sound of men running on the deck. He crossed to the wall, to the dark-glassed mirror. In the top right-hand corner of its mahogany frame a newspaper cutting had been inserted. Details of the coming opera season in New York. *The American Premiere of Signor Verdi's Masterpiece.* Gently he raised the hem of his shirt. A slightly elevated mole about the size of a sixpence. He touched it with his fingertips, then with his thumb. It had a sandpaperish feel but it didn't hurt.

A boisterous cheer sounded from outside on the deck. He went to the porthole and looked out into the blackness. In the distance, a tiny red light could be seen. Halifax Lighthouse. The coast of Nova Scotia.

The surgeon and his sister entered now. Monkton had a grave and harassed look. 'I need you to undress yourself completely and come in here.'

'But why?'

'There's nothing at all to worry about,' Mrs Darlington said peacefully. 'Just follow when you're ready. Everything is all right.'

They went through into what Davidson could see was a small bunkroom. Quickly he undressed and followed them in, bringing his clothes and shoes. The room was very cold; it smelt faintly of pine sap. The boards felt sticky against his bare feet. The surgeon was pulling the blankets from the bed, hanging a lantern from a hook in the beams. 'Would you lie down like a good man. We won't be long.'

Monkton stood on one side of the bunk, his sister on the other. They began examining him closely, every inch of his skin. His chest and groin. His armpits and thighs. Behind his ears. His navel and scalp. Under his tongue. Around his gums. An instrument was produced to hold open his nostrils; a candle was lit so his nasal passages could be scrutinised. Sometimes the physician would utter a word and his sister would write it down in his notebook. Outside on the deck, men were singing a shanty. The surgeon made a one-fingered spiralling gesture, indicating that Davidson was to roll on his front.

'That's the style, My Lord. Now try to relax completely.'

He felt their hands exploring his back; his wire-tense shoulders, his legs and feet, between his toes, between his buttocks. As though looking down on the scene from above, he imagined he could see his own body now: the lowered heads of his whispering examiners, their darting hands like playful birds.

There were prayerlike murmurs in the tiny cabin; words Lord Queensgrove did not understand: Phthisis. Urticaria. Desquamation. Febrilis. The whispering had a lulling, soporific effect and he was so very tired that he began to drift into sleep. The heft of the ship floated him downward; towards his mother. And then he was intensely aware of the heaviness of his frame; the bunk supporting his wearied body. The sea calmed a little. His pain calmed. And he realised, then, that no one was touching him. When he opened his eyes, the surgeon was gone.

Mrs Darlington said gently: 'You can dress yourself now, Lord Queensgrove. Thank you.'

Davidson rose from the berth and did as he was bidden. Suddenly he felt wrung out, completely exhausted. He had an urge to be away from the surgeon's quarters, to walk on the deck and feel the brine-cold air. To look at the golden lights of land.

He entered the sitting room in shirt-sleeves and briskly said: 'You'll let me know what I owe you, Monkton, will you?'

But the surgeon did not seem to be listening to his patient. He had crossed to the table on which stood a globe and was spinning the latter in an absent-minded way. The sailors sang. The globe whirred. It came to rest with his fingertips resting on Africa.

'Willie?' said his sister. 'His Lordship is talking to you.'

Monkton turned. His face was white.

'Lord Queensgrove,' he said quietly. 'You have syphilis.'

Michael, I am in first rate health. I was never better in my life. This Rocky Mountain air agrees with me first rate. I have everything that would tend to make life comfortable. But still at night when I lay in bed, my mind wanders off across the continent and over the Atlantic to the hills of Cratloe. In spite of all I can never forget home, as every Irishman in a foreign land can never forget the land he was raised in. But alas! I am far away from them old haunts.

Letter from Sergeant Maurice H. Woulfe in Wyoming
to his brother in County Limerick

CHAPTER XXXIII

THE BORDER

TREATING OF SEVERAL CONVERSATIONS WHICH TOOK
PLACE IN THE VERY EARLY MORNING OF THURSDAY
2 DECEMBER; THAT BEING THE TWENTY-FIFTH DAY OF
THE VOYAGE. (THESE ACCOUNTS NEVER PUBLISHED
IN PREVIOUS EDITIONS.)

Starboard Near the Bow
— About 1.15 a.m. —

'You're watching the stars, Mr Mulvey.'

'Sir. It's yourself. Good-night, sir. God bless you.'

'See anything interesting up there?'

'Nothin at all, sir. Just thinkin about home.'

'May I join you for a moment?'

'I'd be honoured an you did, sir.'

Dixon came closer and stood beside the killer. The two of them
leaned on the rail of the gunwale, like a couple of companions in a
low saloon.

'Ardnagreevagh, isn't it?'

'*Ard na gCraobhach*, we call it. Or the old people do.'

'Little place, is it?'

'Scantlin of a place, sir. Up near Renvyle. Walk through it so
you would and never know you were afterbeen there.'

'I've been into Connemara but not up that far north. They tell
me the scenery is beautiful there.'

'Ah, there's – not much there now, sir. It was beautiful once.'

'Before the Famine?'

'Long before that, sir. Before my own time.' He drew his collar
closed against the squalling wind. 'So they say anyway. The older

people. But again you sift all the stories you woulden really know. Half it's probably affectation.'

'Smoke?'

'It's kind of you, sir, but I woulden want to be deprivin Your Honour when you've so few left.'

Dixon began to realise something strange about his associate. He was making his accent more Irish than it was. Talking like an actor in a music-hall sketch.

'I have more in my cabin. Be my guest if you like.'

'It's dacent of you, sir. I'm obliged to Your Honour.'

The Ghost accepted a cheroot from Dixon's silver case and bent his head to accept the light. His touch on Dixon's cupped hands was surprisingly soft and the glow from the match made his face seem clownish. Drawing hard, the smoke went into his eyes and he began to cough fitfully. It was as though he was someone who did not smoke but had accepted the cheroot purely because it had been offered. Up so close, he seemed even smaller and more fragile. Sometimes his breathing became a belligerent wheeze. He reeked of the cold and of old shoes.

For a while the two men stood together at the rail saying nothing. Dixon was thinking about life without Laura Markham, the words that might be used when the farewell came. She had told him her decision earlier in the day: whatever had happened between them was over. They would part at New York and not meet again. His letters were returned, and a number of small tokens. No, a friendship would not be possible. It was disingenuous, if not dishonest, to pretend that it might be. He was not to try persuading her; the resolution was unchangeable. Merridith had made it clear that he would never give her a divorce. Absolutely never: it was beyond his imagining. The bed was made; now she would have to lie in it. And she *would* lie, as she had been lying for years. But sometimes you had to live in a lie. No matter what else, the man was her husband.

The strangeness of the stars was his other thought now: the way ordinary things become mysterious late at night. Some people discerned in them proof of a Creator; an impetus which piloted the Earth through the illuminated nullity, and which always would, until it annihilated even that nothingness. While others saw no evidence for anything in their arrangement: a celestial clutter which was beautiful, certainly, but on to which no pattern or purpose should be projected, and for which the word 'arrangement' would therefore not suffice. The stars had not been arranged by any force but hazard, and by those who stared up at them like gaping monkeys from the lonely star they called the Earth. This is what Grantley Dixon had come to believe: that the monkeys' descendants had looked at God's droppings and decided to call them stars. It was mankind and not the Almighty that had ordered the universe; only a man could look at an accident and call it a creation with Himself at the centre.

And he wondered if one day the monkeys might learn to fly, if they might construct ships which would sail around the planets as the one he was standing on at the present moment had sailed around the seas. He supposed that would happen. It was probably unavoidable. They would gawk out their portholes and scratch themselves in wonderment and give each other chimpish grunts of congratulation. And all of it would be seen as something to celebrate.

Grace Toussaint, the elderly Yoruba who had helped to raise him on his grandfather's plantation, had often told him what she felt to be the most consequential secret of life: that all of our trials are caused by restlessness, the refusal to accept the fact that limitations exist. She was the most tender person Dixon had known in Louisiana, a place where people could be ardent as the merciless sun, but on this contention she was ardent herself. Dixon's grandfather, a Jew, a hater of slavery, had argued with her frequently about the point. A man that knew the whispered malignity of neighbours, he had crossed the borders many times: to Mississippi, east Texas, into southern Arkansas. There he would purchase the most broken of slaves and take them back to Louisiana. He would walk his tended meadows as the sun raised the crops and calculate how many could be saved this year. A good field was ten slaves, a bad one maybe two. Every precious harvest of his fifty thousand acres was sold for the purpose of redeeming the stolen.

Mississippi was a Hell for the black man, he told his grandchild; and if Louisiana was far from Paradise, at least it was not quite Hell. The *Code Napoléon* had seen to that. He had purchased Grace Toussaint and her blinded tortured brother in order to restore a version of their liberty; had argued with her frequently about something called free will. He would say that to be human was to accept nothing of proscription, to live only by the boundaries of what your conscience dictated. But Grace Toussaint had not agreed. It was easy to make grand statements from the vantage ground of wealth. Had she remained all her life in the country of her birth she might even be making them herself, she told her purchaser; for her people had once been royalty there.

The arguments were strange. Dixon did not understand them. One night as a boy, he had paused in the hallway, by the half-opened door of his grandfather's study, and eavesdropped on the quarrel that was raging inside: 'You think God has any colour? You really think that, Grace? Jesus Christ was probably a Negro, Grace! His skin was the colour of tobacco, Grace!' And she had answered bitterly that if the old man truly thought as much, he was the sorriest fool that ever saw Louisiana: for Christ was as lily-white as all the powerful.

She used to take Dixon walking on summer mornings, along the drive of yuccas and beeches that led down to the pasturage; past the whitewashed shanties of the upperside meadow and then through the misty heat of the tobacco fields. Sweet the warm air with the aroma of watered leaves; thick with the clatter of crickets. Her brother, whose name was Jean Toussaint, though he was known among the farm boys as 'Handsome John', would sometimes walk behind them with the aid of a stick. He didn't care for company most of the time. In the mornings he didn't care for it, ever.

Despite his great age he was a powerfully strong man, with enormous hands, bulging veins in his temples, his skin the colour of antique gold. He would often pluck a tune from the battered two-dollar guitar he carried on his long, straight back, like a dusty knight in a storybook hefting a shield; but Dixon had never heard him sing or even speak. One day he asked his grandfather why this was so. Dixon was twelve years old at that time, and was told that when Jean Toussaint had been half that age his tongue was cut out as a punishment by his master, a Mississippi son of an Irish bitch who deserved to burn for eternity. That Jean Toussaint was not Handsome John's real name; that Grace Toussaint was not Grace Toussaint's name; that even their names had been stolen away from them when they themselves had been stolen from Africa. It was the instant in Dixon's childhood when everything had changed. More than the realisation that his parents had died. More than the moment when the police came to tell him that there had been an accident at his home, a terrible accident; that his house was burnt and his parents were dead and that now he would have to leave New Haven and live with his grandfather down in Evangeline. It had lodged in him like a bullet that could never be dug out.

'Things are what they are,' Grace Toussaint had often told Dixon. 'Never join anything. Don't ask no questions. The world will still be here when you have left it behind. Those trees, these fields, will still be trees and fields.' And later, as a student, he had seen a version of that thought expressed by savant Pascal in his revered *Pensées*. 'All of man's difficulties are caused by one single thing. His inability to be at ease in a room.' And it wasn't necessarily that Dixon disagreed, but what could be *done* with a thought like that? Could you look at a world where tongues were torn out, where human beings were branded like longhorns, stamped with the names of the savages who had bought them, and say it had nothing to do with you? The clothes on his back, the fine boots on his feet, the very volumes of philosophy in which equality was anatomised – all these had been bought with the proceeds of subjugation, the trust fund established by his slave-trading ancestors. 'Clean money now,' his grandfather would assert. But there was no clean money in a dirty world.

Even now he was in hock to dirty money. Journalism paid little, almost always late. His life in London had been expensive and profitless, and had been possible only because of his grandfather's subsidising it. He had hoped for the 'scoop' that might give him his freedom, the story nobody else could tell; but in six long years it had never materialised. All that had come was further dependence. The plump registered envelopes with the Louisiana postmark. The wads of greasy dollars he had done nothing to earn. The letters from his grandfather so brimming with sympathy for the difficult life of the young man of letters. *You have a talent, Grantley. You cannot hide your gift. Whatever else you do, you must keep writing. Never be discouraged. Do what you have to do. It is not a matter of the ends justifying the means: but of the creation of new means and new ends.* The loathsome defensiveness haunting their lines. The furious guilt of duplicitous compromise. Now there was a way to escape it all.

Other thoughts were boiling like a poison in his mind and he wondered if this might be a good time to mention them. It would be more convenient in some ways to say nothing at all; to stand here in companionable stillness with another of your species and ask yourself what the other might be thinking, if anything, and into which category of stargazing he might be placed. But already Grantley Dixon knew the answer to that. All murderers must be unbelievers, no matter their denomination.

'Do you know – your face seems very familiar, Mr Mulvey.'

Mulvey cocked his head in wonder, like a dog hearing an intruder, then gave a few small nods and brushed the ash from his lapel. 'No doubt you're afterseen me walkin about the ship, sir. I do dander around the ship the odd time at night. Thinkin me thoughts, like.'

'No doubt. But you know, it's the damnedest thing – the first time I noticed you, the night we left Liverpool, I thought I recognised you even then. I actually noted you down in my diary.'

'I can't comprehend how you'd reckon to that, sir. I don't believe we've met before.'

'It does seem a little odd, doesn't it?'

'They do-say every man has a double, sir. Maybe he does.' He chuckled, as though the thought amused him. 'Maybe me own is beyond in America, sir. Your own home place, sir. I might even meet him myself over there, God willing. And shake his hand. Do you think so, sir?'

'Oh he isn't in America. I think he's in London.'

'London, sir? Do you tell me? Isn't that the livin wonder?' He took a long drag on the dampened smoke, like a man who was about to be marched to the gallows and wanted to finish it before having to go. 'But then again when you think –' a longer drag and a deeper exhalation – 'there's queerer conundrums do go on in the world than are dreamed of in philosophy. As Shakespeare has it.'

'Ever been there?'

'Where's that agin, sir?'

'London. Whitechapel. Around the East End.'

A flake of tobacco had stuck to his tongue. It took him a while to pluck it loose. 'No, sir, I wasn't, I'm sorry to say. Woulden suppose I ever will be now. Belfast's as far as I ever rambled from home.'

'You're sure?'

He laughed with unexpected lightness and gazed dreamily out at the darkness. 'I'd say London's one town a man'd remember been in, sir. I believe it's a grand place entirely, so I've been told.' He turned and looked directly into Dixon's eyes. 'They do-say it's full of opportunity, sir. Isn't that right? They do-say a feller might have himself all manner of sport in London.'

'It's just that for a man who's never been to London, I can't help but notice that you talk as if you had been.'

'Beggin your indulgence, sir, but I don't get your meanin.'

'You see, for example – the way you just said the word "feller". Most curious pronunciation for an Irishman, don't you think? "Fellow" or "fella" is what you might expect.'

'I coulden rightly say what Your Honour would expect, sir.'

'And at dinner tonight you used a certain word which I couldn't help noticing. "Costermonger", I think it was. A London word for a street trader, isn't that right?'

'I don't recollect myself ever spakin that word in the whole of me life, sir. Perhaps Your Honour heard me wrong, like. Or misunderstood me accent.'

'Ah, but you did, Mr Mulvey. Let me help your memory. You don't mind?'

'If I minded, I'd not insult Your Honour by sayin I minded.'

Dixon took out his notebook and quietly read a few lines. *'Tonight we dined with Mulvey from Connemara; whose speech patterns in particular I found most interesting, being peppered with colloquialisms clearly picked up in London. Among them: "Coster". "Costermonger". "Chum" for a friend.'*

'It must be a fierce burden for you, sir, writin everthin down.'

'Habit of my profession, I suppose you could call it. I find I forget things if I don't write them down.'

'An honourable profession it is, too, sir: the writin profession. They do-say the pen is mightier than the sword.'

'They do say that. I'm not certain it's true.'

'Tis a great blessin you're afterbeen given, sir, all the same, sir. I wisht I had it meself. There's many as wanted it but it's given to few.'

'What blessing is that?'

'The gift you have for puttin a thing in English, sir. The tongue of the poets and Our Lord himself in the scriptures.'

'I think you'll find the Lord in question actually spoke Aramaic.'

'To Your Honour, sir, maybe. To myself, he spoke English.'

'Or perhaps he spoke cockney. Like the costermongers do.'

The Ghost laughed abruptly and shook his head. 'I must of heard one of the sailorboys usin the word, sir. I could no more tell Your Honour what it means to save me life.'

'Oh, your life hardly needs saving, Mr Mulvey. Not yet, at any rate.'

He blew very wearily and gave a brief frown of bafflement. 'I'd be reline on yourself to explain that one to me, sir. You've a riddlish way of talkin betimes.'

'When I first came to London, there was a case in the newspapers. It interested me a lot, I don't know why. Case of a petty thief in Newgate Prison who murdered a guard and then escaped. You probably remember it. "Hall" was his name. Known as the Monster of Newgate.'

'I don't think I ever heard tell of the case you mention.'

'No. You wouldn't have. You were in Belfast at the time.'

'That's right, sir, I was. The sweet town on the Lagan.'

'You don't remember hearing about the case but you remember where you were when you didn't hear about it.'

Mulvey looked at him coldly. 'I spent a lot of time in Belfast.'

'And I spent a lot of time in London.'

'More luck to you, sir. Now I'll bid you good-night.'

'I was contributing to a newspaper in London at the time. The *Morning Chronicle*. Liberal paper. Well I set myself the task of learning more about the famous Mr Hall. Went to the prison and studied the records. Talked to a few of the old lags in the dens up that end of town. Then down to the East End and rummaged around for a few weeks. Ran into a conversational gentleman by the name of McKnight. Scots gentleman. Something of a drunkard. Well, he says he used to work a dodge around Lambeth with an Irishman named either Murphy or Malvey. From Connemara, apparently. Place near Ardnagreevagh. Strangely enough, he went by the name of Hall.'

'That must of been the right fascination to you, sir.'

'Yes. He got seven years in Newgate – this Murphy or Malvey. Did I mention that already?'

'There's a good many Irish in that place, I'd say, sir. Poor Pat has it hard enough over in England.'

'Not many were admitted on the same day as the Monster. The nineteenth of August, 1837. On the very same charges. Maybe even the same face.'

Dixon flipped open his reporter's notebook and took out a dog-eared cutting. The holed newsprint was yellowed like a scrap of old lace, folded and creased too many times. Gently he opened it, so it wouldn't blow away. A black border. Twenty-point type. The charcoal, monstrous glare of Frederick Hall: Murderer.

'As you say,' said Grantley Dixon. 'Every man has his double.'

Mulvey blinked slowly but there was no visible sign that he was troubled. He never moved his hands from their resting point on the railing. They were small and white, like those of a girl. It was difficult to picture them doing what they had done. 'What do you want?' he muttered very quietly.

'That might depend on what you want yourself.'

'You would not like to hear what I want at this moment. It would give you a nightmare you might not forget.'

'Perhaps we should tell the Captain there's an assassin on his ship.'

'Scuttle along to him, so. More luck if you do.'

'You think I wouldn't?'

'I think a cringing whore like yourself would do anything in the world. And there's all manner of things we could go telling the Captain. And other people, too, if you want them told.'

'Forgive me, Mr Mulvey, I don't get your meaning.'

He gave a brief, derisory snicker. 'If one ship sinks, Buck, all ships can sink. I hope your Countess can swim as well as she rocks the boat.'

'They don't hang you for adultery, Mr Mulvey. They do for murder.'

'Then get him if you've the guts. You know where I am.' His eyes were gleaming with hatred as he grinned. 'Run along, little boy. Before you get what's coming.'

'I mean you no harm.'

'Get to Hell, you bitch's melt. And suck my arse on your way. I've wiped better than you off the sole of my boot.'

'I know about the guard. What you suffered at his hands.'

'And you think what you're doing now is different.'

'I have no weapon.'

'Only your pen.'

'It doesn't do quite the same damage as a rock smashing a face. But you can debate it with the judge at your trial if you like.'

Mulvey spat at his feet. Dixon went to walk away. The snap came after him, cold as a blade:

'I'm after asking you already. What do you want?'

He came slowly back to his quarry and stood beside him.

'I'm a reporter, Mr Mulvey. What I want is the story.'

The killer said nothing. His hands were in his pockets.

'Your life in London. Why you did what you did. How precisely you escaped. Where exactly you went. Your name needn't be included, but everything else. Otherwise I go to the Captain this minute.'

'That's the price nowadays. A story for a life?'

'If you put it that way.'

'And when we get to New York?'

'I last saw you in Belfast eighteen months ago. They were putting you into your grave at the time. You gave me the interview a week before you died.'

The Captain appeared on the upperdeck, strolling with the cook. They seemed to be laughing as they looked up at the sails. He turned and gave a cheerful salute through a frail wisp of mist. Beckoning now. Waving them over.

'Your decision, Mr Mulvey. Either way I get a story.'

'Not Belfast,' he murmured, and he pulled his coat tighter. 'I'm buried in Galway. Beside my brother.'

✳

Portside Near the Stern
— 3.15 a.m. —

'What kind of man am I?'

'A sick one, Merridith. That is all.'

'An evil one, you mean. Lower than an animal.'

The surgeon touched Lord Kingscourt's arm with professional gentleness. 'One cannot see evil under the microscope. What one sees has a name. *Morbus Gallicus*. It isn't a plague, and it isn't a punishment. It does what we ourselves do every day.'

'What is that?'

'Everything it must, in order to survive.'

The flag flapped loudly and furled around the mast. Nearby, two aged beadswomen of steerage were hallowing the blessed glimmer of Coffin Island lighthouse:

> *Ave maris stella, Dei Mater alma;*
> *atque semper Virgo, felix caeli porta.*

'What can I expect?'

'We divide syphilis into four distinct stages. You're nearing the end of the third stage now. The late latent phase, we call it.'

Merridith tossed his cigar butt over the rail. 'And that means?'

'The thing will have lodged in your tissue by now. Lymph glands too. There may be ocular involvement. Uveitis. Vasculitis. Papilloedema.'

'You can give it me straight. No flannel required.'

The surgeon sighed and looked at his hands as though he resented them. 'You will almost certainly lose your sight. It will happen quite quickly. It is happening now.'

'Go on.'

'After invasion it tends to colonise and multiply quickly. You'll develop gummatous lesions – sores – all about your skin. Also on your bones and vital organs. We think it infects the outermost substance of the arterial coat. Basically eats it away.'

'Eats it, you say?'

'In a metaphorical manner of speaking.'

'And then?'

'Lord Kingscourt – you are upset. Naturally this is distressing. Really I –'

'I want to know, Mangan. I am quite prepared.'

'Well then – the nervous or cardiovascular systems are attacked. In the former case there can be quite severe personality changes. Perhaps even GPI.'

'What is that?'

'General paralysis of the insane.'

A memory of his childhood loomed up like a spectre. A madwoman in Galway city, screeching and tearing her clothes, displaying herself to passers-by. His nanny, Mary Duane's mother, had tried to shield him from the sight; had hustled him away across the muddied street. An inebriation of terror. Jam on his hands.

'There is no treatment?'

'We can do a very little to relieve the symptoms with mercury. Certainly we need you not to deteriorate before reaching New York. You must rest completely for the next forty-eight hours.'

'What is in New York?'

'A private hospice for people suffering from your condition. I can arrange for you to be admitted as soon as we disembark.'

'A pox-house I believe such places are called.'

'No matter what they are called, the sisters there are kindly. There is also speculation in some of the literature – only speculation, mind – of hopeful developments with a new thing: potassium iodide. But it's a little way down the road. And the results are extremely inconclusive.'

'So nothing else may be done?'

'If it was primary stage or even secondary, we might try to fight. And we shall, of course. But the chances aren't good.'

'How long do you reckon I have? At worst?'

'Perhaps six months. It might be a year.'

Solve vincula reis, profer lumen caecis,
mala nostra pelle, bona cuncta posce.

A cresting wave threw a handful of yellow spray over the railing. Dense streaks of foam were smacking the barrier. He dried his eyes quickly with the back of his sleeve.

'I should like to thank you for your courage, Mangan. Can't be an easy thing. Situation like this.'

'I am very sorry, sir. I wish I could offer more hope.'

'No, no. Rather feel I should shake you by the hand. Not the executioner's sin that he has to do his duty.'

'May I ask if you've ever had a problem of this nature before, sir?'

Lord Kingscourt said nothing. The doctor spoke quietly.

'I'm an old man, Merridith. I'm difficult to shock.'

'When I was younger I contracted g-gonorrhoea.' The word hung in the air like a floating stone.

The surgeon nodded and looked out far beyond the rails, as though he was trying to make out something moving in the darkness. 'You frequented certain places, I expect?'

'Once or twice. Many years ago.'

'Mm. Of course, of course.'

'Once while at Oxford. Night out with some fellows. Another time in the navy. A third time in London.'

'We used to think gonorrhoea and syphilis were types of the same disorder. Blood relations, if you will. Now we know they're not. Professor Ricord discovered the difference a few years ago now. In '37 I believe. Rather brilliant Frenchman.'

'What about my wife?'

'I could break the news if you'd prefer. Or perhaps Mrs Derrington might be asked to step in. But naturally it would be better coming from yourself.'

'She can't know, Mangan. Not for the moment.'

'Merridith, she might very well be carrying this herself. She – '

'We're not intimate,' he quietly interrupted. 'Not for years now.'

A shadowed moon slid out from behind a vast cloud.

'Nothing?'

He shook his head. 'Our marriage is entirely celibate. I wanted to protect her. After I became infected before.'

'Still.' The surgeon sighed. 'Latency can last from a month to a decade. Much longer, occasionally. She's in very real danger. As is any other woman with whom you have been in familiar contact. Is there such a woman, Merridith? I beg you to be frank.'

The doctor took the silence as permission to continue.

'There is a young woman among us on this ship whom you cannot mention without averting your eyes. We noticed it quite early, Mrs Derrington and I. And I have noticed that this young woman appears never to speak to you. Rather unusual for a servant and her master.'

'What of it?'

'You've had physical intercourse? Please speak frankly.'

'No.'

'But contact?'

'There was – a time when I used go to her quarters at night.'

'What occurred when you went there? I must know all.'

'If you really must – she allowed me to watch as she prepared for bed.'

'To undress?'

'How the deuce else would she prepare for bed?'

'Did you touch her body, Merridith? Did she touch yours?'

He looked at the face of his inquisitor, but no emotion was there. Suddenly he thought of the Roman Catholic confessional. Wasn't this how they were questioned in that coffin-like little box? Always he had found it a strange idea, to tell your failings and lusts to another man, the most secret desires of your heart and body. Now he could see in it a kind of liberation. But no godliness. Quite the contrary.

'I have touched her sometimes. Not in the way you mean.'

'Not in the private sense?'

'I have touched her body. She has not touched mine.'

'You have not had intimate congress with the girl?'

'I have answered you already.'

'Never? Truly? You give me your word?'

He was crying again: very quietly and fearfully. The surgeon offered him a handkerchief but he shook his head and composed himself.

'I speak as your friend, Merridith; not your judge.'

'When we were younger we used to go walking about in the countryside together. At home, I mean. In Galway. I expect there were one or two occasions when we acted unwisely.'

'You mean you had intercourse?'

'No.'

'What do you mean, then? Familiarities and so forth?'

'For Christ's sake, Mangan. Were you never a young person in love?'

Virgo singularis, inter omnes mites,
nos culpis solutos, mites fac et castos.

'Do you love her still?'

'I have very strong feelings. The feelings I have always had. I have not been in a position to live by those feelings.'

'That is not what I mean, as I think you must know. I speak of love in the physical sense.'

'Nothing of the nature to which you allude has happened in over fifteen years.'

'And more recently? It's been a matter of caresses and so forth?'

'Yes.'

'Exploration?'

'If you must.'

'Infiltration?'

'No.'

'There's no question of manipulation of the self whilst in her company or anything of that nature? No emission of fluids?'

'Mangan, can't you leave it? What in Hell do you think I am?'

The surgeon spoke mildly but there was ice in his voice. 'What I think you are is a man in a situation of power. As all men are, in relation to women.'

Vitam praesta puram, iter para tuum.

'Nothing has occurred which might put her in danger.'

'You must never approach her in that way again. Do you understand?'

'There is very little chance of that, I can assure you.'

'May one ask how? I must insist on your guarantee. Otherwise it is my duty to have the girl removed from your quarters immediately.'

'Mangan, I beg you –'

'I will do my duty and that is an end to it. You must give me reason to think the girl is safe from your advances or I shall go to the Captain and have him allocate her a new cabin at once.'

'Please don't do that. I implore you, Mangan.'

'Then speak, Merridith; for pity's sake.'

He nodded. Turned slowly. Looked out at the ocean. The blackdark space where the waves must be. 'There is a fact about my life which I have recently come to realise. A matter of enormous difficulty and shame. I have never discussed it with anyone before.'

'Then you must now.'

'I assume our conversation is confidential.'

'Naturally.'

He hung his head suddenly as though he might vomit. Wind caught his hair and ripped at his clothes.

'Merridith, I beg you to unburden yourself of whatever it is you want to tell me.'

Mea maxima culpa et maxima culpa.

'I am not the first member of my family to become attached in the way I mentioned previously. My parents' marriage was made unhappy by an infidelity of my father's at one point. They separated for some years when I was quite a young child.'

'What does that have to do with this matter?'

'My father's attachment was with a tenant woman on our estate. I discovered its full nature the night I closed up our house in Galway. Certain personal papers came to light. There was a child of the liaison. A daughter.'

'And?'

'She was passed off as a member of the woman's own family. I do not believe her husband ever knew. My late mother did not know either, I believe.'

'Merridith – I'm sorry; I'm just not following your line.'

'No. I didn't myself for too long a time. But the mother was my nanny. A lady called Margaret Duane.'

Sit laus Deo Patri, summo Christo decus,
Spiritui Sancto, tribus honor unus.

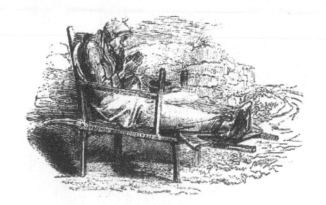

CHAPTER XXXIV

THE DOCTOR

Dies Iovis ii Dec. xlvii

This morning and p.m., assisted by Mrs Derrington, attended a great number (67) of steerage passengers. Many reporting with scrofula, colds, diarrhoea, feverishness, coughs, severe nausea, poor digestion and stomach cramps; head lice, body lice, scurvy, rickets, chilblains, infections of eye, ear, throat, nose and chest, and a number of other minor ailments.

One man with very severe case of dysenteric colitis. Saw him before and gave bicarbonate of potash but now suffers deep-seated pain in epigastrium. Spirit of terebinthinate to belly with citrate of ammonia and ¼ dram of morphia. Very little chance. He will certainly die.

One man with inflamed carbuncle on dorsal penis. Removed it with knife. One woman of twenty-five close to labour. Twins. Husband extremely weak. Has been giving her his entire rations. Told him she needed a father for her children more than she did a few oz of biscuit. Will try to get some milk. Told him if he couldn't I would bring some myself from breakfast tomorrow. Man (about 20) with very bad palsy of the face. Spoke no English. Child (3 yrs) with suspected broken tibia. Gangrenous. V. distressed girl (14 yrs) told Mrs Derrington she feared she was dying. In fact she had begun to menstruate but was entirely ignorant of the matter, her mother having died two years ago. Significant number (about twenty-five, several infants among them) in most urgent need of hospitalisation.

Dysentery widespread. Bowel-colic also. Sloughing sores in throat. Soft and ulcerated gums. Everyone I saw showing symptoms of gross malnutrition and badly underweight, some dangerously so. Diet of biscuit and water completely inadequate. Very poor supply of clean blankets. No safe, clean place to store or cook whatever food they have taken on themselves. No safe, clean place for personal cleanliness and necessary matters. No privacy whatsoever, a matter of obvious distress particularly to the women. Steerage cabin very dark and devoid of clean air. Some of the unfortunate men quite given over to drinking. No proper facilities to wash clothes.

Later made the 'routine call' to First-Class which I had insisted Lord K. agree to. Examined the Honble. Robert and Right Honble. Jonathan Merridith of Kingscourt (Robt 6yrs & 10 mths, Jthn 8yrs). Teeth, eyes, throat normal. Hair clean. J. had often been attended for 'unbearable itching of the skin' by house nurse at Winchester College Hampshire where he previously schooled. (Balming unguent prescribed.) Once chipped collarbone while playing football. Each has a number of small cutaneous inflammations on neck, face and upper body; dry, reddish to brown-grey, slightly scaly or thickened. Some oozing serous fluid. Robt. has large patch on upper back also. Worrying. Yeasty and flaking, but nothing to provoke alarm regarding possibility of congenital inherited S. Children in such distressing cases of an infected parent are often born with no symptoms, going on to develop severe rhinitis (and other conditions) later; but my general impression is that both are safe.

Should like both to have fuller investigations by consultant venereologist when we arrive at NY (have recommended Freddie Metcalf at Mercy who is always discreet) but diagnosis for the moment is that it is a matter of nothing more than simple atopic seborrhoeic eczema. Mrs D. concurs.

R. a little on the chubby side; should have more roughage and cod-liver oil. J. complained of irritating efflorescent rash in his right upper thigh area. Clearly caused by nocturnal urination, complicated by the eczema. Appeared embarrassed to discuss matter openly until I confided that a certain Surgeon W. M. of the Theatre of Anatomy, Peter Street, Dublin, had suffered same heavy affliction until age of twelve. Asked me to explain wondrous workings of doctor-patient confidentiality and Hippocratic oath. Did so. Seemed interested.

Nice alert boy. I said a physician could no more reveal the condition of his patient than a General his battle plans or a Chinese magician his secrets. Wanted to know if the other surgeons would give him a biffing if he broke the rules. Replied that they would beat him like a drum, set him on fire, then stand around pissing on him and yodelling Hallelujah. (Mrs Derrington not in the cabin at that point.)

Examined family servant, Miss Duane, in an unoccupied stateroom, her personal quarters being too small; little better than a cupboard. She is a 35-year-old widowed lady of quiet enough manner. Underweight. A little frightened. Of an intelligence notably above the average. Very fluent English. Strange Chaucerian kind of flavour. Watchful. Strong physical similarity, now one sees it.

Had been attended by a physician only once in her life before; eleven months ago when she came to work at the house of Lord and Lady K. Had fallen on hard times following death of husband (and child) through drowning accident, she said. Was committed to Galway Workhouse in January 1846. Realised in that place she was two months pregnant. Stole away from the workhouse and walked 180 miles to Dublin. Suffered a miscarriage along the way. Lived there in a hostel for women for a time, latterly at a convent where she worked in the laundry. (Could not remember the name of the convent, nor that of the hostel, nor either of their addresses.) Said Lord K. had found her 'at a loss' in the streets of Dublin in January of this year and insisted she return with him to Galway. Lady K. had been concerned for her health and called one Doctor Scolfield or Suffield of Clifden. He diagnosed severe malnutrition. Was taken on as charity case; family servant/nanny. Moved with the family to Dublin in April.

As I commenced the examination she seemed a mite apprehensive; so I attempted a little conversation to put matters at ease. Intends to leave the Merridiths when we arrive at New York. 'No reason, sir.' Merely that she does not wish to remain in domestic service. Had never been a servant until relatively recently; felt it was not the life for her. Perhaps intends to go on to Cleveland Ohio. No relatives there, or none she knows of; but had heard it reported that many Connemara people had made their homes there, which I had not known previously. Otherwise might go on to Quebec or New Brunswick. Brother-in-law had an aunt who had once lived at Cape

Breton but now she might be deceased, or moved away. I said it must be mighty cold in those northern Esqimaux places and she briefly laughed. Quite extraordinarily beautiful when she laughed; not in any silly way of prettiness or such. In fact she is not pretty; but genuinely and deeply beautiful. But she did not laugh long and I could not make her do it again. Had a little money she had saved from her wages. Would like to work as a seamstress or a shopgirl, perhaps, but will take any opportunity 'except for domestic service'. I quipped she might meet a handsome groom or butler or suchlike if she went into service and translate her name to his in the end. Replied that she does not intend to marry again. No bitterness in how she said it; simple matter of fact. A sad loss to the suitors of America, I ventured. 'Perhaps it is, sir; perhaps it isn't.'

Possibility of incipient arthritis or tendonitis in the left wrist. Ingrown toenail which needs attention. Small but nasty burn from a pressing-iron on left inner forearm. Tendency to chest infection and constrained breathing in a harsh winter such as the present one. 'Catching-ness,' she called it. Inherited from late father. 'A farmer and fisherman, sir.'

Number of healed but visible scars on abdomen, upper back, buttocks, thighs and other areas but for these she offered no explanation other than roughhouse play with her two charges. Tendency to occasional mild skin rashes, she said, but again assumed she had simply picked them up from the boys. Had soothed the rashes herself with an emollient decoction of extract of beehive (!) a thing recommended by her mother many years before. Told her I had only recently read a scholarly paper on that very theme, recommending substance gained from *Apis mellifera*, the honey-bee. No reply.

No exanthema at present. No lesions or subcutaneous swelling and can remember none. No discharge or pain. Showed her a number of symptomatic illustrations but she said she had never had any. Asked me as I put the book away if it was S I had been looking for. Taken aback at her question (and her knowledge); but I admitted it was. Had never had anything like that, she said. Would know if she did.

No female difficulties at all, except occasional normal aching at t of the m (she pronounced it 'aguing'), mild melancholia at ovulation and once mastitis in the aftermath of an earlier pregnancy at age 20yrs (1832), treated by a local woman with herbs and drawing-out poultices. (Male child stillborn.) Has a varicose vein in left calf. Some of back teeth v poor. Severe gingivitis of both jaws. Badly corroded and ulcerated ventricular molar must be causing most extreme pain but she complained of none. Overall detected nothing that would give cause to diagnose S but nevertheless v troubled as to reason for evasiveness or dissembling re the scars. Not scrapes or bruises as might result from horseplay, but severe abrasions, welts and striations to the skin. Would say they are a year to eighteen months in age; from before she ever worked as a nanny. Volunteered that her master and mistress never whipped her. (Had not asked her about that, nor mentioned the word whip, though that is quite clearly what caused these defacements.) My suspicion is that the unfortunate girl may at one time have earned her living in a certain manner. Possesses a far greater knowledge of matters of conception and how to avoid it, indeed of the mysteries of the female assemblage in general, than is customary.

As I made to leave she said something which quite knocked me over. 'Thank you, sir. You are very gentle. You are a very kind man.'

All I could think of to answer was that it was my duty to be kind, after all. And she shook her head in the strangest way. 'Your wife is very lucky, sir. Gentleness is a gift.'

I said my wife had passed away a number of years ago now; and in truth would not always have considered herself lucky to be married to a foolish doctor with too many patients. But she did not laugh or even smile. 'Were you happy, sir?' she asked me. I said yes; very happy.

'Did you have children, sir? Yourself and your wife, God rest her.' I answered that we did: two daughters and a son, all now married with little ones of their own. She enquired as to their names and I told them and she nodded.

'I will say a prayer for your family, sir. Thank you. It was good of you to think of me. I will never forget the kindness you have shown me today.'

Words quite failed me for several moments. Then I said the honour of the meeting had been entirely my own, which I truly meant; and I wished her every good fortune. I gave her my calling card with the Dublin address and said that if she ever needed a friend she had only to let me know of it. We shook hands and she left, returning to her work. But I noticed she had left the card on a table. I felt I had been in the presence of a very exceptional person.

Examined the Countess Laura Kingscourt last of all. She is 31 yrs and in absolutely perfect health; particularly for a lady who is in her expectant condition.

As with her elder son, we discussed confidentiality; though perhaps in a more concentrated and intensive manner.

CHAPTER XXXV

THE WARNING BEACONS

Friday, 3 December, 1847
This one night remaining at sea

LONG: 72°03.09′W. LAT: 40°37.19′N. ACTUAL GREENWICH
STANDARD TIME: 02.47 a.m. (4 December). ADJUSTED SHIP
TIME: 10.17 p.m. (3 December). WIND DIR. & SPEED: 42°
force 7. SEAS: rough. HEADING: S.W. 226°. PRECIPITATION
& REMARKS: Air temperature falling. Very strong n. easterlies
all day. Gaining strong speed. Sighted Nantucket Island Leading
Light this morning at 3.58 a.m. Watch reported warning beacons
at Newport, Rhode Island visible by tscope off the starboard by
noon.

Our intrepid old lady is in poor enough health this night, and
creaking along wearily and sorely through a blasting squall; but more
of that anon.

This afternoon, just after two o'clock, a thunderously loud
sound was heard all over the ship, followed several moments later by
another, the latter sending a great reverberation up through the
decks so that the masts shook like trees in a gale. When I left the
wheelhouse I looked overboard and the water was full of thick
bubbling blood of an astonishing redness, several hundred yards
around. It was immediately obvious that we had been struck by a
whale, and a large specimen at that, to judge from the force of the
blow and the copiousness of the blood.

And several moments later my suspicion was confirmed, for the

349

great bloated body was seen in the scarlet water seventy yards to starboard, still thrashing ferociously and spouting and making terrible sounds like human screams, the poor magnificent beast. It was a mature male razorback, *Balaenoptera physalus*, in excess of eighty feet in length, its tail the size of a yacht, its body covered in great tufts of weed and small shelled creatures, and its noble head gashed quite open from its encounter with the hull. Its tortured spoutings were fully fifteen feet in height. Some of the passengers appeared on the deck and were very greatly alarmed. Others asked me to arrange for it to be netted out of the water so it might be chopped up and eaten but I said that would not be possible. I tried to send them away, but the Maharajah had come among them and he told them to rest their gaze on the ocean for a moment if they wanted to see something they would never forget in their lives. Soon the sharks came up to take their quarry, the poor creature now being weakened almost to death, and the water appeared as though it were boiling all around. I very much wish His Imperial Imbecility had considered his advice a little more carefully; given the principal use to which the ocean has been put on this voyage.

Myself and Leeson and some of the engineers hurried below to the downhold and saw that a fissure of about three feet in length had been cracked on the starboard side, and we were taking on water at a fast rate, and soon were up to our bellies. A baling party was quickly deployed and the damage put to rights, though not without the Herculean efforts of the men, the pumps being rusted and in some cases broken and the hold quite alive with many large rats.

Repairs having been effected, a survey was made of the cargo. Thirteen bags of the Royal Mail had been destroyed beyond salvage and I called down George Wellesley the Mail Agent to swear a report. (A most bumptious oaf of a man, maddening arrogant.) Two very large barrels of pork had gone rotten in the downhold and were infested with maggots so I gave orders for them to be thrown overboard. They were hauled up from the hold but in the ten minutes they remained on deck while the men went to fetch the tally-ropes, they were broken open by persons unseen and completely emptied of their contents.

That was not all the adventure we experienced this day, for later this afternoon there was a small fire in the steerage section which very briefly caught the overhead spars and threatened to engulf the maindeck. Seven passengers and two of the men were injured in extinguishing it, not badly. Surgeon Mangan has seen all of them and given opiate treatments for their burns. Considerable damage has been sustained, particularly to the overhead and portside bulkhead, but is capable of being repaired.

More disturbingly it was brought to my attention by First Mate Leeson, following his inspection, that some of the steerage passengers have been breaking planks off the inner cladding and removing portions from bunks and deck boards in the stowage section, in order to use them as fuel for their fires. In one section near the stern almost all of the internal wainscot has been torn away with several large holes hacked in the outer boards also, through which the elements now have unrestricted ingress.

At this impartation I had Leeson go down into steerage again, and gather all the passengers up on the quarterdeck, where I reminded them in the strongest possible terms of the regulations regarding fires, candles and other naked flames below decks. Also, that destruction of any part of the ship was a very serious offence punishable by imprisonment. We might yet have but one short day at sea but the rules on this matter would be vigorously enforced, for a ship may be lost half a league out of harbour as quick as she sinks in the ocean.

Mr Dixon was standing nearby with Lady Kingscourt, who, despite my entreaties to remain in the First-Class quarters, is lately in the habit of visiting the steerage passengers to attempt good works among them. He made several unhelpful interventions, asking me loudly and in full hearing of everyone were the people expected to be cold and wet at night and so on, and generally stirring up their already substantial disaffection.

'What the H*** would you do yourself in their situation?' he exclaimed.

I said profanity would hardly assist their situation, nor would loutish execrations keep them warm or dry; and whatever I might do I would not *destroy the very vessel which was preventing my own destruction*, for such would be the doing of the *emperor of Bedlam*.

He went above with a veritable fanfare of blasphemies and returned shortly afterwards with a blanket from his bunk and another from Lady Kingscourt's, insisting I take them for some of the steerage passengers. This I did. But I thought it curious, I cannot help but own it, that he should feel so easeful removing the coverings from a married lady's bed and apparently without so much as a by-your-leave.

Our American friends have achieved admirably in many fields of endeavour, but in the aspect of manners are often sorely lacking.

11.53 p.m. Beacons burning at extreme easterly point of Long Beach near South Oyster Bay. Getting stormy.

'The Bogus American'

CHAPTER XXXVI

THE ANCHORAGE

─────◆─────

─────◆─────

Saturday, 4 December, 1847
Our twenty-seventh day out of Cove

LONG: 74°.02′W. LAT: 40°.42′N. ACTUAL GREENWICH
STANDARD TIME: 04.12 a.m. (5 December). ADJUSTED SHIP
TIME: 11.17 p.m. (4 December). UNITED STATES NATIONAL
OBSERVATORY TIME: 11.12 p.m. (4 December). WIND DIR.
& SPEED: E. 88°. Force 2. PRECIPITATION & REMARKS:
Extremely cold with biting gusts. Lying at anchor in New York
Harbour.

This morning at a quarter to five we passed Jamaica Bay and Coney
Island and reached the Scotland Light Vessel in Lower Bay; leading
to the South Channel of New York Harbour. There we signalled by
flag-hoist for a pilot to come out. Reverend Deedes conducted a
brief service of thanksgiving for our safe arrival while we waited for
the steersmen and wharfinger to come; and never in all my years at
sea was I happier or more thankful to the Almighty than I was this
morning. Lord Kingscourt joined us at prayer: a mighty unusual
thing. He said he had been having difficulty sleeping of late.

No signal came back for more than two hours but I thought
nothing of it, since the port has been extremely busy in the last several
years. I returned to my quarters and commenced to bundle my kit.
By eleven o'clock no pilot had come and then I began to feel a mite
apprehensive. I returned to the upperdeck and waited with the men.

Finally, just before noon, the tugboats appeared in the distance and a great cry of cheering arose among the passengers. Many embraced each other and began singing hymns and national songs. But their joy was soon to be tempered by a further necessity of patience. On board the leading pilot boat was an officer of the city's Quarantine Division, charged to present me with an order under the Customs Acts not to debark but to come in and await further instructions. He refused to furnish more information; simply I must do as was requested and keep the ship calm. I said nothing to the men or the passengers: only to Leeson. We both of us felt the news might not be happily greeted.

Pilot Captain Jean-Pierre Delacroix came aboard and took the wheel, an Acadian man of Louisiana. He appeared to speak extremely little English so I called Mr Dixon who knows some of the French language. But Delacroix would not say anything about what was taking place in the port, merely remarking that he had a job to do.

Many of the passengers were in a state of tremendous jubilation as we fixed lines to the tugs and began to move through the Narrows and into the bay. After nigh on a month at sea, to be so close to land always seems a blessing. And indeed the land looked so beautiful and verdant in the cold sunlight; Staten Island and New Jersey to the West, the farmlands and little towns of Brooklyn to the East. It is sometimes said by seamen that land has a smell, and this day such seemed indeed to be the case, a wonderful aroma of vegetation and fodder. One could see the town of Red Hook through the lifting mist, and several of the cattlemen on the silhouetted hillsides raised their caps and waved as we passed, to the great rapture of all the passengers.

It was only when we were directed by the pilots into the Buttermilk Channel that I knew something was badly amiss, for in fourteen years making the voyage this has never happened before. A very heavy feeling of foreboding came down. From there we were towed around the island and into the harbour to meet a situation of extreme concern.

Such a scene I never saw in my life. At my estimation, about a hundred vessels are lying at anchor in the harbour at present, all having been refused permission to tie up at the dock. We were led by the pilots' tugboats to a position about quarter of a mile from the South Street Docks, between the *Kylebrack* out of Derry and the *Rose of Aranmore* out of Sligo, with the *White Cockade* out of Dublin lying aft. There we were ordered to drop anchor and await further communications. By the time we had anchored and stowed and written report for the tidewaiter, two more vessels had come in behind, the *Kylemore* out of Belfast and the *Sir Giles Cavendish* out of Mobile, Alabama for Liverpool but mainsail torn from the gaskets off northern Pennsylvania.

I considered the overall situation facing us now. If I said I had many sick on board, which I do, it might make the passengers' chances of being permitted entry that much the lesser. Very hard to know which course to take. I sent a message in to the port to say I was practically out of provisions and water and had well upward of three hundred on board between men and passengers; but a notice came back from the Port Office telling me to wait. Freshwater could be provided, and a surgeon if necessary, but any attempt to come in with the ship would be regarded as an illegal act and met harshly; by the impounding or burning of the vessel if necessary and the imprisonment of every man and passenger on board. I asked for a representative of the company to be sent out to consult with me, but at the time of writing none has appeared.

At two o'clock I had a visit from Surgeon Wm Mangan, who said he was greatly troubled by the situation on the ship. A number of passengers were extremely ill and must be taken into a fever hospital immediately. I explained the circumstances and said there was nothing I could do. He asked if it was true that we had a quantity of mercury amongst the cargo. When I said it was indeed, he asked if he could have some for the preparation of some medicament or another. Of course I acceded. ('Some debaucher down in steerage must have a certain dose,' Leeson joked to myself, when the good doctor had gone. And he added: 'One night with Venus, a whole life with Mercury.' But I did not think such a remark at all amusing. I have seen men die of that evil condition and would not wish such a death on the very worst foe.)

The situation is become alarming, not to say precarious. Many of the passengers have thrown their bedding overboard, in the belief that it is to be inspected by the quarantine officers for lice; and are thus left with no protection from the cold at night. They do not understand that for all the cold of the day, the cold of night can be lethal at this latitude. We are lying so close to the *Ferrytown* and the *Clipper* that the passengers are able to call across to those on the other two vessels. All manner of rumours are now being diffused: viz, any person from Ireland will be turned away from the customs post; all European immigrants must produce a sum of one thousand American dollars before being granted admission; the men are being separated from the wives and children & cetera, and repatriated.

I had Leeson gather all the passengers in assembly and informed them there was no cause whatsoever for alarm, but my remarks were not greeted well. Many heckles and angry remarks were made. I ordered all remaining supplies of wines, ales and spirits for the First-Class passengers to be distributed among steerage. Perhaps that was a foolish course; but it is too late now.

It is to be hoped that some news will come tomorrow, for many are in a condition of surpassing agitation.

*

First Day, 5 December, the sabbath,*
Our twenty-eighth day out of Cove

LONG: 74°.02′W. LAT: 40°.42′N. ACTUAL GREENWICH STANDARD TIME: 11.14 p.m. UNITED STATES NATIONAL OBSERVATORY TIME: 6.14 p.m. PRECIPITATION & REMARKS: Extremely low temperatures all the day, falling to minus 16.71° Celsius this night. Decks and ladders hazardous with thick ice. Ratlines and riggings are frozen solid. Icicles hanging from masts, jibs and shroud-ropes, presenting a danger to passengers; have ordered them broken with spars. Turbulent last night with heavy winds and many passengers sick of stomach.

Still lying at anchor at low tide in New York Harbour. Black, leaden sky all the day. I estimate the number of vessels similarly situated to be now 174, and increasing by every hour. The waters of the

*'First Day': a Quaker term for Sunday. – GGD

harbour badly clogged with feculence and foul matter of all kinds. Hundreds of large black eels in the filthy water. A child of steerage last evening scooped up what she thought to be a large purple balloon with a line-and-hook. Very badly stung by Portuguese man o' war jellyfish. She may die.

I sent a message at noon with an urgent request for a meeting with some person from the Port Office but no reply has yet been given. About an hour ago I had Leeson flag-signal to the Wharfage House for us at least to be allowed to disembark the women and children, many of whom are by now in a pitiful condition, but again no response whatsoever has been forthcoming.

Two steerage passengers died last evening, John James McCraghe of Lee, nr. Portarlington, Queen's County, and Michael Danaher of Caheragh, County Cork. I have ordered the remains to be placed in the hold, since burials within the harbour are strictly forbidden. (In any case, those passengers who profess the Catholic faith consider it unholy to be buried on the sabbath day.) A seaman, William Gunn of Manchester, is badly struck with a fever and is not expected to last the week.

This morning Seaman John Grimesely came to see me and said he had been requested (indeed elected) to do so by his comrades. He said the men were most disturbed by recent developments and could not be asked to bear them much longer.

Last night a number of altercations had broken out in steerage, some of them of very considerable violence. Eight male passengers had been placed in the lock-up, two of them having to be restrained with manacles or leg-irons. He said there was a rumour of a plot among the steerage passengers to scupper the ship or put it to fire were we not granted permission to debark without delay.

At that remark I lost my temper and said I would light the first torch myself: that I went to sea to be a seaman not a glorified undertaker and that if he did not return to his watch immediately I would elect the tip of my boot up his democratic hole.

Food very low. Water almost gone. What we have is frozen to rock.

✳

Monday, 6 December
The twenty-ninth day out of Cove

LONG: 74°.02′W. LAT: 40°.42′N. ACTUAL GREENWICH
STANDARD TIME: 00.21 a.m. (7 December). 'LOCAL TIME':
07.21 p.m. (6 December). PRECIPITATION & REMARKS:
Extremely cold with bitter frost. Temperature at 2 p.m. was
minus 17.58° Celsius. Smoke and soot in the air.

Our comrade William Gunn departed this life early this morning, a
terrible sadness for he was a good honest lad. He was 19 yrs old, from
the city of Manchester, a true friend to all he met.

Heavy snow now falling. Harbour choked up to Governors
Island. Widely rumoured that the port has been closed by the navy;
all vessels being halted and boarded by frigates off Coney Island and
Rock'way Beach. Very large crowds of the poor congregating on
the docks before us in expectation of news of loved ones aboard the
ships. Many constables and troopers fending them back.

At the suggestion of Lord Kingscourt, I have given orders
that all provisions now on board are to be shared equally between
the steerage passengers, the men and those in First-Class. Have
had vigorous complaints from Wellesley the Mail Agent, who says
he shall never again sail with the Silver Star Line. I said I
profoundly regretted his decision (which I do not) but I could not
suffer the passengers to starve to death in order to retain his
custom.

Mr Grantley Dixon has begun to send in by boat a number of
reports and articles he has made on our predicament for the *Tribune*
of New York. As to whether or not this is helpful I venture no
opinion. (The man secretes such an intimate cognition of
righteousness that one would swear he sees an archangel in the glass
when he shaves.)

Gangs of newspaper reporters have been coming out in skiffs
and punts, also large parties of ordinary 'sight-seers'. Though they
are strictly forbidden to board any ship, nor to come within twenty
yards of it, they call up to the passengers asking them questions,
which can only spread alarm and inquietude. I understand that one
reporter has been arrested for attempting to induce a passenger to

jump the *Slieve Gallion Brae* out of Wexford and thereby make himself an entertaining article.

Groups of resident New York Irish have also been rowing out to make enquiry about relatives or friends who are expected, in all manner of vessels from coracles to dories, some little better than floating bathtubs. They sometimes bring baskets of food or parcels of clothing and although we are supposed not to accept these, a blind eye is oftentimes turned. It is a very sad sight, to see people call out the names and home-towns of their loved ones – 'Mary Galvin of Sligo, is she up there with you?' 'Is Michael Harrigan of Ennis there? It is his brother' & cetera – and sometimes to be told that their people are in fact deceased and have been buried at sea. One poor man was seen by Reverend Deedes, gaily calling the name of his father, as in welcome, and saying a happy place had been prepared for him in his son's home at Brooklyn, where he should never know want again. Only to be informed that his relative had never boarded the ship, having died on Derry Quay a month ago. Another man had brought out his infant daughter in the boat, never seen by her grandparents, and was holding the little mite aloft so proud, only to be given the terrible news that his mother and father had died at sea. It is an eerie sound, at night especially, to hear all the names being cried out from the darkness.

This morning I myself was assailed while on deck by a party of humble Irishmen who had come out in a row-boat. They appeared very poor and hungry themselves. They shouted up to enquire if a passenger by the name of Pius Mulvey of Ardnagreevagh was on board and I said yes. Then they asked if we had a certain Lord Merridith on board, also. Again I was happy to confirm that we did. Was Lord Merridith safe and well, they desired to know? I said he was in the best of health, if a little understandably wearied by the journey, and I had seen him only a quarter-hour previously.

At that a little secretive discussion was had amongst them. They said would I tell Mulvey, next time I saw him, that the committee of welcome was waiting to greet him. They very much hoped he had not forgotten them. Would I just say 'the Hibernian lads' had asked to be remembered to him fondly? They would be on the quayside, watching and waiting. They were preparing a whale of a time for him, they said. A time he should never forget so long as he lived. The fatted calf was being prepared for the slaughter now the prodigal himself was coming into America. As soon as he sets foot through the customs post, they would be waiting, they said.

I am sure the poor man shall be extremely gratified; for it is always agreeable at the end of a long and difficult voyage to see a large number of friendly faces.

CHAPTER XXXVII

THE MURDER

One can only speculate as to the thoughts which must have tortured Pius Mulvey on Tuesday, the seventh of December 1847; the last day he would spend on the *Star of the Sea*.

Early in the morning he was seen playing shuffle-penny with Jonathan and Robert Merridith on the aft part of the upperdeck, and then teaching them the words of a nonsensical ballad. They, in their turn, appeared to be schooling him in the mysteries of some strange entertainment later identified as Winchester College Football. He was noticed on the deck, holding a ball made of rags above his head and shouting 'Worms!' – apparently one of that game's important elements.

At about ten o'clock he visited the cookhouse and asked the sommelier if it would be possible to do some sort of work and have a bottle of wine in return for it. He explained that he wished to make a small gift to Lord and Lady Kingscourt who had shown him a great kindness. The ship's cook, a Chinaman, set him to hacking at the frozen water-butts and he was indeed given a half-bottle of burgundy for his labours, which he presented to Lady Kingscourt with a note of gratitude. She thought he was acting very strangely indeed: all smiles one moment and great fearfulness the next. 'He seemed to be speaking at an angle,' she later said; 'as though burdened by some great weight of which he wished to be free.' He kept saying Jonathan and Robert Merridith were 'fine boys', that Lady Kingscourt's husband was 'a decent man'. That it was a pity all the troubles of home had caused such 'separations' between people. There was no need for any of it, especially in such difficult times. We had all done things in the past which we should not have done, but 'an eye for an eye will leave every man blind'. The more she agreed with him, the more he said it. He seemed to be attempting to convince himself about something.

We know he had an intriguing conversation with the Captain that morning, where he wondered if it would be possible to sign as a hand on the ship and return to Liverpool. Lockwood found the question amazing. Never in all his years at sea had he had a passenger make such a request. For it to be made when America was literally a stone's throw away struck him as bizarre to the point of absurdity, but he put it down to the anxiety often experienced by emigrants, compounded by Mulvey's victimisation while on board. He said the ship would not be going immediately back to Liverpool but needed substantial repairs in dry dock at New York and might well remain there until after Christmas. Further he told Mulvey about a curious incident which had happened the previous morning, when a group of apparently friendly Irishmen rowed out to the *Star* and enquired as to his wellbeing. The news was imparted to try to reassure him; but he did not appear reassured at all. Moreover he was said to have grown very pale, and moments later to have become physically ill: a matter he put down to having eaten something bad.

Some time that morning I went down to the lock-up to seek an interview with the prisoner Seamus Meadowes, but did not find him there. Suffering badly from fever in the damp and cold of the lock-up, he had been released into the custody of the Captain, who had warned that he would be shot if he attempted any trouble. He was lodged in the cabin of First Mate Leeson, under lock and key, where he refused to grant me the interview. He had little use for news-papers, he said; still less for those who wrote in them. Furthermore he affected to speak little English, though I knew he could speak it quite fluently if he wanted to. Indeed as I left the quarters I distinctly heard him asking his guard if he could be permitted to go above and take some air.

I then spent about an hour in the steerage cabin, doing what very little I could to help Surgeon Mangan administer to the passengers. Many were in a state of exhausted fear and were begging him to use his influence to get them off the ship. On the way back, I saw Mulvey in the First-Class quarters. He appeared nervous when I met him in the corridor and said nothing at all as we passed. Since he often looked nervous I thought nothing of it.

What he found in his cabin must have greatly increased his anxiety.

We know it must have been placed there some time late that morning or in the afternoon, for a steward had been in to fetch some stored blankets at about ten o'clock and described the lazaretto in a later statement to the police as 'completely empty; I mean there was nothing unusual about it'. The same man went in again just before four and saw the note lying unopened on the bed. Thinking it private, he did not look at it closely.

Mulvey's initial – M – was carefully inked on the envelope, in the cold careful hand of one wanting anonymity. The stark letters forming the note had been cut from a page. To many another it would have appeared impenetrable. To Pius Mulvey it can only have seemed terrifying.

GET HIM
RIGHT SUNE
Els Be lybill

It was nothing less than denial of commutation. David Merridith or Pius Mulvey: one of them would never set foot on Manhattan.

As for the intended victim, it is possible to establish with some precision what he did on the morning and afternoon of the same day.

Just before dawn, at a quarter after seven, he called a steward and reported that he was not feeling well. He asked for Surgeon Mangan to be sent for immediately, but by the time the physician arrived, Merridith seemed a little better. He complained only of a headache, brought on by a bad hangover and the intense cold, and sent the Surgeon back to his quarters saying he intended to sleep a while.

At about half-past eight, he called the steward again and ordered a light breakfast to be taken in his cabin. When the man came back with the coffee and porridge, Lord Kingscourt asked him to draw him a bath. He was apparently in good spirits, though quiet.

When he had bathed, he then asked the steward, a Brazilian named Fernão Pereira, to help him shave and dress. His eyesight had not been good of late, he mentioned, and he did not want to cut his face. He told the steward to leave the razor behind, saying he was in the habit of shaving twice daily, once in the morning and once before dining. He was 'very insistent' about it, the steward would later testify.

Lord Kingscourt remained in his room until about eleven-thirty; his wife and son Jonathan both saw him as they passed. He was searching through a small attaché case in which he kept papers. He greeted them both in the normal way.

Nobody then saw him until about one o'clock when he lunched

with the Maharajah in the small dining area off the Smoking Saloon. Several post-prandial refreshments were summoned. They played a few hands of gin rummy for shillings and unusually enough Lord Kingscourt won. A conversation then ensued about variant rules for poker, billiards and other gentlemanly amusements. The ship's Mail Agent, George Wellesley, remembered several years after the voyage that Merridith had bored him by attempting to explain a word-game called 'doohulla', which he and his sisters had devised in childhood, and had enjoyed a small glass of port wine with the company as he did so. As the conversation came to its end, Merridith ordered up a bottle of the port and returned to his cabin, saying he intended to read.

On his way back, at about a quarter to three, he was seen on the deck outside the First-Class quarters, kicking a football with his two sons. He seemed 'happy enough', according to one witness, an English seaman named John Grimesley.

His younger son, Robert, had eaten too much at luncheon and was feeling unwell, so Lord Kingscourt accompanied him back to his quarters. A conversation took place about the untidiness of the room, Robert being chided by his father for its general messiness and lack of fresh air. Little wonder that the boy had become ill, it was suggested. Also it was said that he must not take advantage of Pius Mulvey's friendliness and have the poor man playing football all morning, when the decks were so icy as to be perilous. Poor Mulvey's handicap was very severe and it was important to show kindliness to one in such a situation. Lord Kingscourt went to the porthole, drew back the curtain and opened it. And at that point Robert Merridith said something which would have profound consequences.

'You know when you were in a funk with me the other night, Papa? About Mr Mulvey?'

'I didn't mean to be angry, old thing. It's just that we mustn't let our imaginations run away with us, that's all.'

'Why did he say he wouldn't fit in through the window?'

'How do you mean?'

'At supper. He said a great big man could never fit in through a little window like that one.'

'And?'

Robert Merridith said to his father: 'I never said anything about the window to Mr Mulvey. So how did he know?'

'Know what, Bobs?'

'Well – that the person I saw had come in through my window.'

For several minutes Lord Kingscourt evidently said nothing. Many years later his son recalled that it was the longest period of absolute silence he could ever remember spending in his father's company. His father seemed 'completely distracted', he said. 'As one in a trance or a kind of hypnotism.' He sat down on the bunk and gazed at the floor. He seemed utterly unaware that anyone else was in the room with him. Finally the boy approached his father and nudged his arm. Lord Kingscourt looked up at his son and smiled, 'as though he had just that moment awoken'. He ruffled his hair and told him not to be worried about anything. Everything was going to be all right now.

'Do you think Mr Mulvey was playing a game?'

'Yes, Bobs. I expect that's it. Playing a game.'

Robert Merridith returned to the deck, leaving his father alone in the cabin. What the Earl was thinking we cannot know. But by now he must have been contending with an unavoidable and shocking fact: Pius Mulvey had indeed entered his son's room with a knife. He meant to do murder on that ship.

After that point the picture becomes confusing. Surgeon Mangan recalled that he visited Lord Kingscourt twice in the course of the afternoon and administered very strong doses of mercury in injection form and a treatment of laudanum to help him sleep. He was apparently in terrible pain, almost cripplingly so. But several of the steerage passengers later testified that they saw him come into their quarters in the following hours. Others insisted that they observed him walking alone near the stern and looking out at the skyline of lower Manhattan Island, which was at that time a tumble of tenements and poor dwelling houses. A great fire had caught in one of the slums that day; the flames and smoke could be clearly seen from the port side of the *Star*. One elderly woman, a widow from near Limerick City, swore she saw Lord Kingscourt seated at his easel and painting a picture of the burning buildings. It was snowing hard by then and he was wearing no coat but she did not approach him, thinking him 'very hag-ridden'.

There was a dangerously charged atmosphere on the *Star* that night. Food supplies were almost completely exhausted; melted snow was by now the only source of drinkable water. By now it was absolutely believed by everyone in steerage that the vessel was to be sent back to Ireland within the next few days. Many in First-Class believed it, too. It was also widely rumoured that some of the passengers were planning to jump the ship and try to swim the four hundred yards across the harbour. Most had sold every last possession to pay for the voyage. Many could literally see their loved ones waiting on the dock. Having come so far, and at such a heavy cost, they did not mean to go back.

For their own part, the sailors were deeply uneasy. To be thrust into the role of jailer suited very few of them indeed; neither did they want to be nursemaids to sick passengers, not having any training to do so. Indeed it was whispered that a number of the men themselves were about to desert, fearful of catching fever from the worsening conditions on board, and resentful of being asked to police hungry passengers for whose continuing imprisonment they saw no reason. One sailor told me that if passengers tried to escape he would do nothing to stop them but would instead wish them luck. Another, a Scotsman, said that if ordered to use firearms on passengers he would refuse, and would throw his weapon overboard. I asked what he would do if his orders were issued at gunpoint. (There was a rumour that the New York police might give such an order.) 'I will shoot any son-of-a-bitch who points a gun at me,' he replied. 'Yank or Limey, he will get himself a bullet.'

At seven o'clock I saw Merridith in the Dining Saloon. He was neatly dressed, as ever, and looked quite strong. The cold was quite savage on the ship that night; nearly everyone in the saloon was wearing an overcoat, but Merridith, a stickler for etiquette, was not. We did not exchange much conversation, but anything he did say I remember as being very clear. As usual he made a few quips at my own expense but that was nothing out of the ordinary.

I dined that night at the Captain's table, with Wellesley the Mail Agent, the Chief Engineer, the Maharajah, Reverend Deedes and Mrs Marion Derrington. Mangan the surgeon was completely exhausted, now violently unwell himself with an infection of the stomach, and he conveyed his apologies through his capable sister.

The Merridiths sat by themselves at a table for two. They did not say much but no argument was had. Lord Kingscourt appeared to eat a hearty enough supper, though even in First-Class we were now down to dried cod and biscuit; and he bade good-night to our company as he left the saloon. A conversation about literature was taking place at the time. He contributed a few remarks, nothing of consequence. And I remember that he shook my hand just before he left – a thing he had never done before; except, perhaps, the first time I had met him, back in London six years beforehand. 'Keep up the good work, old thing,' he said. 'It is not in the material, but the way it is composed.'

Returned to his cabin he made a few drawings: rather neat little studies of aristocratic houses; a sketch of a peasant-boy of the Connemara hills, in which observers have seen some quality of himself. Others have been struck by the resemblance to his sons; particularly, it is said, to Jonathan. To draw from memory must have been difficult that night. And yet the image is not without peace. The boy is clearly poor; but he is clearly not dying. Nobody is dying. His parents might be at home. If it is a depiction of one of his tenants – and many say it is – it must have been done from distant memory indeed.

At about quarter after ten he ordered a glass of hot milk but was told by the duty steward that there was no milk left on board. He requested a glass of hot water or mulled cider instead. He also asked the steward if it would be possible to borrow a bible, from the Captain, perhaps, or the Surgeon. The steward went to Lockwood's cabin but the Captain was not there and no bible was on his shelf. So the man went to the quarters of Reverend Deedes and there he was given what was necessary. Bringing it to Lord Kingscourt, he received a handsome tip. He was told not to remain on guard outside the door. Apparently Merridith joked that he could not sleep if under guard ('nor spring an old leak with another fellow in the room'), both matters which had blighted his navy days. The man said he would rather stand guard, for security. Lord Kingscourt picked up his razor and opened the blade. 'Lay on, Macduff,' he said, and he smiled. 'Not a man on this ship is the match of a Merridith.'

A sailor on deck duty noticed him open the porthole at about half-past ten. It being such a cold night, the man thought it odd. The light was lowered but not extinguished. He placed his shoes outside the cabin door to be polished. Took off his evening suit and hung it carefully in the wardrobe. And he put on the moth-eaten ancient garments he must have brought from Ireland: a peasant's canvas britches and a bawneen '*bratt*': a farmer's smock, as worn in Connemara.

He read and underlined the following verses; from the Gospel of Mark, chapter twelve:

> **1** And he began to speak unto them by parables. 'A lord planted a vineyard and let it out to tenant men, and went into a far country. **2** And at the season he sent to the tenant men a servant, that he might receive of the fruit of the vineyard. **3** And they caught him, and beat him, and sent him away empty. **4** And again he sent unto them another servant; and at him they cast stones and sent him away. **5** And again he sent another; and him they killed; beating some and killing some. **6** Having one beloved son, he sent to them his son. And he said, "I know they will reverence my son." **7** But the tenant men said among themselves: "This is the heir; come; let us kill him; and the inheritance of the vineyard shall be ours."'

*

Just before eleven o'clock that same night, a number of sailors who were nominally on watch duty were overpowered by a group of about twenty men from steerage, led by Seamus Meadowes of Ballynahinch who had broken out of the First Mate's quarters half an hour beforehand. By the time he came onto the frozen upperdeck, Meadowes was 'raging and covered in blood' and 'roaring that a blow had been struck for freedom this night'. They smashed open the chains on two of the lifeboats; heaved them into the icy water and jumped in after them. One man remained in the water and began to swim. The others clambered into the smaller of the two boats and began making hard for the shore. None was an experienced boatman; panic set in quickly. The oars were soon lost and the desperate fugitives were seen trying to paddle with their hands.

Moments later, Pius Mulvey appeared on the deck in an agitated state and pleaded to be allowed to go with the second group. He was pushed away and violently abused. At that point a larger group, comprising another fifty or so, appeared from various parts of the ship. Among their number was Mary Duane.

By now some of the passengers were jumping overboard. Many found themselves in immediate difficulty; the water must have been paralysingly cold, and the majority were unable to swim. An argument seems to have begun on the deck as to which of the remaining passengers should have places in the second boat. The few women and children were accommodated first; next the husbands of the women, or their male relations or fiancés. Mary Duane, being the last woman present at the scene, was offered one of the last two places. She wavered, briefly, and then said she would take it. A very old Galwayman called Daniel Simon Grady was offered the place beside her. He was much admired among the steerage passengers, a gentle sort of old man.

Mulvey stepped forward and said he had prior claim, being a member of Mary Duane's family.

Mary Duane replied, 'May you rot.'

Mulvey was then heard to utter the words, 'Have mercy on me, Mary. Don't deny me the only chance, for pity's sake.'

He began to weep and to clutch at her hands. He seemed absolutely convinced that his life was in danger. He kept saying that he could not leave the ship in such a way as to go through the customs station with the body of passengers, that he had strong reason to believe he would be murdered if he did. Neither could he risk being sent back to Ireland, for a similar fate awaited him there, and anyway he could not bear to face the journey.

She said it was a fate he deserved, and worse.

'Hasn't there been enough of torture, Mary? Enough of bloodshed? *Enough* by now?'

She was asked by the old Galwayman if what Mulvey was saying was correct. Was he indeed related to her? She must speak the truth. To deny one of your own family was a dreadful thing to do. Far too many in Ireland had done it before. So many had turned against their own blood now. He was not blaming anyone; it was just so cruel what had happened to the people. It would break your heart to see it happen. Neighbour against neighbour. Family against family. For a man to turn his back on his brother was the blackest sin. But men were weak. So often they were afraid. For a woman to do it could never be forgiven.

'Is your name Duane, love?' the old man asked her.

She said it was.

'Of over by Carna?'

She nodded.

'That name is a wealth to you. Your people were great.'

When she made no answer she was asked again would she leave one of her own family behind to suffer. Perhaps to die. Was that truly what a Duane would do? The old man said he could not take the place in such a circumstance. No blessing could come from such an action; nor would any be merited. He was only here himself because of natural family love; his children in Boston had sent him the fare. They had little enough but they had scraped every penny to do it. Often they themselves had gone hungry just to save him. There was no need for them to do it, only simple human mercy. 'The only thing that makes our lives here bearable.' He could not disgrace their name by standing in the way of family. His wife in Heaven would weep for his honour if he did.

'Come into the boat,' Mary Duane said to the old Galwayman.

Sleet began falling. He put his hand on her shoulder. 'I have nothing left,' he reportedly said. And some say he briefly continued, in Irish: 'Nothing in the world. Only my name.'

Again Mulvey came forward and pleaded to be given a chance. Again she accused him of deserving none. He had been spat on by now and his clothes were torn. He seemed almost impervious to the kicks and punches being thrown at him. Reportedly he was quaking with fear or pain but he did not raise a hand to shield himself.

'Is there no doubt in you, Mary? Not an ounce itself of doubt? Is this what Nicholas would have wanted, are you saying? Can any of it mend the wrong? Will it turn back the times? I'll die if you want it. *I am already dead.*'

I think I know the answer I myself would have given. I believe I know even the words I would have used, every curse, every spite, every last denunciation. I have heard the anathema I would have rained on Pius Mulvey. I have seen my dagger stab into his betrayer's heart; the dizzying exhilaration of white-hot hatred I would have felt. Or perhaps I would have said simply: 'I do not know you.' I have never seen you. You are no part of me.

But it is not the answer that Mary Duane gave.

It is almost seventy years since the events of that night and not a day has passed in those seven long decades – I mean literally not one single day – without my searching my mind for some explanation of what happened next. I have spoken to every living person who witnessed the occurrence: every man, every woman, every child and every sailor. I have discussed it with philosophers, doctors of the mind. Priests. Ministers. Mothers. Wives. For many of those years I saw it in dreams; sometimes, still, I see it even now. And I believe when my own time comes, I will see it again; an event I never saw, but only heard reported. Pius Mulvey on his knees, begging for his life. Mary Duane above him, shaking with tears; for she wept that night on the *Star of the Sea*, as perhaps only the mother of a murdered child can weep. Nobody ever drew Alice-Mary Duane, whose ruined father snuffed out her agonised life. Her mother wept as she uttered her name. 'Like a prayer', as many of the witnesses said.

And as the name was uttered, some began to pray; and others began to weep in sympathy. And others again who had lost children of their own began to utter their children's names. As though the act of saying their names – the act of saying they ever had names – was to speak the only prayer that can ever begin to matter in a world that turns its eyes from the hungry and the dying. They were real. They existed. They were held in these arms. They were born, and they lived, and they died. And I see myself on the deck in a scream of vengeance; as though it was my own spouse who had been scourged to despair; my own helpless child so cruelly destroyed.

Was it forgiveness? Gullibility? Power? Loss? Some dark aggregation of all these things, or something else more dark again? Perhaps even Mulvey would not have known the answer. Perhaps Mary Duane did not know it herself.

If it was mercy – and I simply cannot say what it was – whatever made Mary Duane show it may only be guessed. Wherever she found it can never be known. But she did show it. She did find it.

When the moment of retribution rolled up out of history and presented itself like an executioner's sword, she turned away and did not seize it.

Instead, still weeping and now being helped to stand, she confirmed that Pius Mulvey of Ardnagreevagh was the brother of her late husband; her only living relation in three thousand miles.

She was asked if she wanted to remain on the ship, to take her chances of being sent back to Ireland alongside him. She hesitated for a moment and then said no, she did not.

They entered the second lifeboat together, taking up the last two places, and were last seen drifting in the direction of the dock.

CHAPTER XXXVIII

THE DISCOVERY

The thirty-first day out of Cove

LONG: 74°.02′W. LAT: 40°.42′N. ACTUAL GREENWICH STANDARD TIME: 00.58 a.m. (9 December). LOCAL TIME: 7.58 p.m. PRECIPITATION & REMARKS: New York Harbour. Low tide.

✝

On this eighth day of December, in the year of Our Lord, Eighteen hundred and Forty-Seven, it is my grievous duty to record the news of the heinous murder of Lord Kingscourt of Carna, our friend David Merridith, the ninth Earl. His body was discovered by Countess Kingscourt this morning, just after dawn in the First-Class quarters. Surgeon Mangan attended immediately but pronounced death to have occurred at about eleven o'clock last night. The cause was seven deep stabs to the upper back, and one to the back of the skull. Yet more horrifically, the throat had been so severely cut that the head was almost completely separated from the body.

No weapon was found and the search for one continues. His Lordship must have been most horribly surprised, for there were no defence wounds to the hands or arms, nor were any cries heard from his cabin.

Full searches were made of the First-Class quarters, a strange note being found torn up into pieces, in the wastage-disposal canister on the Main Lower Landing, as though a kind of blackmail letter. It has been preserved and will be handed to the police at New York.

As Master all responsibility for the security of the vessel weighs exclusively upon myself; and accordingly I hereby tender my resignation from command of this ship, also from the employment of the Silver Star Shipping Line & Co., to be effective from debarkation and unloading at New York.

I sent a boat in to the wharf and explained the frightful happening and asked in the circumstances to be allowed to come in; but permission was strongly denied by the authorities. A large party of police officers and immigration officials came out and took-down testimonies from a great number of steerage passengers and others. It

377

was confirmed that Shaymus Meadowes, formerly of Ballynahinch, County Galway, one of those who fled the ship last night, had indeed threatened extreme violence towards Lord Kingscourt and other landowners of Ireland in the past, and so must be deemed the principal suspect, or at very least, the ringleader of the evil. Mister Mulvey was not alone in thinking him a danger. He was believed by many passengers to be a member of the 'Liable Men' of Galway, and apparently had often himself claimed so to be; on several occasions boasting that he knew for a certitude Lord Kingscourt would never leave the ship alive.

The First-Class passengers may be allowed to land in a few days; but those in steerage shall have to delay until all are questioned and examined and cleared for disease.

I explained to Captain Daniel O'Dowd of the New York Police that we had a number of human remains in the hold, with the inevitable consequences which must attend, and I was anxious regarding the health of those in my charge. I suggested that perhaps a large quantity of rat poison might be supplied but was told that such would not be possible, at least not for the moment, but arrangements would be made for disposal of the bodies.

Two barges came alongside shortly before noon, and the remains we had below were loaded upon them, including those of Lord Kingscourt. We had no colours with which to enshroud him so we lowered the Union pennant from the mainmast and used that. To the great distress of Lady Kingscourt and her sons, a small number of passengers were heard to cheer as the colours were lowered. I appealed to them to have a care for the simple respect of the dead and they desisted. They said it was not the deceased they were jeering, but only the flag. When I said it was the flag under which he had once served his country, one man said many an Irishman had served it too, and had no flag of his own in which he might be buried, as did none of those who had died on the *Star*. No flag nor fuss for them, he said. The very day he had boarded the *Star of the Sea*, nine hundred bodies of those who had starved had been shovelled into a pit in his home town of Bantry. No cross. No stone. No coffin. No flag. I answered that I understood his feelings on the matter, as indeed I do, but this was not the time for such a discussion, since the grief of any widow must surely be the same, as must be the sadness of any little child bereft of his father. We shook hands and he removed his hat as Lord Kingscourt's body was lowered down, though others were seen to turn their backs.

The barge being small, there was little room for mourners. Places were allowed to Lady Kingscourt and her children, to Mr G. Dixon as friend of the family, to Minister Deedes and to myself as Master of the vessel. The steerage passengers who had lost loved ones were greatly upset but the Pilot said he simply had not the capacity on board. Mr Dixon said he would be willing to give up his place but the two little boys seemed very distressed and pleaded with him to remain. The Pilot made to bear off but was affected by the crying of the bereaved on board. He was a kindly man, a Hebridean Scotsman, and one could see he had sympathy for the people. Finally he said he would take one more mourner as representative for all the others, if a choice could be made quickly. They drew lots to decide their representative, and Rose English, a married woman of Roscommon was selected, her husband being among the dead.

We were towed back out a few miles through Gedney's Channel, a short distance west of Sydney's Beacon; and further out past the Verazano Narrows into Lower Bay. There we were ordered to wait for the rising tide. At seven minutes to one, the Pilot gave us the signal. Mrs English asked if we might delay another very few short minutes. The poor lady was by now very distressed but trying to speak calmly. At one o'clock in New York it would be six in the evening at home, she said. The bells would be tolling all over Ireland for the Angelus. The Pilot agreed that we could wait until then.

Mrs English, a Roman Catholic, began quietly to recite the Rosary in Latin and was joined by the Pilot's mate, an Italian man of Naples. The rest of us stood together in silent prayer for a time and added an amen at the end. The two boys were attempting to be brave, but how could they be in such terrible circumstances? Lady Kingscourt began to weep; and I noticed Mrs English, also weeping, take her by the hand.

At the signal from the Pilot for one o'clock, we committed David Merridith's remains to the deep, also those of nine men, women and children of Ireland, and those of our gentle comrade, William Gunn of Manchester. With the assent of Mrs English, Reverend Deedes read quietly from the Book of Common Prayer:

that we look for the Resurrection of the body (when the sea shall give up her dead), and the life of the world to come, through our Lord Jesus Christ; who at His coming shall change our vile body, that it may be like unto His glorious body; according to the mighty working whereby He is able to subdue all things to Himself.

May God almighty grant him peace. He leaves a wife, Lady Laura, and two small sons: Robert and Jonathan, the tenth Earl. It is believed they will stay at Albany, New York, for a time, at the home of a married sister of Mr Grantley Dixon.

The names of the others of our lost companions, on whose souls we ask the mercy of the Saviour this day:

Michael English, a farmer; Peter Joyce, a farmer; James Halloran, a farmer's infant child; Rose Flaherty, a seamstress; John O'Lea, a smith's apprentice; Edward Dunne, smallholder; Michael O'Malley, itinerant labourer; Winnifred Costello, married woman; and Daniel Simon Grady, an elderly man of Galway, who died in steerage early this morning, having intended to go to his children at Boston. The total who died on the voyage is ninety-five.

The compleat register of those who fled the ship last night has not yet been compiled, but their number includes Shaymus Meadowes, Grace Coggen, Francis Whelan, Fintan Mounrance, Thomas Boland, Patk. Balfe, Wilm. Hannon, Josephine Lawless, Bridget Duignan, Mary Farrell, Honor Larkin, and between twenty-five and fifty others – also Pius Mulvey the unfortunate cripple and Mary Duane, nanny of the Merridith family.

The debris clogging the harbour being most severe, both lifeboats were lost some time last night. Most of the bodies were recovered from Gravesend Bay near dawn; but some must be lying on the harbour-bed still. Others may well have drifted back out to open sea. A full report has been made to the Police at New York but little hope if any may be entertained for survivors, the currents in these waters being pitiless strong.

As for myself, I will nevermore to sea. For many years, I had been less than content with this life and torn at by thoughts of what might replace it, knowing only two things for most of those years: that a great sinner am I; but Christ a great Saviour. Now, by His oftentimes terrible grace, I know more.

Upon my return home to Dover I mean to devote the

remainder of my days to some endeavour which will assist the suffering poor of some place, be it Ireland or England or some other nation. What it can be, I know not; but I must do something. The country of the poor can be abandoned no longer.

For I dread what is growing in that country now. I fear we shall reap a venomous crop.

CHAPTER XXXIX

FROM

A MISCELLANY OF THE ANCIENT SONGS OF IRELAND

(Boston, 1904)

Preface by Captain Francis O'Neill of the Chicago Police
Department. Author of the following text unknown.

♣ NUMBER THREE HUNDRED AND SEVEN ♣
"The Grinding Stones" or "Revenge for Connemara"
(Sung to the air of "Skibbereen")

♣

Here is another glittering jewel of Ireland's antique minstrelsy.
Like the greater number of those comprising the present
anthology, the following was first written down on a vessel

journeying here to the United States of Liberty from that green but mournful land across the ocean where freedom, alas, is yet but a reverie. It was heard by a man by the noble name of John Kennedy of Ballyjamesduff, County Cavan, nearly six decades ago now, on his twentieth birthday; the third of December in the year of 1847. The name of the coffin-ship was the *Star of the Oceans.*

Every true-hearted Irishman will bow his head at utterance of 'Black 47', most heinous year of that evil era wherein two millions of our countrymen were martyred by starvation; when the old foe, fearful of Ireland's steel, murdered with the weapon of the coward instead. Every modest woman and girl of Ireland will storm the gates of Paradise with supplications to Our Blessed Mother. O! darkest epoch. How Satan must have delighted to see the Catholic children of Erin decimated like slaves in their own fair land; banished as the Hebrews by the crimes of cultish Pharaoh.

Some comradely dispute has existed between the editors and the sagacious old greybeards of the Chicago Irish Music Club concerning its true age and provenance; but it is evident to any reasonable man that the ballad hails from the ancient bloody times of resistance, when priest and people stood fast together against alien murder and rapine. Not for the first time and neither the last! if the editors know anything about their countrymen's mettle. Hatred can be a holy and a cleansing thing. Please the Lord of Heaven it will not be long before the pallid countenance of violated Mother Ireland is restored to former comeliness by the red wine of vengeance.

This fine lament was heard sung on that vessel of martyrs by a patriotic boy of about six years. Mary bless him! It is best given very slowly and without accompaniment of any kind, having careful respect to the decorum of the words, and is therefore not suitable for group singing or rallies.

♣

Come all ye native Galway boys and listen to my song;
It's of the tyrant Saxon and the cause of Erin's wrong;

The maker of our troubles, and the breaker of our bones;
To keep him up he keeps us down, and grinds us on the stones.

Their taxes and their terrors, boys, they have us nearly dead;
They drink their cup of bloodshed up, they rob our daily bread;
False princes of perdition black, indifferent to our groans;
How long more should we stand aside and let them steal our homes?

The same true gang, they did us hang, they poisoned Eoghan O'Neill;
And sent their hireling cowards, boys, our Mother-land to steal.
The blood be frozen in their veins, their hearts be withered up!
Who robbed the best, and left the rest, the blackened bitter crop.

Is this the land of Sarsfield, boys, the bower of brave Wolfe Tone?
O heroes loyal of Ireland's soil, where fell the seeds they've sown?
Where are they now, who took the vow, that Erin should be free?
In blood and smoke, they smote the yoke of Saxon slavery.

Then come, true native Connaught men, wherever you may be.
A bright new crop is growing up, the flower of liberty.
We'll tend it till it harvests, and they'll ne'er more break our bones;
For we'll slash them down and lift us up, and smash them on the stones.

Cuchulainn, Maeve, those valiant brave, the holy throng of yore,
Who warred with heathen Albion, boys, flinched not in battle's roar;
To fight, to die; Saint Patrick high; the Lords of ancient Tara,
As one cry out, from North to South –

"REVENGE FOR CONNEMARA!"

EPILOGUE
THE HAUNTED MAN

'History happens in the first person but is written in the third.
This is what makes history a completely useless art.'

David Merridith, from an essay written while an undergraduate at
New College, Oxford, Michaelmas term, 1831, on the theme:
'Why is History Useful?'

✱

Here was a story of three or four people. The reader will know that
there were many other stories. An investigation commissioned by
the city fathers calculates that between May and September of that
horrifying year, 101,546 wretchedly poor immigrants entered the
teeming port of New York. Of that number, 40,820 were Irish. It is
not actually known how many lost their lives within sight of what
they themselves often called 'the Promised Land'. Some say the
figure may be as high as two-thirds.

Many years have passed but some things have not changed. We
still tell each other that we are lucky to be alive, when our being
alive has almost nothing to do with luck, but with geography,
pigmentation and international exchange rates. Perhaps this new
century will see a new dispensation, or perhaps we will continue to
allow the starvation of the luckless, and continue to call it an
accident, not a working-out of logic.

1847. Marx's *Poverty of Philosophy*. Verdi's *Macbeth*. Boole's
Calculus of Deductive Reasoning. Emily Brontë's *Wuthering Heights*.
Charlotte Brontë's *Jane Eyre*. Ralph Emerson's *Poems*. Engels'
Principles of Communism. Quarter of a million starved in that year's
nowhere-land: nameless in the latitudes of hunger.

We First-Class passengers from the *Star of the Sea* were ferried
into Manhattan on the evening of Saturday, 11 December, four days
after the murder of David Merridith. As a gesture of apology for the
inconvenience we had suffered, the Silver Star Shipping Line
cancelled our bills and invited us to a champagne reception at an
elegant hotel. It is the only time in my ninety-six years that I have
heard a Methodist minister swear. Reverend Deedes said things to
the Director that the latter will not have forgotten for a long time.
Like many quiet people, he was remarkably courageous, Henry

Hudson Deedes of Lyme Regis in Dorset. He returned to the *Star* the following morning, and would be the last man to leave it, with the exception of the Captain.

Those in steerage had to remain on the ship for almost seven weeks, where they were regularly interviewed by parties of police and officials from the Office of Aliens. Having paid for their own passages in advance of the voyage, they received nothing whatsoever by way of compensation. Neither, I understand, were they given champagne.

In January a programme was commenced to clear the clogged port, which by now had become a floating factory for influenza; but the immigrants were still not permitted entry to Manhattan. Farm buildings and sheds on Long Island and Staten Island were leased as quarantine stations or clearance centres; but the fear of contagion so alarmed the neighbourhoods that many of the buildings were attacked and burned by the locals. A large plot of land on Ward's Island in the harbour was leased by the city government as a secure place to hold immigrants while their applications were processed and their illnesses tended. Before long it had become a permanent facility, this windswept chunk of basalt on which the Atlantic beats like a hammer. It is perhaps a measure of the state of its inhabitants' destitution that 10,308 articles of 'basic clothing' are listed as having been requested by them in one five-month period. Certainly it is a measure of the truer impulse of the New Yorker that those items, so pitifully needed, were provided so quickly.

By the time the *Star*'s survivors were permitted finally to come into Manhattan, every hospital, shelter and almshouse on the island had been overwhelmed. Anti-immigrant feeling was strong and growing. Thousands of new immigrants were simply paid by the authorities to get out of the city and move west. No doubt some were among the 80,000 native Irishmen who would fight for the Union in the Civil War. And others were among the 20,000 of their countrymen who would take up arms for the cause of the Confederacy; for the legal right of a freedom-loving white man to regard a black man as a commodity.

Some Irish earned fortunes and garnered power as a result. Others drifted into the ghettos and were feared and despised. Mary Duane might have been strong enough to endure such an existence, but Mulvey would not have been, or so I believe. He had taken enough of being despised. His crimes were many but he was a scapegoat for more, and being despised had helped to ruin him. David Merridith's ghetto was entirely of another kind; but he had borne more than his share of hatred, too.

What happened took place in 1847, an important anniversary in the history of fictions; when stories appeared in which people were starving, in which wives were jailed in attics and masters married servants. An evil time for the place these three violated people called home. A time when things were done – and other things not done – as a result of which more than a million would die; the slow, painful, unrecorded deaths of those who meant nothing to their lords.

What happened is one of the reasons they still die today. For the dead do not die in that tormented country, that heartbroken island of incestuous hatreds; so abused down the centuries by the powerful of the neighbouring island, as much by the powerful of its native own. And the poor of both islands died in their multitudes while the Yahweh of retributions vomited down his hymns. The flags flutter and the pulpits resound. At Ypres. In Dublin. At Gallipoli. In Belfast. The trumpets spew and the poor die. Yet they walk, the dead, and will always walk; not as ghosts, but as press-ganged soldiers, conscripted into a battle that is not of their making; their sufferings metaphorised, their very existence translated, their bones stewed into the sludge of propaganda. They do not even have names. They are simply: The Dead. You can make them mean anything you want them to mean.

That sometimes there must be struggle is not to be doubted. With which weapons it is fought remains the question; and who shall fight whom, and over which ground. For the poor of one tribe to slaughter the poor of the other, all in the name of a blood-soaked field in which the rich would happily bury them both alive at the precise moment it became profitable to do so: this is no fitting memorial to the landless of the past. But that is the making of another story. One, perhaps, which is yet to be written; with a more brotherly ending and a deal less horror.

✷

As the only professional reporter on the ship where Lord Kingscourt was murdered, my articles were in demand all over the world. Everywhere, in fact, except at the *New York Tribune*, where my editor dismissed me for 'egalitarian sympathies'. There were offers for books; essays; lecture tours. In addition, on the founding of the *New York Times* in '51, I accepted the position of 'Senior Contributing Columnist': the title a piece of hogwash roughly translatable as 'wildly overpaid late-sleeper'. Never again would I have to rely on the blood money garnered by my ancestors' crimes. What happened also removed the label of adulteress from his wife; a badge she had never been happy to wear. It sounds callous to say that his death gave me a kind of freedom, but it would be less than fully honest to allow that fact to remain unacknowledged. Perhaps I was wrong to write about what happened; perhaps I had no other choice than to do so. Certainly any newspaperman would have done the same thing; and at least I tried to do so fairly.

My series on the Monster of Newgate for the *Bentley's Miscellany* was reprinted in my collection *An American Abroad*, first published by my late friend Cautley Newby in 1849, along with my account of the *Star* and its passengers, and some notes on a tour of parts of Connemara. I had insisted three short stories were also included, but no reviewer mentioned them, whether to praise or discommend. A polite silence seemed to hang around them, somehow. From future editions they were quietly removed. Newby never alluded to their disappearance and neither did I. The feeling was that of a sleepwalker who has awoken to find himself at a funeral and must creep away quickly before anyone mentions he wasn't invited. Those three mediocre and justly forgotten short stories were the only fictional writings I was ever to publish.

We argued a lot, Newby and I, regarding the book's title. I wanted to call it 'Reflections on the Irish Famine'; Newby pleaded strongly for 'Confessions of a Fiend'. 'An American Abroad' was an attempt at a compromise; rather a cowardly one, we both felt. On the cover of the second edition was printed, as well as the title, a small sub-line reading: 'Monstrous Revelations'. By the time of the fourth edition the sub-line had grown. By the time of the tenth it dwarfed the title. And by the time of the twentieth edition, the volume's actual name could barely be seen without the aid of a magnifying glass.★

That short section of the book dealing with the Monster of Newgate was of course the most widely reviewed and read. More than that, it seemed to beguile the public's imagination. The appearance of the book created a whole new audience for the monster. Stories of his doings – almost always heavily fictionalised – appeared in every kind of English publication, from ha'penny magazines to pornographic paperbacks, from *Punch* and *The Tomahawk* to the *Catholic Herald*. It became fashionable to attend society fancy-dress evenings costumed as the monster, or even – incredibly – as one of his now multiple victims. At one point there were two different versions of his life playing in London theatres. Soon the monster was to be subjected to the final indignity. That horror among horrors. A musical.

The monster now entered the vernacular of politics. The Irish parliamentarian Mr Charles Parnell, who bravely led the poor of his country towards some variety of liberation, was on one occasion described in the House of Commons as 'little better than the Monster of Newgate'. Reminders were often given that Daniel O'Connell, M.P., an earlier exponent of a form of emancipation, had named the mass gatherings he organised throughout the Irish countryside not rallies or assemblies, but 'Monster Meetings'. Such a baptism now became a matter for frequent discussion in the watering holes and salons of the powers-that-were. The grotesque cartoons depicting the Irish poor in the English journals began to change. Always previously portraying them as foolish and drunken, now they more frequently showed murderers. Ape-like. Fiendish. Bestial. Untamed. How we draw the enemy, what we fear about the

---

★It was Mr Newby and not the author who composed the arresting 'standfirst' texts which introduced the chapters of the original volume, with their hair-raising references to 'SHOCKING DETAILS', 'WICKED DEEDS', 'HIDDEN SECRETS' and so on. Having vexed the author utterly at the time of publication, they now seem rather innocent (though of course they are not). They are left unaltered here as a fond memorial to a friend who could some-times be a little unscrupulous. – GGD

self. Every time I saw one, I saw the Monster of Newgate, whose grim reputation I had done so much to diffuse.

Throughout it all, I had to ask myself was it worth it: to go in disguise into this kingdom of lies. To use the shocking story of the Monster of Newgate to tell another more important and still more shocking story. For many years I convinced myself this was morally acceptable: the ends at least arguably justifying the means. Now, of course, I am not so certain. When we are young these things appear so simple. But they are not simple. They never were.

I was told that the book brought to the attention of some of the reading public the sufferings being endured in Ireland at the time of the Great Famine; but if so, it did little to end those sufferings. It was not the last famine in Ireland by any means, still less in that complicated work of penny-dreadful fiction entitled the British Empire. Modest amounts of money were sometimes gathered by readers and their families. A few farthings, a sixpence, very occasionally a shilling. Generally any monies we received were from women or the poor, though perhaps oddly (and perhaps not) we sometimes received subscriptions from serving British soldiers, particularly those in India. Newby and I established a small trust to administer the funds, the much-maligned (and much-envied) Mr Dickens becoming for a while our excellent chairman. Initially there were high-flown aims of spending what was available on teaching the children of Connemara to read. It was Dickens who snapped that a dead child does not read. He and I quarrelled violently at what I saw as his easy philistinism, and sadly we were never to speak again. The loss was mine, as was the error. He was absolutely correct to argue as he did; politically, morally and in every other sense, that the money ought to be spent on food, not poetry. I should have remembered that his own childhood had been haunted by hunger and terror, whereas mine had not – at least not by my own. If, perhaps, it saved one single life, the book was not an utter waste of everybody's time.

Small but not entirely worthless reforms were put in place in the British penal system as an extremely indirect result of the book's success. Prisoners were given less humiliating work. The number of family visits was raised. Questions began to be asked of the 'solitary incarceration' practised at certain of Queen Victoria's prisons, but it was not to be ended for many years. No doubt these things would have happened anyway, and while I am glad they did, and salute their true authors, I would not be fully honest if I said altruism was my only motive, nor perhaps even my main one if it comes to that. I was a newspaperman. I wanted the story.

David Merridith was quite right to gibe at me as he used to. I think perhaps I wanted to be admired. It is such a brutalising thing, our need for admiration. How very wonderful to have learned that it fades with age.

✳

Seamus Meadowes was arrested for Merridith's murder but found not guilty in a unanimous verdict. I myself was called as a minor witness for the defence and testified that the accused had not composed the death note found in the First-Class quarters. I knew it for a fact and explained how I knew it. At that time Seamus Meadowes could neither read nor write, a fact he had confided with a bizarre kind of pride on the morning I had tried to interview him.

I was not invited to suggest another suspect for the murder; nor did I volunteer to do so. I had promised anonymity to Pius Mulvey and like any honourable journalist I intended to keep my promise. I answered every question, told no lies and was congratulated by the judge for the economy of my evidence.

The trial was a *cause célèbre* in Irish New York and the publicity made the defendant a hero to many. He made an unsuccessful attempt at a professional boxing career, entered the Police Department and then political life; first as an enforcer for Boss 'Honey' Maguire, then as fundraiser, election agent and finally candidate. As 'Southpaw Jimmy Meadows, the working-man's champ',* he was elected eleven times to the East Bronx ward and was only narrowly defeated for Mayor in 1882, a result he always blamed on the inadequate numeracy of his henchmen rather than any desire of the electorate. The vicissitudes of democracy he

---

*He dropped the final 'e' from his surname early in his political career, arguing that 'it made me appear too English.' See Meadows, J. *Fifteen Rounds for Justice: The Story of My Life* (New York, 1892). – GGD

regarded as a minor inconvenience. Often enough, when they tallied up his votes, the total equalled the number of registered voters in the entire constituency; and on two famous occasions actually exceeded it. ('A man should exercise his rights as often as possible,' he used to say cryptically. 'Ain't that what America's all about?')

Two years later he was arraigned for fraud, having been discovered taking the written examination required of aspiring New York postmen, under the name of an illiterate constituent to whom he had promised a job. (The trial was abandoned when the main prosecution witness mysteriously fell out a window and broke his jaw.) Meadows was re-elected the following year, his already monumental majority increased by a third. 'They don't count my ballots, boys, they weigh 'em,' he remarked to reporters. He died very peacefully, aged one hundred and one, in the neo-Regency mansion he had somehow managed to acquire on a lifetime of public representative's wages.

At the time of his death he was said to have been considering an offer from the Edison Motion Picture Company of Orange, New Jersey. One of its executives, an Edwin S. Porter, wanted to produce a short fictional entertainment loosely based on Meadows's life and many adventures. The provisional title was 'The Wild Irish Rover' but negotiations had been stalled in the preceding months. (Apparently the Rover had insisted on playing himself.)

His funeral was attended by an enormous crowd of the poor, many of whom idolised him and always had. If they saw him as a dirty fighter, as some of them did, they argued, convincingly enough, that a clean one would have left them to rot in the slums. The Marquess of Queensberry, Seamus Meadowes was not. (But as admirers of another flamboyant Irishman will know, neither was the Marquess of Queensberry.)

Mass was concelebrated by fifteen priests, including two of his five sons and several other relations. A piper played an ancient Connemara lament as the cortège stopped briefly at the Fulton Street dockside: the place where Southpaw Meadows first set foot on America. Archbishop O'Connell of Boston who led the obsequies remarked: 'Jimmy was a democrat, first and last. All he had to do, to know what the people wanted, was to gaze steadily into the depths of his own magnificent heart.'

A number of matters had come out at his trial for Merridith's murder which were extremely painful to the victim's family. It was revealed that the strange man often seen tailing Merridith around the East End was not in fact an Irish revolutionary but an English detective hired by Laura Markham's father, who had wondered how his son-in-law was spending so much of his money. Unaware that the Kingscourt estate was almost bankrupt, and that Merridith had been financially cut off by his own father, Mr Markham had suspected the existence of a mistress. The truth emerged in court about Merridith's visits to brothels and it was a difficult time for Laura Markham and her sons. Inevitably the details of his medical condition were also revealed, and were pruriently reported in all the newspapers, the usual easy moral derived and explained as though such derivation or explanation were necessary by now. Never was it said that what he suffered was an ailment: not a curse, a revenge, a castigation, but a germ. So strong was the popular lust to attribute supernature to diseases (as much as to famines, perhaps not incidentally) that it was tempting when it came time to set down this story to leave out his illness, or edit its chronology, or change it, somehow, to some other thing. But that would have been wrong; a tacit approval of the game. He had what he had, and was pronounced guilty for having it, though he was not, in fact, on trial for anything. He was posthumously condemned by the violently pious judge, an ascendant star of New York politics who knew how to appeal to the avidity for a villain shared by a number of my saintlier countrymen. If he could have found Merridith guilty of murdering himself, he would have; and hanged his corpse outside a chapel.

As for the note intended to push Mulvey into the act of murder, the reader will already have identified the author; though I did not myself until shortly before the trial. But the moment I actually saw it, I knew who had made it. It was not Mary Duane, nor Seamus Meadowes, nor any of the abject poor who suffered on that ship.

As David Merridith used often to put it, everything is in the way the material is composed.

GET HIM. RIGHT SUNE. Els Be lybill. H.

An expert in doohulla would have noticed the anagram.

WUTHERING HEIGHTS by Ellis Bell.

With the 'M' in 'get him' an inverted W.

It was the victim who assembled that fatal note, fashioned his own warrant for execution. His raw material was the novel I had given him, the gift of the man who had already stolen what was his. The volume was indeed found in one of his suitcases with the jags clearly visible where the title page had been torn out. As to why he made his choice, we can only surmise. Cowardice had been mentioned but I think that insults him. Vaguely Roman suggestions have also been advanced: the falling of the noble on his sword and so on. I think he loved his children too much for imperial gestures.

My own belief is that David Merridith was a remarkably brave man who knew that his life would end very soon and wanted to spare his family the shame of a pariah's death. Perhaps he had other understandable thoughts, too, for the papers found in his desk pertained to the Royal Naval Relief Trust, a fund which supported the private education of the sons of deceased officers whether serving or retired. (Not their daughters, only their sons.) Like all such schemes in that riotously respectable era, it was void in the event of either suicide or syphilis. But not of murder. Murder voided nothing. Murder would give his children some kind of inheritance.

The dividend was to be seized by his creditors anyway, almost his entire estate being swallowed up by debt; the remainder by lawyers' fees, taxes and death duties. It was only discovered after his assassination that bankruptcy proceedings had already been initiated in London, but had been briefly delayed on the entreaties of his lawyers. (They had pointed out that as a bankrupt he would have to resign from the House of Lords. An appalling vista, as somebody said.) The lands at Kingscourt were purchased by Commander Henry Edgar Blake of Tully Cross who broke them up, rack-rented the last few tenants off them, and replaced the farmers and smallholders with sheep. The sheep proved more profitable than the troublesome human beings and less inconveniently solicitous of the right not to die. He made the enormous fortune his grandchildren now enjoy. One of them is active in Irish politics.

On a visit to Connemara in 1850 I met with Captain Lockwood again. He and his wife were living at that time in the village of Letterfrack, near Tully Cross, with other members of the Quaker Society who had gone there to stand in solidarity with the Irish famished. His wife was a cousin of a woman named Mary Wheeler, who had moved with her husband, James Ellis of Bradford, to northern Galway in 1849, hoping to help the local people. They had no previous connection whatever with Connemara; but they saw connections where others who should have seen them simply looked the other way. They built homes, roads, drains, a school; paid their workers fairly and treated them with respect. Lockwood was working with some of the local fishermen, mending nets and repairing boats. He was a modest-hearted man, Josias Lockwood of Dover, and he would have scoffed at being called a hero. And yet he was one of the greatest I have known. He and his sisters and brothers of the English Quakers – he always insisted gently on his preferred word, 'Friends' – saved hundreds and possibly thousands of lives.

It was on the final night of that visit that he made me a gift. Naturally I was more than reluctant to accept it, but once again his gentleness had insistence behind it. Or perhaps he could see that my reluctance was feigned. We had often debated matters of religion – he knew I was not a believer and I knew he was a passionate one – and it was that language he used the last time I saw him; still forging connections as he always had before. 'You are a Jew. Of the people of the book. Here is my book,' he quietly said. 'The things that happened are all written down.' And he added with a look I have never quite forgotten: 'Never let people forget what we did to each other.'

It was as though he knew what I myself had done.

Perhaps I thought his register might contain some clue to what had happened among us on the ship; a thing that was not at all clear at the time. Perhaps I saw it as a grisly souvenir of the thirty days that set the course for the rest of my life. Perhaps – why not say it now, since an old man must confess all his shames – I thought it might make the bones of a story. The novel I had always wanted to write but had failed to.

But take it I did, and I have it by me yet; that terrifying ledger of human suffering, its pages withered and yellowed with time, the calf-skin of its cover blanched with saltwater stains. The reader has seen the words of Josias Tuke Lockwood, who died of famine fever in Dover, England, fourteen months after the last night I saw him. Those words have the advantage of being contemporaneous, where my own recollections, still bright as they seem to myself, must inevitably be questioned so long after the event. That is entirely and properly as it should be. I have tried not to distort but no doubt have not always succeeded.

I would like to think I am objective in what I have put down, but of course that is not so and could never have been. I was there. I was involved. I knew some of the people. One I loved; another I despised. I use the word carefully: I did despise him. So easy to despise in the cause of love. Others again I was simply indifferent to, and such indifference is also a part of the tale. And of course I have selected what has been seen of the Captain's words in order to frame and tell the story. A different author would have made a different selection. Everything is in the way the material is composed.

From papers found, from documents discovered, from certain investigations and recollections and interviews; from enquiries made among others who sailed that ship, from questions asked on many return visits to those rocks which maps call 'The British Isles', other matters came to light which may safely be lodged in the column of fact. For the benefit of the curious, let me set them down:

There was once a Galwayman called Pius Mulvey, another named Thomas David Merridith. They sailed to America in search of new beginnings. The first had been charged to murder the second, a man who was blamed for the crimes of his fathers. In a different world they might not have been enemies; at a different time, perhaps even friends. They had far more in common than either of them realised. One was born Catholic, the other Protestant. One was born Irish, the other British. But neither of these was the greatest difference between them. One was born rich and the other poor.

There was once a beautiful woman called Mary Duane, who came from a village called Carna in Connemara; the middle child of Daniel Duane and Margaret Nee, the former a fisherman and sometime small-farmer, the latter a nanny and mother of seven. She once loved a boy she didn't know to be her brother. Before knowing she was his sister, he loved her in return; or would have done, maybe, were he capable of loving her. He and the girl who once cherished him so dearly were separated in the end, as perhaps all are, not by what divided them, but by what they had in common – the tangled facts of a past they did not make. What is sometimes called in Ireland: 'the lie of the land'.

Some will judge his lack of that capacity to be entirely his own fault; others will see in it a kind of victimhood. As for myself, I dare advance no judgement on the sins of another, my own sins being sufficiently consuming of reflection. Call him the son of the father who destroyed him. Call him an untouchable; the lowest of the low. He was a man who could have done good things if only he knew it. I believe Mary Duane saw such a miraculousness in him when they were young enough to believe that power does not matter; before wealth separated them, and class stepped between them, and then made her abuse at his hands become a possibility. They were not Romeo and Juliet. They were master and servant. He had choices in life that she had not. That he chose as he did is a matter of record. That each man is the sum of his choices is nothing less than the truth. And each, perhaps, is also something else.

Of Mary Duane's immediate family, her father, her mother and all three of her sisters died of starvation in the land of their birth, as did her youngest and eldest brothers. Her one surviving brother was killed in an explosion while attempting to escape from Clerkenwell Prison in London in December 1867. He had been jailed for membership of a revolutionary faction seeking an end to British rule in Ireland. At the time of his death he was awaiting trial for his part in the murder of a Manchester policeman.

What became of Mary Duane in America I cannot say. She worked the streets of lower Manhattan for a time; was arrested twice, briefly jailed once, and then seems to have simply disappeared from view. I know she was begging in Chicago in the winter of '49 and was admitted to the vagrants' ward of a Minneapolis chest hospital for two days in 1854. By the time we had travelled there, she had quietly moved on. Advertisements seeking her whereabouts remained unanswered. Rewards offered remained unclaimed. Enquiries through detectives over the decades placed women who matched her nationality and description in thousands of places across

America, and in as many different circumstances of life. New Orleans, Illinois, Minnesota, Colorado, Wisconsin, Massachusetts, Maryland, Maine; a sister in an enclosed convent in northern Ontario, a sweeper in a lavatory, a maid in a brothel, a cook in an orphanage, a frontiersman's wife, a scrubwoman on trains, the grandmother of a Senator. As to which, if any, was Mary Duane from Carna, I simply cannot say and will never know now.

Only once, in response to a newspaper advertisement, did I receive anything she might have written herself. A third-person account (though clearly autobiographical) of the life of a woman who had worked as 'a night-girl' in the heartless Dublin of 'the hungry forties', following her abandonment by the son of an aristocrat. It was unsigned, inconsistently spelled, with no return address or identifying clue, but laden with the speech patterns of southern Connemara. It was mailed from the post office in Dublin, New Hampshire, on Christmas Eve, 1871, but a search of that small town by the local authorities yielded no result; nor did a fresh search of the entire state, and then of the whole of the New England region.

Many will feel that the story is not complete without knowing all its endings. No doubt they are right. I feel the same way. Looking back over these pages, they seem to say almost nothing about her; it is as though she was merely a collection of footnotes in the lives of other, more violent people. So many years I attempted to find her that now if I did I would feel a kind of loss. But I will not find her now. Perhaps I never could have. I would like to have been able to say more in the present account, to do more than record the few known facts of her existence in terms of the existences of the men who hurt her. But I am simply not in a position to do so. Some things I have invented but I could not invent Mary Duane; at least no more than I have already done. She suffered more than enough composition.

There were times over the years when I would think I saw her. On a railroad platform, once, in San Diego, California. Sleeping in a doorway in downtown Pittsburgh. A nurse in a hospital in Edenton, North Carolina. But I was always wrong. It was never Mary Duane. It can only be assumed that she did not want to be found; that she changed her name and began a new life, as did so

STAR *of the* SEA

many hundreds of thousands of the Irish in America. But I do not know. Perhaps that is wishful thinking.

The last time I thought I saw her was last November in Times Square: a shade moving slowly through a forest of black umbrellas. The playhouses were emptying into the streets; a strong winter rainstorm had swept in from the Atlantic. A great crowd had gathered to cheer a troop of ambulance volunteers who were marching away to the war in Europe; and it was on the edge of the throng that I imagined I saw her; alone under a street light in the pearl-like rain. She was selling something from a tray – flowers, I think. But she was so fragile and young, the girl I saw that night, and Mary Duane would be old now, if still she lives. The only creed I have ever believed in is reason, a faith that must tell me it was not her I saw. But if her spirit indeed walks the glittered streets of Broadway it is far from alone; so any actor would claim. Ghosts, it is said, are sometimes drawn to theatres; as much as they are to war.

The dire fate of her lover, Pius Mulvey, is easier told. He died some time on the dismally snowy night of the sixth of December, 1848, a year almost to the day after landing in New York; knifed to pieces in a Brooklyn alleyway near the corner of Water Street and Hudson Avenue, in the ragged Irish shanty town of Vinegar Hill. Across a broken wall was the freshly whitewashed sentence: IRELAND IN CHAINS SHALL NEVER BE AT PEACE.

In the pocket of his greatcoat they found a leather-bound bible, a five-cent coin and a handful of earth. There was a cheap copper washer on his wedding-ring finger but we shall never know whom he married in America, if indeed he did. He had been going under a variety of assumed names, among them Costello, Blake, Duane and Nee, but many in the neighbourhood knew exactly who he was. It was said that he had been shunned and often assaulted; had been sleeping on the benches of local parks, begging passers-by for scraps of food. Often at night he had been seen on the waterfront, staring out at the ships coming into the harbour. He had taken to drinking and was desperately thin. Prior to death he had been tortured and horribly disfigured. It was reported by the City Coroner who examined the remains that the heart had been cut out and flung in the gutter, probably while the victim was still alive. A few of the more superstitious of Connemara New Yorkers were said to see

400

meaning in the admittedly eerie coincidence that the murder took place on the feast-day of St Nicholas.

Nobody was ever charged with the crime and nobody remembers for certain where its victim was buried. It is hard to believe that he even existed. I would doubt it myself had I not met and known him, this monster who murdered his enemy in Newgate Gaol and his friend in a forest on the outskirts of Leeds. Had he murdered David Merridith he might have been a hero. The subject, perhaps, of a valiant song. Instead he is forgotten: a minor embarrassment. The coward who could not bring himself to murder for a cause.

Part of the land a few miles west of Vinegar Hill was compulsorily purchased by the city some twenty-two years ago, including a shabby plot of waste ground called Traitor's Acre, where local paupers or prostitutes were often flung into shallow graves. Some say he lies there: Pius Mulvey of Ardnagreevagh, younger child of Michael and Elizabeth, brother of Nicholas, father of nobody. The tombs are unmarked; the rocks overgrown with weeds. On that precise spot and its many buried shames now stands the Brooklynside anchorage for the Manhattan Bridge.

Others who sailed the *Star* had secrets of their own. One fellow traveller I last saw in South Dakota in 1866, to which state I had been sent by my editor-in-chief to write a series of articles on immigrants in the Midwest. My enquiries had taken me to a travelling Bandolero Show where a great many of the roustabouts were said to be Irish. I conducted a number of interesting interviews with cowboys from Connemara and other parts of Connaught. But just as I made to leave, something fascinating happened. My attention was drawn to a wrestling booth in the far corner of the field where, for the reasonable sum of half a dollar, the brave could pit their skills against 'the greatest conqueror who ever lived', one 'Bam-Bam Bombay, the Sultan of the Strangle-hold'. His former butler (actually his elder brother) was now doing admirable duty as ringside second and barker.

They appeared mighty happy to see an old friend, and many a glass of moonshine was raised in South Dakota that night. Their names were George and Thomas Clarke and they were born in Liverpool, of a Galway scullery maid and a Portuguese sailor, the latter bequeathing them their dark complexions (and conspicuously little else). They had spent most of the 1840s criss-crossing the Atlantic in imperial disguise, performing small-time robberies and feats of minor card-sharping; until one day in Boston they were recognised by a hefty Irish policeman, which apperception necessitated a rather unimperial retreat into the slums. We shared a few reminiscences about our days on the *Star*, a voyage, apparently, less profitable than most. (It was the Maharajah and his servant who had roamed through First-Class, relieving us of what they regarded simply as their tribute. Moreover, they regarded it as a spiritual service. 'Buddhism teaches a putting-away of material possessions,' they remarked.) Apologies were sincerely offered and sincerely accepted. They rode me to the station, bade me farewell with many vigorous grapples and implored me to keep in touch on a more regular basis.

It was only on the train back home to New York that I noticed my watch was missing.

I didn't begrudge it. They had insisted on paying for the booze. But eleven years later, in 1877, an envelope arrived from the wilderness town with the melancholy name of Desdemona, Texas. Inside was my watch, now inscribed with the memorable message: *Fondest Greetings from Injun Country.*

There was certainly a woman named Laura Merridith, for she and I were to marry a year after the death of her husband, and no kinder-hearted woman ever lived. Our marriage was not in fact happy but I never think of those times now. We divorced after eighteen months but never quite managed to separate. I still have the final papers somewhere in my files, devoid of the necessary signatures. For fifty-four years we were companions and comrades, each year a little better than the one before. Love came late; but it did come. It takes so long even to know what it means.

In later times, if friends asked for the secret of our closeness, she would remark that she still intended to sign those papers but was waiting for the children to die.

She was blinded in a streetcar accident in 1868, the same accident confining her to a wheelchair for the rest of her days. But it did little enough to prevent her doing what she wanted. All her life in America she worked for the advancement of the poor, and was a powerful champion of the suffragist and Negro causes especially.

She was involved in a great number of important events, but I think her proudest achievement was to be among the women jailed for attempting to vote in the presidential election of 1872 (for Ulysses S. Grant). When the judge asked how it felt for a dowager Countess to be sharing a cell with the daughter of a slave, she said it was the deepest privilege she had known. She fought prejudice and bigotry wherever she saw it, most angrily whenever she saw it in herself; which others, including myself, never did. She died in 1903, on her eighty-seventh birthday, at the inaugural meeting of the American Ladies' Garment Workers' Union, an organisation she had helped to found. To have known her was the greatest honour of my life: to have loved her the only truly good thing I have ever done.

Our beautiful child was born prematurely, and only survived long enough to be baptised with the names of two brave women who stood in her background: Verity Mary Merridith Dixon. We learned soon thereafter that we could never make another child, a fact that was far from easy to bear. Neither were we able to foster or adopt. 'Coloureds' were not permitted such rights at that time, and though the colour of my body is the same as President Wilson's, the colour of my soul is legally not. My father being quarter-Choctaw weighed heavily against us. When the papers came back from the Office of Minors, the place headed REASONS FOR UNSUITABILITY had been stamped with the single word 'negritude'.

Her two remarkable sons are the joy of my days. They never talk about Ireland now. They tend to say they were born in America.

Robert married three times, Jonathan never. Long ago he confided that he prefers the companionship of men; and if he does, his living truthfully seems to have brought him happiness, and perhaps helped to make him one of the finest men I know. They bear my own name, those two aged fellows, a choice made by themselves in their early twenties; an election as unexpected as entirely undeserved. People even say they look like me, and in a certain light, indeed they do. Often we have been taken for three silent old brothers as we sit outside a café in a companionable huff at the world. ('Shadrach, Meshach and Abed-nego,' says the waiter – when he thinks we cannot hear him.) That gives me such pleasure that pleasure is not the word.

In the winter, when the leaves have fallen from the lime trees, I can see their mother's tombstone from the window where I now sit and write. The beautiful daughter we lost is at rest there, too. I visit most days; sometimes daily now. I like to hear the truckles of the trams going past; and the hoots of the tugboats drifting in from the river – reminder that this noisy city is an ancient island; a prehistoric outcrop in a concrete disguise. Strange birds sing in the cemetery garden every morning. The old priest has told me their name many times but lately it never seems to stay in my head. Perhaps it does not matter. Anyway they sing.

Couples often stroll there in the spring afternoons, workers from the offices or students from the university. I sometimes see a child netting the astonishing butterflies that cluster in the nettles near the back of the chapel. He sells them in fruit-jars at his shoeshine station on 12th Street; this bright little mulatto boy who whistles southern gospel as he tiptoes between the gravestones chuckling to himself. Before long the birds will sing over me, too. My physicians have told me my time is very short. I like to think of the boy whistling gospel above me, and his sons whistling, when he grows to a man. But I know this will not happen. I will hear nothing, then. There is nothing to hope for and nothing to fear.

The above events all happened. They belong to fact.

As for the rest – the details, the emphases, certain devices of narration and structure, whole events which may never have occurred, or may have happened quite differently to how they are described – those belong to the imagination. For that no apology whatsoever is offered, though some will insist that one is needed.

Perhaps they are correct, by their own lights anyway. To take the events of reality and meld them into something else is a task not to be undertaken coldly or carelessly. On the question of whether such an endeavour is worthwhile or even moral, readers may wish to pronounce for themselves. Such questions must hover over any account of the past: whether the story may be understood without asking who is telling it; to which intended audience and to what precise end.

As for David Merridith's murderer, his answer is this: on the wall of his study hangs the image of a monster which he cut from a newspaper seventy-five years ago, when he was young enough to believe that ends justify means. Love and freedom are such hideous words. So many cruelties have been done in their names. He was a very weak man; and a rational man: a combination capable of realising the unspeakable. He believed he could not live without what he desired, and what he desired was owned by another. When he wept in the night, that was what he wept for. And still he weeps now, though for different reasons. As to whether he would have desired beyond that terrible limit had the prize been free, he does not know. He called this deformity 'love' but part of it was hatred; another part was vanity and yet another fear: the same reasons why men have always done murder. His life was unimaginable without possessing the prize. Some call that patriotism; others call it love. But murder is murder no matter the translation.

He is an old man now with very little left to him. People are kind when they see him in the street. They know he once wrote something, but they do not know what. There was a time long ago when he garnered citations for his work, when he met with Presidents and eminent men. But the times did not last; and he was glad when they ended. He visits the tomb of his wife every morning. In the evenings he sits in his window and writes; and the portrait of a killer glares down from his wall. Sometimes it reminds him of Pius Mulvey; sometimes of Thomas David Merridith; but mostly of other untouchables he has known who lived to great ages and died in their beds.

Many on the *Star* had their secrets: their shames. Few have kept them hidden for quite so long.

The stare of the murderer intimates many things, but one thing mainly, which he sometimes forgets. That every image committed to paper contains the ghost of the author who fashioned it. Outside the frame, beyond the border, is often the space where the subject is standing. A shifting and elusive presence, certainly, but a palpable one for its camouflages. He is there, the killer, in the pictures he paints. But they also contain the untold histories, as every man who ever hated contained the blood of his innumerable fathers. Every woman. Every man.

All the way back to Cain.

G. Grantley Dixon.
New York City.
Easter Saturday, 1916.

SOURCES &
ACKNOWLEDGEMENTS

BACKGROUND: Mary Daly, *The Famine in Ireland* (Dublin Historical Association, 1986); R.F. Foster, *Modern Ireland 1600-1972* (Allen Lane, 1988); Joan Johnson, *James and Mary Ellis: Background and Quaker Famine Relief in Letterfrack* (Religious Society of Friends in Ireland, 2000); Helen Litton, *The Irish Famine: An Illustrated History* (Wolfhound, 1994); Kerby A. Miller, *Emigrants and Exiles: Ireland and the Irish Exodus to North America* (Oxford U.P., 1985); Cormac Ó Gráda, *The Great Irish Famine* (Macmillan, 1989); Tim Robinson *Connemara: Map and Gazetteer* (Folding Landscapes, Roundstone, 1990); William V. Shannon, *The American Irish* (Univ. of Massachusetts, 1963); Kathleen Villiers-Tuthill, *History of Clifden 1810-1860* and *Patient Endurance: The Great Famine in Connemara* (Connemara Girl Publications, 1997). Larger bibliographies are available in the above works and at the website of the University of Wales, www.swan.ac.uk/history. Other websites featuring primary source texts and illustrations include www.ucg.ie/depts/history/famine0.html and www.historyplace.com/worldhistory/famine.

EYE-WITNESS ACCOUNTS OF THE FAMINE: William Bennett, *Six Weeks in Ireland* (Gilpin, London, 1847)[1]; *Distress in Ireland: Narrative of William Edward Forster's Visit* (Friends' Historical Library, Morehampton Road, Dublin 4); *The Irish Journals of Elizabeth Smith 1840-1850* (Oxford U.P., 1980); Alexander Somerville, *Letters From Ireland During the Famine of 1847* (Irish Academic Press, 1994, K.D.M. Snell ed.); Asenath Nicholson, *Lights and Shades of Ireland* (1850)[2].

SHIPBOARD EXPERIENCES: Details of individual voyages, some with passenger manifests, are at www.theshipslist.com. Many emigrant ballads are at 'Irish Folksongs', www.acronet.net/~robokopp/irish Thomas Gallagher's *Paddy's Lament: Ireland 1846-1847* (Harvest, 1982) quotes the unmediated recollections of numerous emigrants, many from the collection at the Folklore Department, Univ. College Dublin. Further material is held at the Irish National Archives, Bishop Street, Dublin 8 (www.nationalarchives.ie). *Voyage*

[1] Extracts at www.people.virginia.edu/~eas5e/Irish
[2] Quoted frequently in Litton's *Irish Famine*.

from Dublin to Quebec by James Wilson is at 'Immigrants to Canada', http://list.uwaterloo.ca/~marj/. Robert Whyte's *Journey of an Irish Coffin Ship, 1847* is at fortunecity.com/littleitaly/amalfi. A work of which questions have been asked as to provenance is Gerald Keegan's *Famine Diary* (or *Summer of Sorrow 1847*), first published in 1895.

ILLUSTRATIONS: L. Perry Curtis's *Apes and Angels: The Irishman in Victorian Caricature* (1971) is a pioneering work on the subject, though some of its assumptions are questioned at www.people.virginia.edu/~dnp5c/Victorian/index.html, where a gallery of 'simian' Irish images is available. Steve Taylor's website 'Views of the Famine' at www.vassar.edu/~sttaylor also features a collection of visual materials. I thank him for providing copies of certain illustrations and granting permission for their use. Artists, dates and original publications are listed if known. *(HW: Harper's Weekly. J: Judy* magazine. *ILN: Illustrated London News*; JM is the *News*'s resident Irish artist, James Mahony. *PT: Pictorial Times. PU: Punch* magazine; JT is *Punch's* principal cartoonist, John Tenniel.)

Title Page: 'Scientific Racism', *HW*. From www.nde.state.ne.us/SS/irish/unit. **Prologue:** 'Emigrants Boarding a Ship at Waterloo Dock, Liverpool', *ILN*, 6 Jul 1850, signed 'Smyth S.' **Chapter I:** 'Poor House from Galway', *HW*; by W.A. Rogers. From www.people.virginia.edu/~eas5e/Irish/Famine. **II:** 'The Pig and the Peer', *PU*, 7 Aug 1880; JT. **III:** 'Meal-Cart Under Military Escort', *PT*, 30 Oct 1847. **IV:** 'The Fenian Guy Fawkes', *PU*, 28 Dec 1867; JT. **V:** 'Below Decks — Feeding Time'. From http://vassun.vassar.edu/~sttaylor/famine. **VI:** 'The Scalp of Brian Connor, near Kilrush Union House', *ILN*, 22 Dec 1849; JM. **VII:** 'Keillines, near General Thompson's Property', *ILN*, Jan 1850; JM. **X:** 'Searching for Potatoes in a Stubble Field', *ILN*, 22 Dec 1849; JM. **XI:** 'A Scalp at Caeuermore', *ILN*, 29 Dec 1849; JM. **XIII:** 'The Village of Tullig', *ILN*, 22 Dec 1849; JM. **XIV:** 'Bridget O'Donnel and Children', *ILN*, 22 Dec 1849; JM. **XV:** 'Boy and Girl at Cahera', *ILN*, 20 Feb 1847; JM. **XVI:** 'Funeral at Skibbereen', *ILN*, 30 Jan 1847; 'From a sketch by Mr H. Smith, Cork'; [the signature is 'Smyth']. **XVII:** 'Cottage Interior', *PT*, 7 Feb 1846. **XVIII:** Detail from 'Three Irish Affections: Force, Folly and Fraud', *J*, 8 Dec 1880. **XIX:** 'Pentonville Yard', from *The Criminal Prisons of London and Scenes of London Prison Life* by Henry Mayhew and John Binny, London, 1862. **XXII:** 'A Farming Family Defending Their Home', *PT*, 2 Jan 1847; and 'The Ejectment', *ILN*, 16 Dec 1848, signed 'Landells'. **XXIII:** Cover of *Harriet Staunton; or married and starved for money*. Artist and date unknown. **XXVI:** 'Miss Kennedy Distributing Clothes at Kilrush', *ILN*, 22 Dec 1849; JM. **XXVII:** 'Begging at Clonakilty', *ILN*, 13 Feb 1847; JM. **XXVIII:** 'Irish Armed Peasants Waiting for the Arrival of a Meal-Cart', *PT*, 30 Oct 1847.

XXIX: 'The Day After the Ejectment', *ILN*, 16 Dec 1848. **XXX:** 'The British Lion and the Irish Monkey', *P*, 8 April 1848. **XXXI:** Detail from 'Two Forces', *PU*, 29 Oct 1881; JT. **XXXII:** Detail from *PU* anthology, Vol. LXXXII, 1882; JT. **XXXIII:** Detail from 'Anything for Peace and Quiet', *J*, 13 Apr 1881. **XXXV:** 'The Kind of Assisted Emigrant We Cannot Afford to Admit' by F. Graetz, date unknown; possibly from *HW*. **XXXVI:** 'The Bogus American', *J*, 15 Jan 1868. **XXXVII:** 'The Irish Frankenstein', *PU*, 20 May 1882; JT, after similar work by J. Kenny Meadows in *PU*, 3 Mar 1843. **Page 371:** 'Herd Boy of the Purple Mountain', *ILN*, 1849. **XXXVIII:** Detail from 'The Irish-American Skunk', *J*, 3 Aug 1881. **XXXIX:** 'Idiot and Mother', *ILN*, 12 Aug 1846. **Epilogue:** 'The Village of Moveen', *ILN*, December 1849; JM.

QUOTATIONS: Many of Mulvey's words for stealing are quoted in Robert Hughes's *The Fatal Shore* (Collins Harvill, 1987). The remarks of London traders (pp. 178 and 227) were recorded by Henry Mayhew in his *London Labour and the London Poor* (1861) and quoted in Donald Thomas's *The Victorian Underworld* (John Murray, 1988). That compelling work also describes the 'solitary' system in British prisons of the era and the 1836 escape of a Newgate prisoner who climbed over the cheval-de-frise; I borrowed the latter detail for the flight of Mulvey, so again I acknowledge Donald Thomas. The real-life letters extracted throughout the novel are quoted in Kerby Miller's *Emigrants and Exiles* and *Out of Ireland: The Story of Irish Emigration to America* (Aurum, 1994, with Paul Wagner). I thank Professor Miller for his kind assistance in identifying the owners of some of the documents, and I thank the institutions and individuals below for granting permissions. **Chapter II**: From Patrick Dunny, 1856; Collection of Arnold Schrier, Emeritus Prof. of History, Univ. of Cincinnati. **IV:** From Mary Brown; Schrier Collection. **V, VI** and **VIII:** From Mrs Nolan (first name unknown); by permission of the Deputy Keeper of Records at the Public Records Office of Northern Ireland (PRONI) T2054. **XI** and **XIII**: From James Richey; quoted from Miller; ownership of original document unknown. Possibly at PRONI T/2035/2345/2671 or D3561 (Richey Family Papers). **XVII:** From Daniel Guiney; Irish Nat. Archives (Famine Letters from the Quit Rent Office, Kingwilliamstown Estate). **XXXIII:** From Maurice Woulfe (or Wolfe), circa 1870; microfilm copy in Nat. Library of Ireland (mf p.3887); current ownership of original document unknown.

ACKNOWLEDGEMENTS: I thank my wife, Anne-Marie Casey, for so many kindnesses that I could not catalogue them without writing another book. For her patience, wisdom and endless charm, I am more grateful than the dedication of this novel could begin to convey. To Geoff Mulligan, my editor at Secker, I once again express my thanks for his insight and skill. To my literary agent, Carole Blake, I add my gratitude; as I do to Conrad Williams, my screenwriting agent, also at Blake Friedmann Literary Agency in London. I thank Caroline Michel, my publisher at Vintage, Hans Juergen Balmes at Fischer Verlag, Germany, Lolies van Grunsven at Nijgh and Ditmar, Holland, Jean Pierre Sicre at Editions Phebus, France, Luigi Brioschi at Guanda, Italy, and Drenka Willen, my publisher at Harcourt Books, New York. Special thanks are due to my father, Seán, whose jaunts with me into Connemara three decades ago were the joy of my childhood. Advice on certain Irish translations was given by Dr Angela Bourke, Dr Diarmuid Breathnach, Peadar Lamb and Niall Mac Fhionnlaoich. I offer each of them the sincere *maith agat* of an almost monolingual whose own garblings will be identifiable to careful speakers of Irish. The book was designed with great skill by Peter Ward.

I also thank the following: John and Monica Casey; Denise Clack; Dr John de Courcy Ireland; Philomena Connolly at the Irish National Archives; Ciara Considine; Dr Mike Cronin of De Montfort Univ.; Joe and Jillian Cunningham; Isobel Dixon; Adrienne Fleming and Anthony Glavin; Seamus Hosey; Beth Humphries; Professor Declan Kiberd; Grainne Killeen; Noel Kissane (Keeper of Manuscripts at the Nat. Library of Ireland) and his colleague Justin Furlong; Michael McLoughlin; Ann McVeigh at PRONI; Kim Miley; Eimear O'Connor; Viola O'Connor; Faith O'Grady; Jonathan Owens (Oxford Univ. Press, New York) and Shelagh Phillips (OUP, London); Prof. Robert Patten at Rice Univ. Houston; Deirdre Shanahan; Stuart Williams at Secker, and Barbara Walker. Kay McEvilly of Cashel House Hotel, Connemara, discussed local surnames with me, and I thank the McEvilly family for their hospitality over a number of years. I thank the Arts Council of Ireland for awarding me the Macaulay Fellowship in 1995, which allowed me to do initial research for this novel in New York. I thank Dr Philip Smyly of the National Maritime Museum at Dun Laoghaire, who gave me access to the museum's extensive collection despite the building being closed for renovation. Landlubber's mistakes, and all other ones, are my own.

HISTORY: *Wuthering Heights* by Ellis Bell was indeed published by Cautley Newby in December 1847 (not very well and rather unscrupulously). V.S. Pritchett, in a 1946 essay, was among the first critics to discuss the connection between Emily Brontë's masterpiece and Ireland. It has been further explored by Terry Eagleton *(Heathcliff and the Great Hunger,* Verso 1995), John Cannon *(History of the Brontë Family from Ireland to Wuthering Heights,* Sutton 2000) and Christopher Heywood (Appendices to his 2001 edition of WH, Broadview Press). I have dared to allow Pius Mulvey to suffer the 'separation' system at Newgate in the late 1830s, but in fact it was not introduced until 1842, and at

Pentonville. No organisation called the Else-Be-Liables or Liable Men existed, but many others of cryptic names and violent activities did, and had done so in Ireland for at least eighty years.[3] The sending of anonymous or pseudonymous threatening letters to landlords was frequent. Litton's *Irish Famine* quotes several. Often their authors were new to written English, thus their texts had mis-spellings or phonetic renderings of the kind appearing in the letter to Merridith. Its diagram of the coffin is borrowed from a note sent to a Kildare landlord in January, 1848.[4]

MUSIC: Captain Francis O'Neill did not contribute to any work called *A Miscellany of the Ancient Songs of Ireland*. A Chicago policeman and native of Cork, his *Dance Music of Ireland* (1907) and endearingly titled *Waifs and Strays of Gaelic Melody* (1909) did much rescue a beautiful repertoire from a fatal diminishment. Admirers of Irish singing will know that the paradigm of Mulvey's Recruiting Sergeant ballad is 'Arthur McBride', a 19th century song restored to the canon by Paul Brady and later recorded by Bob Dylan. (Brady's version is on *Andy Irvine and Paul Brady*, Mulligan, 1976; Dylan's on *Good as I Been to You*, Columbia, 1992). The ballad Mulvey sings on page 95 is 'In the Month of January'. A version is included on Paddy Tunney's *The Irish Edge* (Ossian Recordings, 1991). Tunney's version is not 'a macaronic' (which Mulvey's is), though many such songs exist in the Connemara *Sean-Nós* or 'Old Style' tradition. Several were recorded by Seosamh Ó hÉanai (like Mary Duane, a native of Carna). Examples may be found on *Joe Heaney: Irish Traditional Songs in Gaelic and English* (Topic, London, 1988). 'Revenge for Skibbereen' (or 'Skibereen') (Chapter XXXIX) is often given in live performance by that Caruso of the genre, Seán Keane of Galway. It features on his acclaimed album *Seánsongs* (*Circín Rua Teo*, 2002). Ciaran Carson's *Last Night's Fun* (Cape, 1996) is a brilliant work about traditional Irish music. It mentions a Loyalist drummer, Right McKnight, who borrowed his drum from a Nationalist band and forgot to give it back. I borrowed his name for Mulvey's Glaswegian sidekick. I hereby give it back.

---

[3] Miller's *Emigrants and Exiles* and Foster's *Modern Ireland* list many.

[4] See Litton, pp. 42 and 101. Phrases similar to those quoted here appear in the note to Merridith.

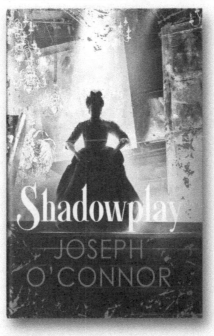

penguin.co.uk/vintage